THE TALISMAN OF WRATH

The first tale in the saga of the twins of Arl

S. P. Muir

Copyright © 2014 by S. P. Muir. All Rights Reserved.

All rights reserved. No part of this book may be reproduced in any form or by any electronic or mechanical means including information storage and retrieval systems, without permission in writing from the author. The only exception is by a reviewer, who may quote short excerpts in a review.

This book is a work of fiction. Names, characters, places, and incidents either are products of the author's imagination or are used fictitiously. Any resemblance to actual persons, living or dead, events, or locales is entirely coincidental.

S. P. Muir
Visit my website at www.spmuir.com

ISBN: 978-1499583823

The Saga of the Twins of Arl

1 – *The Talisman of Wrath*

2 – *A War of Destiny*

3 – *Kamarill: The Earthsoul*

For my wife, Rosemary, who always believed

S. P. MUIR

My deepest and sincere thanks to Brian Slack for all the original artwork

S. P. MUIR

THE TALISMAN OF WRATH

A bleeding sky, a freezing fire,

Then comes the time for righteous ire,

An oath's upheld from bygone age,

While hunters prowl and howl with rage.

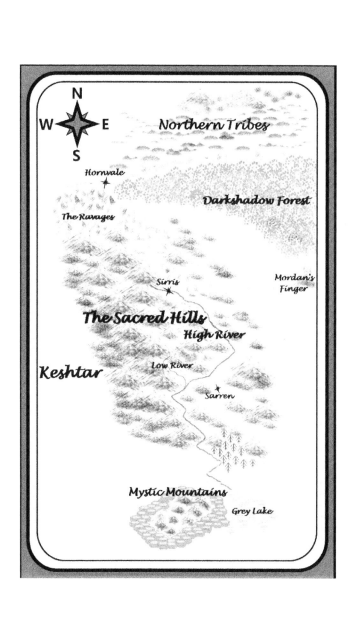

PROLOGUE

The magnificent palace of the old kings towered majestically over the sprawling ancient city of Arl, and its throne room was one of the true wonders of the world. Its lofty, vaulted ceiling was stunningly decorated with exquisite murals that depicted rare exotic flora and dramatically animated beasts. There was a distinct lupine theme to the artwork, with savagely noble wolves being the predominant species in every one of the glowing frescoes. The walls were hung with impossibly elaborate tapestries that shimmered with every imaginable colour, shade, and texture. The floor caressed the eyes with the lambent shine of softly polished black granite and twinkling white marble tiles that were set in a deliberate and intricate arrangement.

The only discordant detail was the long straight line of rough-hewn stone slabs that led from the tall, heavily embossed double doors right up to the imposing oak and leather throne. This lowly pathway served as a reminder that even the poorest and most humble citizen of the land of Keshtar, retained the right to approach and petition the king.

The vast hall was echoing to the melodic and captivating singing of a sylph-like girl child standing twenty paces to the front and right of the throne. Sitting in the great seat itself, was an improbably handsome man. He appeared paradoxically both ancient and youthful, and both masculine and feminine. Dark hair fell onto his broad, powerful shoulders in a cascade of loose, shimmering curls. His long flowing robes were of the softest, pure white linen that highlighted the golden-brown tone of his finely chiselled features.

He sat with his eyes closed, his head resting in his left hand as he savoured the sweetly soaring voice of the pretty young singer. His right hand rested lightly on a softly shining silvery crystal which nestled in a specially shaped hollow set in the throne's ornate arm. Its colour and shape gave the impression that a small star had fallen from the heavens to be caught and treasured by the kings of old. Scattered strategically around the hall stood several servants, patiently waiting to obey any command that was put upon them. The fact that all the attendants, both male and female, were young, pretty, and scantily dressed in sparse, loose fitting white robes, attested to the often-unsavoury nature of their master's demands.

The scene remained unchanged until the huge doors at the far end of the throne room opened and a small lone figure walked purposefully along the rough stone pathway that led to the royal seat. He was a strange looking creature, standing no taller than an eight-year-old child. His smooth dark skin was hairless and had the appearance of thick, tanned leather. His unearthly features were sharp and pointed. At odds with this unnatural, almost evil appearance however, were his large round eyes. They were soft and gentle and seemed to carry the sad wisdom of one who had lived far too long and had witnessed far too much. His clothes were fashioned from thick brown hide and consisted of a tunic and tight leggings. From his shoulders flowed a long black cloak that reached almost to the floor. He leant lightly on a plain ebony staff that he held in his right hand, while in his left he carried a small, black, rune-covered box.

As he approached the throne the seated man opened his eyes and sat bolt upright. A look of excited expectancy lit up his beautifully sculpted features, but his eyes, heavy-lidded and dark, remained cold and empty, as devoid of warmth and emotion as a lifeless corpse.

"Mylock!" he cried as he impatiently motioned for the girl to be quiet. "Have you found it? Do you have it?" His voice was as soft and light as a young woman's, yet it carried a masculine quality that conveyed a natural strength and authority.

"We have it, oh great one," the creature replied bowing deeply. Its voice was thin and harsh and cut the air like a sharp blade. "Although it cost the lives of many in my sect, the task has been accomplished."

"Show me," the man commanded eagerly. The tiny figure carefully laid his staff on the ground, opened the box and held it out to his god-like king. There, resting on a bed of scarlet silk lay a plain grey pebble, no larger than a small egg.

"Is this it?" the king asked, his voice laden with scepticism.

"Without a doubt," reassured the small leather-clad creature. The king looked at him dubiously then motioned to the nearest of his many servants.

"You," he said to the dusky-skinned, fresh-faced youth. "Pass it to me."

The boy trotted obediently over and reached into the box; but the moment his fingers touched the stone, his bright and innocent blue eyes rolled back in his head and every trace of life flooded from his body. Without a sound he collapsed to the floor and lay in a crumpled heap on the exquisite black and white tiles.

"Excellent!" exclaimed the king delightedly. Without a glance at the youth's lifeless body, he lifted the star-like crystal from its recess and held it tightly in his right hand. The silvery light within it grew steadily brighter until it dazzled all in the vast hall, forcing the many servants to turn their backs and shield their eyes with their hands. With trembling cautiousness, he reached into the box with his left hand, hesitated for a moment, and then snatched the innocuous looking stone from its silky nest.

Immediately, the blinding silver light from the crystal faded until it was almost out and a look of intense pain strained his tanned and handsome face. Jewel-like beads of perspiration appeared on his forehead then trickled down into his cold, dead eyes. After some time of gasping with the strain of such a tremendous effort, his contorted features gradually eased and the dim light in his right hand grew steadily brighter until finally it settled back to its original gentle glow. Holding the stone and crystal high, he looked around the hall until his eyes fell upon the young girl whose delightful singing had so captivated him only moments earlier. The tiny vocalist shuffled uncomfortably under his hardening gaze until suddenly, a burst of intense green light flashed from his eyes and struck her full in the chest. The unfortunate child was blasted from her feet and sent flying across the immaculately polished floor. She slammed into the far wall where her shattered body lay in a shapeless heap with faint wisps of smoke rising slowly into the air.

"At last," cried the king throwing back his head and laughing triumphantly. "I am more than divine, I am God! I'll seek out that accursed race wherever they're hiding and I shall blast them to ashes. Soon, all men will bow down and worship only me. Then, the whole world will tremble at the name of Limnash the Great!"

THE TALISMAN OF WRATH

The small leather-clad figure threw itself to the floor and prostrated itself before the deity it had helped to empower.

CHAPTER ONE

The old man climbed slowly up the snow-clad hill, deep in the sacred eastern mountains. He stopped frequently to catch his breath leaning heavily on the rough wooden staff that he'd cut from a tree in the sparse pine forest far below. His laboured breathing was transformed to ephemeral clouds of mist by the crisp, cold air.

He looked far too frail to be journeying so deep into such inhospitable territory; for although he was of average height, he was only slight in build. Wisps of long white hair peeked out from beneath the shapeless fur hat that he'd pulled well down over his ears. His bushy eyebrows and wild, unkempt beard were also white but were shot through with dirty looking silver streaks. His gaunt, dusky-skinned face was so time-worn and wrinkled that it carried every one of the hundred and ninety-two years that had passed since the day of his birth.

In spite of the unnatural great age etched into every line, his features were soft and friendly with a gentle openness that could inspire immediate and unhesitating trust. In sharp contrast with this amiable countenance though, were his eyes. For although far from hostile, behind the enigmatic blue-grey there lurked a dangerous light that glittered illusively, hinting at an inner strength to be ignored at one's peril.

His clothes were of simple skins, durable and warm but clumsily tailored and as devoid of style and form as his hat. Even his rough fur boots looked home-made.

He suddenly stopped and raised his eyes heavenward. Then in a quiet and beseeching voice, he offered a simple prayer to his god. "Oh Mordan, wise and powerful as you are, couldn't you have found a more suitable servant for this task? Or perhaps commanded me to act when I possessed the youth to ensure success? I fear now it's beyond my strength; and what then for the world? Will you allow all your creation to fall into darkness?" He cocked his head and listened as if waiting for a reply, but none came save the wind and the mocking cry of eagles far off in the distance. After a short while he sighed gently and continued on his way.

The morning was almost gone when to his immense delight, he stumbled upon a wide path running in almost the same direction as he was travelling. Briefly, he knelt in the snow and gave thanks to Mordan for this blessing; for surely it was the answer to his earlier prayer. A tingle of excitement ran through him as realised that he must be nearing his goal. The thought of a warm bed and hot food filled him with eager anticipation, although the thought of human contact – his first for many decades – filled him with trepidation.

As he trudged on in the bright, late winter sunshine, he studied the path that was making his progress so much easier than before. It was surprisingly well trodden and extremely well maintained. It suddenly dawned on him that it was not so much a wide path as a narrow road, easily capable of carrying a reasonably sized cart. Yet curiously, although he could see well into the distance, there were no signs of traffic, either wheeled or pedestrian.

His puzzlement ended abruptly when he noticed thin wisps of smoke rising from beyond the next ridge. Was it a sign that he was within touching distance of his destination? Inwardly he smiled as he imagined harassed mothers, bent over the cooking fires which were surely the source of the grey haze staining the clear blue sky. He pictured them stirring cauldrons of aromatic stew while calling to their laughing, mischievous children, impatiently imploring them to behave. Oh, how he missed the laughter of children!

He tried to increase his speed but his tired old legs were far less enthusiastic than his mind. The gradient was not that steep but in his feeble, enervated condition, it was a daunting obstacle that separated his aching limbs from a much-needed rest.

Eagerly, he arrived at the summit only to come to a shuddering, horrified halt. He cried out in dismay as he surveyed the terrible scene laid out before him. There, no more than three or four hundred strides below and beyond where he stood aghast, lay the shattered remains of a small, once picturesque village.

"No, no, no," he cried as he stumbled down the gently sloping path that led to the appalling scene of devastation – a devastation that seemed to mark an end to the world's last and only hope.

As he staggered down the hill, he reached inside his loosely fitting clothes and pulled out a small white object that he clutched tightly in his right hand. His ungainly and erratic stride then strengthened and all the encumbrances of age and frailty fell from him. He sprinted headlong toward the ruins, his pounding feet scattering snow in all directions. Even the fastest of runners in the flower of their youth would have been hard pressed to match his speed. The killing pace did not ease until he had passed well beyond the fringes of the wrecked village that had once stood so proudly in the gentle, secluded vale.

As if lost in a terrible waking nightmare, he slid the white object back inside the folds of his garments and shuffled numbly through the remains of the wide, spacious streets. His disbelieving eyes took in the full horror of the scene unfolding around him. It was a scene of frenzied bestiality which defied all description.

Savagely mutilated bodies lay everywhere, most no longer recognisable as human. Here and there, however, he could see corpses that were more intact than most, and in some of these it was possible to make out the gender. He found himself wishing that he couldn't, for the womenfolk had clearly been sickeningly violated before their brutal slaying.

His endurance finally came to an end when he spied the body of a small child; a girl of no more than two or three years of age who seemed to have been half eaten. He sank to his knees in utter despair and buried his head in his thin, bony hands.

"Too late, too late!" he wailed. Helplessly, he raised his eyes to the cloudless heavens where the innocence of the bright, clear sky seemed to mock the awful desolation, so stark was the contrast. "Mordan," he wept, the tears streaming down his distraught, time-worn features. "Why me? I'm too old and too slow. The destruction of all that's good lies on my feeble, unworthy shoulders."

Again, he buried his head in his hands, lost in a private world of unendurable pain as knelt in the brilliant winter sunshine. Great shuddering sobs wracked his frail body so violently, it seemed impossible that his heart could continue to beat. Somehow though, it did, and eventually the convulsions began to ease and a gradual change came over him.

S. P. MUIR

For a long time, he sat motionless, staring unseeingly at the cold, hard ground. But then slowly, he began to raise his head. His hand slid slowly and deliberately toward the strange white artefact hidden beneath his warm, roughly tailored skins. His tear-streaked face was ashen and gaunt but the elusive, dangerous light behind his eyes blazed with a fury to rival the dreadful holocaust around him. As his fingers touched the cold hard source of his power, he began to rise.

Suddenly, he stopped and became deathly still as something sharp jabbed painfully into the back of his neck and a cold hard voice said: "Move not one hair of your head lest I cleave your neck and part it from your body."

CHAPTER TWO

"Would you strike down a defenceless old man without first hearing him speak?" asked the ancient theurgist. Although his voice was thin and trembling, his eyes flashed angrily, burning with a cold and bitter fire.

"Old men who can outrun a hunting wolf may not be as defenceless as they claim," came a second voice from behind. "Nevertheless, it is our custom to be just. You may speak."

"And may I rise?" There was no reply but the sharp object was removed from his neck and taking this as permission, he climbed slowly to his feet and turned to face his captors.

Standing before him was an improbably slim and graceful looking man of perhaps twenty or twenty-five years of age. His clothes were completely white, contrasted only by the black leather of the straps on his leggings, his belt, and the headband which held the long golden hair from his face. In the centre of the headband was a silver, seven-pointed star. His eyes were fierce and passionate and this, together with his bright, keen edged sword, added all the weight to his bearing that his slight frame lacked.

Slightly behind and to the right of the stranger, standing on a low stone plinth was the owner of the second voice. He was dressed in identical garb to the first man and their faces were so alike, that were it not for a vast difference in build, he could not have told them apart. But in contrast to the slim swordsman, this man was broad and muscular, looking as solid and impervious as the rock upon which he stood. In his left hand he carried a large, heavy hammer.

The old man's heart leapt at the sight of them. Could he dare to hope that all was not lost after all? Could something be saved from the blood and desolation that surrounded them? Excitement flooded his body but when he spoke, his voice was deliberately calm and level.

"You have my gratitude," he said with an almost imperceptible bow. "Mordan's children have always been a courteous race."

The larger man's brow furrowed as he jumped down from the plinth and moved questioningly forward. "You've had dealings with my people before?" he asked sceptically. "You know us?"

"Alas no," the old man said sadly. "But I have knowledge *of* you and *for* you."

"And do you have knowledge of...of this?" spat the first man, waving his sword at the desecrated corpses lying scattered all around them.

"It was precisely to prevent this catastrophe that I've been sent; but to my eternal shame, I've arrived too late."

The first man pressed his sword to the old man's throat but the second gently pushed the blade down until it pointed harmlessly at the snow-covered ground.

"Then tell me," the powerfully built one asked. "Who would commit such an atrocity, and how did you hope to prevent it?"

The old man sighed. "The one responsible for this crime has long sought to find your people and wipe them from the face of the land. Surely you've heard of him? No? Well, his name is Limnash the Great, the cruel god-king of all Keshtar; and now that he's found you, he'll not rest until you're utterly destroyed."

The muscular, white-clad stranger tucked his hammer into his belt, put his hands on the ancient's thin, frail shoulders and peered into his face.

In contrast to the intense fire of the swordsman's eyes, the eyes that now studied the old man's features so carefully were gentle and thoughtful – despite being identical in both colour and shape to those of his slim companion. Meticulously they searched every line and every wrinkle, staring deep into the ancient's perilous blue-grey orbs as if seeking to penetrate his very soul. The old traveller felt naked and vulnerable beneath the intense yet somehow benign gaze.

"I see within you much we should know," he said thoughtfully. "You must share everything with us so we may act appropriately."

"That which I have to share is for the ears of the High-Lord alone – if he still lives. Do you know if he survived this destruction?"

"He was in rude health when we left Sirris two days ago," the slim warrior replied sneeringly.

"You mean there's another village?" the old man asked, a note of excitement creeping into his voice.

The sword bearer snorted and looked at his companion. "Village!" he scoffed. "And he claims to know of us."

"Patience Eh'lorne," soothed the gentle eyed stranger. "For once in your life let me take the lead." He returned his attention to the curiously dressed ancient in front of him. "Sirris is the home city of our people. To call it a village is like calling these mountains a molehill. But in answer to your question, yes, there is another."

"Then we must leave for Sirris at once!" the old man cried. "As it is, we may be too late to prevent it suffering the same fate as this place."

The hard, strong hands left his shoulders and the soft noble eyes looked sadly around the smouldering ruins. "This place, as you call it, is – or rather was – the village of Sarren. It was home to many of our friends and our kin." The pale young face turned back and focused on the old man again. "But come," he said in a kindly tone. "Let's begin again. My name is Eldore Starbrow and this is my twin brother, Eh'lorne. High-Lord Lorne is our father, so whatever you must say to him, you can also say to us; so why not begin with your name?"

His name? Yes, he did once have a name but it had faded into the mists of time so long it was since he'd heard it spoken. For a moment or two it escaped him but then the memory of a former life came flooding back. He remembered his mother, dark and elegant; his comfortable chambers... He closed his eyes for just a moment to contain the feelings of loss as he recalled the sumptuous palace; the warmth and the comfort; but most of all he remembered his father. He'd been strong and proud, powerful and wise.

"My name is Bandil, son of Bail, and I bring a grave warning of a terrible power that threatens the whole world. But I also bring tidings of hope and redemption for the ancient race of Arlien kings; so we must reach Sirris and warn your father before it's too late."

"Well, Bandil, son of Bail," Eh'lorne sneered coldly. "You must tell *us* these tidings and how you came by them." He put his sword to the old man's throat again. "*We* will then judge if you're worthy of an audience with our father."

"Did you not hear me?" Bandil asked impatiently. "The whole world is in peril! Every moment we spend standing here makes Limnash's final victory all the more certain. We must go – and we must go now!"

The two brothers exchanged a glance and momentarily closed their eyes before returning their attention to the strangely clad figure in front of them. Eldore, the larger of the two, shook his head.

"I'm sorry Bandil," he said regretfully. "But Eh'lorne's right; we must first establish that you're free of any involvement in this foul slaughter of innocents."

"Speak or die." Eh'lorne added threateningly.

Bandil looked as though he was about to explode. He spluttered incoherently, struggling to find the words to articulate his frustration.

"Fine!" he suddenly cried angrily. "We will tarry here bandying futile words of proof and death while the sky comes crashing down around our ears!"

The two brothers didn't reply and seemed completely unmoved by his ire, although at least Eh'lorne lowered his sword. The old man looked from one to the other as if awaiting a response, but finally, with a deep sigh of resignation, he began his tale.

"Since before living memory I've lived as a recluse, devoting my life to the service of Mordan, our god. Through divine inspiration and prophetic dreams, he revealed to me the location of the Arlien race of kings – your people. I was given the task of preventing your destruction and preserving the royal bloodline. If we survive Limnash's onslaught, your people may even go on to liberate all Keshtar from his long, tyrannical reign. Mordan has instructed me to show the High-Lord the means by which all this could be done."

Eldore raised an eyebrow. "And why would *our* god disclose all this to a Keshtari heathen such as you, when we, his chosen people, are kept in ignorance?"

Bandil sighed heavily. "That I do not know; but I've lived far beyond my natural years, sustained for this purpose by his power as I dwelt deep in the Mystic Mountains."

"You lie!" roared Eh'lorne, forcing the old man back a step with his sword. "The way to those mountains is barred by the impenetrable pillars of Mordan's Maze. None may enter that place and live. To spend even one night within its fringe will drive a man insane."

"Even so, it is the truth," the old man said simply.

"Blasphemy!" cried the young swordsman, apoplectic with rage. "Brother, he trespasses in these sacred hills and mocks our god with his falsehoods. You know the penalty for such encroachment and heresy. It's written that his life's blood is forfeit and must be spilt into the cleansing snow."

"That is the law," Eldore replied tersely.

It was the first time Bandil had heard anger in the muscular Arlien's voice and he realised it was a warning of just how much danger he was in. But his response was swift and startling. His right hand was a blur as he pulled the small white object from the folds of his garments and thrust it towards the sky. It burst into life with a blinding light that blazed between his fingers like a fallen star.

"Do not think that one sword and two hot heads are enough to daunt me!" he cried in a voice crackling with barely restrained power. "I am an emissary of the great god Mordan himself. Were it his will, fire would rain down from the sky and reduce you to ash!"

Eldore took a surprised step backwards but Eh'lorne stood firm, dangerously poised like a cat waiting its chance to pounce. Tense moments passed until gradually the dazzling glare faded to a soft luminescence and the wizened hermit let his arm fall.

"But that is not his wish," he said quietly. "You shall have your proof that he speaks through me." With his left hand he pulled at a leather thong which hung around his scrawny, dirt-stained neck and drew out a small leather pouch. "Do you know the legend of how the Mystic Mountains were formed?" he asked wearily.

"Every child knows that," Eh'lorne replied, his voice thick with wounded pride. "After creating the world, Mordan's physical body passed away leaving his spirit free to roam across the surface of the Earth unhindered. His body lay at rest and became the Mystic Mountains. The rocks are his bones and the soil his blood. The great maze then sprang from the grateful earth to guard his remains for all eternity."

"And what do you think of that legend?"

"It's an infant's tale, a myth. Mordan was always a spirit and never flesh. He is immortal and could never have died."

"That is correct," said Bandil. "But the tale does contain a grain of truth, although how such knowledge could have reached the ears of mortal men is beyond me. The Maze *did* spring from the earth to protect the secrets of that holy land." He opened the pouch wide and then held both hands out for the brothers to see. In his right hand, still glowing gently, was a smooth, egg-sized stone the colour of polished ivory. The pouch in his left hand contained a handful of deep-red coloured earth.

"Observe," he said solemnly. "This is the Mystic Stone. It was infused with strength and hope at the founding of the world and then hidden in the Mystic Mountains until Mordan's spirit led me to its secret location. This pouch contains the soil from that most sacred of places; it's the only soil in the whole world stained by his sanguineous power. Here then is your proof: behold the blood and bone of our god."

Eldore gasped. Slowly and reverently, he reached out and gently touched the radiant white stone. "You speak the truth," he said in a soft, hushed tone.

His brother, Eh'lorne, stared dumbfoundedly at the artefacts. Suddenly, he sank to his knees. Then, hilt first, he held out his sword towards the old hermit.

"I swear this oath to you, Bandil, son of Bail," he said with fierce sincerity. "My sword is yours to command and where you lead, I will follow. I'm your servant from now and forever more; for surely our god speaks to us through you."

"Bless you, Eh'lorne, but it's *I* who must serve *you*. So now, if we have all that sorted to your satisfaction, let's press on to Sirris and pray that we're not too late."

The young warrior leapt to his feet and sheathed his sword. "So be it. Can you run?" Bandil nodded, marvelling at the sudden and profound change in the slim swordsman's attitude. Yet even with that change and his sword safely in its scabbard, there was something unnerving about this tall, extraordinary man. "Then let's away! Brother, will you manage the supplies?"

"I'll manage them," Eldore replied moving quickly back to the plinth. He reached behind the low stone platform and retrieved a large, heavy pack that he effortlessly strapped to his back. "Now," he said, adjusting the heavy load to a more comfortable position. "We must complete a two-day march in less than one; so we must run as we've never run before!"

Soon, the three men were sprinting through the centre of the smouldering ruins following the path that led roughly north-eastwards. They kept their eyes fixed firmly on the road in an effort to shut out the grisly horrors lying scattered all around them like a terrible waking nightmare. Thankfully, it wasn't too long before they cleared the far side of the village and the path began to ascend out of the secluded vale and away from the gruesome visions. As they climbed, they settled down to a slower, more sustainable pace.

Only once was there a pause when Eldore stopped and looked back at the devastation in the valley below. He stood for a few moments, his expression a mixture of sorrow and regret before spinning around and hurrying after his companions.

As the race continued, Eh'lorne smiled in wonder at the frail, wizened old man beside him, the snow flying from his feet as he effortlessly matched him stride for stride. Bandil noticed the amazement on his new companion's face and smiled back at him.

"It's the Stone," he explained, puffing very slightly. "While I hold it Mordan grants me the strength of youth. I'll pay for this exertion later though; and the more power I draw, the greater the price. I'll be a sorry sight at journey's end!"

On and on they flew, desperation lending wings to their heels and the wide, well-trodden path easing their way. At around mid-afternoon Eldore called a halt.

"A short break," he panted, pulling the pack from his back and opening it. "We must eat and drink or we'll lose the strength to succeed."

Eh'lorne sank gratefully to the ground and tried to catch his breath, envious of the old man's energy. Eldore, meanwhile, rummaged around in his pack and then passed over a large stone flask and some round brown cakes. The old man uncorked the flask and sniffed warily at its contents.

"Water," he muttered and took a long pull. He suddenly spluttered violently, coughing and gasping for air as the odourless, tasteless liquid seared his throat like a strong spirit.

"Wow!" he croaked as a fiery glow spread through his body. He stared at the flask in amazement as he realized that unlike any other spirit, this drink actually quenched his thirst.

"My apologies," laughed Eldore, his eyes twinkling. "I should have realised that this would be your first taste of firebrew."

"It's amazing!" wheezed Bandil.

"It's more than amazing if you drink too much of it," laughed Eh'lorne. "It's concentrated water, so I suggest you eat some of that honey cake or it'll feel like it's burning right through your belly."

The old man smiled ruefully and took a bite from the hard, dry-looking cake. His eyes widened as the unappetizing crust gave way to a soft and fragrant interior. As he greedily finished it off, Eldore closed his eyes, a gentle smile playing on his lips. Eh'lorne grinned and then chuckled as he too closed his eyes. Both brothers then opened them in unison and looked affectionately at the strange, eccentric-looking recluse. Bandil looked from one to the other as the truth suddenly dawned on him.

"You can speak without words," he said, his voice full of wonder.

"Of course. Mind-talk is nothing unusual," explained Eldore. "Every Arlien has the capability to some extent; most are very adept."

"But none are as expert as my brother and I," bragged Eh'lorne.

"Then can't you use it to warn your people in Sirris?"

"If only we could," Eldore replied wistfully. "As my brother says, no one can use mind-talk as skilfully as we can – perhaps because we're twins. Yet even between the two of us we can reach no further than a stretch or so. But if either of us tries to reach anyone else – even our own father – we're little better than the next man or woman. Then we're limited to a range of no more than three or four hundred strides."

"Then let's continue to close the distance," said Bandil, climbing back to his feet and squaring his shoulders. Eldore repacked the provisions and the three travellers continued their journey at the swiftest maintainable pace.

As the sun began to dip towards the western peaks, the Arlien twins began to slow the pace until they were travelling at no more than a gentle trot. They glanced uneasily around, searching every rock or snow-covered bush in an effort to pinpoint the source of their growing anxiety.

"Hold!" cried Eh'lorne at last, drawing his sword. "Do you sense it brother?"

"Aye; I smell a trap!"

Bandil looked anxiously around them. "I see nothing," he whispered. "Where are they?"

"I fear they are everywhere," the swordsman stated dryly.

As if taking their cue from his words, scores of outlandish figures seemed to rise up out of the snow, surrounding them on all sides. The hellish creatures then began to move slowly and menacingly towards them.

CHAPTER THREE

The creatures were vaguely human in shape, but were naked apart from the coarse dark fur which grew on their hunched, misshapen bodies. Each one carried a wicked-looking, tooth-edged sword, tightly gripped in a long, claw-tipped hand. Their feral eyes burned with a savage hatred as they crept slowly forward, snarling ferociously.

"Lich!" spat Bandil in disgust.

"What are they?" Eldore asked, his voice a mixture of fascination and horror.

"Foot-soldiers of Limnash. They were human once but he reduced them to animals with his dark, forbidden arts."

As Eldore slipped the heavy pack from his shoulders, Eh'lorne looked around, quickly calculating the odds. His face hardened as the hopelessness of their situation became all too apparent.

"There are too many for us," he said grimly. "But I give you my word old man, you'll not fall while there's breath left in my body."

"We're not lost yet!" Bandil snapped. "If you can guard me for just a few moments, I'll break this noose. When the time comes, run for the High River, we must be close to it by now."

"It's just a stretch or so to the west; but it's far too wide and swift to cross."

"If we can gain enough time it'll not be a barrier; but we must outrun these demons first, for what I must do cannot be done quickly."

The two brothers nodded their understanding and placed themselves back-to-back with the old recluse standing between them. He held the Mystic Stone in both hands and began quietly to hum in a soft, monotonous tone. Steadily, the note grew louder and louder and as it did, the stone grew brighter and brighter as if sound and light were fused into one.

Suddenly, the lich charged, snarling and shrieking as they ran. Soundlessly, Eldore braced himself against the onslaught then smashed his hammer into the faces of their bestial attackers. At the same time, Eh'lorne skilfully whirled his sword around his head. "Mordan!" he thundered as he cut and slashed at the wall of hairy bodies. His sword flashed brightly as it reflected the Stone's brilliance, weaving a net of light as he fought.

Momentarily, the lich were halted by the unexpected ferocity of the two Arliens' defence, but almost immediately, they pressed forward again. They were so hungry for blood and so angered by the stiff resistance that they hampered each other's movements in their eagerness to kill. Even so, their sheer weight of numbers would soon overwhelm the gallant, white-clad champions.

But the twins had earned Bandil all the time he needed. He drew himself up to his full height and held the brightly shining Stone high in the air.

"*Vernarsh!*" he cried in a deep and powerful voice. A dazzling white light flashed from his raised hand and every one of the foul creatures went mad, biting and hacking at each other in blind confusion. Yet as incredibly bright as the sudden flash was, it proved harmless to the twins' eyes, leaving their vision completely unimpaired.

The three men took their chance and barged through the writhing mass, sprinting full pelt for the western horizon. It took several moments for the stricken lich to regain their sight and to realize their quarry had bolted. This gave the fleeing companions a small but precious lead. All too soon, however, the grotesque half-beasts came howling after them.

Once off the path, the snow was much deeper, and in many places had gathered into chest-high drifts. Here, Eldore led the way using his powerful, muscular arms to shovel the snow aside; but on the clearer stretches, the power-filled old man and the slim, athletic Eh'lorne pulled out a clear lead. Eventually though, the power of the Stone began to have a detrimental effect on Bandil's fragile frame. It made him feel both hollow and overstretched as though he could either deflate or snap at any moment.

None too soon they blundered over the last of an interminable series of ridges, and to their immense relief, they saw their goal. The High River flowed roughly from north to south and looked from their vantage point like a wide dark ribbon winding across their path. With renewed vigour, they flung themselves down the steep slope, slipping and sliding as they went, desperately trying to keep their footing on the treacherous surface. Eh'lorne outstripped them both but then lost his lead when he tripped on a hidden rock and was sent sprawling headfirst down the hill. Grimly he held on to his precious sword and somehow managed a tucked half-roll that enabled him to regain his feet and race on after his companions. Finally, he slithered to a halt beside them on the icy riverbank.

Quickly and calmly, he scanned the riverbank looking for a more defensible position, but there was none to be found. Mentally he shrugged his shoulders. At least with the river at their backs they couldn't be surrounded. The odds, although worse than poor, had at least halved.

"What now?" Eldore asked, struggling to catch his breath.

"Now you must guard me while I create a bridge," the old man panted as he knelt beside the rushing water.

"A bridge? You can do that?" In spite of everything he'd seen the old hermit do, there was still a note of incredulity in Eldore's voice.

"I can," Bandil called over his shoulder. "But I'll be beyond spent afterwards. The burden of our journey must then fall on you, for I'll be as unconscious as the dead!" He then plunged the Stone into the freezing river, wincing with shock as he fought the urge to pull it out again. The rushing, icy water seemed to burn his flesh and slice his wrist like a cold knife.

"Then I'll carry you," the muscular young lord assured him before adding bitterly, "After all, I no longer have a pack to burden me." The old man didn't reply so Eldore turned and placed himself beside his brother, ready to defend the now chanting theurgist. He glanced at his twin standing proudly beside him impatiently testing the balance of his sword. Eh'lorne was a born warrior and since early childhood had been a fighter; first with his fists and then, under the tutelage of their father, he'd begun to learn the art of swordplay. Soon after that, the great Arms-Master Rennil himself had taken on the young lord as his protégé. For as long as Eldore could remember, his brother had longed for the glory and fame of the old kings.

Eldore felt the weight of his hammer and wished he could share his brother's passion for fighting. He tried telling himself that the pounding of his heart was due to the exertion of their run, but in truth, he was just plain scared. It was tradition for the heirs to the High-Lord's seat to learn a trade and he'd chosen the art of forging metal. He'd gained for himself an enviable reputation for the quality of his workmanship, and his swords and armour were much prized in the north and in southern kingdom of Mah-Kashia. He'd drawn satisfaction from creation rather than destruction. Not that that would be of use in this situation. He took a deep breath and planted his feet firmly in the snow – it wouldn't do to slip now!

"Here they come!" warned Eh'lorne, a belligerent smile playing on his lips.

The lich came flooding down the hill like a hairy tidal wave, whooping and screaming with bloodcurdling fury as they came. With reckless abandon they crashed into the skilfully wielded weapons of the two brothers. In spite of his fear, Eldore stood like a rock, a grim expression on his youthful face as his heavy hammer swept their attackers aside two or three at a time.

Eh'lorne on the other hand, moved with all the style and grace of a dancer. "Mordan!" he roared as once again his sword bit into flesh. His speed and dexterity were astounding as he ducked and whirled, cutting and slashing with extraordinary skill and precision. As he fought, he sang the warrior's song Rennil had taught him to control his breathing. If truth were told, he was actually enjoying himself.

The bodies that began to pile up around them soon became an asset, hampering the lich's frenzied, clumsy attempts to strike a telling blow. Even so, Eldore knew it was only a matter of time before one of the wildly swinging tooth-edged blades found its mark.

"Bandil," he called. "Time is short, we need that bridge!" there was no answer save the hermit's strange, rhythmic song – barely audible above the clamour of battle.

Quickly ducking behind his brother's whirling blade, he risked a glance at the old man's progress and gave a sharp exclamation of surprise and hope. From the point where Bandil held the Stone in the freezing water, a thick layer of ice was spreading towards the far bank. Already it was three quarters of the way across. Another fifty strides and it would be complete.

All this Eldore registered in the blink of an eye, but that was far too long to turn his attention from the battle raging around him. A sharp pain erupted in his side with a force that sent him staggering into Eh'lorne. But somehow, his brother reached out with his free hand and steadied Eldore while at the same time hacking off the head of the creature that had struck the blow.

Eldore tried to continue the fight but was now hampered by a deep gash in his side. Eh'lorne too was leaving himself open as he tried to cover his brother's slow, pain-filled movements. He was no longer singing – he was fighting for their lives! Despite the cold he was sweating profusely and his sword arm was beginning to ache. They could not hold on much longer,

But Bandil did not let them down. As soon as the ice reached the far side of the river, he pulled his hand clear of the water and lurched to his feet.

"It's done," he croaked, then staggered exhausted across the bridge. At the far side he turned and collapsed to his knees, shaking with fatigue but ready to carry out his final task.

The two Arliens were now backing slowly across the ice, not daring to turn their backs on the wildly swinging swords of the lich.

"Go," urged Eh'lorne. "I'll hold them." Without a word, Eldore immediately ducked behind his brother and ran to join Bandil. As soon as his brother was clear, Eh'lorne leapt high into the air and with a loud cry, cut down three of the hellish creatures in one sweep. As he landed, he spun on his heels and raced across to the far bank. The suddenness of his retreat gave him the precious strides he needed to escape unscathed.

As Eh'lorne leapt onto the bank, Bandil slammed his fist down on the bridge. The ice bucked and fractured into a thousand pieces, throwing all the creatures on it into the fast-flowing water. Only a handful of the grotesque beasts were left alive on the eastern bank. All the rest were either slain or swept away by the swift current to a freezing, watery death. Eh'lorne turned and held his bloody sword high in the air.

"Go!" he called to the remaining lich standing uncertainly on the far side of the river. "Go, lest Mordan lose his patience and strike you all to dust!"

Screaming their frustration, the human-like beasts turned and fled, bounding back up the slope from whence they'd come. Eh'lorne dipped his sword in the river, dried it on his leggings, and then returned it to its sheath. Only then did he look to his companions. Bandil lay prostrate on the bank beside the water while Eldore stood leaning against a boulder, his face screwed up in pain.

"We can't stay here," Eldore said between gritted teeth. "We can't allow those disgusting animals to find Sirris unprepared."

The young warrior nodded in reply, then went and knelt beside his brother. He examined the wound in his side. It was a nasty gash, at least two hands long and disturbingly deep; but it was clean and although his white tunic was stained with blood, it wasn't bleeding too heavily.

"If you can bear the pain you can travel, although running will be beyond you."

"We've gained more than a march by crossing the river," Eldore growled. "Even if we had to crawl all the way to Sirris, we'd arrive sooner than if we'd followed the road and run."

Eh'lorne grunted and then moved on to the old man lying crumpled in the snow. He examined him carefully then looked at his brother with a puzzled expression on his face.

"I don't understand it; I can find no sign of injury yet he doesn't wake."

"He spoke to me about this earlier. He has a frail body to carry so much power; but he will recover and until he does, I said that I'd carry him."

Eh'lorne shook his head "No brother; you're hurt and in need of rest, and we can't even bind your wound. It'll be enough that you carry yourself. He's slight and not heavy; *I* will carry him."

"If you insist," Eldore agreed, pushing himself away from the rock. "Come on then, let's go. A journey not started is never completed."

The full moon shone coldly down on the nightmare journey of the Arlien brothers. Eldore staggered along, his teeth gritted against the searing pain in his side; and although each step was a personal triumph, it was a hollow victory for it had to be followed by another, then another.

Eh'lorne fared little better for he was already exhausted by his extravagant style of fighting and by the long afternoon run. Now, as he trudged through the snow with Bandil's inert body in his arms, it felt as though his every muscle was screaming in agony. Every sinew in his tall, slim frame was shouting in protest against the extremes to which it was being pressed.

By midnight, they'd both had enough. Eldore collapsed against a cliff-like outcrop and sank to the snow-covered ground while Eh'lorne carefully placed Bandil in a sitting position beside his brother. Tenderly, he brushed the matted wisps of white hair from the old man's dusky, wrinkled face and straightened his crude fur hat.

"You've grown fond of him already," Eldore commented with a slight note of surprise in his voice.

"Somehow I have," Eh'lorne replied as he gazed into the moonlit, wrinkled brown features. "I'm convinced he'll prove a powerful ally, but there's something sad and pitiable about him as well." He carried on staring at him for a moment longer then shook himself out of his reverie and wearily squeezed himself between his two companions. "I must say though, care as I might and as light as he is, I can carry him no further. Perhaps we should be grateful that we lost our supplies – it would be far beyond my strength to carry both."

"You've spent too much time with Rennil," Eldore replied with a pained smile. "While you played soldiers, I worked at my forge. By sweat and toil I grew broad and strong. Waving a sword around does not build muscle, my brother."

"And muscle does not turn sword thrusts! Consider your wound before lecturing me."

Eldore burst out laughing, clutching at his side as waves of searing agony exploded through his body. "Oh, my brother, your wit is as sharp as your weapon. Your wisdom is beyond me."

Eh'lorne frowned. "I've been telling you that since we were children; and if your mind was as powerful as your arms, you'd have realised it long before now."

Before Eldore could reply they were interrupted by a low moan from Bandil. Eh'lorne turned and then knelt beside him. He peered intently into the old hermit's deeply shadowed eyes.

"How are you my friend?" he asked, his voice full of concern.

The old man groaned. "I'll live – just! I've never before called up so much power; I fear I've found my limits."

"You're not alone," Eldore commented wryly. "We're all spent; but Sirris will fall unless it's warned. As soon as you're able we must continue the journey."

"Then we'll begin at once. Eh'lorne, will you help me to my feet?" The young lord obliged. "There now, I can stand. Just give me a moment or two to get the life back into my legs and we can go." He stood stamping his feet while Eh'lorne turned to assist his brother. By the time Eldore was upright, Bandil was ready. He nodded to the two Arliens and the journey continued.

They no longer ran – it would have been beyond them if they'd tried – but doggedly they trudged on through the moonlit night, carefully picking their way through the shadows. Without using the Stone to give himself strength and speed, Bandil was once again just a tired old man, head down but determined.

The going was easier for the twins though, for without Bandil to carry, Eh'lorne was able to support and assist his brother. But even so, their progress was painfully slow.

When they were only half way to their destination, Eh'lorne called a halt. "The moon's full and high," he said before pointing to a tall, steeply rising rock-face that stood nearby. "From that peak over there I should be able to see most of the way to Sirris. Wait for me here, I won't be long."

Eldore nodded and sank carefully to the ground. Bandil joined him and watched the graceful young Arlien climb the steep slope, marvelling at the speed of his ascent.

"How can anyone so tired be so agile?" he asked, his voice full of wonder.

Eldore followed his gaze and shook is his head. "There indeed is a question. He's an amazing man, full of contradictions. Our people love him dearly and would follow him into the fires of Halgar if he asked it of them – I know I would."

"Do you always follow his lead?"

"Usually, yes," laughed Eldore. "He acts while I'm still thinking; it's been that way since we were children – although I must say, he often got us into a lot of trouble."

Bandil grinned. "I can imagine."

They lapsed into silence as they followed Eh'lorne's progress. It wasn't too long before he reached the summit. He stood outlined against the black sky; a small white figure shining in the cold, bright moonlight. Suddenly, he turned and threw himself recklessly back down the slope, slipping and sliding alarmingly as he went. Without a word, the two companions rose and went to meet him. As he careered towards them, he called for them to run.

"Lich!" he shouted. "Too many to count but there must be thousands. Without warning, Sirris will fall and they'll be slaughtered in their beds!"

The two men sprang into life and tried to run after their nimble companion, but although they both tried to sprint, all they could manage was a ragged trot. Their efforts soon came to an abrupt end when Eldore tripped and fell sprawling into the snow. Twice he tried to regain his feet and twice he fell back to his knees, a fresh flow of blood spreading from his wound and staining his tunic.

"Eh'lorne wait!" the old man called breathlessly. We can't go a step further – your brother's too badly hurt and I'm beyond my limits. We can't hope to catch them now."

Eh'lorne's quick temper suddenly flared and he came storming back towards them, shouting angrily. "I will not stop here and leave my people to be slaughtered! If I have to fly all the way to Sirris to save them, then that is what I'll do – alone if I must!"

"Calm yourself," the old man said, holding his head in his hands. "I must think. There has to be a way of sending a warning. I cannot believe Mordan would abandon his chosen people to such a fate."

"Think fast old man," Eh'lorne grated. "Time is running out."

Bandil stood tugging at his beard until suddenly, his eyes lit up. "Of course!" he exclaimed excitedly. "Oh, I'm such a fool! Quickly, come and sit beside your brother for it'll take the strength of all three of us." He knelt beside the stricken Arlien and impatiently motioned for Eh'lorne to join them. With a doubtful look, the tall, slim warrior did as he was urged. He sank to his knees facing the old man who had now pulled out the Stone and was rubbing it between his hands.

"How is this going to help?" he asked irritably.

"Foolish youth," Bandil cried angrily. "Do you mock me? You are Mordan's children and this Stone is a vessel for his spirit. With its power your mind-talk can reach Sirris and warn your people. I feel it could carry your minds all the way to Arl if the need arose. Now hurry; I'll hold the Stone while you both place your hands on mine." The twins obeyed with hope beginning to shine in their eyes. "Now open your hearts, let the Stone channel Mordan's spirit into your souls and let your minds soar."

For a few heartbeats nothing happened. But then as the stone began to glow between the old man's gnarled fingers, a warm wave of energy crept up the brothers' arms until it cradled their entire bodies. Closing their eyes, they reached out with their minds; further and further; far beyond any distance they had achieved before. And still they travelled until at last, they knew they'd arrive and began seeking out the heart that was closest to their own. When the contact was made, they quickly and concisely relayed the details of the imminent threat. Then, with an almost audible snap, the contact was broken. The shock of it sent Eldore and Bandil sprawling back into the snow; but Eh'lorne continued to kneel with a fierce light burning in his dark, passionate eyes.

"It is done!" he stated triumphantly.

CHAPTER FOUR

High-Lord Lorne sat on the edge of his large, four-posted bed and tried to shake off the sticky syrup of deep sleep that was slowing his thoughts. He looked around the comfortable bedchamber that was dimly lit by the embers of the fire still glowing in a small grate set into the far wall. He rubbed his eyes, and in his mind, he reran his sons' desperate message. Sarren was gone; razed to the ground by an unspeakably cruel and ruthless enemy. All of its inhabitants slaughtered and the womenfolk... He shut that terrible image away; it was too distressing and he needed his mind focused on the swift action he needed to take to prevent Sirris from suffering the same fate. An improbable army of savage man-beasts – many thousands strong – were less than half a march away.

It suddenly occurred to him that his sons had spoken to him from a great distance, which was of course impossible. Mind-talk could not reach any further than a hundred strides or so, therefore his sons had to be close by – probably in the Halls of Duty itself. With a sudden burst of relief and anger, he decided it must be one of Eh'lorne's ridiculous tricks – and a particularly cruel one at that! It had been a long time since he'd been on the receiving end of one of Eh'lorne's practical jokes. He had believed that the rash, headstrong youngster was now enough of an adult to put aside such childish games; but obviously not. With an irritated sigh, he swung his legs back onto the bed, pulled the covers up and settled back down to sleep. There was going to be trouble in the morning – that much was certain!

Suddenly, just a few moments later he sat bolt upright. Eldore had always had far more sense than to indulge in such nonsense. And the urgent, desperate tone of their mind-talk was definitely not an affectation.

He threw off the covers, moved quickly to the fire and used its embers to light one of the tapers that he took from a receptacle on the mantelpiece. Guarding the flame with his free hand, he carried it over to a low plain table that stood near to the imposing bed – a bed which seemed far too large for a single man; but since the death of his beloved wife, Veyanna, some twenty-four years ago, he could not bear to consider sharing it with another. The table held only two objects: a lamp and a large hand bell. Carefully, he lit the lamp and once it was shining satisfactorily, he picked up the bell and rang it as loudly as he could.

The chamber revealed by the soft, warm lamplight was strangely at odds with his sumptuous berth. It was sufficiently spacious and comfortable enough, but its contents, although marvellous in quality, were sparse and plain in design. Carefully folded on the small armchair that nestled in a corner close to the fire, were his clothes. Hurriedly he stripped off his sleeping gown and began to pull them on. In design and colour they were almost identical to the attire of his sons; white tunic and leggings tailored from a cloth that comprised of three separate layers, quilted to form an amazingly warm material. The lining was made from soft and comfortable brushed linen; then came a thicker layer of pliable woollen fibres to provide insulation, and finally a shastin outer.

Shastin was a wonderful material, unique to the Arlien people. It was valuable enough to be traded with the only two nations of the Earth that shared the secret of the Arlien's existence. This soft, hardwearing material was woven from the long, coarse coat of the shastora mountain goats that the Arliens tended as livestock. Its manufacture involved a long and complex process of repeated beating and combing that resulted in a tight, water resistant cloth of incredible durability.

He was only halfway through dressing when he stopped and listened intently for sounds of stirring from outside the room; but he could hear nothing other than the occasional faint crackling from the dying fire. With an impatient curse, he picked up the bell and rang it even louder and longer than before.

He cocked his head and once again listened for any signs of life but there were none. He stormed across the room and threw the door open.

"Bishtar!" he called at the top of his voice whilst ringing the bell so hard it seemed in danger of losing its clapper. "Bishtar! Where in Halgar-come are you?" He stood in the doorway, legs splayed, bell in one hand and the other resting impatiently on his hip. He muttered about the dire consequences that awaited the household's chief servant if he did not appear soon.

In the half-light of the lamp shining through the doorway, he looked every bit the image of his slim, athletic son. His impatient, intolerant demeanour only added to the close resemblance. Then from a darkened corridor that led off from further along the hallway, he heard the slamming of a door and saw the faint gleam of an approaching light. The light was accompanied by the sound of running footsteps that grew rapidly louder as they approached until at last, Bishtar appeared.

He was a tallish man, not a great deal shorter than Lorne himself, but his slight corpulence disguised the reality of his true stature. Neither was he very much older than the lord he served, but his thinning grey hair – now matted and uncombed – along with his loose, sagging jowls, made him appear very much the senior of the two. His bleary, red-rimmed eyes were full of surprise and concern for his beloved master. The sight of him standing there, half-dressed and apparently half-crazed filled him with an apprehension that bordered on dread.

"My lord I…"

"There's no time to explain," the High-Lord interrupted. "Doom is upon us! You must wake every member of the household – everyone, mind, even the children."

"The children?" Bishtar asked agog.

"There's no time to argue, just do exactly as I say. I want everyone gathered in the great hall before I've finished dressing. They must be ready to leave here at once, so they must be shod and warmly clothed against the night air. Is that clear?"

"But my lord…"

"No buts!" Lorne interrupted once more, this time with his voice rising in frustration. "Their very lives are at stake; if you would save them you must act now!"

Bishtar still hesitated but only for the briefest of moments; his complete trust in the lord he'd served for so long quickly overcame any misgivings. With a quick nod he turned and scurried away. Lorne could hear him as he faded into the distance, shouting and banging loudly on doors. With a satisfied grunt, he turned and re-entered the bedchamber. He finished dressing more slowly and carefully than before, for he knew that few of the household would be ready before him; but at least his impossible command would add some urgency to their preparations. The deliberate care of his movements however, were completely at odds with his wildly racing mind. If what his sons had told him was true, this was no impudent raid on a trade caravan, nor even one of the rare, daring incursions by the larger bands of tribesmen from beyond the eastern wilds. No, this was war!

When he was fully dressed, he passed through another doorway and into an adjoining room. It was far smaller than his sleeping chamber, containing nothing more than a desk and a chair. This was his private office and the walls were lined with shelves stacked with dozens of scrolls and several old, loosely-bound books. He settled at the desk, took out a quill and ink and started to scribble a note on a handy sheet of blank parchment. He then folded it, sealed it with wax melted over the lamp and stamped the seal with the ring of Duty that he wore on his right hand.

He was about to leave when he suddenly paused. With a thoughtful look on his face, he scanned one of the many shelves until he located the precise scroll he was looking for. Being careful not to disturb any of the others, he pulled it out, opened it, and after finding the particular section he was searching for, he began to read. After a while he angrily closed it and threw it against the wall.

"Damn the law!" he shouted as he stormed out of the room. He exited the bedchamber then hurried along the hallway. He soon reached a landing which stood at the top of an impressively sweeping stairway that he proceeded to descend at a dangerous, breakneck speed. The stairs led down to a large central atrium containing many closed doors – doors that concealed corridors that led away to the various other parts of the sprawling Halls of Duty. He raced across the atrium and headed towards the great hall which was located near the main entrance of the great house.

The great hall itself was a multi-purpose area which was used mostly for balls, parties, and the regular gatherings during which the High-Lord would address the assembled representatives of the populace. The floor was of a polished-wood, parquet design and the walls were draped with plain but visually pleasing tapestries. Along each of the walls ran long, fixed wooden benches that were scattered with strategically placed cushions.

Around twenty or so members of the household had already arrived and by the light of their lamps he could see that every one of them looked dazed, confused, and not a little frightened. A young fair headed boy of around ten or eleven years of age caught his eye. The youth was pressed tightly against his mother's side, his face pale and his eyes wide with fear.

"Hello Yewan," Lorne said in a calm, level voice while forcing a reassuring smile to his lips. "Can you come over here for a moment?"

The boy hesitated at first but with a little encouragement from his mother, he trotted over and looked up at the High Lord expectantly.

"Now then young man, can I trust you with a very important errand?" The boy nodded uncertainly. "Excellent!" Lorne cried, pumping the air with his fist. "Now then, do you know the home of Rennil the Arms-Master?" Again, the boy nodded but this time with more confidence. "Of course you do! I knew you were just the man for the job." Yewan beamed, his face radiant with pride. Placing a hand on the boy's shoulder, Lorne bent forward and spoke softly and conspiratorially in his ear. "I'm going to give you this note which you must hand to the Arms-Master himself. Not his servants or his retainer, but only to Rennil. When you do, you must tell him that the word from me is '*immediate.*' He will know what you mean. Now, you must hurry and when the message is delivered, you must come straight back here to me. Is that clear?"

"Yes, my lord."

"Good! Then in Mordan's name go. And be careful, there's a frost tonight and the cobbles will be icy."

With a final nod the boy snatched the note from Lorne's hand and scurried from the hall. The High Lord watched him go, sighed heavily, and then scanned the faces of the assembled servants and residents. He tried to work out who was missing but as far as he could tell, everyone was now present. Standing to the fore was Bishtar with his wife, Freiya, close beside him. Somehow, the chief servant had found time to wake everybody, wash, dress, and comb his hair. Had the Arliens ever had a need to shave, Lorne was certain he would have managed that as well! Inwardly he smiled; Bishtar had always been vain.

He cleared his throat and in a strong clear voice, addressed the huddled company. "You'll all no doubt be asking yourselves whether I've lost my mind. Well I can assure you that that's not the case. I've always done my utmost to earn your respect and your trust, and in this I do believe I've succeeded." Many in the assembly nodded their agreement. "We now face a moment of great peril, so I must ask you to honour that trust and do exactly as I tell you as quickly as possible.

"I've received word that a large and terrible army is bearing down on us seeking our total and utter destruction. I pray that we've been warned in time and that the armshost will prevail against our enemies; but they are many and merciless. It's therefore imperative that the population be evacuated to the Refuge. You must go out from here and rouse your closest friends and family, and they must in turn do likewise. Then you must all go straight to the caves. I've given word to the Arms-Master to call the militia to arms and no doubt you will hear the horns of summoning very soon. Don't forget that the old and the sick will need assistance.

"Although we've not practiced this for some time now, I'm sure that with Mordan's blessing, all will go well. Do you all understand what's required of you?" There came the sound of frightened muttering accompanied by many scared and confused looks. "I said, do you understand?" Lorne repeated sternly.

"Yes, my lord," the crowd replied in unison.

"Good. Then be off with you and may Mordan guard you all." The company turned and began to file noisily from the hall. All that is save Yewan's mother.

"My lord..." she began nervously.

"Don't worry, Sharna," Lorne said with another of his reassuring smiles. "I'll have him brought to you as soon as I've finished with him."

"Yes sir," she said with a small and unnecessary curtsy. Then reluctantly, she turned and joined the exodus.

"Not you, Bishtar," Lorne called to his chief attendant, who along with his wife was busily ushering everybody out. They both turned and gave him an enquiring look. "There's still a great deal for us to do before I can let you go."

Bishtar's wife began to protest but the loyal attendant stopped her by gently placing his fingers to her lips. "Peace, my love," he said quietly. "I have my responsibilities. I'll be joining you soon enough." For a few moments Freiya stared anxiously into her husband's ryes, then after quick kiss on the cheek, she hurried from the hall. Bishtar watched her go and then turned to Lorne.

"I'm sorry, my lord, but she's frightened."

"And with good reason. Our whole race is in danger of annihilation; but we must trust to our god, stout hearts, and sharp blades. Speaking of which, I need you to go and find my sword. It's been a long time since I last saw it, so I have no idea of its whereabouts. If it cannot be found, I want you to go to the armoury and bring me the finest weapon you can see."

"My lord?" An expression of deep confusion clouded Bishtar's round, loose-jowled features. "Why would you want a sword?"

"Don't question me, just go and get it!"

"But...the Lord-Guard?"

"Damn the Lord-Guard!" Lorne snapped angrily. "Just do as you're told."

Still Bishtar did not move for it broke one of the most sacred and ancient laws for the High-Lord to use any form of weapon; he was after all, not a king.

Lorne sighed impatiently then tried a different tack. "Look," he said condescendingly. "All I want is my own sword. I'm sure you remember what it looks like. It's a long, pointed thing with sharp edges. *Now go and get it!*"

Bishtar was crestfallen. "Yes, my lord," he said in a wounded, shaken voice. He then spun on his heels and scampered away.

Lorne ran his fingers through his hair and shook his head in self-disgust. He had just insulted his oldest and most faithful servant; one in fact he could even call a friend, although such an idea would horrify a strong traditionalist such as his chief attendant. It suddenly occurred to him that he would be ruffling a great many more feathers before daybreak. Mentally he shrugged; it couldn't be helped. The most important thing was to ensure the survival of his people. He would make any due apologies in the morning – assuming for him there would be a morning.

He moved to the wall opposite the corridor that led to the main entrance and sat down on the bench. Wearily he rested his head against the wall and prepared to wait.

Now he was clearly visible in the light of the lamps left by the assembly, his resemblance to his two sons was even more striking. His hair was of the same length and style – albeit a little darker and shot through with the white highlights of age. Apart from the many laughter lines and the two incongruous, deep, vertical furrows in the centre of his brow (lines that gave the impression of a permanent frown) their features were remarkably similar. Facially though, he was closer to the broad and muscular Eldore, for his eyes held the same benign and gentle thoughtfulness. But in build he was the image of Eh'lorne, being slim and athletic with the same ability to move with speed and grace.

He heard a door slam at the main entrance and within a heartbeat, Yewan came running, flushed and breathless into the hall.

"I've done it my lord, just as you said," he panted.

"Did you remember to give him the word I gave you?"

"Yes sir. '*Immediate*'. I said it twice just to be certain that he'd heard me correctly."

"Well done!" Lorne said warmly, clapping the boy enthusiastically on the back. "Now have a seat and get your breath back. Bishtar will be along soon and he can take you to the refuge to join your mother."

Yewan nodded gratefully and sat on the bench as close to the great man as he dared. He looked up at him with a mixture of respect and adoration in his tired young eyes.

The High-Lord began to drum his fingers impatiently, gradually becoming more and more agitated as time wore on. Eventually, he jumped to his feet and began to pace back and forth across the room. The frown lines on his brow became progressively deeper as his concerns continued to grow. Something was very wrong. He'd given the code word for the summoning of the militia and by now the whole vast valley plain should have been echoing with the strident cry of horns. Instead, there was just a thick silence punctuated by the steady clomp-clomp of his boots on the gleaming wooden floor. Eventually, he could stand it no more and turned to the young boy sitting patiently waiting for Bishtar's return.

"Yewan my lad, can I count on you for one more errand?"

The boy nodded, eager to please the man he'd looked up to for all of his short life.

"I want you to back to Rennil's home. If he's still there, tell him I want him here right away. If he's already left, find any of his soldiers and tell them to pass that message on."

Without a word, Yewan sprang to his feet and ran towards the door, but before he had gone even halfway across the hall, an imposing figure emerged from the gloom beyond the doorway. The young errand boy skidded to a halt and returned to his seat with a faint air of disappointment.

The newcomer, although tall by the standards of other races, was somewhat squat for an Arlien. He was powerfully built with huge, shovel-like hands. He appeared to be of late middle age with his steel-grey hair cropped in the traditional military fashion. From his left profile his features could be said to be distinguished, but from any other angle his visage could only be described as terrifying. A horrific scar disfigured his face, running from the corner of his right eye all the way to the point of his chin, slightly twisting the corner of his mouth as it passed close to his lips. He was dressed for battle in a long, chain hauberk, and under his arm he carried an ornate helmet. At his side he wore a long broadsword.

Lorne strode angrily towards him, his self-control finally shattered by the pressure of leadership and the feelings of impotence.

"Where in Halgar have you been?" he shouted. "Where are the horns? Why have you delayed when my instructions were clear?"

The newcomer's face betrayed no emotion and when he spoke, the deep rumble of his voice was calm and impassive. "Because your instructions were flawed," he said simply.

"Flawed!" Lorne cried, apoplectic with rage. "Flawed! Your inaction is flawed. It may have cost the lives of every man, woman, and child in the city. Their blood will be on your hands and the guilt will be on your head!"

The grim warrior remained unmoved, his steady hazel eyes remaining fixed on the dark, flashing orbs of his irate lord.

"I have not been idle," he replied in the same level tone. "Even now the Lord-Guard stands outside waiting to escort you to the safety of the Refuge. The summoning *is* underway but with silence and care. If the horns had been sounded, our enemy would know that we're aware of them. I thought it would be appropriate to surprise those who seek to surprise us."

Lorne stared into his Arms-Master's face then nodded in agreement. The anger in his eyes dissipated with the realisation that the burden was not his alone.

"Forgive me Rennil, I should have had more faith in you. We've been together too long for me to doubt you now."

Rennil gave a slight bow then fixed his eyes over the High-Lord's shoulder as Bishtar came running up behind him. In his hands he carried a longsword sheathed in a black, jewel-encrusted scabbard.

"Here it is, my lord; I've found it," he panted. "It was kept in the relic-store of all places, so it's been well cared for."

Lorne turned and took the weapon from his attendant. He examined the exquisite sheath and then with a great flourish, he drew the gleaming blade and held it up to the light. Bishtar had not lied. It was as clean and sharp as when he had last seen it some twelve years before. His fingers thrilled at the feel of the heavy but well-balanced sword that had once so delighted him.

"What's this?" Rennil asked raising his eyebrows. "A sword in the hands of the High Lord? That is completely unacceptable; the covenant of duty forbids it. You must hand it back."

"I will not!" Lorne declared firmly. "I am the High-Lord; I will not slink away to the Refuge taking fifty of our finest warriors with me. My people are in peril therefore *I* will stand at the head of the armshost with *you* at my side."

"It's not your task to lead our army," the Arms-Master growled. "That responsibility is mine alone. Not once in five hundred years has a High-Lord wielded a weapon. *You are not the king!*"

"No, but you are my subordinate and I do not answer to you!"

The two men glared at each other, their eyes locked in a battle of wills until eventually Rennil gave a curt bow.

"As you wish," he said coldly. "But the battle plan is mine."

Lorne smiled and the tension eased. "I'd have it no other way." He turned to the servant standing uncomfortably at his side. "Bishtar, I've no further need of you tonight so you can go and join Freiya. Take Yewan with you and make sure that he's reunited with Sharna – she'll be beside herself with worry by now."

"Yes, my lord; thank you." The relieved servant wasted no time in grabbing his new charge's hand and leading him quickly away.

Lorne returned his attention to the Arms-Master. "Do you have a plan?" he asked.

"I do," Rennil replied. He motioned to the exit. "Shall we walk as we speak; time is short after all." The High-Lord nodded and the two men strode out into the crisp, clear night. "I assume the enemy approaches from the south?" the old warrior asked putting on his iron helmet.

"So the twins say. Apparently, they're on the Sarren road less than half a march away."

"Good. In that case they'll have to squeeze through the southern pass and that'll leave them disorganised and vulnerable to attack. I'll divide our forces into three separate units placing one on each side of the road. Once they emerge from the pass, we'll strike simultaneously from both sides, catching them while they're still in disarray."

"And the third unit?"

"They'll stand on the road between the enemy and the city. Once the battle is well and truly under way, they will mount a frontal assault with loud horns and bloodcurdling cries. That should cause enough panic in the enemy's ranks to leave them helpless. With luck and Mordan's blessing, we will slaughter them by the thousands."

"It sounds a good plan," Lorne commented with a tinge of doubt. "But aren't you leaving too few men between the city and its attackers?"

"That's why you should be in the refuge," Rennil growled. "Your place is with the people while the battle is best left to those who can win it."

"Meaning you I take it."

"Meaning me. Rest assured, this is not the first time I've used this ploy – although never against such overwhelming odds. I'm counting on your boys exaggerating their numbers; which is quite normal in these cases."

"I hope you're right, but it doesn't sound like Eldore to be so emotional, nor for Eh'lorne to be so inaccurate in matters of war."

"That," Rennil said grimly, "is what worries me."

By now they'd emerged into the cold, moonlit night where they were greeted by the Lord-Guard. They were waiting stiffly to attention at the shadowy base of the wide stone steps that led to the Duty Halls' forecourt. These fifty soldiers were the elite of the armshost. Their sole responsibility was the protection of the High Lord; and in this they enjoyed a degree of autonomy – even from the Arms-Master himself. At the head of the tight, hard-faced formation stood their commander, Gildor, Prime-Officer of the Lord-Guard.

He was a striking figure of a man. Slim and wiry in build, he stood more than a head taller than even the loftiest of his men. As the two men approached, he snapped a salute to the Arms-Master and then turned to Lorne.

"My lord, if you will come with us, you'll find that your quarters in the caves have been prepared. I've sent instructions for a fire to be lit and a hot drink to be prepared."

"The High-Lord won't be going to the Refuge," Rennil informed the Prime in his deep, gruff voice. "He'll be requiring a hauberk and helm, so if you could send one of your men to fetch them."

Gildor took a step forward and peered indignantly into Rennil's face, half hidden in the gloom. As he did so, his own features were caught in the moonlight revealing an improbably youthful visage. To all appearances, he seemed just out of his teens, but in fact he was well on the wrong side of thirty.

"And where exactly *is* he going, and why does he need the trappings of war?"

The Arms-Master was unmoved. "At his own insistence the High Lord will be joining the armshost under my command."

Gildor looked at Lorne and for the first time noticed the sheathed sword in his hand. He turned back to Rennil and shook his head.

"I'm sorry Master Rennil but I cannot allow that. The High-Lord will need to surrender his weapon and come with us."

Rennil reached up, put his arm around the Prime's shoulders and led him aside. He spoke softly and quietly into his ear. After a short while, Lorne distinctly heard Gildor say, "No, I still don't like it." Rennil then added a few more words after which Gildor gave a reluctant nod of agreement and the two conspirators returned.

"You heard the Arms-Master," Gildor said to one of his men. "Fetch helmet and chainmail for the High Lord."

The confused soldier hesitated for a moment but then saluted smartly. "Prime!" he snapped, then raced off into the darkness.

Rennil smiled at Lorne. "That's it then; you're now just Lorne Starbrow, section officer of the armshost and mine to command. So, section officer, here are your orders: you've quite rightly pointed out that the city will only be lightly defended against a frontal assault. Therefore, you'll take the Lord-Guard along with every man I can spare and you will stand guard at the city's edge. You will continue to hold that position until the battle is won."

"But this is trickery!" Lorne protested angrily. "You're deliberately keeping me away from the fighting. Remember, I'm the High-Lord and I'll go where I please."

"You are a section officer under my command. Either you obey my orders or you'll go to the Refuge where you belong."

"How dare you speak to me in such a manner! I'll...I'll..."

"A simple 'yes Master' will suffice, section officer," Rennil replied with calm authority.

Lorne glared furiously at the Arms-Master; and for the second time that night the two men's eyes locked together in a contentious struggle. This time however, it was the High-Lord who yielded.

"Yes Master," he ground out between gritted teeth.

CHAPTER FIVE

Sirris. The City of Shame. Home to the exiled Arlien people for more than five hundred years, it stood cradled at the northernmost end of the vast, oval-shaped valley-plain of Cor-Peshtar – or 'Vale of Plenty' in the common tongue. As cities go, although not small, it was an unassuming capital for a race of such royal lineage. The homes, business premises, and workshops were of a simple design and were mainly built of wood. Almost all were single-storey affairs and were arranged in wide, well planned cobbled streets with none of them displaying even a hint of grandeur.

The only really imposing building, the Duty-Halls of the High-Lord, was a magnificent – if somewhat diminutive – palace of black, polished granite. It stood at the heart of the southern half of the city which was separated from the northern

THE TALISMAN OF WRATH

part by the wide and fast-flowing High River – the very river in fact, that Eh'lorne, Eldore, and Bandil had so miraculously crossed earlier that evening. It was spanned by seven bridges over which the last stragglers of the evacuated people were now struggling as they made their way to the miraculous labyrinth of caverns that made up the Refuge. The river entered the city from the west over a tall, spectacular waterfall, and then left it in the east via a deep gorge cut by time or seismic shift into the steep, cliff-like boundary.

Cor-Peshtar was in fact a huge elliptical caldera – the relic of an ancient, long-extinct volcano. The land there was rich and fertile, and in the summer, lush with green pasture and golden fields of wheat and barley. Now however, late in the long mountain winter, the plain was covered in a thick blanket of snow that reflected the cold, silvery moonlight which made the early hours as bright as a dull, overcast day.

A wide, well-trodden road ran arrow-straight from the city's southern fringe and led all the way to the deep gully-pass from which the army of lich would eventually emerge. It was at this point that Rennil's men lay in ambush, pressed into the snow on either side of the long thoroughfare.

Rennil himself was kneeling in the centre of the eastern line of soldiers who were ranged along the roadside. He was surveying the proposed battlefield and making some last moment calculations in his head. He questioned himself as to whether his men were positioned at the correct distance from the road. Too near and they would be in danger of being seen before they were ready to spring their trap; too far and they would have to cover too much ground before they could press home their attack. He scanned the area once again and nodded to himself. He was as sure as he could be that he had got it right.

He knew the plan was a good one. As he'd said to Lorne, he'd used it with great success many times in the past – a past he was loath to let his mind dwell upon for too long. With a satisfied grunt he lay back down to wait.

This of course, was the worst part for a soldier. The agony of anticipation when the imagination became a whirlwind of what-ifs; the tightness of the chest, the gnawing flutter of the stomach, and the dryness of the mouth. Then would come the mad, bloody confusion of battle in the midst of which came the terrifying realisation that fatigue was going to leave you at your enemy's mercy. He grinned savagely; he loved every moment of it!

His thoughts returned to the High-Lord. He knew he'd overstepped the mark by belittling him so harshly but Lorne had left him no choice. Every High-Lord since the office had been created had sworn the Oath of Duty. Gorand himself, the last Arlien king and Lorne's ancestor, had demanded it be so. And now Lorne was prepared to break that oath? He shook his head. No, he couldn't allow him to defile himself in that way; he had far too much respect for his old friend. Not to mention, of course, the danger he would be putting himself in. Although before inheriting the Seat of Duty he'd been a formidable swordsman, to have not lifted a weapon for so many years would leave him helpless in the wild chaos of combat. Yes, he may have belittled him, but it was better to have wounded his pride than to have him dead!

A slight movement at the pass entrance pulled him from his reverie. Sure enough, a great number of dark, indistinct figures were beginning to file out from the deep shadow of the gully. They marched along the road in a loose, undisciplined formation that gradually began to spread out as they moved further into the plain. As they moved closer, Rennil was able to see the figures more clearly and a wave of revulsion swept through him as his mind registered their loathsome form. The misshaped, fur-covered bodies, the fierce savage faces, and the long, claw-tipped fingers were all the stuff of nightmare. The moonlight glinted threateningly on their jagged, wicked-looking swords.

And still they came. More and more of the disgusting creatures were pouring into the valley in a never-ending stream. Tens became hundred, hundreds became thousands, and still no end was in sight. Rennil had hoped that Eh'lorne had miscounted their numbers, and indeed he had; but he had woefully *underestimated* the strength of the enemy's legions.

The Arms-Master's Arlien senses could feel the ripples of fear spreading through his own ranks – especially amongst the hurriedly pressed militiamen. If he didn't attack soon, they'd simply melt away like snow in the spring sunshine. Of the fifteen hundred men deployed evenly on each side of the road, a third were made up of these irregulars. Although they were the pick of the part-time soldiers, they were after all just farmers and goatherds – and this threat was far beyond anything they could possibly have imagined.

But then mercifully, the last of the evil beast-soldiers appeared and joined its fellows, marching in that strange, animalistic, loping gait which seemed typical of this unnatural breed. Rennil climbed to his feet with his sword gripped tightly in his right hand. He lifted his horn to his lips and with a mighty blow, sounded the charge.

From both sides of the road the Arlien troops sprang up from the snow, and with a loud cry, threw themselves at the stunned malevolent horde. They crashed into the enemy's exposed flanks and swept through their disorganised ranks leaving a bloody trail of gore in their wake. The armshost's success, however, was almost its undoing.

Rennil's plan had envisaged striking the enemy in a broad attack along their whole length, but such were the lich's numbers, the Arlien onslaught could only hit them in the centre of their long formation. As they penetrated deeper into the mass of tooth, claw, and steel, the two separate units quickly met up to become one, while the rapidly co-ordinating lich were able to sweep around and envelop the valiant attackers. Losses began to mount as the armshost found themselves surrounded by their viciously screaming, feral foe.

Disaster seemed inevitable; but then, clearly audible above the nerve-shattering din, came the sudden strident calls of a hundred horns followed by the terrifying roar of fierce war cries. Once again chaos spread throughout the lich army – chaos that quickly turned to confused panic as the planned frontal assault charged headlong into the fray. Every last vestige of cohesion vanished as the four hundred grim, determined warriors slammed into the invading multitude. What had begun to look like certain defeat had turned into what was surely going to be an unstoppable victory!

Lorne paced to-and-fro in front the line of the two hundred and fifty soldiers he nominally commanded. With each step he slapped the flat of his sword impatient against the side of his leg. The main body of his men stood in a single row with the fifty men of the Lord-Guard in a line in front of them. Then came the tall, willowy figure of the Prime who was standing watching the High Lord's movements with a faintly amused expression on his boyish features. Gildor had taken the liberty of disobeying Rennil's instructions and had given in to Lorne's desperate pleas to leave the city's outskirts and move closer to the action. He'd decided that to do so did not put his charge in any more danger than before; and besides, he fully understood the High-Lord's frustration at his enforced inactivity.

"The plan goes well, wouldn't you say, my lord?" the Prime asked brightly. But Lorne's only reply was an irritated grunt. Gildor's smile grew broader for a moment, but then as he turned his attention to the battle not four hundred strides away, his face became deadly serious. No matter how complete the victory looked to be, there were still going to be heavy casualties.

Suddenly, there came a bright, red flash as if scarlet lightning had split the air and turned the snow to the colour of blood. The blinding burst of light seemed to have an instant and devastating effect on both sides of the bloody conflict so near to where they were standing. The lich were suddenly transformed into an efficient and well-disciplined army, while it was the Arliens' turn to be thrown into confusion and panic.

"What was that?" Lorne asked, his voice thick with trepidation.

"I don't know," Gildor replied striding forward to stand at the High Lord's side.

Both men peered across at the battle, eyes squinting to try and see what had caused such a catastrophic turn of events. Another flash momentarily dazzled them but the tall Prime had managed to pinpoint the place from where the strange, silent blast had emanated.

"There!" he said, pointing to a spot somewhere towards the centre of the melee. "A great mountain of a man in full armour; and by Mordan, I swear he stands head and shoulders above even me!"

"Where?" Lorne asked, following Gildor's outstretched arm. "I can't make him out... wait... yes, I can see him. Look, he's directing the lich with his staff and I'll wager that that's the source of the light."

As if to confirm his suspicions, yet another burst of light blazed from exactly where the two men were looking, leaving them momentarily blinded.

"Sorcery!" the Prime declared. "Look how the red light disrupts Rennil's men and disorientates them. He must be stopped!"

"*We* will stop him!" Lorne declared firmly. "I'll lead an attack right into the heart of their ranks and we'll cut him down. Quickly, form a battle-wedge behind me; we've only moments before the armshost is annihilated."

"No," Gildor said placing a restraining hand on Lorne's shoulder. "*I* will lead the attack. You are the High-Lord and can have no part in this fight. You must wait here."

Lorne's expression hardened and a steely glint entered his eyes. "Leave me here if you want, but I'll only follow in your wake. Would you rather I fight alone?"

Gildor stared at the High-Lord with his mind racing. Abruptly, he came to a decision.

"Very well, but I'll take the lead. I'll form the point of the spear with you behind me. The wedge will form up behind us and with luck, we'll keep you out of harm's way."

"Agreed!" Lorne replied with grim satisfaction.

Gildor nodded curtly then turned his attention to his men and barked out his orders. With practiced speed and precision, they fell into formation behind him with Lorne at his back and the bulk of the tough, experienced Lord-Guard giving close protection. With a single hand signal from the Prime, the tightly packed body of men began to move forward.

Although a traditional Arlien formation, it was one which had been much improved upon with the benefit of Rennil's experience. Each man on the cutting edge of the 'blade' was able to both smite the enemy and defend the back of the man to his front. Its purpose was to act like a spear and drive deep into the main body of an opposing army and strike at its very heart. And that was exactly what Gildor now intended to do.

They approached the disastrously one-sided contest at a brisk trot. Then, when just fifty strides away, they surged forward with a defiant roar. Almost unopposed they cut through the startled lich's ranks, taking the creatures from behind as they concentrated on crushing the beleaguered armshost. On and on the wedge drove until, when just a few short paces away, the huge, staff-wielding general became aware of the threat. He shouted a loud, harsh command and turned to face them.

At his word, dozens of the hideous, bestial creatures threw themselves recklessly at the Arlien wedge. They slashed at it with their swords while biting and clawing in their desperation to protect their fell master. Screeching and wailing, they battered the tight formation with their bodies and brought the valorous charge to a standstill almost within touching distance of their gigantic, armoured commander.

Gildor made a determined lunge in an attempt to break through the last few lich that stood in his way, but so fierce was the creatures' desire to defend their master, they managed to brush aside his attack and leave him isolated and surrounded.

With the Prime separated from the wedge, Lorne found himself at its point, exposed to the vicious fighting all around him. The lich however, were so intent on stilling the whirling accomplished sword of Gildor that they left a small but distinct opening in front of their mystical leader. Without hesitation, Lorne stepped into the gap, tightened the grip on his sword, and prepared to face the monstrous warrior.

He was a colossal foe standing almost half as tall again as the High Lord. He was completely encased in strange red armour which consisted of many loose, overlapping plates. His face was completely hidden by his spiked enclosed helmet. In his left hand he held a long staff, tipped with a large ruby-like crystal. In his right hand he wielded a huge, curved, rune-engraved sword. As Lorne charged forward, the titanic general swung the massive blade with all the skill and dexterity of a master swordsman.

Rennil's worst fear had come to pass: the unpractised, inexperienced High-Lord now found himself alone and defenceless in the face of a ruthless and powerful foe.

Except the Arms-Master was wrong. True, Lorne had not touched a weapon for twelve long years, but he was not unpractised. Using wooden training rods, he had drilled almost every day with his son, Eh'lorne. At first and in secret he had trained the boy, teaching him all he knew; but as the lad had grown ever more proficient in his art, the pupil had become the master. So, for many years now, the High-Lord had been taught by the most accomplished swordsman in living memory – perhaps of all time.

With a deft, efficient touch, he parried his opponent's mighty brand and with all the grace of a ballet dancer, he turned a full circle and struck the warrior-mage's side with the speed and potency of a deadly snake. Such was the power of the blow, it would have cut an unarmoured man in two. Even had that man been wearing regular chainmail, he would surely have suffered a mortal wound. But the red plates of this adversary were anything but regular. In a shower of red sparks and with a shock that Lorne felt right up to his shoulder, his sword ricocheted harmlessly aside.

Within the space of twenty heartbeats, Lorne's blade found its mark again and again to no avail. Each time his huge antagonist laughed derisively at his futile attack. Then the crystal flashed again, dazzling the High-Lord and in that instant, with a mighty thrust, the gigantic, malevolent warrior ran him through.

Lorne sank to his knees as all the strength flooded from his body. The urgent clamour of battle receded to a distant, hollow echo. Did he hear Gildor's voice calling his name from far away or was that just a trick of his imagination? As the dark veil of death fell across his eyes he began to pray. He prayed forgiveness for his arrogant folly, but most of all he prayed for the people he had failed – *his* people. Somehow, he managed to raise his head, and there, standing gloatingly over him, stood his assassin. He was laughing in mocking triumph with his staff and dripping sword held to the sky.

Then, from his lowly, defeated position, Lorne spied what had so eluded him in combat. The warrior-mage's raised arms had separated the uncanny red plates and revealed a tiny chink in his armour.

The stricken High-Lord whispered a final, desperate prayer. He prayed that he could accomplish in death what he had failed to achieve in life. He grasped his sword in both hands and braced himself.

"Mordan!" he roared echoing his son's ringing war cry. Then with the last vestige of his strength, he thrust his sword upwards, deep into the evil warrior's heart. A bright white light flashed from within the armour as the blade hit its mark.

With his life-force then expended, Lorne fell back to his knees where he seemed to sit, head bowed in a final communion of gratitude.

As his giant opponent toppled backwards, the red gemstone exploded with an ear-splitting crack, showering the battlefield in tiny crimson shards that scintillated in the moonlight as they fell. Without the cohesion of their occult general, the lich went mad with fear and rage. They fell upon each other, howling and screaming as they slashed and clawed in their frantic efforts to escape. The relieved armshost had little to do except watch the slaughter and pick off any of the creatures that managed to break free.

Gildor, miraculously unscathed, rushed to Lorne's side. It was clear for anyone to see what had transpired. The lifeless High-Lord was sitting on his heels with his head bowed and his arms limp at his sides. The sword, wrenched from his weakened dying grip, still protruded from the dead giant's chest.

As Prime of the Lord-Guard, Gildor had but one responsibility: the preservation of the High Lord's life, and he had failed. Not only had he allowed his charge to walk into grave danger, he himself had suffered no injury. He hung his head in shame and wept bitter tears for the man he had loved and respected.

Thus passed Lorne Starbrow, seventeenth High-Lord of Sirris and steward of the Arlien race.

CHAPTER SIX

Eh'lorne knelt beside his brother who was propped against a smooth rock face in the welcome shelter of an overhanging cliff. He peered intently into the pale, pain-etched face and noted the closed eyes that seemed to have sunk deep into their sockets. His skin was grey and parchment thin. The deathly appearance was made all the worse by the cold, shadowy light of the moon. Eh'lorne gently took hold of one of Eldore's rough, calloused hands and held it between his own. It was ice cold. The broad, powerful Arlien's condition had deteriorated markedly after they'd used Bandil's Stone to warn their father. Without fluid and warmth, he was unlikely to see the morning.

He looked over at the old man sitting huddled beside the stricken Arlien. He looked nothing more than a large fur bag full of dirty bones. He too had his eyes closed and seemed more comatose than asleep. Eh'lorne knew that if he didn't act soon, he would have two bodies on his hands when this longest of nights finally ended. He took a deep breath and wearily got to his feet. As impossible as the task appeared, he was going to have to find water and firewood. True, Bandil did have a flask but it was small and they'd drained it of its last few remaining drops not long after crossing the river. There was plenty of water lying all around them in the form of snow, but without a fire to melt it they might as well have been in a desert. But even with a fire they had no receptacle in which to heat it.

"Whatever your woes, trust in Mordan." That was the mantra he had heard so often from Hevalor, the city's Spiritual Overseer and Eh'lorne had always been devout in his worship. Well they certainly had a surfeit of woes now. His brother's serious, thoughtful face flashed into his mind. "There's a lesson in everything," he would say – and he would say it often! In even the slightest of adversities, out would trot that same old adage. He'd heard it so often that it had become almost like gibberish in his ears. How did the rest of the old proverb go? Ah yes, that was it: "There's a lesson in everything for all to see, but only the wise learn from it." Well he, Eh'lorne, would need to be wise now.

He drew another deep breath and slowly let it out between pursed lips. Deliberately, he calmed himself and tried to think in the steady, logical way of his brother. It was not something that came naturally to him.

First, he needed fire; and for fire he needed tinder and kindling. The former was not a problem for he always carried the silver tinderbox which his father had given him on a chain around his neck. Kindling was the real difficulty. In this part of the mountains, trees and shrubs were almost non-existent. That in fact was the reason the Sarren road did not cross the High

River until it drew close to the Cor-Peshtar valley. But he was sure he had seen growth of some kind recently; but where?

Then it came to him. As they had struggled up a particularly steep passage between two broken and crumbling escarpments, he had spied some small, scrub-like trees, valiantly clinging to the precipitous crags. He tried to remember how far back it had been. He was not over familiar with this region but it couldn't be too far. Perhaps a stretch, maybe even fifteen hundred strides but certainly less than two stretches. And it was mostly downhill of course – but that would mean a long uphill slog on the return trip. And then he would then be weighed down with armfuls of firewood. Assuming that is, he was able to climb up and reach the stunted bushes at all! It was totally pointless to even make the attempt.

He squared his shoulders and set off, but before he had gone more than a few paces, he heard Eldore's weak, croaking voice behind him.

"Eh'lorne?"

He turned around to see his brother's eyes upon him with a questioning expression on his gaunt, ashen features.

Eh'lorne smiled reassuringly. "It's alright, I shan't be long. You just rest easy and I'll be back before you know it."

With an almost imperceptible nod of assent, Eldore reclosed his eyes and then drifted back into deep unconsciousness. Eh'lorne watched him for a moment or two, then walked briskly and determinedly away.

The lithe warrior-lord had not been wrong. It was little more than a stretch to where he'd seen the shrubs high up on the unstable looking rock face; and he arrived there far sooner than he had dared hope. Looking up to where they were growing however, filled him with the sickening realisation that his walk had been in vain. The ascent would entail an almost vertical climb of forty or fifty cubits and the rock itself was loose and treacherous. To make matters worse, much of the climb would be made in the darkness of deep moon shadow. It was suicidal and impossible.

Without hesitation, he began to climb. Time and time again his heart came into his mouth as rocks crumbled beneath his hands or feet leaving him hanging precariously by his fingertips. Soon his arms and legs began to ache unbearably. Once again that night, his overtaxed muscles screamed out in protest.

Few men could have made such a climb, even if fresh and rested and in broad daylight. But then their twin brother wasn't lying close to death, and nor were they Eh'lorne Starbrow. Eventually, he reached the craggy outcrop from where the shrubs grew; but he then found himself facing another problem. His hold on the rock face was precarious to say the least, and the force he would need to break or cut any of the dry, brittle limbs would surely send him crashing down to his death. For a while he dangled there at a total impasse, but then he began to climb once more. When he was high enough, he manoeuvred himself across until he was directly above the small trees. He then descended enough to be able to kick out at the fragile boughs. It needed great care to stamp down hard enough to snap the branches without loosening his frighteningly insecure grip, but somehow, he managed it.

At last, although he would have liked to have sent more wood tumbling down to the valley floor, he decided that what there was would have to suffice. To delay any longer would have left him too weak to make a successful descent. As it was, when he was still around ten cubits from the ground, his strength finally gave out and he toppled backwards, crashing down heavily and striking his head on a loose rock. A bright light flashed before his eyes and for a moment, everything went black. When he came to, he found himself lying painfully on his back and staring up at the moon. His head was throbbing and something was digging unpleasantly into the back of his neck. Cursing quietly to himself he sat up and carefully checked his limbs.

Mercifully, none were broken or sprained. Then he gently probed the back of his head. There was a lump there which felt as though it were the size of an egg, but when he checked his fingers, they were at least free from blood.

Angrily, he picked up the large flat rock which had caused the bump and made to throw as far as he could down the narrow gorge. He suddenly stopped and peered closely at the offending stone. It was a very unusual shape indeed.

"Whatever your woes, trust in Mordan," he muttered, then slid the rock into his tunic where it nestled cold and uncomfortable against his belly.

It took far too long to gather the fallen branches, for his movements were now frustratingly slow and painful. But with a superhuman effort to emulate his brother's patience, he doggedly carried on. In the end, he was ready to begin the return trip with his tired arms full of the hard-won firewood.

The temptation to give up and to accept the inevitability of failure was overwhelming, but the thought of his stricken brother gave him a strength born out of love and desperation. Eldore, he knew, would never have given up on him. They were so closely linked, they had always felt as though they were two opposite halves of a single person. Besides, he had sworn an oath to protect the old man and Eh'lorne Starbrow did not take oaths lightly.

"There's a lesson in everything!" he shouted at the top of his voice. His brother's mantra echoed around the peaks and valleys, repeating the adage over and over as if Eldore himself was with him, encouraging him on.

With a grim smile, he began the long, soul-sapping trek back to his companions. He thought the earlier journey with Bandil in his arms had been hard enough, but this made that torture pale into insignificance.

"Just one more step," he told himself each time his exhausted body pleaded for rest, and each time, "one more step" was followed by another.

Finally and miraculously, the end was in sight. He put his head down and gritted his teeth. One last effort was all it would take.

A sudden flash illuminated the ground at his feet as if a brief bolt of lightning had ripped across the sky. He raised his head and scanned the mountainous horizon waiting for the thunder. None came. But that of course, was hardly a surprise for the sky was as clear and cloud-free as any he had ever seen. Puzzled, he continued on his way with his eyes fixed on the point ahead where the peaks met the stars. Then, there it was again! This time he noticed a distinct red hue to the strange burst of light. He frowned. What could it mean? Another flash caused him to experience a curious sinking feeling in the pit his stomach as he trudged the final few strides back to their meagre camp.

Just as he arrived, there came a fourth flash followed almost immediately by an intense wave of despair that swept over him and seemed to tear his heart out of his chest. He dropped his burden and sank to his knees. Then sitting back on his heels, he raised his eyes to the twinkling, moonlit heavens and prayed.

"Mordan," he whispered, unable to identify the terrible feelings of sorrow that had so suddenly struck him down. "Help me now." He searched the sky, vainly seeking an answer in the cold beauty of the stars, but as the feeling began to subside, the urgency of his party's predicament overrode any other thoughts.

As quickly as his overspent reserves of energy would allow, he gathered up the wood once more and took the last few steps to complete his impossible quest. He dumped it close to where his two unmoving companions were still sitting, threw the stone down beside it, and then crouched down to check on his brother and newfound friend. To his intense relief, neither seemed to have deteriorated significantly so he hurriedly set to work.

THE TALISMAN OF WRATH

Carefully, he arranged the smallest of the twigs and used his tinderbox and flint to set them aflame. With practiced skill he added larger and larger sticks until he was satisfied that the fire was well and truly alight. He then hunted out some loose rocks and used them to form a protective circle around the growing blaze.

He picked up the large, flat stone which he'd carried from the gully and examined it more closely. It resembled a wide, shallow bowl, far too shallow in fact to contain more than a few drops of water; but a deep groove in one edge had given him an idea. Deliberately, he placed it on the largest of the rocks and stood back to admire his handiwork. He tutted to himself and shook his head. Then, after bending down and adjusting the stone's position so that it overhung the rock slightly, he nodded his satisfaction and turned to the old man.

"Bandil," he called softly while gently shaking the old hermit. Then more urgently, "Bandil!"

"Mmm?" the old man mumbled, blearily opening his eyes.

"I'm sorry to wake you my friend, but I need your water bottle."

The old man looked confused. "What? Why would...? It's empty."

"I know. That's why I need it; I intend to remedy that situation."

Bandil looked as though he were about to ask more questions but instead dragged the flask from his shoulder and handed it over. Eh'lorne took it with a smile and returned to the fire. After removing the stopper, he carefully positioned it under the stone. He then began to gather large handfuls of snow that he deposited onto the shallow bowl. Then he sat himself down beside it and settled down to wait.

"Very clever," the old man called weakly from behind. Then, "How did you manage to build a fire?" His cracked, ancient voice was full of a mixture admiration and deep curiosity.

"Now that," Eh'lorne replied with bitter irony. "Is a tale I would rather forget."

"Still, I would hear it if you'd care to share it with me."

"Maybe another time," Eh'lorne replied, surprised at his own reticence. He did not usually hesitate to boast of his heroics, but for some reason this time it seemed inappropriate. "Let's just say that in all our woes, I trusted in Mordan."

"I didn't realise you were so wise."

Eh'lorne gave no reply but continued to stare at the slowly melting snow. As it did, the water began to run along the channel-like chip in the stone and drip into the flask. It would take a while but there would soon be enough to give Eldore a lifesaving drink.

As he sat, he pondered the strange red light and the strong feelings of grief and anguish it seemed to have evoked within him. Although those feelings had now gone, they had left him with a terrible sense of doom that hung threateningly over his head like a thundercloud. It suddenly occurred to him that although they had managed to warn Sirris, there was no guarantee that the armshost would be victorious. He put such negative thoughts out of his mind and went back to concentrating on the water. The snow had almost gone yet precious little liquid had flowed into Bandil's water bottle. It was going to take a great many more handfuls to fill the flask; a rest was still some way off.

Again and again he replenished the stone dish, and gradually the bottle's water level rose until eventually, there was enough. He took the flask to his brother and held it to his lips.

"Eldore, wake up. You must drink or you'll perish. "Eldore!" His brother didn't stir. Gripped with anxiety, Eh'lorne felt his forehead. It was neither feverish nor too cold. He held his hand. That too felt better than it had. He checked the gash in his side and found the bleeding had stopped again and it looked no worse than it had before. He breathed a sigh of relief. His fear of infection appeared groundless, but even if they were to reach safety, Eldore would be in a lot of pain for a considerable amount of time. Eh'lorne allowed himself a selfish smile, glad that he didn't have his brother's uncanny 'gift' of sharing his pain. It may have been unfair that it only ran one way, but he had never felt inclined to complain!

Closing his eyes, he used his mind to reach out to Eldore, calling to him with mind-talk. Eventually he found him and coaxed him back to consciousness.

"Hello brother," he said gently. "I have some water for you. Will you drink it? I've gone to great pains to find it."

"You look awful." Eldore croaked, trying to crack a smile.

"Whereas you of course, are a picture of health. Now be quiet and drink!"

Eldore's grin grew a little broader as he obediently followed his brother's instructions. After gulping down most of the precious liquid, he turned to look at the old hermit who appeared to have drifted back into a deep sleep.

"How is he?" he asked.

"Better than you. He's exhausted beyond measure and dangerously cold, but now we have some warmth, he'll live."

"Tomorrow you must tell me how we came to have such miraculous luxuries; but I can see you too are beyond your limits. Come, sit by me and rest.

Eh'lorne smiled gratefully and after throwing the last of the wood on the fire, he settled himself between his two companions and pulled them both close to share their warmth.

"There is a lesson in everything…" he muttered as he slipped into a bottomless slumber.

CHAPTER SEVEN

The morning after the great battle dawned bright and crisp, and as the sun climbed slowly into the sky, the magnitude of the previous night's slaughter became horrifyingly clear. The battle had spread over a huge swathe of the plain as the crazed, frantic lich had tried desperately to escape both the vengeful Arliens and each other. For more than two stretches in all directions from the southern pass, the snow was stained red with the creatures' blood and gore. Thousands of their corpses – a stomach churning mixture of matted fur and glistening mutilation – littered the killing field. Dozens of large oxcarts, each with an attendant team of several men, were busily collecting the carcasses and carrying them away. They were transporting them to a gigantic pyre built close to the rim wall, about a stretch to the west of the narrow gorge where the invaders had first entered the great valley-plain.

The bodies of the fallen armshost and militia had been the first to be recovered. At first light they'd been gathered up and reverently carried back to the city for an honourable burial. Although the Arlien forces had achieved a resounding victory, the terrible scale of their casualties bordered on the catastrophic. Of the two thousand or so armshost and militia that had taken part in the battle, almost seven hundred were either dead or critically wounded. On top of that, at least another five hundred had received some kind of incapacitating wound, and almost no one had escaped unscathed.

An air of gloom and despondency hung over the work details as they went about their gruesome business. Although most were wearing large protective aprons, even these could not prevent them from becoming smothered in blood and guts from their disgusting chore. Many a man turned aside from his task to be physically sick.

At around midday, one particular group were toiling not too far from the entrance when a loud, shrill whistle caught their attention. They all turned to see three figures staggering out of the gully, all supporting each other as they came. Several of the labourers went running over to them. They then turned and motioned frantically for the cart to be brought over. To Eh'lorne, Eldore, and Bandil, the stinking, gore covered burial party were the most welcome sight of their lives.

Ironically, the old man was in a considerably better condition than his two strapping young comrades. Such was his sorry state, Eldore was being half carried and half dragged between his two companions. At his side, Eh'lorne was so tired and enervated, he shouldn't have been able to stand, let alone share the considerable burden of his injured brother over so great a distance. Quickly, the unlikely rescuers dragged the lich corpses from the cart and helped the three exhausted travellers onto it.

Then as fast as the two oxen could pull, they headed along the road towards the city.

As they entered the outskirts, Bandil looked around him in wonder. Although insignificant compared to the regal majesty of Arl where he'd spent his youth, Sirris still filled him with awe. It was, after all, the first town he'd seen in well over a century and a half. He marvelled at the low wooden houses with their long, sweeping, snow covered roofs, and their large, leaded windows. Where did so much glass come from, he wondered. And the people! Although the wide cobbled streets were hardly crowded, after so many decades of solitude, the old man couldn't help but feel a little intimidated. Despite the terrible ordeal the people had just been through, they couldn't resist staring curiously at the strange old hermit as they numbly returned to their homes. All but a very few had ever seen a beard.

The men were dressed in a similar fashion to Eh'lorne and Eldore but instead of white, there were a great variety of colours – although most were dull, earthy shades of brown, green, and grey. The women's clothes on the other hand, were a far gayer affair. Their long dresses of bright-red and summery-green cheered the old man's heart in spite of the gravity of his mission.

The Arliens themselves were a tall race, light of skin and fair of hair. Their brown eyes varied from pale hazel to a deep chestnut, so dark as to be almost black. Bandil's heart thrilled at the sight of a people he'd only ever seen depicted in faded murals and cracked, broken statues. He'd spent many a long afternoon in the derelict temple near the great palace where he'd grown up, staring wistfully at the images of the old kings. The priests of Ruul – the great eagle god of the Keshtarim – had declared the Arliens a myth, but the young Bandil had known in his heart that this was a lie.

But the demeanour of the men and women he was looking at now hardly resembled that of the proud, noble kings and queens portrayed in those artworks. These people looked dazed and frightened. Many, he knew, would be mourning the loss of their sons and husbands, killed in the previous night's hostilities. He guessed that they'd never known the fear and uncertainty of war. He sighed compassionately; they would soon grow very used to it indeed.

Eventually, the cart trundled into a wide, gravelled drive which led to a vast wooden hall which although still only single storey, had high walls and tall, wide windows. The large forecourt was crowded with bloodied men, either sitting or lying on blankets while several uniformed women busied themselves cleaning and binding their wounds. They were obviously overwhelmed by the sheer number of their charges.

The cart came to a halt outside a set of double doors that Bandil took to be the main entrance. A large wooden sign hung over them with the word 'Viltula' engraved into it. He turned to Eh'lorne. "Viltula?" he asked.

"House of healing," the young lord explained. "By the look of things, the battle was far more costly than I'd feared."

The two travellers climbed wearily down and then turned to help Eldore. As they did, Eh'lorne heard someone calling his name. He spun around to see Rennil hurrying towards him. The Arms-Master ran up and put his huge hands on the slim warrior-lord's shoulders.

"Eh'lorne my friend, it's so good to see you." Although genuinely pleased, the deep rumble of Rennil's voice was tired and strained – and there was something else too. Eh'lorne peered into his mentor's disfigured face and tried to read the expression hidden behind the terrible scar. Several deep, bloody scratches had added to the warrior's unfortunate appearance, courtesy of a lich's wicked claws.

"You're hurt," he stated flatly.

"It's nothing; most of us bear the marks of battle." He motioned to the wounded men all around them. "I've been fortunate compared to some."

"I wish I could have been here. I ached to take revenge for Sarren."

"Then it's true, it's gone?"

"Aye, it's true," Eh'lorne sighed.

Rennil nodded soberly. "I've always said it was vulnerable. I wish I'd been wrong." He looked at Eh'lorne's bloody clothes, the stricken Eldore leaning heavily against the cart, and the strangely dressed bearded old man who was supporting him. "I see you've had some battles of your own."

"We have indeed. Can you have one of the tenders take Eldore inside? He's sorely hurt and in need of Aldegar's attention. Also, this odd-looking fellow is Bandil, son of Bail. He's in need of food and a bed – oh, and a bath wouldn't go amiss. But Rennil, make sure he's treated well, for although he's Keshtari, he's Mordan's emissary and but for him, you'd now all be cold in your graves."

"As you wish." He called to a soldier to fetch one of the uniformed girls.

"Now my friend," Eh'lorne continued, wearily rubbing his eyes. "Take me to my father. There's much I need to tell him and I'm in dire need of rest myself."

Rennil's eyes filled with sorrow and the rough growl of his voice became thick with sadness and regret. "My friend, your father has gone to the long sleep. He fell in single combat against the enemy's evil general."

The quick fire of Eh'lorne's volatile spirit erupted like a volcano.

"Dead?" he shouted, grabbing his friend and tutor roughly by the shoulders and trying unsuccessfully to shake him. "Dead? How can he be dead – what of the oath? What of the Lord-Guard; were they all slain too?"

"Eh'lorne," Rennil said gently. "You knew your father better than anyone. He would not be told. He took up his sword and demanded to fight alongside his army. Despite all our efforts to keep him safe, he would not be guarded."

"And Gildor?" Eh'lorne spat. "Does he still live?"

"To his shame, he does."

"Then I can remedy that!" Eh'lorne shouted, his anger spiralling dangerously out of control. "Where is he? My blade can soon put an end to his misery!"

"Eh'lorne!" Eldore's voice, although weak and pain laden, carried an unaccustomed, firm authority which immediately stopped his brother's furious ranting. Eh'lorne stood with his back to his brother, his eyes blazing fiercely. He was shaking with a rage that burned just as hot, but was at least no longer uncontained.

"My brother," Eldore continued more gently. "You of all people should understand. Had you been in father's position, could *you* have forsaken your sword? Could the Lord-Guard have kept *you* from battle? I think not. I share your pain. He was my father too, and I also feel the need to lash out in my grief; but stop for a moment and think. We don't know all the facts. Let Rennil explain them to us and then we can judge if any man carries blame."

Rennil sighed and shook his head. "Ah, my lords, my friends. There's so much to tell that I can't easily relay all that transpired – at least not so you'd understand properly."

"Then use mind-talk!" Eh'lorne snapped, turning to the Arms-Master and glaring into his disfigured face.

Rennil gulped and looked nervously from one twin to the other. He was frightened of no living man, but this? Mind-talk was an intensely private affair. When two people opened their consciousness in that way, no one else could intrude. It was a fact as sure as life itself. Yet somehow the twins had the disturbing ability to both enter another's mind at the same time.

It was something few had dared to experience and none more than once. To have three personalities in one head made it feel as though it were about to explode!

With a huge effort, he forced down his reticence. "Very well but have a care; you're both emotional and I'm not at my best."

Eh'lorne grunted derisively but Eldore managed a strained smile. "We'll be gentle," he said reassuringly.

They closed their eyes and stood for some time, sharing not just the information, but also the sensations and the sentiment of the previous night's events. Beads of perspiration broke out on the Arms-Master's forehead and the slight distortion of his lips twisted even further until it became a taut grimace. At last, contact was broken and Rennil staggered back, gasping for breath.

"You see brother," Eldore said in a voice breaking with emotion. "Father died an honourable death which no one could have prevented – not even the Lord-Guard. Gildor cannot be held responsible, and neither can anyone else. Even father can carry no guilt –oath-breaker though he undoubtedly was; for had he not forsaken the law, all would have perished. Now his name will be revered as highly as even the greatest of the old kings."

Eh'lorne stood for a few moments with his head down, choking back the tears that threatened to flood down his face. Abruptly, he lifted his gaze and locked his fierce, grieving eyes on Rennil's. "Do as I've said," he said harshly; then he turned and strode quickly away.

"Eh'lorne!" Rennil called anxiously as he made to follow after him.

"Let him go," Eldore said wearily. "It's safest for everyone for him to be alone."

The Arms-Master stared after his prodigy and shook his head sadly. He then turned to the pretty young tender now hovering at Eldore's side.

"Take Lord Eldore to the healer and make sure he's seen to immediately."

The girl curtsied, then with another's assistance, helped the debilitated Eldore through the viltula's doors.

Numbly and unsteadily, Eh'lorne walked through the city, oblivious to the horrified stares of the people he passed. He certainly had a gruesome appearance. His leather headband had slipped allowing his long, untidy hair to fall across his dirt-streaked face. His blank, staring eyes were bloodshot and dark rimmed. His once white clothes were now filthy and covered in the dried blood of both the lich he'd slaughtered and the brother he'd carried.

He stumbled on through the cobbled streets until he reached the riverside path. There, he turned to his left and walked alongside the wide, fast-flowing water. When he came to a bridge he crossed over to the northern bank and continued beside the river until he came to the towering waterfall at the western rim of the huge caldera. He then followed a steep, hidden path which led to his own private place of solitude. Even his brother knew nothing of the small cave cut into the precipitous cliff face where he would go to be alone with his wildly conflicted thoughts. There he would often sit, staring out over the city he both loved and resented, his mind plagued by a paradox of deep anger and fierce loyalty.

He'd furnished the cave with a lamp, a large flask of firebrew, and a bed of skins that now, after unbuckling his sword he threw himself on to. He lay staring at the low, rocky ceiling trying to make sense of the kaleidoscope of images whirling around in his head. The unimaginable brutality he'd witnessed in the ruins of Sarren; that strange, weak old man with his formidable power who'd so touched his heart; the desperate race to warn Sirris of its impending doom; and overshadowing everything else, the terrible loss of his beloved father.

Although he'd loved both twins equally and had never shown favouritism in any form, somehow Lorne had always been closer to the headstrong, impetuous Eh'lorne than to the quiet and thoughtful Eldore.

To try and stem the tide of unbridled sorrow and loss that was threatening to overwhelm him, in a voice surprisingly soft and clear in tone, Eh'lorne started to sing.

Many times, he'd heard his father sing the same rhyme of mourning. Every time Lorne had taken the two boys to visit the tomb of the mother they'd never known, he'd heard the words. But he'd heard them with no understanding of the heartache they contained. As he sang them now however, their full bittersweet meaning became clear to him.

> *Now your life is done and your love's touch is past,*
> *How for you will I not weep?*
> *In thoughts that are treasures no mere gems can match,*
> *Nor gold any mortal can give,*
> *Till the flame of my life flickers and dies,*
> *Your bright spirit always will live.*

Then, unable to hold back the waves of pain and anguish any longer, he curled up on the rough bed and cried himself to sleep.

CHAPTER EIGHT

The main dormitory of the viltula was a simple but efficient affair. It was little more than an enormous hall filled with row upon row of modest but comfortable beds. A preparation area for salves and potions took up one corner while a space for the tenders to rest while still watching their charges took up another. It was warmly heated by a large stove at each end of the huge room, the temperature being kept at a comfortable constant courtesy of six large, leaded windows that were ranged along one of the walls. Each of these was separated into several opening vents by thick mullions and transepts. The double doors of the viltula's entrance were set into the centre of that wall, while the opposite wall contained several more doors that led through to the storerooms and to the private quarters of the healer and his family.

S. P. MUIR

Although usually greatly under-occupied, the hall was now perilously overcrowded from the consequences of war. Scores of the most seriously wounded men filled the beds, while almost as many were on blankets on the floor, crammed into any available space that could be found. The air was filled with the groans and cries of agony and despair. The tall, thin healer, Aldegar, was working methodically through the carefully triaged patients, his balding head shining with sweat and his sharp features pinched with strain. Dozens of the hard-pressed uniformed women – some little more than girls in their teens – rushed here and there, doing what they could to dress wounds and alleviate suffering.

One of the tenders, however, was conspicuously different from all the others. It wasn't just the red sash of seniority worn over her light-grey uniform that set her apart. It was her appearance. She was unlike any other female in the city. All Arlien women were tall and pale with brown eyes and fair hair; but Morjeena was very different. She was short and slight in build, and had it not been for her womanly figure, she could easily have been mistaken for a twelve-year-old girl. Her long, shining, ebony hair and rich, light-brown skin only served to accentuate the brightness of her deep blue eyes. Even the tension and fatigue etched into her young, delicate features could not detract from her striking beauty. Despite her obvious youth, her cool competence was remarkable, and the deference of those under her firm authority bore witness to her outstanding ability.

Although Aldegar claimed her as his daughter, she was not in fact Arlien at all but was actually of Keshtari descent. Twenty-two years previously, an Arlien patrol had found a heavily pregnant Keshtari woman wandering alone in the western foothills. Barefoot and lightly clothed, she was only half alive, staggering through the snow and rambling incoherently. The patrol had taken her straight to the viltula where she'd soon given birth to a healthy baby girl. The poor unfortunate woman, however, had died shortly after. The young apprentice healer, Aldegar, had delivered the baby and had taken it upon himself to find the girl a home. But in the end, he could not bear to part with the tiny, dusky-skinned bundle. After securing the services of an obliging wet-nurse, he'd formally adopted the child and had named her Morjeena, which means 'Gift from God'.

Dedicating his life to his work and his new daughter, Aldegar had never married, but had soon become incredibly adept as both a healer and a father. As Morjeena grew, he'd showered her with love and knowledge, training her in the arts of potions and anatomy – arts for which she'd shown a prodigious appetite and aptitude. A constant companion to her adored father, her skills now almost equalled his and would soon outstrip even his tremendous expertise. But despite all that talent, the present situation was getting completely beyond her control. At least, she thought, the wounded had stopped arriving and she knew exactly what she was dealing with.

Her heart sank when she heard the doors open behind her. She turned around to see the blood-soaked, half-dead form of Eldore being helped into the already overstretched medical centre. It was a moment or two before she recognised the High-Lord's son, but when she realised exactly who the latest casualty was, she gave a small cry of horror and ran to assist the two struggling tenders.

Expertly, she assessed the severity of his wound and quickly realised exactly how seriously injured the young nobleman really was. She looked around the impossibly overcrowded hall and immediately made up her mind.

"Take him to my quarters," she ordered sharply.

"Your quarters? But..." The tender was cut short by Morjeena's fierce, withering look. "Yes mistress," the hapless girl finished meekly.

The diminutive head tender watched them go for a moment then looked over to where her father was working on the far side of the hall. He'd seen the stricken lord arrive and now realised exactly where he was being taken to. He turned to her with an enquiring look on his face, but Morjeena merely motioned around the packed hall and shrugged helplessly. Aldegar studied her for a moment then gave a resigned nod. His eyes followed her as she left the huge chamber, his expression both thoughtful and troubled. His daughter had not spoken to Eldore for many a long year now, and he would have preferred it to stay that way.

When Morjeena reached her quarters, she found Eldore in her sleeping chamber and sitting on her generous single bed with the tenders helping him out of his stained, filthy tunic. The young lord winced and grunted with the stabbing pain of each movement, but still did all he could to assist. When at last he was free of the offending garment, the two girls stepped aside to allow Morjeena to crouch beside him and assess the wound more carefully.

It didn't look good. The deep gash started behind and above the hip and reached almost to the sternum. The cut itself looked angry and inflamed and was encrusted with dried blood and dirt. None too gently she prised open the wound to see exactly how far the grime of his torturous journey had infiltrated. As she probed, Eldore gave out a loud, agonised cry which he quickly cut off by clenching his teeth. He looked down at her in dismay but she completely ignored her patient's obvious distress. She then stood up and addressed her subordinates.

"Strip him and clean him up," she instructed coldly. "I'll see to his wound when I return." She turned and strode briskly from the room leaving the two girls to exchange a worried look. Although she often had a tendency to be aloof and curt in her manner, their mistress was rarely rude and never rough with her patients. To make them even more uncomfortable, this particular patient was the late High-Lord's son! Carefully and respectfully they did as she'd requested, using the washbasin and pitcher that stood on a table in one corner of the room to wash the blood and dust from his powerful frame. They also had time to find a spare sheet to drape over his lap and cover his dignity.

As they were clearing away, Morjeena returned carrying a large tray loaded with soft cloths, bandages, and various salves and ointments. There was also an alarmingly substantial needle and thread.

"Leave us," she demanded abruptly. The two girls who had never before witnessed such intimidating behaviour from their tiny Keshtari supervisor, wasted no time and fled silently from the room

Without a single glance at his face, Morjeena placed the tray at Eldore's feet and knelt beside him. Once again, she inspected the wound, making little sounds of approval at the way her underlings had swabbed around the horrendous laceration without interfering with her task of sanitising the injury itself.

Eldore watched the top of her head as she worked. His face was understandably full of pain and grief at the loss of his father, but there was something else too. His dark, gentle eyes also held an almost wistful and nostalgic melancholy. Eventually, for the first time since he'd entered the house of healing, she spoke to him. Her voice was cool and detached with an exaggerated efficiency that made him wince.

"The wound is deep and contaminated. It must be thoroughly cleaned before I close it." She looked up at his face, deliberately avoiding his eyes. "I'll apply oil of leaf to numb the area, but it won't be a pleasant experience."

"Do whatever you must," Eldore replied softly, trying to hold her gaze. "I'm in your hands now little Delsheer."

For a moment she froze as she heard the old nickname he'd given her. Then inwardly she cursed herself and set about her task once more; this time though, with noticeably more consideration and care. The more she heard her patient strive to contain his agonised cries, the more her demeanour softened. Her carefully constructed emotional barriers were beginning to crumble, despite her efforts to reinforce them with anger.

"Delsheer indeed!" she thought scornfully. "How dare he call me that name." Then it occurred to her that she'd felt that self-same indignation the first time he'd used it eight, or was it nine years ago? She tried to push the memory aside but it was no use.

Unbidden, the picture flashed into her mind of the young girl of thirteen, standing in the main square with her hands covering her eyes to hide the tears of anger and shame. Her ears were ringing to the all too familiar taunts of 'heathen bastard' and 'harlot's spawn'. She'd been surrounded by six boys from the same crowd that had made her life a misery for most of her life. Most of them – girls as well as boys – were a year or two older than her. It was one of the reasons she'd spent so much time with her father.

Suddenly, there'd been a shout, a scuffle, and the sound of running feet disappearing into the distance. Then a hard, commanding voice had said, "Get you gone lest *I* strike you too!" She'd opened her eyes to see the eldest and largest of her tormentors sitting on the ground before her, blood streaming from his nose and crying like a baby. Behind him was the ludicrous sight of his five fellows running as fast as they could, closely pursued by a single tall but slightly built lad of around fifteen. Her fallen persecutor had then scrambled to his feet and run off wailing in the other direction. She'd turned to see who'd spoken and had been confronted by a tall, thin, blonde-haired boy with dark, softly smiling eyes.

"It's alright," he'd said in a gentle, reassuring voice. "They've gone now."

"What have you done!" she'd wailed, horrified. "Are you a complete imbecile? Now they'll taunt me all the more. How could you be so stupid?"

"My, my," the tall boy had said with an amused twinkle in those benign, compassionate eyes. "That's an awfully sharp tongue for one so small and delicate. I know, I shall call you 'Delsheer' and you can call me Eldore."

She'd glared indignantly up at him, angrily wiping away the tears. How dare he give her such a ridiculous nickname! The delsheer was a tiny flower, unique to the Sacred Mountains. It had deep-red and black petals whose fragile delicacy was offset by the wickedly sharp thorns on the broad, dark-green leaves. They'd locked eyes, the intense fire of hers countered by the warm, friendly humour of his. Gradually the flames of her ire had been quenched by the infectiousness of his amiable smile. She too had then started to smile and as she had, he'd started to chuckle. It hadn't been long before they were both in fits of laughter and the feelings of hurt and shame had dissipated like a summer mist.

Just then, the other boy had returned and she'd found herself open mouthed and staring from one to the other and back again. There'd seemed no way to tell them apart. But later, as she'd got to know them better, she'd had no difficulty, for not only were their demeanours at opposite ends of the spectrum, their eyes always gave them away. Not in shape or colour but in the soul behind the dark brown orbs that could never be hidden.

"Did you catch them?" Eldore had asked.

"Indeed I did," the newcomer had said happily. "It's high time those scoundrels were taught a lesson in manners."

"Aye," Eldore had replied sagely. "There's a lesson in everything."

Morjeena had looked at them aghast. "But there were five of them. That isn't fair."

The lad had looked down at her with wild joy shining in his eyes.

"You're right of course, little lady," he'd said with a laugh that had sent a flutter through her tummy. "But you know the one with the big ears and the pug nose?"

"Yes, his name's Carrigan."

"That's him. Well, I caught them as they reached his house. His big brother seemed to take exception to my method of teaching and came out to join them. That made the odds a little more even."

"But his brother has just joined the militia, didn't he hurt you?"

The wild-eyed youth had thrown back his head and roared with laughter. "Mortally!" he'd said, holding up his hands and showing her the grazes on his knuckles.

"But why would you fight for me? And against so many of them. Weren't you scared?"

"You should understand my brother," Eldore had said putting his arm around her and causing an eruption of feelings she'd never known before. "To those ruffians, it was a desperate fight but to Eh'lorne here, it was entertainment."

"Eh'lorne," she'd gasped as realisation had dawned on her. "You're the High-Lord's sons."

"At your service, my lady," Eh'lorne had said with an elaborate bow.

Morjeena had flushed and had tried to disentangle herself from under Eldore's arm. "But...please let me go," she'd cried, fearing that she was the victim of an even crueller game.

Eldore had gently turned her to face him so he could look into her eyes. "Little Delsheer," he'd said tenderly. "We mean you no hurt but would be honoured to count you as a friend. But if you feel we're unworthy of that honour, then so be it. Go safely on your way and forget you ever met us. But we for our part, will count ourselves blessed that we've had these few moments in your company."

"Aye," Eh'lorne had added. "But rest assured, *we* will never forget *you*."

The sincerity in both their voices and the warm reassurance in Eldore's eyes had left her in no doubt. "Very well then," she'd smiled. "I am your friend."

And so, she'd found herself escorted merrily back to her home at the house of healing, arm in arm with two identical handsome young men, laughing happily as they'd teased each other as to who had been the most gallant. When they'd arrived at her door at the rear of the viltula, she'd turned to thank them, and on a sudden impulse had reached up and kissed them both on the cheek. She'd then run inside, slammed the door shut and rushed to her bedroom. There she'd lain on her bed with her heart pounding and her mind racing to secret, thrilling places it had never been before.

Sometime later, her father had called her to tell her she had visitors at the door. She'd flown excitedly from her room and had flung open the door hoping to see her new friends; but instead was met by the sight of her six tormentors. They were standing on the doorstep, shuffling uncomfortably, their bruised and battered faces red with shame and embarrassment. After muttering their apologies they'd assured her that nobody would ever pick on her again. Gracefully, she'd accepted the apology, and then smiled to herself as out of the corner of her eye she'd spotted two blonde heads peering surreptitiously around the corner of a building. Never before had she felt so safe and so cared for outside the confines of her own home.

For more than a year she'd spent as much time in the company of the twins as her studies and their duties would allow. She'd grown to love them both of course, but although the wild and reckless Eh'lorne's infectious laughter, quick wit, and even quicker fists had thrilled her in ways she could never have imagined, it was always Eldore that she'd preferred. As she'd approached her fifteenth birthday – the full age of womanhood

–he'd kissed her for the first time and she was sure he would soon ask for her hand. That was the terrible day that she'd told her father.

"And who is the poor unfortunate boy," he'd joked, delighted that she'd found a suitor. "Does he come from a good family?"

"The best," she'd gushed excitedly. "He's the son of the High-Lord himself!"

Her father's face had fallen. "I'm sorry my child, but that cannot be allowed." His face had been full of deep and genuine regret. She remembered how the life had drained away from her cherished dream, leaving a gaping void that had threatened to swallow her very soul.

"Why?" she'd asked desperately. "I love him and I know he loves me."

Aldegar had put his hands on her shoulders and had looked into her eyes; his face had been full of sorrow and concern. "Because my dear sweet daughter, he is an Arlien lord and you are a Keshtari maiden. It is the law."

"Then the law is wrong!" she'd declared angrily. "How could it stand in the way of love; is my race so despised that we're to be denied happiness?"

"You are not despised by any right-minded man or woman in this city. The fault is mine; I should have told you before now but I failed to see how you were becoming a woman." By now the tears were flowing down his thin, hollow cheeks. "Arliens cannot have children with any other race. No one knows why but in all history such a union has never borne fruit."

"So I can never marry?"

"Bless you, of course you can. It was always considered the highest expression of devotion that two people should forgo any hope of having a family for the sake of love. But he is a Starbrow – the line of kings. It's their sworn duty to provide an heir. It's a duty that is set in holy law. He has misled you for he surely must have known this."

The sense of loss and betrayal had almost killed her. For days she'd shut herself away, crying non-stop and refusing to eat. Eventually though, the resilience of her spirit had helped her to survive the devastation. She'd emerged from her room, her expression cold and hard. She'd thrown herself into her studies and had soon enrolled as a tender. She'd buried her emotions in an icy tomb and had only spoken to Eldore once more. He'd called round, concerned that he'd not seen her for so many days. She'd opened the door and had given him a dispassionate look. "I'm sorry," she'd said in a firm, frigid tone. "But I'm afraid I'll be far too busy to see you again. Perhaps, 'my lord', you can find another 'friend' to play with."

So tight was the grip on her heart that even the deep hurt in his eyes at the scornful way she'd used his title had not swayed her resolve.

And now here he was so many years later, naked and vulnerable, grieving the terrible loss of his father and suffering great pain from a wound that was her responsibility to treat. Her eyes filled with tears making it almost impossible to thread the needle. Angrily she brushed them away, threaded it, and set about closing the wound.

When the task was completed, she looked up at his face to see he was weeping softly. She felt her emotions writhe as they struggled to break free of the icy grip that had held them in check for so long. Carefully she eased him into the bed and pulled the covers over to conceal his nakedness. For a long while she stood over him, watching the silent tears running down his pale cheeks and onto the pillow cradling his head. Then she spoke.

"Eldore," she called softly. He opened his eyes. The gentleness in them was accentuated by his suffering. "I'm sorry about your father."

The floodgates of his soul burst open leaving him sobbing so hard, she feared he would reopen his wound.

"Oh Delsheer," he'd cried bitterly. "What am I to do?"

To Morjeena's surprise, she found that she too was weeping uncontrollably. As the ice around her heart finally melted, she climbed onto the bed beside him, and forsaking her duties, she held him until at last sleep took him.

CHAPTER NINE

Bandil sighed contentedly and stretched out his legs to find a cool spot for his toes. His bed was large, luxurious, and the single most comfortable thing he'd experienced in more than sixteen decades. In spite of the trials of recent days, for the first time in many years he'd woken pain free and relatively loose limbed. He sighed again and eased himself up into a sitting position. After arranging the soft, fluffy pillows behind his withered, bony shoulders, he settled back and revelled in the glorious luxury of it all. He allowed his eyes to wander approvingly around the sumptuous room that was so different from everything he'd seen in Sirris so far. In spite of being superb in design and beautifully crafted, the city had given the impression of function and efficiency at the expense of elegance and style. This chamber however, was the epitome of opulence.

Although the curtains were drawn across the wide, arched window, enough light filtered through the shimmering red and gold organza to reveal the exquisite detail of the room. The light-oak panelled walls (where did they obtain oak at these altitudes?) were hung with radiant tapestries that reflected the rich warmth of the rugs scattered strategically around the polished, dark wooden floor. Set into the far wall stood a magnificent fireplace, its large grate still aglow with the embers of the roaring fire which had been lit in his honour. To the left of the bed, a wonderfully carved door led to a dressing room through which could be accessed the washroom. This contained a lidded commode, a washbasin, and a pile of soft, absorbent towels. Luxuries he thought he would never see again.

A tough-looking soldier had escorted him to the Duty Hall just as Eh'lorne had requested. In spite of a bandaged head and the obvious fatigue etched into his grim face, the soldier had been surprisingly amiable. On arrival, he'd handed the old man over to an impeccably groomed Bishtar who'd organised a lavish hot bath and a splendid meal of goat stew, pickled vegetables, and fresh crusty bread. This had been followed by dried fruit that seemed to have been fried in butter, drizzled with warm honey, and topped with thick cream. He had devoured the banquet as if he'd not eaten for a whole moon.

His dirty fur clothing had been taken away for cleaning while in the meantime, he'd been presented with a warm simple robe complete with a pocket for his Stone. Content but exhausted, he'd then been shown to his bed in the 'envoy suite' by a serving girl.

At first the girl had not really registered on his awareness. She was an unremarkable maid in her late teens or early twenties (it's difficult to determine the age of the young when you're so ancient yourself) but after turning down his bed she'd smiled at him. He'd felt his heart skip a beat and the breath had caught in his throat.

"Will that be all?" she'd asked with a desire to please that was clearly sincere. Unable to reply, he'd nodded dumbly, aware that his face must have been a picture of imbecility. The girl, seeming not to notice his inane expression had merely motioned to a large hand bell resting on a beautifully carved dresser. "If you change your mind, just ring that and someone will be along shortly." Again, he'd only nodded. She'd then turned away to leave but as she'd reached the door, he'd finally found his voice.

"Child, what is your name?" he'd asked curiously.

"Gretya," she'd replied with another of her dazzlingly beautiful smiles. But this time, beneath the radiance, he'd detected not only the understandable grief felt by all Arliens at this fateful moment in time, but something else as well: a bittersweet sorrow born of intense devotion and fruitless hope. He'd felt a desperate desire to put his arms around her and comfort her; for despite her lowly position, there was something *very* special about this girl. It was something that made his heart ache with compassion and empathy.

"Gretya; that's a beautiful name. Well Gretya, always remember to trust in Mordan and he will bless you; for he always rewards love and loyalty."

She'd given him a long searching look as if she'd realised that he somehow understood her pain.

"Thank you," she'd said quietly before hurrying from the room.

For a while after she'd gone, he'd stood at the window staring out over the city to where the sun was about to disappear behind the mountainous horizon. Then after exploring his suite, he'd closed the curtains, disrobed, and climbed into bed. Within moments he'd fallen into a deep and restful sleep.

And now he was awake, comfortable and refreshed. He settled himself even further into the cossetting luxury of his plump pillows and tried to ignore the pressure in his bladder. He was definitely going to have to get up soon but not yet; please not yet. His reluctance to surrender to the urgent call was mainly due to the knowledge that, no matter how well deserved, such splendid indulgence would be depressingly brief.

Even though his journey from the Mystic Mountains had been fraught with danger and had come so close to failure, it had in truth been the easiest part of his mission. The real trials were yet to come – and soon! He couldn't complain of course. The only reason Mordan had saved him from certain death and preserved his life so far beyond its natural span was for this very purpose. "But surely," he asked his god silently. "Would a few extra days be so disastrous?" He needed no reply for he already knew the answer; but even so...

He was brought back to reality by a polite knock on the door.

"*Koreen* Bandil, are you awake?" It was a youthful male voice, hesitant but respectful.

"One moment," the old man replied sliding out of bed and slipping into his robe. "Come in."

The door opened to reveal a tall, skinny lad, his arms laden with white clothes. With alarming clumsiness, the gangly youth entered the room and deposited his burden on the end of the bed.

"With your permission, *nir koreen*," he said in that curiously cracked and undulating voice of adolescent boys. "Bishtar has had these garments made for you. They're the traditional attire of Arlien lords and he says it would honour us if you wear them. He also said to tell you that he's added a concealed pouch, if you take his meaning."

I understand exactly what he means," Bandil smiled. "And the honour would be all mine. I'll dress at once and then I must speak with either Eh'lorne or Eldore."

The boy looked confused and horrified. "Yes, *nir koreen*, but...but Master Rennil has requested that you breakfast with him, and I...erm... what shall I tell him? I..." The poor lad was obviously terrified of the Arms-Master.

"Don't worry," the old man interrupted reassuringly. "I'll be delighted to join your Master Rennil for breakfast. I assume he'll be in the hall where I supped yesterday?"

The relieved boy nodded.

"Good. Tell him that I'll be there shortly."

"Yes, *nir koreen*." The thankful boy made for the door but then suddenly stopped. He turned and bowed awkwardly, and then rushed out, completely forgetting to shut the door behind him as he went.

Bandil chuckled to himself. He walked over, softly closed the door, and then headed for the washroom. It wasn't until he was half dressed that he suddenly realised the boy had addressed him as 'my lord' in old Keshtari. They probably thought it would show the greatest of respect to elevate such a scruffy old man to so high a rank. He laughed out loud. If only they knew! He suddenly became deadly serious; he was painfully aware that Mordan had little patience with those who showed such hubris. He muttered an earnest prayer of remorse and finished pulling on his new clothes.

Once fully dressed, he stood in front of the full-length, polished silver mirror that stood in the dressing room and admired himself. He marvelled at the cloth and cut of the pure white garments and touched the place near his heart where the Mystic Stone nestled comfortably in its secret pocket. Bishtar had not only noticed both the Stone and its hiding place in his old clothes, but had managed to organise the alterations required to replicate it in his new ones – in spite of the upheaval and loss around him. Bandil's respect for the High-Lord's chief retainer grew considerably.

Satisfied with his appearance, he took a deep breath and marched out to his rendezvous with the Arms-Master.

It wasn't long before he found himself in the plain hall where several men and women – mainly off duty servants – sat eating breakfast. The bare wooden tables and long benches bore witness to the fact that this was no formal dining chamber. Rennil sat alone in one corner with a large steaming bowl in front of him. He motioned for the old man to come over and join him and called to a female servant to bring the newcomer some food. Bandil sat down opposite the Arms-Master and waited for him to speak but Rennil ignored him. Keeping his head down, he continued to spoon the thick porridge from his bowl into his mouth.

"I must eat here more often," he eventually rumbled between mouthfuls. "The food here is far better than anything my lazy cook manages to burn."

Bandil didn't reply but continued to stare at the old warrior's disfigured face, trying to gauge the quality of the man behind the scar. When his own food appeared, he stirred the unappetising gruel dubiously. It was grey and glutinous with unidentifiable lumps lurking in its uninviting depths.

"It tastes better than it looks," Rennil reassured him without lifting his head. Suddenly, he looked up and fixed the old man with a penetrating glare. "Sometimes things are different to how they appear."

Bandil felt the incredible force of will behind the hazel eyes but didn't flinch. Instead, he returned the Arms-Master's scrutinising gaze with his own.

"That is my experience also," he said cryptically. Without taking his eyes from Rennil's, he took a spoonful of the porridge and cautiously tasted it. He smiled. "You're right, it is good."

Rennil returned the smile and relinquished his hold on the old man's eyes. "Eh'lorne said that you're the one who saved us from annihilation, and that you're Mordan's emissary."

"True, I am his emissary but I can take no credit for your salvation. That is Mordan's doing alone for I am but a tool. Can the brush take credit for the artist's masterpiece?"

"Hmm," Rennil replied thoughtfully then returned to his breakfast. After a moment Bandil followed suit and the two men continued their meal in silence. When Rennil had finished, he sat back in his chair and studied the frail, ancient old man eating in front of him. He wasn't the least amazed by the sight of his beard, for he'd seen plenty of those in his eventful lifetime – although admittedly none quite as long and wild as Bandil's. He took in the long, unkempt white hair and the spectacular eyebrows that framed the blue-grey eyes – eyes that seemed full of both amity and peril in equal measure. Eyes that seemed to leap out at one, contrasted as they were against his brown Keshtari skin. Despite his natural wariness, Rennil found that he liked the strange old hermit.

When Bandil finished his food, the Arms-Master attracted the attention of the serving girl, held up two fingers, and pointed to the table. The girl nodded and hurried off in the direction of the kitchens. He then turned back to the old man.

"So then, Bandil, son of Bail, other than your name and the fact that you were sent to us by the one great god himself, I'm in ignorance. So enlighten me; who are you, from where do you come, and how did you come to be in the company of the High-Lord's sons? You must tell me everything."

"Everything?" the old man sighed. "There's no time to tell you everything. Neither, with respect, is all that I have to say for the ears of a soldier – no matter how esteemed and honourable he may be. But I will tell you what I may.

"I was sent forth with a warning of impending doom and with instructions for your High-Lord." Rennil raised his eyebrows incredulously at the suggestion of Lorne being given orders by a Keshtari hermit. "Eventually, I arrived at the ruins of Sarren where I encountered Eh'lorne and Eldore."

"Too late to save the lives of its inhabitants," Rennil growled bitterly.

"Aye too late," the old man murmured with heartfelt remorse. "But you understand, I knew nothing of Sarren. When I came upon it, I despaired for I thought it must be Sirris. I knew of no other settlements in these sacred hills and was sure that I'd failed in my mission. In none of my dreams and visions did Mordan reveal its existence or instruct me to go there." He paused to give the Arms-Master an opportunity to comment but Rennil made no reply. Intriguingly, he nodded sadly but sagely as if he fully understood the reason for such a fateful omission. A few moments later the old man continued his tale.

"It took a while for me to convince the young lords of my fidelity, but once that was established, we began the desperate race to..." The Arms-Master stopped him in midsentence as the serving girl returned with two large mugs of a hot yellow beverage. The air was filled the pungent, although not unpleasant, aroma of vinegar mixed with honey and herbs. He nodded his thanks to her then motioned for the old man to continue.

And continue he did, sparing no detail of the exhausting run and the courageous battle fought by the valiant twins. His description of Eh'lorne's swordsmanship brought a gleam of pride to the scarred warrior's eyes. However, his attempt to gloss over his own part in the heroics did not go unnoticed.

"How exactly *did* you cross the river?" Rennil asked with a puzzled frown.

"Does it matter? Is it not sufficient enough to say that I facilitated the means of our escape?"

Rennil gave him another of his penetrating looks but decided not to press the matter any further. He was sure that all answers would eventually be forthcoming, and he was nothing if not patient.

"Continue," he said curtly and the old man obeyed.

Some of Bandil's tale of course, was not first-hand but relied on what Eh'lorne had related to him as they'd undertaken the final nightmarish stage of their journey; but he relayed it as accurately as he could, trying hard to remember all that he'd been told. At last, when Bandil reached the point where they'd arrived at the viltula, he fell silent. The two men gazed at each other until eventually the Arms-Master spoke.

"I can see we've a lot to be thankful for. But what now? I have the impression you're not finished with us yet, so what else can you tell me of Mordan's designs?"

"As I've already told you, whatever else I had to say was for the ears of the High-Lord alone; but now he's gone, I'm at a loss. I must speak to Eh'lorne and Eldore and hear what they have to say on the matter. Ultimately though, I must wait for Mordan to instruct me."

Rennil drained his mug and stood up. "Well, while you wait I have much to organise. Not least because Eldore lies stricken in the viltula and Eh'lorne is missing; so you'll not be meeting with either of them any time soon."

"Missing?" the old man asked, his voice full of concern.

"Don't worry," Rennil reassured him. "He'll turn up soon enough. He'll be mourning his father in private. I know him well enough to realise he'd see any show of grief as a sign of weakness. In the meantime, it falls partly on my shoulders to finish the preparations for the High-Lord's funeral. There's also a memorial for the fallen soldiers to arrange. You're welcome to accompany me if you feel able; it may be useful for you to meet some of the city's officials – particularly Hevalor, our Spiritual Overseer. He'll be most interested in you and the manner of your worship."

"Thank you, I'd like that."

"Good. Drink up then; it's going to be a long day and I'll wager a long night too. I'm thinking there'll be a meeting of the High Council this evening and you'll be its guest speaker."

"The High Council?" the old man queried warily.

"Don't worry," Rennil replied with a tired smile. "They don't bite."

Bandil nodded dubiously, finished his sour-sweet drink, and followed the Arm-Master from the hall.

CHAPTER TEN

Eh'lorne opened his eyes and groaned. His cave of solitude faced toward the southeast and the bright morning sunshine streaming in through its entrance was causing him to blink and squint against the painful light. He was cold, stiff, and sore. For one blessed moment he couldn't remember why he was there, but then the floodgates of his memory opened and the past two days came back to him in an agonising rush. The loss of his beloved father was almost too much to bear. Drawing his legs up, he hugged his knees and began to rock gently back and forth. He closed his eyes against the dazzling sun that was causing him so much pain. His head felt as though his brother had laid it on his anvil and was pounding it with that infernal hammer of his.

His eyes flicked open in horror. Eldore! In his own grief he'd forgotten all about his stricken brother. Not only would he be suffering the same emotional anguish, but he had that slash in his side to contend with as well. When he'd first inspected the wound after crossing the river, it hadn't seemed too bad. Indeed, if he'd been able to rest and had received immediate treatment, all would have been well for Eldore; but the forced march had taken a terrible toll on him. His condition had deteriorated with each step that he'd taken.

Eh'lorne climbed to his feet, walked over to the cave entrance, and looked out over the city. Instantly he picked out the main landmark that was the Duty Hall and then followed the road with his eyes until he located the large wooden viltula. It was a fair distance from the cave, far beyond the range of mind-talk for anyone save the Starbrow twins; but even then, contact wasn't a certainty. He closed his eyes and made the attempt, concern etching deeper and deeper into his face as his brother's mind eluded him. Then with a burst of relief, he found him.

For a long time, he stood motionless, silently conversing with his distant twin until at last they broke off. He took several deep breaths. It was alright. Eldore was safe and relatively comfortable, although obviously in a lot of pain. Eh'lorne allowed himself a selfish grin, for whenever he hurt himself, Eldore shared his pain; yet the reverse had never been the case. Countless times in his life he'd thanked Mordan for such a mercy and never had that gratitude been as heartfelt as now.

He could tell that emotionally his brother was as distressed as he was, yet there was something different about the way Eldore was coping. Somehow, his brother had found a kind of strength and hope that he couldn't understand. But wherever he had found it, Eh'lorne was glad for him.

Returning to the cave he took a large swig of firebrew and buckled on his sword. He then took several more deep breaths as he tried to focus his thoughts. He needed to pull himself together for the sake of the people for they would be justifiably frightened and as adrift as a rudderless ship. The loss of the High-Lord had left them leaderless – a vacuum that would have to be filled and he was the only one who could take on the role. Eldore was too sick and no other had the blood-right. No, he would assume the mantle of High-Lord – in deed if not in title. Squaring his shoulders, he strode out of the cave.

He went directly to the Duty Hall, resisting the temptation to drop in at the viltula. He would see Eldore soon enough. As he marched through the city streets, he at first tried to reassure the inhabitants with an encouraging smile, but almost all he came across seemed either to look away or to recoil in horror. Puzzled by their behaviour he eventually gave up and kept his eyes fixed firmly on the road ahead. Looking neither left nor right, he hurried to the Hall as fast as he could walk. Once there, he proceeded straight to the foot of the grand staircase and called loudly for the head servant.

"Bishtar!" he bellowed, his voice echoing around the huge atrium. "Bishtar!" He could never understand why some kind of communication device hadn't been installed over the years. How difficult could it be to rig up some bell cords? Standing in the middle of the Hall, bawling to the servants was so inefficient, let alone undignified. When he officially became High-Lord, he decided that this was one of the first things he would address. He was about to call again when he heard a door open along one of the many corridors that led from the atrium. A short time later, Bishtar's wife, Freiya, came hurrying along, her face a picture of anguished concern and intense relief.

She was not a particularly tall woman and her once willowy figure was, to be polite, now somewhat rounded. Her greying hair was tied up in a neat efficient bun that revealed features that were care-worn at the best of times, but now looked distinctly haggard. Despite all this however, she'd retained enough of the fresh beauty of her youth to still be regarded as a good-looking woman.

"Lord Eh'lorne," she wailed. "Where have you been? We've been so worried about you. Poor Gretya was inconsolable when you vanished yesterday. You didn't even send word to her that you were safe."

"Gretya," Eh'lorne groaned. The serving girl had been his closest friend since she'd joined the household as an orphaned eight-year-old, about a year younger than the twins. Both boys had taken her under their wings, but it was Eh'lorne that had spent most time with her, for the charming, happy little girl had shown a prodigious aptitude for his war games. The two of them had spent many a happy hour poring over row upon row of the model soldiers that they'd then pitted against each other in vast, devastating campaigns. All very much to Bishtar's disapproval of course; servants should *never* fraternise with their betters.

"Tell her that I'm fine. I just needed a little time to myself; but as soon as I get the chance, I'll come and find her and we can sit down and I'll tell her all about my adventures. Will that be alright?" he asked with pleading eyes.

"I suppose so," she replied a little reluctantly. "But I don't know what Bishtar will say if he hears you've been interrupting her duties again."

"I know exactly what he'll say," Eh'lorne said with a wry smile. "He says it every time. And talking of Bishtar, where is he? I've got a great deal to discuss with him and only a little time to do it."

Freiya's visage became clouded with distress. "Oh, my Lord," she lamented, wringing her hands furiously. "I'm afraid he's gone to the house of prayer with Master Rennil and that old man of yours."

"The house of prayer; why?"

Well there were things to do and…you must understand what with you missing and lord Eldore laid up in the viltula…" she trailed off into an uncomfortable silence.

"You mean he's gone to help with the arrangements in my stead."

"Yes, my lord; but he meant no disrespect. He would never willingly overstep his authority but he thought…" Eh'lorne cut her short by placing his hands on her shoulders and peering into her eyes.

"My dear Freiya," he said soothingly. "I would never dream of suggesting such a thing. The fault is mine; I should have been here. Anyway, there's no harm done; I'll go straight there now and send him back to you. I'm sure he'll be relieved to be spared such a responsibility."

"Eh'lorne Starbrow!" she scolded, just as she had when he'd been naughty as a boy – and to be fair that had been often. "Don't think you can go to the house of prayer looking like that!" Her eyes suddenly widened in horror as she realised how disrespectfully she'd spoken to him; but Eh'lorne appeared not to have noticed.

"What?" he said, genuinely confused. But when he looked down at himself, he realised why the people in the streets had reacted to him so badly. His clothes were no longer white but a filthy grey stained all over with blood. His hands, badly grazed from his midnight climb, were black and ingrained with dirt, and he guessed his face was not much better either.

"Freiya," he said with real affection. "What would I do without you? I think perhaps I should leave Bishtar to represent the Halls while I have a bath. Can I ask you to organise one for me?"

"At once, my lord," she replied with a huge smile of relief. She ran off calling over her shoulder as she went, "And I'll tell Gretya to make you a meal."

Eh'lorne watched her go and shook his head. Perhaps he wasn't quite as ready to be High-Lord as he'd thought.

CHAPTER ELEVEN

The existence of the Arlien race and their city home, deep in the Sacred Mountains, was a secret that had been maintained for more than five hundred years. Only a select few outsiders knew the whereabouts of Sirris – and these only because of the necessity for trade. The success of this policy of concealment was made possible by several factors such as the inviolable holiness of the mountains and their reputation for deadly spirits and eerily frightening entities – a reputation that was reinforced by the many patrols of the armshost. The main reason for Arlien anonymity however, was quite simply geography. The approaches to the Sacred Mountains were steep and difficult to negotiate – especially so in the west. But more importantly, the huge caldera that was Cor-Peshtar was almost completely inaccessible. It was of course for this very reason that Sarren, the 'Settlement of Hope', had been so controversial. Many had argued against it. Some had even called it a heresy, but just fifty years before its destruction, two hundred and twenty-four rebellious souls had left the safety of Sirris and had established a new home where they could renounce the notion of guilt and shame.

Apart from the southern pass through which the lich army had entered the valley, the only other road into the hidden plain sloped down from the rough eastern moorland and into the northern half of the city, close to where the river flowed out through its deep gorge. There were several other paths, the main one being a pass that led over the western rim, well to the south of the city. But these were all well-guarded and not easily negotiated. The rim wall itself was at its steepest along the northern-most perimeter where it cradled the city like a mother hen protecting her chicks. Cut into the solid rock of this precipitous rock-face, a stretch outside the city limits, were the tombs of the High-Lords.

The entrance to the catacombs was set at the rear of a huge, semi-circular atrium; its great stone doors counterbalanced to provide ease of movement. The walls around this massive portal were engraved with the faces of the sixteen High-Lords interred inside, including Gorand, the last Arlien king and the first to swear the Oath of Duty.

The doors to this ancient mausoleum were usually shut tight, bolted and barred against unwanted intrusion. But on this particularly momentous day, they were pinned wide open, ready to receive the latest and arguably most notable resident – second only to King Gorand himself. High-Lord Lorne's body lay resting on a simple bier perhaps twenty strides in front of the hallowed burial vault. On a raised platform behind it stood Hevalor, Spiritual Overseer of Sirris.

Although the late afternoon sun was already casting a deep and lengthening shadow over the plain, the huge assembly of townsfolk could clearly see their religious guardian as he addressed them with his eulogy to their fallen leader.

To look at he was an unremarkable man. Of average height and build with somewhat forgettable features, it was only the thick mane of brownish-blonde hair that gave his appearance any noteworthy characteristics at all. At forty years of age he was one of the youngest ever to hold such a responsible office, but a more selfless and caring personage could not be found in all the lands of the earth. The boundless love and respect that the people held for him was hard earned and well deserved.

In keeping with tradition, he wore no trappings or insignia to set him apart from the people he served and guided, for he was one of them, not over them. He had many assistants to help him in his work, for Sirris was large and populous but even so, there were few of the city's inhabitants that he didn't know by name. He was tasked with ensuring that all worship and moral conduct remained pure and acceptable; that no heresy or sin went unchecked, and that any who strayed were counselled and helped back to the true path.

The forefront of the crowd he faced was reserved for some of the city's dignitaries but mainly of course, for the deceased's family and close friends. Lorne however, had just two living relatives and of these, only Eh'lorne was present as the initial prayers were said. On his left stood the grim, solid Arms-Master accompanied by the ancient and frail theurgist, Bandil. For some strange reason, the old man had formed an inexplicable, almost spiritual bond with the tough, disfigured warrior.

Standing somewhat uncomfortably at Eh'lorne's right hand was the slim, towering figure of Gildor. The moment when the Prime and Eh'lorne had first come together had been tense to say the least. The volatile, hot-headed young lord had glared up at Gildor, his dark fiery eyes blazing with raging accusation. The Prime however, despite his own immense feelings of guilt, had squarely met Eh'lorne's fierce gaze and offered out both hands, palms uppermost in a gesture of conciliation. For some time, the two had stood face-to-face whilst those around them had waited in an uncomfortable silence. Eventually, Eh'lorne had relented and with an almost imperceptible nod of acceptance, he'd taken his place between the two warriors. An intense wave of relief had swept through all those that had witnessed the standoff.

After leading his mammoth congregation in prayer, Hevalor looked up and studied their faces with an overwhelming pity in his heart. He could see their uncertainty, their fear, and their grief. Most had suffered the loss of at least one member of their family; or at the very least, their close circle of friends. It was the second time that day that he had stood before them conducting a funeral, and they were still in a state of shock. They were numb from the sight of the mass funeral pyre that had sent their loved ones into Mordan's hands. At last he cleared his throat and began to speak to them in a strong, clear voice. He had no need to shout for the atrium at his back seemed to amplify his words and project them out over the attentive throng standing before him.

"Brothers and sisters," he began. "My dearest friends, when dire times..." He trailed off as a growing disturbance spread through the crowd from the direction of the city. Eventually the murmuring host parted to allow passage for the unlikely figures of Eldore and Morjeena. The former was struggling heroically just to walk, his face pale and strained from the agony he felt with each step. He was clinging tightly to the diminutive Keshtari tender, without whose help he would surely have crashed heavily to the ground. Morjeena's dusky, delicate features were flushed from the unequal effort of supporting the great bulk of Eldore's powerfully muscular frame. When they reached the front of the congregation, Gildor moved aside so that Eldore, still holding desperately to Morjeena, could take his rightful place beside his brother. Eh'lorne made to take the burden of his twin from the tiny girl but Eldore ignored him and embraced Morjeena all the more tightly. This action could hardly go unnoticed and drew a ripple of surprise from the crowd, and a frown of disapproval from the Arms-Master.

Hevalor saw all this and hesitated to resume his speech. What, he wondered, could be the meaning of such an unnecessary display of affection? He was of course, well aware of the bond that could develop between a man and his carer – especially if she was young and pretty – but so soon? It was an impropriety that would definitely need further investigation, but for the moment he had more important things to attend to.

"As I was saying," he continued. "When dire times strike and all seems beyond our comprehension, we are wise to remember that we are Mordan's children. If we place ourselves in his care, no matter how hard the road or how great the suffering, he will always provide the strength to endure.

"We have faced a great evil that we are yet to understand, and many brave souls have fallen protecting our lives and our homes. We have already bid them farewell, sure in the knowledge that we will meet them again when Halgar comes. But now we have one more valediction to make.

"Behind me lies the body of a man; just a man. No more valuable or treasured by kith and kin than any other we have mourned this day. The pain his sons feel, unbearable though it may be, is no greater than that of the sons of any other that died so valiantly just two nights since. And yet to us as a people, to our future as a race, his loss is more costly than any.

"How often have we whispered to each other that surely, the spirit of Gorand himself lived on in Lorne's brave and noble heart? But in his shame, the last of our kings gave up his crown and laid down his sword, swearing never to lift it again. That oath has been sworn by every High-Lord that followed him and was the same oath sworn by Lorne on the day he took the Seat of Duty. And yet against all we hold holy, he broke that sacred vow, took up his sword, and went into battle.

"Now, we as a people hold all vows to be solemn and unbreakable, so how can we honour the passing of High-Lord Lorne when his breach of promise is unforgivable? In all scripture and all law there is no provision to excuse such a heinous crime. Yet had he kept faith, not one of us would be standing here now and the last of our race would be gone from the earth. So what can I tell you?

"Well, this is *my* word, and whether it is right or wrong, I'll leave it for Mordan to judge. But whatever the scale of Lorne's transgression, he shall never be named the 'Oath Breaker'. From this day forth he will be forever known as 'Lorne the Glorious', and until Halgar comes, songs will be sung of his valour and no one will be allowed to sully his reputation.

"And so now, in Mordan's name, let us all sing praises to the High-Lord while those who were his nearest and dearest bid farewell to the man."

Then, in a remarkably strong and clear baritone, he began to sing the traditional funeral hymn reserved only for those who had shown conspicuous loyalty and fortitude in the service of their god. As the congregation began to take up the refrain, Eh'lorne was handed his father's naked sword and the two brothers moved towards the bier. Eldore – to the consternation of many – still refused to be parted from Morjeena's supporting embrace. A few faces however, shared an expression of understanding and even approval.

Both brothers had firmly resolved to maintain their dignity, but as more and more voices joined together, the singing became so powerful and moving that neither could prevent the tears from cascading down their cheeks. Upon reaching the bier, they paused for a moment and gazed down at their father's lifeless form. He lay supine, arms at his side and looking for the whole world as if he were taking no more than a well-earned afternoon nap. His pale, noble face – so much like their own – was framed by the long, grey-white hair that was held in place by the same black leather headband as worn by the twins. The silver star set in its centre seemed to shine all the brighter under the shadow of the vertiginous cliff that rose high above them. His features, in life so often severe and conflicted in spite of his supreme confidence, were now in death content and at peace.

Eh'lorne was the first to move. Reverently, he placed the sword on Lorne's chest and gently folded his limp arms across it as if to embrace the potent blade for all eternity. Then fighting down a heart-rending sob, he stepped back, stood stiffly to attention, and gave a crisp, firm salute.

Then it was Eldore's turn. With his features distorted by pain, and with Morjeena's help, he bent forward and kissed his father's forehead. "Till Halgar-come," he whispered huskily. Then after a respectful pause, all three returned to their previous positions in the assembly.

As they went, one wizened, old and wrinkled man, a heavy chain of office around his scrawny neck, watched the tiny Keshtari girl's progress with a scowl of disapproval and derision. His name was Verryl, Guardian of the Law and Keeper of the Past. It was his task to preserve and interpret the ancient texts, and this situation was precisely one that he considered it his duty to eradicate. The look in his fierce, yellowing eyes indicated that he would go to any lengths to do just that.

When the singing finally ended, Hevalor let his eyes roam across the silent crowd, trying to catch the eye of as many of his grieving, frightened flock as possible until eventually he spoke.

"Brothers and sisters, I cannot promise you that your lives will go back as they were before, or that despite our sadness, tranquillity will return to Cor-Peshtar. But one promise I can make you is this: no matter what, Mordan will always stand with you, as long as you stand with him.

"Now, go on your way with peace in your souls and hope in your hearts. I for my part, will go to the house of prayer, and if any of you wish to, you may join me there. Give praise to Mordan!"

"Let it be so!" the congregation responded. And then satisfied, they began to disperse.

Rennil turned to Eh'lorne. "Come," he said as softly as the gravel in his voice would allow. "We have to compose ourselves and make our way to the Moot Hall; the High Council will meet at once and it falls on you to take the chair. Eldore here is in no fit state to join us."

"I will be there," Eldore stated firmly between gritted teeth. "Even if I have to be carried, I will not shirk my duty."

"Eldore, no!" Morjeena implored. "You've pushed yourself too far already; you need to rest now."

"She's right brother," Eh'lorne agreed. "As much as we may need you there, we need you alive more. So go with your lady and recover your strength; I can manage things for the both of us."

"No," Eldore insisted. "I will not miss this. I must hear what our new friend here has to tell us, and I must be a part of what is decided. I'll not be persuaded otherwise."

His brother shrugged. He knew there was no point in prolonging the argument but Rennil wasn't finished.

"I think you're making a mistake, lord," he growled, his deep rumbling voice seeming to resonate even more than usual. "I'm aware that if you insist, I can't stop you, but I strongly urge you to reconsider and return to the viltula. But whatever you do, you cannot take '*your lady*' with you." His use of the phrase 'your lady' was loaded with sarcasm.

"I'm sure Eldore is fully aware of council etiquette," Eh'lorne interjected, a note of anger beginning to creep into his voice. "He has attended enough of them after all."

It was at this point that Bandil, still standing quietly at the Arms-Master's side, decided to intercede.

"Would it not be acceptable for the young lady to accompany Eldore *to* the Moot Hall but not enter? Then, if she has no objection, she could wait outside until we're finished. Then if our injured companion takes a turn for the worse, she's on hand to help, while council etiquette is preserved. That way surely everyone is satisfied?"

"Not everyone," Rennil growled sourly. Then he strode angrily away.

Eh'lorne smiled and patted the old man gently on the back while Morjeena looked at him gratefully. It was the first time she had seen another member of her own race.

"Thank you," she said quietly.

For the second time since entering the city, and for no fathomable reason, Bandil felt as though his world had been rocked by a softly spoken young girl.

CHAPTER TWELVE

There were only four chambers in the Duty Hall that were specifically set aside for official purposes, and of these, the Moot Hall was by far the smallest. Measuring no more than fifteen strides by ten, it was sparsely furnished with two tall, narrow cabinets and lined with several shelves carrying the ubiquitous scrolls and parchments. Heat was provided by a diminutive black stove, which in spite of the room's modest dimensions, seemed far too small to be sufficient. Apart from one door and a large leaded window that was now covered by heavy drapes, there was little else in the room of any note – except of course, for the table.

It was not overlarge, having room enough for only twenty chairs, but it was ancient and solid with beautiful marquetry crafted into its oft-polished surface. Its dimensions were such that eight people could sit each side along its length while it was wide enough for two more at each end. One of these ends however, was completely taken up by the High-Lord's large, impressive seat.

Sitting around the table, freshly arrived from Lorne's memorial service, were eight of the twelve permanent members of the city's High Council. Between them they represented and governed all aspects of life in the city and therefore the whole of the Arlien race. Apart from the High-Lord and his two sons, only Hevalor was absent, busy as he was comforting the grief stricken in the house of prayer. The six men and two women present were responsible for agriculture, law, defence, manufacture, and trade. As they waited for Eh'lorne's small party to arrive, the air was filled with the low hubbub of expectant and apprehensive chatter.

It was taking Eldore some time to reach the Duty Hall from the catacomb. It was not a short distance but he stubbornly refused to accept any assistance other than that provided by Morjeena. The great discrepancy in their relative sizes however, made progress even more difficult. Eventually though, they did arrive at the door to the meeting chamber and it was at this point that Eh'lorne stood firm.

"Little damsel," he said gently but firmly, addressing Morjeena the same way he had so many years ago. "This is as far as you can go; I'll take him now. As Bandil suggested, you can wait here until the meeting is over, or you can return to the viltula. If you decide to stay, I'll have a chair brought up for you but if not, I swear that your patient will be returned to you in no worse a condition than you leave him."

"I'll stay," she replied defiantly, but Eldore shook his head and relinquished his hold on her. He managed to stand unaided but only by placing a hand on the wall to steady himself.

"No, Delsheer, there are many men more in need of you than I; so go back to the viltula and see to them. Besides, who knows how long this meeting may last."

"But they *are* being seen to, whereas you're..." He cut her short by placing a finger on her lips.

"Hush now," he said softly. "I'll be back with you as soon as I can. Off you go and do your job; your father will be lost without you."

She peered into his eyes, distress giving her features an unaccustomed air of vulnerability. Then, to his brother's amusement, she reached up and kissed Eldore's cheek.

"Take care," she breathed, then hurried away.

"Well now," said Eh'lorne giving Bandil a sly wink. "This is a rum turn of events brother. I envy your choice of admirer but not the position she places you in. At least you've had eight years to prepare your explanations."

"Leave it be," Eldore warned. "We've more serious problems to consider; so stop acting like a child and help me inside."

Eh'lorne grinned, and placing his brother's arm around his shoulders, assisted him to walk into the room. Bandil followed along behind, his wrinkled, bearded face wearing an expression of puzzled amusement.

The council members took to their feet as the three men entered and remained standing until the two brothers had taken their accustomed places at either side of their father's honoured seat. Bandil positioned himself beside Eh'lorne, noting as they sat down that his companion was still wearing his sword – as indeed were Gildor and Rennil – something unimaginable in Keshtari ruled Arl.

Under normal circumstances it would have been Lorne's responsibility to control council proceedings, but with the High-Lord's seat vacant, Eh'lorne found that all eyes were turned expectantly towards him. He glanced at his brother sitting in the seat opposite and realised from his expression that he too was waiting on him to begin. It was an immense responsibility – and responsibility was something he was not too familiar with – but in his usual rash and heedless way, he unhesitatingly threw himself into the role. He returned to his feet and looked around at the strained and frightened faces. Only Gildor and Rennil seemed to have retained any measure of their composure. The Prime was sitting next to Eldore with the Arms-Master beside him, both of them watching the youthful Lord with relaxed and unwavering eyes. Whatever the tension between himself and Gildor, he found the Prime's towering presence (even sitting down he dwarfed the rest of the company) and his composed, boyish features reassuring. And Rennil? One look into those steady, piecing hazel eyes and it seemed anything was possible. Even that hideous scar and the fresh, deep scratches only served to reinforce the notion.

"My fellow councillors," he began. "I know the events of the past few days have left us all unsettled and in need of answers, but I hope our guest here..." he laid a hand on Bandil's bony shoulder, "...can shed some light on what has befallen us and also on what lies ahead. But before I call on him to speak, I think we need to know if our defences are still adequate, for who knows how soon they might be tested again. Rennil, will you relate to us the details please?"

"Indeed, my lord," the Arms-Master said formally, getting to his feet. As he did, Eh'lorne retook his own.

"The particulars of the battle itself are known to most of you and are inconsequential to this evening's discussions, so I'll move straight on to the battle's aftermath. Our casualties, I'm afraid to say, are severe. We were able to field just over two thousand one hundred men in total, and out of those, we lost more than six hundred and fifty either dead or critically wounded. Another five hundred and seventeen have suffered less serious but still incapacitating injuries. Fewer than half the hostmen and militia that took part in the battle are available to me today. To add to our woes, almost none of those are completely unscathed." Gildor shuffled uncomfortably in his seat, acutely aware of his own lack of injury.

"However, things are not quite as hopeless as the bare facts would make it appear. At least six hundred militiamen were not called to arms and are completely fresh. With these added to the men that survived the battle, we still have an army that consists of around six hundred hostmen, nine hundred-and-fifty militiamen, and thirty Lord-Guard. A grand total of almost sixteen hundred men."

"More than five hundred fewer than took part in the battle," someone interrupted dryly. The speaker was one of the two females present; a tall and stately-looking woman in her mid-fifties. Her grey hair framed fine, aristocratic features, and even in her twilight years, she was still a great beauty. Although her statement was discouraging to say the least, her voice was serene and betrayed no trace of fear.

Rennil smiled at her. "Yes Hesta, five hundred fewer."

"And only six hundred hostmen?"

"Only six hundred. Plus, of course, thirty Lord-Guard."

"Of course," Hesta replied, returning the smile. "That makes all the difference."

"I've spoken to Aldegar," Rennil continued, pretending not to have heard her gentle sarcasm. "And he tells me that many of our wounded will recover. In time we can expect as many as four or five hundred to return to duty. So, as you can see, day-by-day our resources will continue to grow.

"Considering the total annihilation of our enemy, I feel it unlikely that we'll face another such onslaught anytime soon. Nevertheless, I've sent out patrols to watch all the approaches to the vale, so we won't be caught unprepared again.

"I've also enlisted every able-bodied man into the militia and their training will commence at once. I'm sure you'll all provide every assistance in ensuring that all those who qualify will report to the relevant officers. And as time is of the essence, shall we say the day after tomorrow at the latest?"

"And what of the fields?" snapped a stocky, ruddy-faced man near the far end of the table. "The spring thaw will arrive any day now, and if the field hands are recruited into the militia, there'll be no one left to till the soil and plant the crops. How will we feed the people without grain or vegetables?"

Rennil remained unmoved. "There'll be no people to eat the grain if there are no soldiers to stop them from being murdered," he replied levelly.

The man leapt angrily to his feet, his ruddy cheeks burning crimson with outrage. "And there'll be no need to murder us if we're all to starve. *All our deaths will be on your head*!" he shouted pointing an accusing finger at the Arms-Master.

"Sit down Gurd!" Eh'lorne interjected forcefully. "Remember where you are and show some restraint. Master Rennil is correct; defence *must* be our first priority."

"With respect," Gurd cried, swinging round to face Eh'lorne. "You *would* agree with him because he's your mentor and has been for many years. You think as a warrior because you *are* a warrior. Well I for one would like a different perspective on the matter. Perhaps Lord Eldore would like to share his thoughts with us. At least I'd have faith that his judgement is impartial." There came a murmur of agreement as every eye turned toward the pale, stricken young noble."

For some time Eldore sat quietly contemplating his response. His face was strained and etched with pain and his brow was furrowed with concentration. When at last he spoke, his voice, although quiet, was steady and his words considered and well chosen.

"Neither argument is entirely wrong, but nor are they entirely right; and there can be no doubt that both Gurd and Rennil have nothing but the people's welfare in their hearts. Indeed, I'm sure all of you have concerns about your own responsibilities. But aren't we all forgetting one thing? We are all mere mortals with every imperfection and lack of wisdom that our humanity entails. If we're to be sure that our decisions are the correct ones, should we not rely on Mordan? Normally, we would turn to Verryl, our esteemed Keeper of the Past..." He nodded to the old man who had so disapproved of Morjeena at the funeral. "...and to Hevalor, our Spiritual Overseer. They would then scour both scripture and law until an answer was found – if indeed one *could* be found. But today we have no need for such time-consuming deliberations. We have a more direct communication with our god through his own emissary, Bandil, son of Bail.

"Also, we sit here making decisions of such import that they could affect the very survival of our race, but we do not yet have all the facts. That is why I believe we should hear what Bandil has to say before reaching our conclusions. After all, do any of you know who attacked us or why?"

All save Verryl nodded in agreement and looked towards the ancient hermit with hope in their eyes; but the old Lore-Master climbed slowly to his feet and fixed Bandil with an icy stare.

"Eldore is correct in only one thing," he said in a thin, cold voice. "As Keeper of the Past and Guardian of the Law it is my responsibility to ensure that all decrees made by this council or the High-Lord do not contravene statutes or endanger life – assisted by the Overseer of course. But in all else he is mistaken or misled. We alone are Mordan's children, and only we have both the history and the right. Yet you, a foreigner, come here claiming to represent him and we are to abide by your word. I think not! If the Keshtarim have drawn closer to our god than we, his chosen people have ever been, then there is no hope for us. Just because you have an Arlien sounding name, it does not make you an Arlien!

"I can assure everyone here that since your arrival, I have spent all my waking hours in the vil-carrim, the House of

Scrolls. There I have searched every book of lore and every parchment of scripture. Nowhere can I find any mention of a prophet arising from among the heathen nations. The Keshtarim have never been true followers of Mordan. Even in the days of the Arlien kings they paid him no more than lip service while secretly keeping to the ways of their old gods. So now I must ask: how has *our* god judged *you* worthy to carry *his* word to *us*?"

Verryl hesitated for a moment as if wondering if he'd completed his point; then with a satisfied grunt, he sat back down and glared defiantly at the perceived interloper.

The ensuing silence seemed to stretch on for an eternity while the amazed council members looked from one old man to the other. Verryl sat glowering at the bearded stranger with stiff and angry indignation, while Bandil did nothing except stare at his own hands. Although his face remained expressionless, his perilous blue-grey eyes glinted dangerously. When at last he spoke, his voice was quiet and level, yet it carried an ominous potency that made all in the room shift uncomfortably in their seats.

"Not everything is written down in scrolls or books, Master Verryl. If they were, your vil-carrim would need to be the size of these mountains just to hold them all. Important though your texts undoubtedly are, Mordan has other, more direct ways of communicating his plans to us. Unfortunately, he has charged me with passing on those designs to you, and believe me, I would prefer it were not so. But it's not for me to question his commands, so I have a great deal to tell you, but also, I have a great many questions to ask and time is very, very short.

"As for my fidelity, I've already proved it to Eh'lorne and Eldore and I have no intention of doing so again with every man and woman in this city. If your lords' word is not good enough to dispel your doubts, then all *is* lost and your men have died in vain."

He suddenly snapped his head up and fixed the unfortunate Verryl with a fierce and penetrating stare. His voice became strong and hard while the whole room seemed to crackle with the threat of its power. "Is it not enough that I have saved your lives, or must Mordan himself come down and teach you a lesson in discernment and humility?"

The hapless Lore-Master shrank back in his chair, his eyes wide with a mixture of fear, embarrassment, and anger. All traces of his arrogant opposition evaporated in the cold, withering blast of the ancient theurgist's ire. Eh'lorne and Eldore shared a knowing look. They too had been on the wrong end of the old man's righteous impatience.

Once he was assured that no more obstacles were to be placed in his way, Bandil resumed staring at his hands and continued in a more measured tone.

"I hardly know where to start. I don't know how much knowledge you have of events outside these mountains, and it's more than five hundred years since you began your exile. The world has changed a great deal in that time." He lifted his head and smiled at the expectant faces around him. "Perhaps then, I should begin at the moment when Gorand surrendered his crown and led your people into obscurity.

"His last act as king was to seek out the worthiest family amongst the Keshtari nobility. When he was sure that he'd found the most righteous and honourable dynasty, he placed that clan's patriarch on the throne, and then along with his race, vanished from the face of the earth. To his great credit, he chose well and for more than three hundred and fifty years, that bloodline ruled, for the most part, with fairness and equality for all. Keshtar continued to shine out as a beacon of virtue and wealth throughout the known world. All the kings that followed kept the laws and statutes that the Arlien kings had first implemented; and for the population itself, life continued the same as it ever had.

"Your worthy Lore-Master is correct in one thing though. The Keshtarim never were devout in their worship of Mordan, and within a few short years, the houses of prayer were abandoned. Some were pulled down while even worse, others were converted into temples of the old gods. The cult of the eagle god, Ruul, became the dominant religion, and almost everyone worshipped either him or one of the lesser gods that serve him. Mordan's very name was soon lost to memory and even the Arlien kings were soon no more than a half-remembered legend. By the time I was born, that legend had passed into a myth that was believed by only the most gullible or deranged.

"In spite of all that, the last of the Keshtari kings was perhaps the wisest and most honourable of them all. Under his rule, Arl shimmered with a glory that rivalled that of the old legends – legends that had so captivated him as a child. Indeed, they thrilled him so much that he named his only son after one the characters in his favourite tale. As that child grew, he too shared his father's fascination with the past; and then one day, while exploring the most ancient part of the city, he found a hidden, half-buried entrance. It led to an ancient and secret shrine to Mordan himself. He then took it upon himself to clear it of rubble and to clean three hundred years of dirt from the walls and floor. To his amazement, his labours revealed bright, colourful frescoes depicting tall, fair-haired kings and nobles, bravely striding into battle with gleaming swords and streaming banners. The images of the Arlien queens and ladies held a beauty so captivating, they took away his breath and stole away his heart. Every king held in his hand a star that shone so brightly, it seemed as if he'd reached up into the night sky and plucked it from the very heavens. Wisely, he decided to keep his discovery a secret, for the Ruul-priests would have wasted no time in tearing it apart or filling it with idols of the great eagle and his minion gods and demigods.

"It was at this time, before even the eldest of your elders had been born," he shot Verryl a pointed look. "Before even the birth of your great grandfather, there came news of a terrible unrest far to the south of the city. A whole village had simply vanished. Every man, woman, and child had disappeared without trace. Soon, another followed, then another, and another. The king knew it was time to act so he sent for his champion, Darakeem, the greatest warrior of the age. He was a huge mountain of a man, taller even than Gildor but broad and strong with it. He was a skilled swordsman and fierce in battle; yet Darakeem had a warm smile and a gentle laugh. The king's son had spent many a happy hour as a child play fighting with this gentle giant.

I was around the same age as Eh'lorne and Eldore when I stood among the crowd, cheering wildly as he led his men out of the city to hold the evil to account. Two hundred and fifty of the king's most valued warriors marched south with him, and were never seen again."

Bandil stopped and hid his face in his hands. For some time, he sat like that, breathing deeply as if fighting back tears. The puzzled onlookers glanced at each other uneasily. Rennil looked at Eh'lorne and raised his eyebrows questioningly, but the young lord merely shrugged and turned back to wait for the old man to come to his senses. Eventually, he did just that and taking his hands from his face, he gazed around the table smiling apologetically.

"I'm sorry," he said in a somewhat shaky voice. "Until two days ago I'd forgotten almost everything of my own past. Now, as the memories come flooding back, they bring emotions with them that are as strong as if it had all happened only yesterday.

"Now, where was I? Ah yes, the evil. The king decided that there was no option but to lead his whole army south and put an end to the trouble once and for all. The affected villages had one thing in common: they were all just a short distance from the fringes of the Green Oak Forest that borders the kingdom; so it was to there that he went.

"For three days he led his men up and down the tree line issuing loud challenges for whoever or whatever to come out and be judged. On the fourth day, that challenge was answered. Hundreds of the disgusting creatures that we now know as lich, poured out from among the trees and threw themselves at the king's men. Although the lich were heavily outnumbered, they brought with them an invisible and irresistible form of sorcery that paralysed even the most hardened warrior with abject terror. The misshapen force cut through the king's army as if they were no more than helpless children leaving him no option but to retreat.

"He fell back to the city but now the evil no longer held itself in check. Although it didn't pursue him as such, it was moving inexorably closer by the day. Survivors were constantly arriving at the gates, all telling the same story of bestial demons led by a beautiful, man-shaped demigod who wielded a terrible and irresistible power. The king knew the city walls could not hold the enemy out for long, so he gathered all his priests and priestesses, the sages and the oracles, and asked them what could be done. He implored them to call on Ruul; that the great eagle might swoop down and carry their enemies away. But in despite all their prayers and incantations, nothing happened.

"Then the young prince led his father down to the secret shrine he'd found and showed him the murals of the great kings. Perhaps they were more than just a folktale; perhaps somewhere they still existed and could come to Keshtar's aid. Unlikely as it seemed, the king had nothing to lose so he gave his son the mission of searching the world, to try and find the lost Arlien race. Also, he had all the most valuable treasures and artworks sent away to save them from the approaching marauders, and in hindsight, I believe he did the same for his son. I don't think he had any real hope of his son's mission succeeding, but he knew there'd be no other way of persuading him to leave.

"And so, while the king prepared to die in a glorious final battle, the young prince left the city on what seemed to be nothing more than a fool's errand. Yet no matter how pointless it appeared, he knew that his quest would be fraught with peril."

"By Mordan!" Eh'lorne cried, his eyes shining. "This was a mighty king indeed. And his son! What courage. To make such a sacrifice and walk away from battle; I could never have done it. Tell me, old man, what were the names of this great king and his valiant son?"

"I think I know," Rennil said quietly, fixing the old man with a steady gaze.

"I believe you do," Bandil smiled, staring back into the Arms-Master's piercing hazel eyes.

"Well I don't," Eh'lorne retorted in an exasperated voice. "Does anyone?"

All those around the table shook their heads in bewilderment while Rennil and Bandil continued to gaze at each other in a form of mutual understanding.

"Tell them, old man," the Arms-Master rumbled softly.

"Very well," Bandil sighed. "The name of that king was Bail-ahk the Just, and his 'valiant' son sits before you now, stripped of his title and his youth; a humble prophet and servant of the one true god, Mordan."

CHAPTER THIRTEEN

A stunned silence filled the room as everyone stared at the ancient, wizened old hermit as though seeing him for the first time. His long white hair and wild, unkempt beard were so at odds with the notion of a proud young prince that none of the council members seemed able to bring the two images together. All that is save three. Eh'lorne and Eldore had been through too much with the old man to not recognise the nobility that lay beneath Bandil's eccentric appearance; but somehow, Rennil too could sense both the power and the royalty of the old man. What puzzled the stoical, pragmatic Arms-Master, however, was exactly *how* he knew. From the moment they'd met he'd felt some kind of bond between them; a sense of purpose that bordered on brotherhood.

Such intuition went completely against everything the hardened warrior had witnessed or experienced in his extraordinary life.

It was Hesta that finally spoke for them all. "*Nir koreen*," she said with dignified regret. "I fear we have done you a great disservice. None of us have given you the respect you deserve and have even spoken to you with discourtesy – some more than others," she added giving Verryl a withering look. "Yet from what you tell us, there can be no doubt that you are the rightful king of Keshtar."

"I suppose I am," Bandil replied wistfully. "But that's of little consequence now; Mordan has other plans for what's left of my life."

"But what happened next?" Eh'lorne demanded with excited impatience. "How did you come to reach the Mystic Mountains when the way is barred by both pillars and power? Our scrolls tell us that it's impossible to even tarry at the edge of the Maze without losing one's mind."

"And your scrolls don't lie, but you're leaping ahead. I haven't told you about the manner of my departure from Arl.

"My mother wept bitterly when my father told her of the secret quest he'd set me. Yet she didn't try to forbid it. I'm positive she knew the real reason why the king was sending me away – he had, after all, made every attempt to persuade her to escape to safety; but despite all his pleas, she'd refused to go.

"And so it was that on the day I left, my father took me to the main temple of Ruul. There we knelt before the huge statue of the great eagle..." he ignored Verryl's snort of derision. "...and prayed for his protection and guidance. Then my father presented me with his most prized artefact, the '*Reshah-I-Ruul*' or 'Way-stone of Ruul'. This was a black stone pendant in the form of the great eagle-god himself. When freely suspended the tiny idol would always turn its beak to the north. With the '*Reshah*' in my possession and after a final embrace, I departed with a heavy heart but a confident step.

THE TALISMAN OF WRATH

"For many moons I travelled, trying to glean even the tiniest clues from the folktales that I heard on my way. But as time went by, I witnessed a great change spreading throughout the land. Fear and despair were growing in every town and village and my life became more and more imperilled until one day, I had to flee from an angry mob who were bent on my bloody and savage murder. They pursued me relentlessly and it soon became apparent that far from giving up the chase, the hunt was actually growing.

"Twice I had to fight my way free of small bands intent on collecting the bounty on my head – a bounty I was told, that had been set by a tiny demonic imp. Thankfully, both times my captors were few and were ignorant of any war-craft and fell easily to the edge of my blade. Although I made my escape without too much difficulty, the noose was tightening and I could now do nothing except run.

"Thus, I found myself driven southeast until, against my will, I was cornered at the edge of the great Maze. The towering pillars of stone filled me with dread, but to be torn apart by a vicious mob was a thought that was even more terrifying.

"Putting my faith in Ruul and the '*Reshah*', I plunged into the Maze and left my tormentors behind. If any were foolish enough to follow me, I neither knew nor cared; as far as I was concerned, they deserved whatever ills befell them. I think differently now; they were no less victims of Limnash than I.

"My idea once inside the Maze was simple enough. I was familiar with the lay of the land in that region, for cartography had been among my many studies. I planned to turn east, then north and exit the pillared labyrinth at the southern foothills of these very mountains.

"At first all went well; my eagle pointed solidly to the north and my progress, although slow and difficult, was at least steady. But then as darkness fell and I settled down for the night, a fell wind came up and on it I could hear the voices of a thousand angry spirits calling my name. Terror filled my soul such as I'd never felt before and I slept not a single wink. By morning I was exhausted and half crazed. Then, to add to my utter despair, the *Reshah* began to spin wildly leaving me totally lost and disorientated."

"Tell me," Eh'lorne interrupted, a breathless thrill in his voice. "What's it like in the Maze? I've heard that the spirit of Mordan roams between the pillars and that it burns away the mind of any who encounter it."

"It's a place I would rather forget," Bandil replied heavily. "It was cold and it was bare; a place of gloom and dark shadows. Only at midday when the sun was at its highest did any light reach my face – and this was the height of summer. The air was charged with a power that prickled my skin and seared my lungs with every breath that I took. My hair stood on end and strange lights danced before my eyes. The longer I was there, the stronger the forces assailing me became until..." He paused and closed his eyes. His voice had begun to crack and he needed a moment to rein in his emotions. When he reopened them and continued, his tone was once again measured and controlled. "I can't say for exactly how long I wandered. It was days certainly, but how many...? Suffice it to say that I eventually succumbed and fell into blessed unconsciousness. My last coherent thought was one of bitter regret, for I had failed both my father and my people.

"I've no idea how long I lay there at death's door. Perhaps I died and my body lies there still. Perhaps I was given a new one, just as all the dead will when Halgar comes. All I'm certain of is I awoke to find myself lying on a bed of straw in a small, dry cave. From the quality of the light streaming in through the narrow entrance, I could tell that it was early in the morning. I lay there for some time, marvelling at the peace and the quiet. You can't imagine how delicious it was after the battering my senses had endured in the Maze. I soon realised however, that the silence was illusory, for on straining my ears, I could clearly hear the music of glorious birdsong and the distant babble of running water.

"On checking myself, I was delighted to discover that apart from a few scrapes and bruises, I was completely unhurt. I was not so pleased to discover that I had lost my sword, my pack, and the *Reshah*. Apart from my clothes, all that remained of my possessions were my tinderbox and a small knife. I trusted that whoever had placed me in the cave was better equipped than I.

"Suddenly, my peace was shattered when a loud, terrifying rushing and fluttering erupted from just beyond the cave's entrance. I cowered on the bed, my heart racing with fear and dread, but to my relief, it lasted only a few short moments, ending as suddenly as it had begun.

"I lay there for some considerable time before I'd gathered enough of my tattered resolve and courage to venture out and investigate. When finally I crept from the safety of my shelter, my trepidation turned to joy and wonder. For there on a flat boulder was a veritable feast of berries and nuts, and most welcome of all, the still-warm body of a dead rabbit. Thirty strides beyond the table-like boulder ran a cool clear stream and not far beyond that was a large thicket of trees and brushwood. I had everything I needed for survival and comfort. I had food and shelter, water and firewood. Soon I was warm and fed and my thirst was quenched. My body was satisfied but my curiosity was growing. 'Where am I?' I wondered, completely bewildered.

"At daybreak the next morning I was greeted by the same loud cacophony as before and on exiting my cave, I found the same bounty of food as I had the previous day. The next day was the same, as was the next. Eventually, I resolved to witness the source of the noise that miraculously provided the provisions that were sustaining my life. Thus it was that on the sixth morning, I roused myself before dawn and waited at the entrance for the sun to rise. When it did, just as it cleared the distant mountain peaks, a great flock of bird swept down and covered the stone table; birds of all shapes and sizes, each carrying a single berry or nut. I marvelled at this wondrous gift and then, to my overwhelming delight, a huge eagle swooped overhead and dropped a large hare at my feet. To my eternal shame, believing that Ruul himself had come to rescue me, I fell down and worshipped it. My error became apparent the next morning when the birds failed to appear, and I was left to fend for myself.

"Now, although I'd had a privileged upbringing, I considered myself to be a fair hunter. But no matter what I stalked or what traps I laid, I caught nothing. True, I found some berries but nothing that could sustain me. The moon waxed and waned and still I could find nothing to eat. I felt betrayed by my gods, and upon finding one last empty trap, I raised my face to the sky and cursed Ruul for saving me from a quick death, only to torment me with a slow and lingering one.

"It was at this point, in a blinding flash, I had my first vision. In it, Mordan revealed himself to me and assured me that he would provide for me in every way. In return, I was to worship only him and become his emissary when the time was right. I felt as though a great burden had been lifted from me and with my soul soaring, I readily agreed. Instantly, the birds appeared and once again I was saved.

"True to his word, I was given every conceivable necessity. I had food and shelter, even friendship from all the animals I encountered – except the wolves," he added wistfully. "I could never approach the wolves."

For a moment he seemed to disappear into his own private reverie, but then with a sudden shake of his head he came back to the present.

"For all its solitude, it was a good life; and through dreams and intuitions I learned much of the world outside the Mystic Mountains, for that was where I was. I learned of your people, of the fall, and of your subsequent exile. I witnessed the tyrannical reign of Limnash, the evil god-king, and I saw my beloved Keshtar turned into a land full of corruption, terror, and intrigue." He looked around at the faces of his audience with painful sadness in his eyes. "In truth, I learned too much.

"As the years went by, my beard grew long and my hair turned white with age. The recollection of my past life – even my own name – faded from my memory. Over a century had passed since I first awoke to find myself in that cave – and yet still I lived! Then, when I was one hundred-and-ninety-two years of age, Mordan revealed to me my mission. I was to leave my home in those holy mountains, seek out your people and preserve your lives."

"For which you have our undying gratitude," Hesta said graciously.

"Eh? What...?" The old man looked confused for a moment then pulled himself together. "My dear lady, you misunderstand me; you all misunderstand me. I've not yet completed my mission for you're not yet safe from destruction. Now that Limnash knows of both your existence and your whereabouts, he'll not rest until you are wiped from the very surface of the earth."

"Why?" Verryl asked haughtily, trying to regain some of his lost dignity. "Why would he want to bother with us when we're no threat to him?"

Several voices chorused their agreement.

"Oh, but you *are* a threat; a very real threat. If Gorand's heir was to lead an army down from these hills, he could depose the tyrant and reclaim his rightful throne."

"Old man," Rennil said in a tired and jaded growl. "We've not even the strength of arms to hold these hills securely; so how then could we possibly lay siege to Arl and defeat a foe that even a king as powerful as your father could not. If this Limnash thinks otherwise, he is a fool!"

"Oh, he's no fool. He knows of a weapon that only the true Arlien king can wield. A weapon so mighty that in the king's hands, even *he* could be overthrown. He'll stop at nothing to prevent the king from obtaining it; and it's my mission to ensure that he does."

Eh'lorne shook his head and placed a conciliatory hand on Bandil's shoulder. "Ah, my friend, my friend," he said gently. "You've been misled. There is no king. There can be no king. We Arliens ruled Keshtar by the artefact Mordan gave us to prove our right to do so. Only an Arlien could touch it and only the king himself could use its power. Gorand, to his shame, lost that artefact forever. No Star, no king.

"So why then do you think I'm here?" Bandil asked angrily, rising to his feet. "Does Mordan mislead?" He glared around the table, daring anyone to answer. "Master Rennil, how about you, will you not side with me?"

Rennil shook his head. "How can I? Lord Eh'lorne is right; without the Star there can be no king."

"And that," the old man cried slamming his fist down on the table, "Is precisely why you *do* have a king. The artefact has been found. Limnash holds the Star of Destiny!"

CHAPTER FOURTEEN

The Moot Hall erupted with shouts of angry denial punctuated by the clatter of falling chairs as the assembly leapt to their feet. Above the pandemonium there was at least one clearly discernible cry of "liar!" but Bandil was unaware of exactly who had made such a slanderous accusation. As the storm raged around him, the old man calmly retook his seat and looked across at Eldore. The muscular young lord had retained both his seat and his composure and was watching him with a thoughtful expression on his pain-etched face. In spite of the seriousness of his injury, he seemed as calm and as solid as a rock in a maelstrom.

Order was only restored when Eh'lorne drew his sword and hammered the hilt on the table so hard that it dented its delicate surface, forever marring the intricate marquetry.

"I am ashamed!" he cried furiously. "Have you no dignity? This is the High Council and you are its members. If you cannot behave in a manner befitting such an honour, I command you to leave this chamber now!" He glared furiously around the room, his whole body shaking with rage. His outburst, although outrageous and shocking, had the desired effect and a stunned silence descended on the chamber. The upset chairs were set straight and the errant councillors returned, somewhat shamefaced, to their original places. After a few moments, Eh'lorne sheathed his sword and turned to Eldore.

"Brother," he said, struggling to keep his volatile emotions in check. "Perhaps, if you're up to the task, you could conduct proceedings from now on. I feel your steady hand will steer a straighter course than mine."

Without taking his eyes from the old man's face, Eldore nodded in agreement and as Eh'lorne sank heavily back into his chair, a hushed expectancy descended on the chamber. As Eldore continued his tacit, intense scrutiny of Bandil's ancient features, the silence became oppressive and gathered in the air like a thundercloud waiting to unleash its fury. When at last he spoke, Eldore's voice was tight and controlled as he struggled to overcome both the pain in his side and the turmoil in his soul.

"You're certain he has the Star?" he asked.

"There can be no doubt," the old man replied steadily. "I've seen it in my visions and in my dreams. He sits on Arl's throne with the Star in his right hand and cruel malice in his black heart."

"But how can this be?" a tall, aristocratic-looking man asked incredulously. "The Star is not evil. It was a gift from Mordan himself; no hand may touch it save it belong to an Arlien, and then only the king himself can bend its power to his will."

"Tilmar is right," scoffed Verryl. "Your visions have obviously misled you, for what you say is impossible!"

"Nevertheless, it is the truth."

Eldore took a deep breath and slowly let it out through pursed lips. As the old man's words echoed ominously around the room, the injured lord leant back in his chair and stared thoughtfully into space. At last, he returned his attention to Bandil.

"I've no doubt that you *are* Mordan's prophet; so as unlikely as your news appears to be, how can we doubt your word? You say that Mordan himself sent you here to instruct us; so then, Bandil, son of Bail, we're listening; instruct us."

With a wry smile, the old man rose to his feet and walked around to the head of the table. Standing beside the High-Lord's grand chair, he took only a few moments to scan the ten faces staring expectantly up at him. He then addressed them in a tone that managed somehow to convey both humility and authority.

"I'm fully aware of the dismay my news has brought you," he said. "But I can only tell you the things I'm commanded to tell you. Mordan has shown me that Limnash not only *holds* the Star, he wields it with great mastery. Indeed, it was by utilising its power that he overthrew my father and seized all Keshtar for himself. He has always planned to spread his evil empire throughout the whole world; but first he had to find and eradicate your people. He knows the Star belongs to the rightful king and only Gorand's heir has the means to take it from him.

"How he came by the star or learned how to control it is a mystery to me, but how the king can tear it from his grasp is not."

"You spoke of a weapon," Rennil interrupted, his deep, booming voice resonating like distant thunder. "What is it?"

"Indeed I did, and I'll come to that soon enough. But first I must ask you all a question: do any of you know exactly what the Star of Destiny is? Anyone? Surely master Verryl knows?"

"Ah well, um..." The old Lore-Master's cheeks burned crimson with embarrassment. "Yes, of course I do. It's the um... the symbol of...um..."

"It's far more than a symbol," Bandil interrupted, putting an end to the old scholar's discomfort. "It holds one of the four elemental forces unleashed at the founding of the world. Unchecked, those forces would have torn creation apart and returned everything to the chaos from which it was wrought. So Mordan took those four uncontrollable forces and bound them by law, each in its own artefact. These forces are completely beyond anything our imaginations could possibly understand, but I'll do my best to explain them to you.

"You must realise that the words I use to describe them are oversimplified and limited by the inadequacies of human language." Slowly and deliberately he pulled out the Mystic Stone and held it up for all to see. "This is one of the four. The power of hope and strength are bound within its confines. The Star of Destiny holds dignity and might, while the third power is Mordan's righteous anger; and this he poured into a different kind of artefact. It takes the form of a fabulous gemstone, a large diamond that he set into the blade of a mighty sword. This is the Talisman of Wrath, the most powerful weapon ever forged. Once completed, he hid it in a secret location only to be revealed to the true king when the world was in its greatest peril. That time is now."

"You mentioned four forces," Eldore asked curiously. "Yet you've only told us of three."

"The fourth power is hatred and spite and of that I will not speak. Suffice it to say that its artefact is secured in a place far beyond the reach of any man."

"So that's it?" Eldore asked. "Do I take it that one of us must now retrieve this 'Talisman of Wrath', bring it back here, and use it to defend ourselves?"

"That is correct; but not just anyone. Only the rightful Arlien king can claim it. So then, tell me, who has that right? Is it you Eldore, or is it Eh'lorne? Which one of you was to be the next High Lord?"

He looked impatiently from one to the other, puzzled by the twins' embarrassed silence. "Well?" he pressed. "Which one?"

"That is...undecided." Eldore eventually replied choosing the word carefully.

"Undecided? How can it be undecided? It's not a matter of opinion it's a matter of fact. One of you is the elder, and even if it's only by a single heartbeat, that one is the heir to the throne. Or is the Seat of Duty inherited differently? Is that the case Lore-Master?" he asked fixing Verryl with a fierce, questioning look.

This time the ancient academic didn't flinch and answered with all the dignity he could muster.

"The law of succession with the High-Lord remains the same as that regarding the king. But this particular case presents a unique problem. The boys' mother died traumatically in childbirth, and with the ensuing commotion and the twins being so alike, no one is quite sure which one of them *is* the rightful heir. We were considering drawing lots on the matter."

"Lots!" Bandil cried incredulously. "How can you decide such an inheritance with lots? This is no mere game of chance; it's a matter of life and death. The whole world is at stake. If the wrong man touches the Talisman, he will die an instant and horrible death!"

Once again there was silence. Then Eh'lorne took to his feet and placed a hand on the old man's shoulder. "Well, Bandil my friend," he said brightly. "You've made the decision for us. Doom is at hand so the talisman *must* be acquired without delay. And as Eldore is in no fit state to travel, it falls on me to make the attempt. You and I will leave at first light."

"I'm sorry, my lord," Rennil said with a firm shake of his head. "But that's out of the question. You'd be just as likely to die as to succeed, and we can't risk your life with such a gamble."

"Then we're all doomed, for without the Talisman, Limnash can finish us off whenever he pleases."

"We've defeated him once without it," the dour warrior replied grimly.

"And you yourself have conceded that we were lucky to do so. Can we beat him again? And if we can, what of the time after that?" He turned to Bandil. "Will he ever give up?"

The old man shook his head. "Not while one single Arlien lives. If any of your race still survives, the threat of the Talisman remains like a knife to his throat."

"Exactly!" the young lord declared triumphantly. "The argument is settled; we leave at dawn."

"My dear brother," Eldore sighed. "I admire your enthusiasm but once again your impatience has outstripped your reason. Who knows how long it'll take to reach the Talisman; and if you die, what then? We'd have to wait until Bandil returns here to lead me back to it. No, we'll wait a while and when I'm up to it, all three of us will travel together."

"And when will that be?" Eh'lorne demanded angrily. "Look at you, you can hardly stand unaided – you shouldn't even be out of bed. It'll be several moons before you're fit enough even to walk across this plain, let alone embark on an arduous quest!"

"Just give me a day or two to recover some strength. I'll not slow us down."

"A day or two!" Eh'lorne cried incredulously. "Even if you *are* able to walk, what if we have to fight again? I tell you brother, there is no alternative; we leave tomorrow without you. Bandil, how far is it to the Talisman's hiding place?"

The old man smiled. "Not as far as you'd think; in fact, you can see it from the eastern rim of this very valley. You all know the tallest peak in these mountains, the one that looks like a huge knife pointed at the sky?"

"Aye, we call that one, 'Mordan's Finger'. It's just a two-day journey away – three at the most – but it's not a location we'd willingly go to. It's an uncanny place, full of strange sounds and eerie lights. It's said that malicious spirits abide there, waiting to suck the souls from anyone foolish enough to trespass."

"Well, we must go there now, for deep beneath that pinnacle we'll find a labyrinth of tunnels so vast and intricate, that any who'd dare pass beyond the entrance would quickly find themselves lost forever. At the heart of that impenetrable maze there lies a huge cavern, and that is where we'll find the mystical sword with its crystal artefact. It hangs there suspended from nothing, waiting for the king's hand to pluck it from the air and carry it into battle."

"And then I'll make this Limnash pay for his crimes," Eh'lorne said with a savage glint in his eye. "I look forward to wresting the Star of Destiny from his evil claw."

"Unless the Talisman kills you the moment you touch it," Eldore retorted with bitter irony. "And we'll be left in ignorance wondering if our salvation is on the way or whether we're left helpless and vulnerable to our enemy's attacks."

"Of course you'll know if I've survived!" Eh'lorne retorted angrily. "You remember when our nurse took me to visit her relatives in Sarren? You remained here because you had the child pox; yet when I fell from a roof and broke my arm, you felt my pain as if it were your own."

"I remember," Eldore replied with a wry, nostalgic smile. "Aldegar was at a complete loss to explain my discomfort."

"And haven't you felt every scrape and bruise I've received for all of our lives?"

"Indeed. And there's been more of them than I care to remember."

Eh'lorne's voice softened. "So, if I *were* to die an agonising death, it's only reasonable to assume that you'd know of that too."

His brother closed his eyes and drew a deep breath. "Very well then," he said, suddenly making up his mind. "Have it your own way. Bandil will lead you to Mordan's Finger while we make preparations for war. Rennil shall have all the recruits he requires regardless of any other concerns. The welfare of the livestock is a major problem though, so perhaps Gurd and Corah..." he motioned to the second of the females present – a plain, middle-aged woman responsible for the city's apiaries, "...could come up with a plan to keep them safe." The two councillors nodded their agreement although Gurd did so with a marked expression of truculence on his round, red-cheeked face.

"Now, unless there's anything else, I'm going to take the medical advice I've repeatedly been given today and return to the viltula. If you'll assist me please brother."

"Of course," Eh'lorne replied as he walked around Bandil to the other side of the large and ornate High-Lord's chair. He took his brother's arm and prepared to heave his muscular bulk to his feet.

"There is one more thing," Verryl said placing his elbows on the table and clasping his hands together officiously. "A matter of some...delicacy, should I say."

"Can't it wait?" Eh'lorne asked somewhat impatiently. "My brother needs rest and there's a certain tender who'll be going out of her mind with worry."

"No, it can't wait and that '*certain tender*' you speak of is precisely the matter that needs to be addressed."

"What about her?" Eldore asked warily.

"Well, my lord," the Lore-Master continued, his thin, cracked voice dripping with false deference. "While your affection for that young lady is completely understandable, the public display of such an emotion is not – especially with regards to your different... erm... situations."

"Get to the point."

"Well, my lord, it's a question of...erm...well, law and...erm..."

"He means her race," Rennil intervened, coming to the stumbling old scholar's aid.

"Precisely," Verryl said with a condescending smile.

Eldore's cheeks flushed. "That's none of your concern," he said warningly.

"Oh, but it is," Verryl replied perfidiously, keeping his voice as inoffensive as he could. "Although I'm certain there's nothing untoward going on, it would be quite improper to give the impression of any kind of romantic attachment with a...a *Keshtari* girl." Although he tried to keep his tone neutral, the Lore-Master couldn't hide the contempt in his voice at the mention of Morjeena's race. Bandil frowned, deeply offended by the inferred slight.

"If I wish to have a relationship with her, I will!" Eldore retorted, raising his voice. "And I'll brook no interference from anyone. *And I mean anyone*!" he added glaring pointedly at the Arms-Master.

"I'm sorry," Verryl argued, now dropping all pretence of respect and veneration. "The scrolls are quite clear. While union between an Arlien and a member of another race has always been acceptable, the sterility of those relationships makes it impossible for any of the royal line to have such a marriage. It is the law."

"Damn the law!" Eldore roared, echoing the words his father had used before calling for his sword. "I'm going to marry her!"

Verryl sank back in his seat, speechless with fear and indignation but Rennil took to his feet. Roughly, he pushed Gildor's over-tall body aside and shouted down at the young lord. His deep voice exploded like a thunderclap bursting in the room.

"IT IS FORBIDDEN!"

The two men glared at each other with eyes blazing, faces red, and their breathing heavy with passionate fury.

The crushing tension was then broken by a slow handclap and a sardonic, "Bravo," from Eh'lorne. Everyone looked towards him, surprised to see the look of wry amusement on the slim warrior-lord's face.

"'Forbidden' is a word that seems a little over-used of late," he said drily. "But I'd like to point out that if the letter of the law had always been applied, we wouldn't be here to have this discussion. Had my father not broken one of our most sacred laws, the enemy's fell captain would never have been slain.

"And you Master Rennil. The law 'forbids' any Arlien to take up arms in the service of a foreign power, yet had you not learned your craft in the service of King Xyron of Mah-Kashia, who would have led us to victory? You Gildor? Could you have defeated the lich horde?"

The Prime shook his head. "I'd have sounded the summoning and placed our men in front of the city. Thus forewarned they would have cut us down like wheat before the scythe."

"That's all very well," Rennil argued. "But the royal line MUST be preserved!"

Eh'lorne smiled. "Of course it must, so let me put this to you: if I take hold of the sword and live, *I* will be king and the burden of producing an heir will fall on my shoulders. But as king, I'll *command* my brother to marry Aldegar's daughter. Then as my loyal subject, Eldore will have no option but to obey."

Both Rennil and Verryl began to object but Eh'lorne silenced them by raising his hand. "Hear me out before you speak."

He then turned to Eldore. "And you my brother, would you be prepared to obey such a command without delay or complaint?"

"Of course I would," Eldore replied with a wide grin.

"Good. But then I'm afraid we must address the other possibility. If I should die in the attempt, then *you* would become king, and as the sole survivor of the royal bloodline, it would become *your* duty to provide an heir. In that event, my dear brother, you'd have no option but to choose a different bride."

Eldore's smile vanished. "I'll be damned if I would," he growled.

"We'll all be damned if you won't," his brother replied flatly.

Bandil stared at the two men in amazement. It seemed as though they'd swapped bodies, for the usually placid Eldore was glaring up at his volatile brother's calm, implacable features with eyes that blazed with passionate fury.

The whole assembly waited breathlessly agog for the outcome of the titanic battle of wills. In the end it was Eldore that capitulated.

"Very well," he ground out, his voice bitter with resentment.

"Will you swear to it?"

"My word's not enough?"

"For me, without doubt. But the Council may need reassurance that your heart won't overpower your resolve."

Eldore swallowed hard and closed his eyes. The anguish of his inner struggle was painful to behold, yet his brother was merciless.

"Well?" he pressed firmly.

"Alright!" Eldore cried suddenly. "I swear it. In Mordan's name I vow to continue the bloodline if I should become king." He glared around the table. "Is that enough? Are you satisfied?"

Verryl looked across at Rennil and the two men nodded to each other.

"It will suffice," the old Lore-Master replied with obvious reluctance.

"In that case," Eh'lorne said sounding a little too pleased with himself. "This meeting is closed. Bandil, will you assist me with my brother?"

"It will be my pleasure," the old man replied graciously.

CHAPTER FIFTEEN

It was close to seventh turn of the time-glass when Eh'lorne and Bandil finally returned Eldore to the viltula. The journey from the Moot Hall had not been a pleasant one for it was soon apparent that Eldore was in a far worse condition than his companions had feared. Their progress had become slower and more difficult with each step and by the time they'd arrived, Eldore was shivering and sweating while his breathing had become distressingly laboured.

They entered the crowded house of healing to find Morjeena midway through examining the terrible injuries of a seriously wounded soldier. The poor man was lying in a bed at the centre of the hall, and although only semi-conscious, her attentions were still causing him to cry out in pain, despite the tenderness of her touch.

The pretty head tender gasped when she caught sight of Eldore. Immediately, she recognised how sharply his health had deteriorated in the short time since she'd left him. With a point of her finger, she indicated to Eh'lorne that they should take him straight through to her chambers. She finished seeing to her patient as quickly and as painlessly as she could, then hurried after them, an expression of anxious concern darkening her dusky, delicate features.

She entered the room to find that he'd already been undressed and was now lying in the bed. His face was flushed with fever and his eyes were sunken amid ominous dark circles. Eh'lorne was perched carefully on the edge of the bed with Bandil hovering beside him.

"Let me see to him," she said, trying unsuccessfully to keep her voice professionally detached. The two men moved aside to give her room. Gently, she felt Eldore's face and forehead then put her ear to his chest. As she listened to his breathing her face darkened and a deep frown furrowed her brow.

Quickly, she straightened and turned to Eh'lorne. "Go and find my father," she said urgently. "Tell him I need a strong infusion of bitter bark laced with five... no make that *ten* drops of stink-bulb oil. Tell him I could also use his advice on anything else that can fight high fever, lung-water, and poisoned blood."

"How bad is it?" Eh'lorne asked fearfully.

"Bad," she replied curtly.

For a moment it looked as though he was going to ask more questions, but then with a sharp nod, he turned and hurried from the room.

Morjeena took Eh'lorne's place on the edge of the bed and grabbed hold of Eldore's hand. "Why did you have to leave here?" she asked with tears in her eyes. "You should have stayed in bed and rested. Now look at you; you're in a terrible state."

"I had my duty, Delsheer," Eldore replied weakly, his voice almost inaudible in spite of the quiet in the room.

"Duty be damned," she snapped, her face flushing with anger. "What use is duty if you kill yourself in the process?" The question was left hanging as Eldore closed his eyes and seemed to drift into unconsciousness.

"Eldore?" she said giving him a gentle shake. Then more urgently, "Eldore!" Getting no response, she jumped to her feet and pressed two fingers against his neck then breathed a deep sigh of relief.

Heavily, she sat back down and looked up at Bandil with silent tears running down her cheeks and dripping from her chin into her lap.

"Help him," she pleaded.

The old man placed a consoling hand on her shoulder and whispered a short prayer. Once again, he had the sense that in some undisclosed way, this Keshtari girl was of great importance to Mordan's purpose. It was a mystery why such a purpose – if indeed there was one – had not been revealed to him; but then he'd learned over the years not to question his god's ways. When his prayer was finished, he gazed down at her with growing feelings of attachment and familiarity, and to his surprise, found that he too was weeping softly.

A short time later, Eh'lorne returned carrying a tiny, steaming cup in one hand and an even smaller stone pot in the other. He took one look at the scene and let out a cry of despair.

"It's all right," Morjeena said wiping away her tears. "He isn't dead, he's just sleeping very deeply; it's probably the best thing for him now." She glanced at the receptacles in Eh'lorne's hands. "It's a shame we have to wake him but essential nonetheless."

She reached into a pocket in her uniform and pulled out a tiny metal box that she proceeded to open. The air became thick with a pungent reek which was out of all proportion to the size of the small container from where it came. With a look of disgust on her pretty, light brown face, she reached out and held it under Eldore's nose. After a moment or two the stricken young lord gave a feeble gasp, coughed, and then opened his eyes.

Morjeena smiled. "Welcome back," she said tenderly. "You have to take some medicine now if you can manage it." Her patient returned the smile, nodded, and then struggled to sit up, wincing with pain. Morjeena returned the evil-smelling pot to its pocket, and then with practiced skill, assisted him in his efforts. She then rearranged his pillows to provide support. She reached behind her, took the cup from his brother and then helped Eldore to drink it one sip at a time. Once the cup was empty, she swapped it for the stone pot and sniffed its contents curiously. Of course; fierce mint and bane oil. She chided herself for not having thought of it before. The strong, heady vapours would do nothing to heal but would at least ease his laboured breathing. After rubbing the contents of the pot on his chest and neck she eased him back into a lying position.

"We'd best leave him to sleep for now," she said over her shoulder. "If you wait outside while I settle him, I'll join you in a moment."

Reluctantly, Eh'lorne did as he was told. The old man followed and shut the door behind them.

The two men waited outside in gloomy, despondent silence, both of them lost in their own private thoughts. After what seemed an age the door opened and Morjeena came out to join them.

"How is he?" Eh'lorne asked anxiously.

"Very sick. I've done all I can but it's possible he won't survive the night." Although her voice was amazingly calm and matter of fact, Bandil was acutely aware of the underlying heartbreak in her tone.

"NO!" Eh'lorne exploded and made to rush past her but she caught his arm.

"He doesn't want to see you," she said firmly.

"What do you mean he doesn't want to see me? I'm his brother!"

"I know," she said, then added more softly, "but he's asking for Bandil. He wants to speak with him privately." Eh'lorne spun away and began frantically pacing back and forth along the short, narrow hallway.

She turned to the old man. "Go in." Then she added pleadingly. "But don't stay too long."

Bandil nodded, entered the room and closed the door.

Morjeena let out a long, wavering sigh and then caught Eh'lorne's arm. "Please stop," she said. Then as the distraught young lord glared at her, she finally succumbed to her emotions. Great waves of uncontrollable sobs wracked her body and the floodgates of her tears fully opened. Eh'lorne's expression melted as helplessly, he looked down at the weeping girl. Once so strong and determined, she was now broken like a delicate, fragile vase. His innate desire to jump in and fight for others was of no use to him here; there was no enemy to strike as there had been when they'd first met. Not knowing what else to do, he took her in his arms, held her tightly, and gently rocked her to-and-fro. As she buried her face in his chest, soaking his tunic with her tears, he stared into space, tight-lipped and his dark eyes burning with a glacial fire.

Suddenly, he pushed her away, held her by her shoulders and peered excitedly into her eyes. "Marry him," he said defiantly. "Marry him now. I'll go and fetch Hevalor, even if I have to bring him here with the point of my sword and force him to perform the ceremony. Marry him while you still can!"

She shook her head. "He won't," she replied between sobs. "I've suggested it myself but he says that he swore an oath to both you and the council. He told me to tell you one thing though. He said that you're to take hold of the Talisman and live, for only then can we marry."

"Then, little damsel, I'll make a vow of my own. I swear before Mordan himself that come what may, I'll take hold of that sword and I *will* live. I'll make it my own, if for no other reason than for the happiness of my brother and his bride. And for your part, you must make certain that he also lives."

With her tears subsiding she smiled up at him and stroked his cheek. "And that is why I love you more dearly than a brother. I promise; I'll stop at nothing to preserve him for us both."

As Bandil approached the bed, Eldore opened his eyes and forced a smile to his pale, blood-drained lips. He patted the bed. "Sit," he croaked.

Obediently, the old man eased himself carefully beside his dying comrade and took his hand between his own. It was as cold and as limp as a dead fish. "Morjeena says you want a private word with me. What can I do for you? I'm listening."

"Your Stone; I've seen the power it holds. Can't you use it to heal my wounds? Not for my sake you understand; the long sleep holds no fear for me, but for Morjeena's. To have come together after so many years only to be torn apart again so quickly. I can't bear the thought of her suffering so. That's why ask; for her."

"My friend," the old man sighed. "If it were possible, I would have done it on the day we met. The Stone holds hope and strength, not creation and healing. Your fate is in Mordan's hands so you must ask him for your life. If it's part of his plan, he'll not let you die."

"Aye," Eldore replied heavily. "It's as I thought." He closed his eyes and concentrated on keeping his breathing steady.

Bandil watched him for a few moments then drew out the Stone and looked at it closely. "It may not be able to heal you," he said thoughtfully. "But perhaps I can use it to ease your suffering. Here, take it."

Eldore opened his eyes again, hesitated a moment, then took the proffered artefact from the old man.

"Now hold it as tightly as you can while I wrap my hands around yours." Once again Eldore complied and Bandil began to chant softly and rhythmically. As he did, the Stone began to glow gently and a comforting wave of warmth swept up the injured lord's arm. Gradually, the colour returned to his cheeks while his breathing quietened and regained a more natural cadence.

"There now, how does that feel?" Bandil asked taking back the Stone and returning it to its pocket. "You certainly look stronger."

"I feel it," Eldore replied. "Perhaps it is healing me after all."

"I'm afraid not. The beneficial effects will soon fade. Then, as I say, your life is in Mordan's hands."

"Then pray for me, old man."

"I will. Every day. Every morning and every night; and while I walk and while I eat; if I can control my dreams, I'll even pray for you while I sleep."

"Then I can ask no more."

The two men smiled at each other, then a sudden thought came into the old man's mind.

"Here," he said, taking the pouch of red earth from around his neck and placing it around Eldore's. "Keep this with you. It holds no power within it but let it be a symbol to remind you of our quest, and of the new world that awaits after the hounds and fires of Halgar have done their work. Perhaps, if nothing else it'll give you the courage to hold on."

"Thank you, old man," Eldore replied with a tear in his eye.

"No, my friend, it's I that should thank you." He stood up and moved towards the door. As he reached it, he turned and gave his friend one last smile.

"Eldore Starbrow," he said in a warm, earnest voice. "I'm honoured to have met you. Whatever now transpires, I know we'll meet again, if not in this world, then in the new. Fare you well my friend." With that he opened the door and left.

CHAPTER SIXTEEN

Bandil sat at the large solid table and let his eyes wander around the Duty Hall's expansive kitchen. It was obvious from the great number of work surfaces and ovens that there were far more residents and visitors to the government halls than he'd imagined. He took another mouthful of his excellent breakfast and continued visually exploring the room.

Apart from himself and the two young kitchen maids busily lighting the ovens, the only other person present was the cook. He eyed her warily for she was a huge, intimidating woman being tall, fat, and distinctly irritable. The way she was setting about a large slab of meat with her enormous, sharp cleaver made him wince with every brutal stroke. As she chopped, she muttered crossly to herself, punctuating each word with a particularly fierce swipe. The old man caught the eye of one of the maids with a questioning look and guessed from her returning grin that this behaviour was quite normal and completely harmless. He wasn't entirely convinced.

In spite of the early hour, the kitchen was pleasantly warm, due mainly to the cheerful fire burning in a grate set into the wall opposite the ovens. A hinged hotplate could be swung around over the flames for the cooking of small meals when the ovens were cold. Indeed, it had been on this very contraption that the cook had prepared Bandil's breakfast of spiced goat-meat patty, eggs, and fried oatcakes. After so many years of solitude and living off the land, the past few days had seemed like a dream to the old man, but he knew there was a good chance he would never experience such luxuries again. He sighed and took another sip of his now familiar sour-sweet hot drink.

He was startled by a loud crash behind him and turned around to see the door thrown open and Eh'lorne struggling through it with what looked like a large, heavy backpack. The young lord's flushed face lit up when he saw that the old man was already there.

"Bandil!" he called out happily. "I hadn't thought to find you here so early. Have you been here long?"

"Long enough to break my fast."

"Breakfast?" He looked across at the cook who was now setting about a pile of vegetables with the same gusto with which she'd assaulted the meat. "Is there any left for me, cookie?"

The huge, terrifying woman whirled round and angrily waved her cleaver at him.

"Breakfast is it? As if I haven't enough to do, I've now got to feed you as well as your visitor."

"But cookie dear," Eh'lorne replied pleadingly. "I've got a long hard road ahead of me and who knows when I'll eat again."

"Long hard road indeed," she scoffed indignantly. "With your father just passed and your brother desperately ill, off you go on another of your 'adventures' without a care for anyone. Still," she added reluctantly. "I suppose I can't leave you to starve; there's nothing of you as it is." She threw the cleaver aside and walked towards the fire. Eh'lorne gave Bandil a huge wink, placed his pack on the floor, and sat down.

Bandil gawped at him, unable to comprehend the drastic, inexplicable change in his companion's demeanour. Last night he'd been understandably distressed and downcast – even angry – but today? He was acting like an excited child about to be taken on a thrilling daytrip. Even for one so unpredictable and erratic, it was a difference that bordered on metamorphosis.

Almost immediately the cook brought Eh'lorne's food to the table. For all her bellicose protestations, she'd actually prepared it at the same time as Bandil's and had merely been keeping it warm for him.

"There," she said grumpily. "Eat it while it's hot."

"And a drink?"

"He wants a drink as well!" she cried, throwing her hands up in mock despair. "Some of us have been up since before second turn you know." Tutting loudly, she swung her great bulk around and stalked off.

"She loves me really," Eh'lorne whispered to the old man, grinning widely.

Unmoved, Bandil studied him for a moment. "You seem remarkably cheerful this morning," he commented soberly.

"Of course. We're about to embark on the greatest adventure of my life; one that could result in me being crowned king. How could I be anything else?"

"And your brother?"

"My brother? Oh, I see; no, he's fine. I've spoken to him already and he seems much stronger. I think he's going to make a good recovery. All the more pressure on me then, yes?"

"You've been to the viltula already? At this early hour?"

"Of course not," Eh'lorne replied; then tapping his head added, "I've 'spoken' to him."

"Ah, mind-talk."

"Exactly."

Bandil nodded sagely and gazed silently into the fire. He decided it best not to explain that the improvement in Eldore's condition was due to the Stone's influence and therefore only temporary. In the ensuing lapse in the conversation, Eh'lorne enthusiastically set about devouring his breakfast. As he did, the cook brought his drink over and banged it down on the table, spilling some in the process. Once again, he gave the old man a mischievous wink.

At that moment the door opened and Bishtar entered carrying an extremely large leather water bottle. He acknowledged Eh'lorne with a nod and a short "My lord." Then with great respect, he addressed Bandil.

"Here you are *nir koreen*, a flask of firebrew, just as requested. Are you sure there's nothing else you need for your journey?"

Bandil gave him a grateful look and wondered how it was that even at this early predawn hour, the chief servant could be so immaculately dressed and groomed.

"Thank you, Bishtar, but no, that's all I require. I gather that the other thing I mentioned couldn't be organised at such short notice."

Bishtar slapped his forehead. "Of course. I'm sorry but no... I mean yes... I mean..." The flustered retainer drew a deep breath and started again. "Yes, I did make the arrangements for it to be made. I gave your exact instructions to a seamstress and a fence maker. They've been labouring all night and I'm told it'll be ready before you leave."

"Please give them my thanks; and of course, Lord Eh'lorne's too; we'll both be grateful for their efforts in the coming days I'm sure."

"What on earth are you both talking about?" Eh'lorne asked in a puzzled voice.

The old man smiled cryptically. "You'll see, you'll see."

"Well if that's going to be your attitude, the sooner we start off, the sooner I'll find out." He got to his feet and with some difficulty, picked up his huge backpack. "Are you ready?"

Bandil nodded, and following Eh'lorne's lead he stood up and took the flask from Bishtar. He tested its weight and then laughed at his companion who was struggling with the burden he'd given himself.

"When we planned this journey last night, I went to great pains to emphasise the need for speed and secrecy. Somehow I think your idea of travelling fast and light is somewhat at odds with the accepted meaning of the phrase."

Eh'lorne dropped the pack to the floor and placed his hands on his hips. "You may scoff old man, but if things don't go according to plan, you'll be more than grateful for my foresight."

"Of course," Bandil replied with a twinkle in his eye. "In which case, perhaps I should bring along a table and chairs to eat our meals at. Or maybe even a bed?"

Eh'lorne was about to respond to the old man's sarcasm but was cut short when the door crashed open with such force it made everyone jump. It seemed to Bandil a miracle that its hinges had survived such an onslaught for the second time that morning. He turned to see who this culprit might be and was confronted by the improbable sight of a young woman rushing into the kitchen, hair uncombed, and still in her nightgown. As she ran up to Eh'lorne and threw her arms around him, he recognised her as the young maid that had so affected him that first morning.

"Gretya!" Bishtar shouted in outraged dismay. He made to take hold of the errant girl and drag her away but Eh'lorne's fierce warning look made him stagger back as though he'd been physically struck. For a few moments, Eh'lorne stood looking awkwardly down at his friend as she clung to him with her cheek pressed against his neck and tears in her eyes. Unsure of what else to do, he put his arms around her and patted her back consolingly.

Eventually, as gently as he could, he pulled her arms away and looked into her face. There was no sign of the joyous beauty that usually shone out through her smile. Her cheeks were pale and her pretty, dark eyes, still bleary from sleep, were full of trepidation and concern.

"You're going without saying goodbye," she said in a quivering, hushed voice.

"Gretya, my dear, there's been no time to say goodbye to anyone."

"But you've only just got back."

"I know, but there are things I must do. Anyway, I'll be back in a few days and then we'll finish off that war game we started. And this time, just for a change, I'll beat you; alright?"

"No, it's not all right," she wailed. "You're NOT coming back, I know it. I've got a terrible feeling that I'll never see you again!"

"Of course you will. With a sword in my hand and Mordan's emissary at my side, I'll be as safe as if I were in my own bed."

"Then take me with you. If it's so safe there's no reason I can't come along; and you said yourself that I always beat you in war games, so you know I'm not helpless."

"Gretya, you know that's not possible. You've got your own duties here at the Halls and Freiya would never forgive me if anything happened to you."

"So it's *not* safe!" she declared with a slight stamp of her foot. "I'm right, you won't be coming back. Your last trip *was* safe and look at Eldore. And I've seen nothing of you since you returned."

"Nonsense. We shared a meal only yesterday."

"You did what!" Bishtar exclaimed, unable to contain his outrage any longer. The two friends seemed not to have heard him.

"And we'll share another when I return," Eh'lorne continued.

"*If* you return."

"*When* I return," Eh'lorne repeated firmly.

"Promise me," she demanded, peering deep into his eyes.

"I promise." His voice was so sincere and positive that no one could possibly have believed that he'd let her down.

"Alright then," she said resignedly, sniffing back her tears. "You can go." Reluctantly, she turned to walk away but then on a sudden impulse, she spun around, threw her arms around his neck and kissed his cheek. Then, with Bishtar's scandalised cries of protestation ringing in her ears, she fled the room.

Eh'lorne stood in open mouthed silence, staring after his friend with his hand on his cheek and confusion in his eyes.

Bishtar stepped forward and addressed the young lord in a voice that, despite the respectful tone, could not conceal the retainer's overwhelming sense of indignation.

"My lord, I must protest. This behaviour has gone far beyond the unacceptable and with your permission, I'll have a strong word with her. If she can't behave as a servant should, then she'll have to go."

"Hmm," Eh'lorne replied absently still staring thoughtfully at the door. He turned to the old man who was grinning widely, apparently enjoying his companion's bewilderment. "What just happened?" he asked, genuinely mystified.

"What can I say?" Bandil replied, struggling to keep his face straight. "I've been alone for more than a hundred and sixty years. If *you* don't know, then how could I?"

"Women!" Eh'lorne muttered shaking his head. Once again, he heaved his pack up from the floor and slung it over his shoulder. "Come along then, old man," he said brightly. "Show me this thing you've had made through the night."

He then looked at the head servant and smiled. "That's it then, old friend, we're off. Look after things until we return and keep an eye on my brother."

"Yes, my lord."

"Oh, and one other thing," Eh'lorne continued in the same light tone.

"My lord?"

"With regards to Gretya's behaviour, if when I return, I hear that you've given her a single word of chastisement, my displeasure will have no bounds. Do we have an understanding?"

Bishtar gulped. In spite of his lord's conversational tone, the perilous look in his eyes told a very different story.

"Yes, my lord," he answered meekly.

As he watched the two men leave, he let out a long sigh of relief then turned on the gawping kitchen maids.

"What are you looking at?" he snapped, then stalked indignantly out of the room.

CHAPTER SEVENTEEN

It was in the shadowy, predawn half-light that the two men left the Duty Hall and made their way through the city's wide cobbled streets. Although the eastern sky beyond Cor-Peshtar was already brightening, down in the caldera, gloom still lingered. Eh'lorne first led them north towards the river. There they turned right and followed the wide bankside path. They crossed the river by means of the most easterly bridge, which in contrast to the other crossings, was a narrow wooden affair. They then began to ascend the long winding path beside the gorge that took them up and out of the vast valley-plain.

By the time they reached the rough moorland at the end of the climb, the sun was just clearing the peaks that marked the eastern horizon. Eh'lorne paused and turned back to gaze at the city still half-hidden in the shadow of the caldera's precipitous rim. The first rays of the morning sun that were falling on the narrow streets of the western quarter only served to emphasise the gloom that clung resolutely to the rest of the city. Even the claustrophobic drabness of the workshops and warehouses that characterised those parts seemed to have been cleansed and polished by the golden light. As he stared thoughtfully out over his home, he heard the clear chime of the time bell, followed almost immediately by the muffled ringing of the many repeat bells scattered around the town.

"Third turn," he muttered half to himself, then added in a louder voice, "I had hoped to be further along than this by now."

Bandil placed a hand on his companion's shoulder. "Then why wait, my friend?"

Eh'lorne seemed not to have heard him and continued quietly peering down, his face wearing a serious, reflective expression. Eventually, he looked at the old man waiting patiently beside him and sighed.

"Do you think she could be right?"

"Who?"

"Gretya. Is it possible that I'll never return?"

"Yes, it's possible. But you've known that from the outset, so why do you hesitate? It's not like you to be so uncertain."

Eh'lorne smiled wryly. "No, it's not is it." He returned his gaze to the city. "I just have a strange feeling..."

He suddenly brightened. "Enough of this melancholy. Let's carry on with courage and hope. With Mordan's blessing we can be halfway to our goal before nightfall."

The path they followed was obviously little used but still clearly defined and relatively even. Their progress was therefore satisfyingly good in spite of Eh'lorne's discontent with his heavy burden. He constantly shifted the weighty pack in an effort to stop it cutting painfully into his shoulders. He was not accustomed to carrying his own load, let alone the extra he'd decided to bring for his companion. Usually, he left the task to the seemingly limitless strength of his powerfully built sibling. He glanced enviously at the old man walking lightly beside him. Even without utilising the power of the Stone there was an almost youthful spring in his step; especially as he was burdened with nothing more than his voluminous water skin, a blanket, and a strange lightweight bundle of sticks rolled up in a roll of waxed linen.

"It's just a tent!" Eh'lorne had cried in disappointment when it had been presented to Bandil just before they'd left.

"Aye," the old man had replied with a twinkle in his eye. "And a good one too."

As they continued along the trail, the rising sun began to shine on their faces and the snow around them began to melt away into a watery slush. Here and there patches of green appeared, joining the low scrub in a glad declaration of winter's end.

"Spring thaw," Eh'lorne stated as the sweat ran down his flushed face. "Gurd will be beside himself with his farm hands training under Rennil's command."

"When the Talisman is safely in your hand, perhaps Rennil will allow some of the men back to the fields."

"My hand or my brother's," Eh'lorne replied dourly.

Bandil studied his young companion's grim expression. He tried to think of a way to explain that Eldore would certainly be dead before they reached their goal; that whichever of the twins was the firstborn, Eh'lorne would then be heir to the throne. But try as he might, he couldn't find the right words so he decided to hold his tongue.

After little more than a stretch along the path, they came upon another trail that branched off to the left and curved away to the northwest as it went.

"It leads to Hornvale," Eh'lorne explained. "A full three days march away."

"Hornvale? I've not heard of it. Is it another settlement like Sarren?"

"No, Sirris is the only Arlien home now. Hornvale's a very unusual place. It's half temple, half fortress, and inhabited by the strange priests of the Horn-Watch. They're a curious race; dour and secretive, having no dealings with any outsiders except us. Even then it's only for trade and then not often. I've never even met a Hornvaler."

They continued along the path until just as the sun reached the zenith of its arc across the sky, the trail curved sharply around to the southwest.

"Well that's it, old man," Eh'lorne stated ruefully. "Unless you wish to go to Mah-Kashia we must leave the path here and strike out across open country."

Bandil eyed the barren, devastated terrain ahead and scowled. "Your idea of 'open' leaves a lot to be desired."

Eh'lorne roared with laughter and slapped his ancient companion's back. "You've grown soft since you came to us. Perhaps we treated you too well."

"Not at all but time's short and I hadn't realised the journey would be so difficult. Looking at that…" He pointed at the torturous ground that barred their way. "…two days seems somewhat optimistic."

Eh'lorne grinned. "Indeed it does, but as Eldore always says, 'there's a lesson in everything'. Perhaps we'll learn something from such a trial. Maybe we'll see that not everything is as impossible as it seems. But," he continued, shrugging off his pack. "I for one have no appetite for learning anything until I've rested a while. What do you say, a drink and some food to give us strength?"

"How can I refuse? I'm far too old for this kind of adventure."

"Ah yes, but you have your Mystic Stone to give you energy. All I have is a heavy pack and sore shoulders!"

"Hah!" scoffed the old man as he sank gratefully to the ground. "I'd trade my Stone for your youth any day. And as for sore shoulders, I'll wager you'll consider them a worthy sacrifice before journey's end. In fact, I'm sure we'll both be glad of your foresight in bringing such a wealth of supplies."

Eh'lorne stopped rummaging through his pack and stared at his friend incredulously.

"What's this? Are you actually admitting you were wrong to ridicule my preparations? Surely my ears deceive me."

"I may have been a little hasty, but remember, Mordan has always provided for my every need since the day I awoke in the Mystic Mountains all those years ago. Even on my journey to find your people I carried no provisions."

"What, nothing?"

"Other than a small water skin, I put all my trust in our god."

The young lord shook his head in wonder. "You never fail to surprise me, old man. Your faith is truly humbling."

After their small meal and a good draught of firebrew, the two men continued their journey with great trepidation. Their fears however, proved to be relatively groundless, for although difficult, the going was far from impossible. Picking their way carefully around the large, wickedly jagged rocks, they found it surprisingly easy to avoid the pits and gullies that threatened to ensnare them. Had the rising temperature not melted most of the snow, however, things would have been very different; but as it was, their progress was reassuringly steady.

As the sun disappeared beneath the western horizon and twilight approached, it became more and more difficult to negotiate a safe route. Eventually, Bandil was forced to call a halt and seeing the necessity for caution, Eh'lorne reluctantly agreed to stop and make camp. It took some time to find a suitably dry and sheltered spot however, for the melting snow seemed to have sent tiny rivulets of water running into every conceivable nook and cranny.

Eventually though, the rapidly fading light forced them to settle on a flat, raised outcrop beneath a dangerously sharp and jagged overhang. With no possibility of erecting the tent or lighting a fire, their resting place was far from snug. Coupled with the sudden, drastic drop in temperature, it looked as though they were in for a long and miserable night.

They settled themselves as best they could and tucked into a meal of dried meat and honey cakes washed down with fire brew. Bandil still couldn't believe how just a few sips of the strong, tasteless spirit could quench even the fiercest of thirsts. When he'd asked his companion how it was possible to concentrate so much water into so little liquid, Eh'lorne had merely shrugged. "How should I know?" he'd replied indifferently. "I'm a warrior, not a brewer."

As they sat huddled in their blankets – and to his companion's intense delight – the old man recounted some of his experiences of life in the Mystic Mountains. He told of how the initial intense loneliness had gradually subsided as more and more of a vast array of animals had befriended him. He shared many tales of his adventures with the animals he'd come to know by name. Although some of the stories were sadly tragic, most were quite humorous and enchanted Eh'lorne with visions of the youthful prince playfully wrestling with bears and mountain lions.

"Did you tame all the animals you met?" he asked eagerly.

Bandil frowned. "It's wrong to say that I tamed any of them. All remained as wild and as free as they'd ever been; but by Mordan's grace they treated me as one of their own. Whether bear or boar, eagle or lion, I was their kin, not their Master."

"But not the wolves?"

"No, not the wolves. For some reason they wouldn't come near me and even after a century-and-half, I'd caught no more than a glimpse of them. I was deeply disappointed for the pictures on the ceiling of the throne room in Arl had captured my imagination and stirred my heart. I longed to look into their fierce, noble eyes and run my hands through their thick, coarse fur. But sadly, it wasn't to be."

"Tell me more," Eh'lorne demanded, his voice burning with curiosity. "How did you clothe yourself? How did Mordan instruct you? Where did you find the Mystic Stone?" The questions were relentless and Bandil did his best to answer them all. Eventually, though, fatigue got the better of him and he could take no more.

"Enough!" he cried. "Go to sleep. If you can't sleep at least rest your tongue so that I can. Today was hard enough but your constant interrogation is even worse. There'll be plenty of time for talking tomorrow." With that he drew his blanket even tighter and grumpily lay down with his back to his inquisitive friend.

Eh'lorne grinned in the darkness and wrapped himself in his own blanket. "Goodnight old man," he whispered affectionately. Then he too settled down for the night.

They roused themselves before dawn and ate a miserable breakfast of pine nuts and dried fruit. By the time they'd finished and were ready to move on, there was just enough light to proceed – albeit slowly due to the caution that safety dictated. But as the sun rose, the going got easier and the morning proved to be very much a repeat of the previous afternoon. It wasn't long before the last vestiges of snow had completely disappeared and once again Eh'lorne found himself sweating profusely.

They carried on without a rest until well past midday when they stopped for another bite to eat and a chance to slake their thirst. They were now so close to their goal's towering peak, it seemed they only had to reach out a hand to touch it, and that one last push would see them arrive well before sundown. The reality, however, proved very different, for once their brief rest was over and they continued on their way, the terrain became progressively more difficult to negotiate. Eventually, in the shadow of the colossal pinnacle that was Mordan's Finger, they were brought to a complete stop by a seemingly impassable chasm.

"This is somewhat awkward," Eh'lorne commented with dry understatement. He leant over the edge and peered into the ragged fissure. It was a little too wide to jump across, and although not over-deep, the sides were so broken with tiny, razor-sharp outcrops, that even for him it would be an impossible climb.

"Awkward indeed," Bandil replied, scanning the lay of the land. "We need to find a way across but in which direction? To the south, the going becomes even more unnavigable while to the north, the chasm runs for as far as the eye can see."

Eh'lorne carefully gauged the distance to the far side. "At its narrowest it's only just beyond me to make the leap. Perhaps with a long enough run up…"

"Look around you," the old man countered scornfully. He pointed to the surrounding crowded boulders and treacherously uneven ground. "Where exactly will you find room to run? It's almost impossible just to walk. And if do make it across, by what miracle do you expect me to follow?"

"Can't you use the stone?" Eh'lorne asked hopefully.

Bandil shook his head. "If the Stone had the power of flight, we wouldn't need the Talisman. I'd fly straight to Arl and overthrow Limnash myself."

Eh'lorne nodded and looked around them thoughtfully. Suddenly, he threw off his pack and with a curt, "Wait here," he hurried off in the direction of a nearby tor.

He vanished for a while, eventually reappearing as he pulled himself up onto the summit. Bandil found himself a rock to sit on and watched his agile young friend in awe. Heedless of danger, he was standing on the precarious, unstable vantage point and searching the area for a way to continue. At last he turned to climb down but as he did, he suddenly stood stock still. Then to the old man's horror, he seemed to throw himself from the rock, disappearing from view in the blink of an eye.

Bandil jumped to his feet, concern etched deep into his gaunt, wrinkled features; his eyes fixed on the point where he expected his friend to reappear. His concern turned to puzzlement, however, when Eh'lorne burst into view, zigzagging wildly between the larger boulders and recklessly leaping over the smaller obstacles. At any moment he was in danger of tripping headlong and smashing his head on the keen, knife-edged rocks.

As the speeding, white-clad figure approached, Bandil realised that he was shouting something while repeatedly pointing towards the western sky. Mystified, he followed the direction of his companion's desperate gesticulating and gave a horrified gasp of alarm. The whole western horizon was a boiling mass of dark, yellow-tinged clouds that were racing menacingly towards them. From deep within the gathering storm, lightning flashed its disturbing portent of the violence to come.

CHAPTER EIGHTEEN

Bandil frantically turned this way and that in a fruitless search for anything that could offer a vestige of shelter from the approaching storm. The whole landscape was a mass of splintered boulders and huge shattered rocks, and although many were several times the height of a man, nothing he could see would provide more than a little respite from a moderately steady wind. Looking up at the fast approaching maelstrom, he guessed the wind it would unleash was going to be anything but moderate or steady. He sank back onto his rocky seat with his heart leaden and his mind numb.

But then he looked at the white-clad figure sprinting recklessly toward him and his hopes rose. Perhaps Eh'lorne had spotted something from his lofty vantage point; something that could offer them the sanctuary they so desperately needed. With a quick prayer he got back to his feet and with immense difficulty, heaved his companion's enormous pack onto his shoulder. Staggering under its weight, he walked over to meet him.

"What did you see?" he called as soon as he was in earshot.

As he ran up, Eh'lorne shook his head. "There's no way forward; the rift continues as far as the eye can see."

"But did you see anything that can shelter us from that?" Bandil asked, pointing up at the boiling sky.

Eh'lorne took the pack from his struggling friend and grinned mischievously. "Indeed I did, but you won't like it."

"Like it or not," the old man snapped tersely. "As long as it gives us some protection, it'll have to do."

"Then follow me as fast as you can. Perhaps using your stone would be a good idea, yes?"

The old man grunted sourly but nonetheless, he drew out the artefact and called on its power to give him the speed he needed to keep up with his friend. Swiftly they retraced Eh'lorne's steps and soon arrived at the base of the rugged tor.

"Here we are," Eh'lorne declared triumphantly.

Puzzled, Bandil searched the area. "Don't toy with me, time is too short. Where is the shelter? I don't see it."

"Up there," Eh'lorne replied pointing upwards.

Bandil followed his outstretched arm and gasped. Set into the vertical rock-face, at least thirty cubits above their heads, a dark rent marked the entrance to a cave. The old man shook his head in disbelief. As safe and welcoming a sanctuary as the cave might be, it may as well have been on the moon.

"And how do you propose that I get up there, fly? I've already told you, I don't possess that particular ability."

"But it's an easy climb," Eh'lorne responded sounding crestfallen. To him, the short ascent with its myriad of handholds was no more difficult than an afternoon stroll. "And you have the Stone to help you," he added hopefully.

"Which I need to hold in my hand."

The young lord looked downcast but then suddenly brightened. "Then it's fortunate that I thought to bring a rope. I'll go up first and drop it down to you. Then I can pull you up and you'll be safe and snug in no time at all."

"It's possible, but even so..." Bandil's voice was full of trepidation as he eyed the rock-face again. His fears were hardly allayed when he saw the thin, supple coils that his companion pulled from his pack. "It's not much of a rope is it?" he said nervously. "It looks as though I could pull it apart with my bare hands."

"Have no fear," Eh'lorne laughed as he slipped the thin coils over his head and shoulder. "*Stencord* is immensely strong." The old man looked unconvinced. "Honestly, it won't break. If it does and you fall, you'll be the first man ever to die from its failure. Just think of the fame," he added with a roguish grin,

Before Bandil could reply the agile young lord was gone, scaling the rock with a speed that was as astonishing as it was reckless. Within moments, he reached the cave and disappeared from view. His fair head reappeared a few heartbeats later as he sent the *stencord* rope snaking down to the apprehensive old hermit. Quickly, Bandil tied it around the pack, and then as an afterthought, he added his own tent and blanket for good measure. He called out to Eh'lorne to pull up. Immediately the bundle shot into the air as it was hauled arm over arm to the waiting sanctuary. The old man watched its progress with mounting unease as it repeatedly bounced off the rocks, spinning wildly as it went.

All too soon the rope was back and with deliberate care, Bandil tied it around his chest and tested the knot. It was well tied and completely secure but still he hesitated. Even in the flower of his youth he'd never felt a great need to climb anything; so now as an old man, the reluctance was almost insurmountable. A quick glance over his shoulder however, gave him all the impetus he needed. The sky had grown black with seething menace and the air had become deathly still as the storm gathered itself like some huge predator preparing to pounce. He swallowed hard and began to climb.

In truth, it was actually a great deal easier than he'd feared. The numerous handholds were deep and solid, and Eh'lorne had a skilful ability to pull on the rope just enough to take his weight without threatening to tear him away from the rock. In no time at all he reached the cave's entrance and was hauled unceremoniously inside. Once there, he crawled well away from the edge and then climbed breathless and shaking to his feet

"There now," beamed Eh'lorne as he undid the knot at Bandil's chest. "I'll warrant that was exciting, yes?"

"No it was not!" came the emphatic reply. "It was both unnerving and humiliating."

"But where's your sense of adventure?" Eh'lorne laughed as he rewound the silky rope into tight coils.

"Adventure is one thing; if I had no taste for it at all I wouldn't be here; but to find pleasure in such danger is nothing more than foolhardy!"

"But there was no danger," Eh'lorne protested, still grinning widely. "The rope was secure and the climb was simple. I rather enjoyed it to be honest."

"Come back and say that when *you* are a hundred and ninety-two years old! See how agreeable you find it then!"

Eh'lorne's smile vanished. "I'm sorry, my friend," he said in a contrite voice. "I keep forgetting your great age. Let me make amends. Here, you take your ease while I prepare a meal. I'll even make you a feather bed if that's what it takes to earn your forgiveness."

Before the old man could reply, however, a blinding flash, immediately followed by a deafening crash of thunder stunned him into silence. As if it had waited for just this signal, the storm suddenly struck with a ferocity that was far beyond anything the two men had feared or imagined. The wind shrieked around the rocky tor, screaming like a thousand angry she-demons as it drove an impenetrable blizzard across the cave's entrance. Instantly, the temperature plunged, numbing their hands and turning their breath to a thick smoke-like vapour. Freezing blasts repeatedly drove stinging hail and snow into their faces.

"Quickly, the tent," Bandil shouted at the top of his voice. Despite struggling to hear what he was saying above the shrieking roar of the storm, Eh'lorne understood his meaning and retrieved the old man's tent and blanket, as well as his own pack. They moved to the back of the cave which was now so dark that without some form of light, the erection of the tent would have been impossible. Bandil solved this problem by holding the shining Stone aloft as if it were a lantern. But this meant the burden of the task fell to Eh'lorne who had never before seen such an unusual design. With the old man's instructions drowned out by the growing cacophony outside, it took quite some time before they were able to crawl inside and settle, huddling together for warmth.

"I must say," Bandil bellowed. "Your idea of a feather bed is somewhat disappointing."

"My apologies," came Eh'lorne's shouted reply. "But the fault is hardly mine. I can provide the meal I promised though. Here," he said offering his companion some dried meat and biscuits. "Eat and enjoy." The old man gratefully accepted the food and sat munching thoughtfully.

"This storm troubles me," he eventually hollered between mouthfuls. "Even with the Star in his grip, Limnash can't control the weather; yet this tempest hardly feels natural. I've certainly never seen its like before."

"Nor I. Let's hope it's nothing more than a freak of nature."

As if in answer to his words, the 'freak of nature' suddenly escalated to an even greater intensity. The lightning flashed and the thunder roared so loudly, they had to cover their ears against the painful concussion of sound. The very rock beneath them vibrated with such violence, it seemed only a matter of time before the whole tor came crashing down. Conversation, already more than difficult, became impossible. So after their last few mouthfuls and a swig of firebrew, they settled down to try and sleep.

Just before the old man extinguished the Stone, however, a particularly strong gust of wind swirled around the cave and threatened to tear the tent down. At the same time, it felt as though a massive thunderbolt had exploded right outside the cave's entrance. As he looked at the proud and reckless warrior at his side, Bandil saw something in his eyes that he thought he would never see – fear!

CHAPTER NINETEEN

The storm – if 'storm' be a strong enough word for such violent and unbridled fury – raged unabated all through the night and for most of the next day. Not until late the following afternoon were the two men given any respite from the ceaseless, nerve-shredding assault. Throughout the ordeal Bandil sat rocking back and forth while tugging at his beard and praying fervently for deliverance. Eh'lorne, on the other hand, crouched at his side, muttering constantly with his mood swinging wildly from burning anger to wide-eyed fear. More worryingly, he occasionally broke out into fits of uncontrolled laughter. Unable to relax in any way, the constant onslaught left them both even more exhausted than their race to warn Sirris.

Then, as suddenly as it had struck, the tempest was gone. The abrupt silence came as such a shock that had they been standing, they would without doubt have been knocked from their feet. Bandil held up the shining Stone and for some time they gawped at each other with incomprehension stamped on their pale and enervated faces. Then, as one, they scrambled from the tent.

Their sanctuary was as black as night but by the light of the Stone they could see the cause of the darkness. The entrance was blocked by snow that had been driven in to the cave by the howling wind. Desperate to escape, they somehow found the strength to dig their way out, their bare hands becoming first painful, then dangerously numb. As they toiled, each man was reminded of the way Eldore had waded so powerfully through just such drifts when the lich had chased them to the High River. They both wished he was here with them now; but the old man realised that Eh'lorne's quiet, muscular twin was almost certainly now dead.

When at last they reached the opening, the sight that greeted them caused their newly found flame of hope to flicker and die. Although the air was now as still as the grave, the snow was still falling – and falling so thickly that they could see no further out of the cave than a single arm's length.

"I wouldn't have believed the sky could hold so much snow," Eh'lorne said heavily.

"It can't," Bandil replied bitterly. "We must face the fact that this *is* Limnash's doing."

"But you said it was beyond him to control the weather."

"Indeed I did. And so it should be; but he has found the power from somewhere, although from exactly where is beyond me."

"Perhaps he's beaten us to the Talisman."

"Impossible. Even if he knew where to find it, he can't touch it."

"Are you sure? After all, he possesses the Star, and that in itself goes against all we know to be true."

For a few moments Bandil gave no answer but stood thoughtfully staring out at the thick white curtain of falling snow. When he eventually did speak, his voice was slow and measured.

"I can see the logic in what you say, but if you're right, although perhaps the storm would not be beyond him, it would certainly make no sense. I'm positive the purpose of the storm and this snow is to prevent us from reaching the Talisman. If he already possessed it, then this weather would be pointless."

"So where *has* he found the power?"

"I have no idea, but if it was his intention to prevent us reaching our goal, he's succeeded." He waved a hand towards the falling snow. "We're trapped here until he lets us go."

Eh'lorne grunted and stared into the thick white veil, his expression grim and tense with frustration. Then slowly his face softened and a twisted grin spread across his lips. Then his grin grew into a chuckle, then a guffaw, and finally a full-blooded belly laugh. He laughed so hard that he stumbled backwards and fell into the piled-up snow making him roar even louder.

Bandil stared at him in alarm fearing the strain and lack of sleep had driven the unpredictable youngster insane.

Seeing the concern on his friend's face, Eh'lorne did his best to supress the gales of laughter that had rendered him so helpless. "I'm sorry," he said, wiping the tears from his eyes. "But after all the hardship I find such good fortune almost too much to bear." Bandil looked at him blankly. "Come now, old man, you're Mordan's emissary. Surely you can see the blessing in our predicament?"

"I can see nothing of the sort. If you call our enemy's success a blessing then you've lost your mind and we're in even more peril than I feared."

"You really can't see it?" Eh'lorne asked incredulously. The old man wearily shook his head. "And I thought you were a man of faith," Eh'lorne chuckled, delighted with his own perceived wit. Eventually, after taking several deep breaths, he managed to bring himself under enough control to sound more serious. "As you are unable to see Mordan's helping hand in our plight – despite being his prophet – I will explain.

"Limnash, the mighty god-king and our terrible enemy, has raised against us a storm such as the world has never seen before; a storm powerful enough to tear down forests and shake the mountains to their very roots. You say his plan succeeded but I say it's failed miserably for I'm certain that he sought to destroy us; yet here we stand!"

"Or sprawl," the old man commented dryly as a smile of understanding began to curl his lips.

"Or sprawl," Eh'lorne agreed, his exhausted, bloodshot eyes twinkling with merriment.

"So tell me, my young sage, apart from failing to kill us, why is this evil weather such a blessing?"

"Because the snow falls so thickly, it's impossible for us to continue."

"So?"

"So look at the pair of us. Are you able to carry on? I very much doubt it. Speaking for myself, I'm far beyond spent; yet if the weather had permitted, we would have had no choice but try and reach our goal. In our parlous state and in this fearsome terrain, how far do you think we would get before suffering serious harm? No my friend, let's take advantage of the peace and get some sleep. Perhaps when we awake, things will have a more positive outlook."

The old man looked down at his companion lying ridiculously on his back. He was half buried in the snow and chuckling away to himself like a madman. He shook his head in wonder. Yes, Eh'lorne was unpredictable and unnerving –

sometimes to the point of being frightening. Undoubtedly, he was impetuous and rash – some would even say foolhardy. Yet without question he was courageous and loyal, charismatic and inspiring. It was no wonder his people loved him so. He would, Bandil decided, make a fine – if somewhat unorthodox – king.

Smiling more broadly, he reached down and pulled his friend to his feet and brushed the snow from his back. Silently he offered a humble prayer of thanks for such an unexpected lesson in faith. The two men then crawled back into the tent and fell into a deep and peaceful sleep, not waking until well past dawn on the following day.

They emerged eager and refreshed but the sight that greeted them was even more disturbing than before. True, the snow had stopped falling but the sun was hidden behind an ominous layer of thick, deep-red clouds. As far as the eye could see, the evil, unnatural sky had turned the snow that now blanketed the land to the colour of blood. The smoothly undulating, sanguineous covering was so deep, it reached almost to the lip of the cave.

"Trapped again!" Eh'lorne spat in disgust. "If there's no reprieve soon we'll be imprisoned here until we starve."

This time it was the old man who laughed. Eh'lorne turned to him and raised an inquisitive eyebrow.

"Am I missing something?"

"Indeed you are. Unknowingly Limnash has eased our path and we should reach Mordan's finger before nightfall this very day."

"You really think so?"

"I'm sure of it."

Eh'lorne leant out and peered down at the surface of the blood-red snow little more than half a man's height below them. "I don't see how. The snow is almost thirty cubits deep. If we climb down, we'll sink through it and become stuck until we either freeze or starve." He turned back to his companion and gave him a sceptical look. "I know I've learned to trust you, my friend, but other than fly all the way, I can't see how you propose we get there."

"We shall see, we shall see," the old man chuckled. He retreated into the cave and pulled out his knife, muttering happily to himself as he went. Puzzled, Eh'lorne followed along behind and then gasped in horror as Bandil started to slash at the tent with his sharp blade. He watched curiously as the ancient theurgist cut four diamond shaped sheets. Then, using more strips of the tough fabric, he tied some of the supporting sticks into frames of the same shape, only a little smaller. As the old man fastened the sheets to the frames with more strips, Eh'lorne's face suddenly brightened.

"Of course," he cried delightedly. "You're making wings. We *are* going to fly!" Bandil just smiled enigmatically and continued with his task.

When at last he'd finished, he gathered up his four strange creations, straightened and turned to his companion.

"That's it then," he said cheerfully. "Pack your belongings and let's be on our way."

"But how...?"

"Trust!" Bandil interrupted firmly. The younger man shrugged his shoulders and obediently did as he'd been asked.

When they were ready, they moved back to the entrance and to Eh'lorne's surprise, using even more strips of tent material, the old man sat on the edge and tied one of the frames to each foot. For a few moments he remained there with his strangely shod feet dangling over the sickly red snow. Then with a laughing parody of his friend's battle cry, he thrust himself from the edge and jumped down.

To Eh'lorne's delight, instead of disappearing from sight, his friend sank no more than half a hand into the surface and was now happily stamping around in his makeshift snowshoes.

"What are you waiting for?" he shouted cheerfully. "I thought we had a war to win."

Whooping with joy, Eh'lorne followed Bandil's lead and in no time the two travellers were striding towards their towering goal with broad triumphant smiles across their faces. Just as the old man had predicted, far from being a hindrance, the deep snow was actually proving an asset. Even the gaping fissure that had so thwarted them two days ago was now nothing more than an easily traversed, shallow depression. Once across it, the tall slim warrior-lord slapped his frail, ancient friend on the back.

"Well, Bandil, son of Bail, with you to guide us how can we fail? Even Limnash's most malignant machinations are no match for your great wisdom."

Bandil sighed. "Don't be too quick to mistake knowledge for wisdom, for they are not the same thing and are easily confused."

"But surely," Eh'lorne argued. "The difference between a wise man and a fool *is* knowledge."

"Is it?"

"Of course it is. It's as plain as the nose on your face."

"Is that so? Then answer me this: There are two men, one uneducated with little understanding and the other a great scholar with a vast wealth of knowledge. One day – and to no great purpose – they both decide to do something incredibly dangerous. The uneducated man has no idea of the peril he's in, but the scholar realises, not just what a terrible risk he's taking, but also its pointlessness. Which of them is the bigger fool?"

"The scholar?"

"Exactly. Wisdom is not knowledge in itself but the *application* of that knowledge. And there's more. If someone is content with their knowledge, no matter how well applied, they still can't be deemed wise; for if they were, they would not be content. Knowledge is infinite, and the wise one doesn't see answers to be content with, but sees only more questions."

Eh'lorne frowned. "You're speaking in riddles when all I've said is that we're fortunate to have your wisdom to guide us – or are you telling me that *you* are a fool?"

"Who knows?" Bandil replied cryptically. "Perhaps I am – or will be. Wisdom is not carved in stone, and even the wisest of the wise can lose their way. If they do, then they become the most foolish of fools."

"Enough!" Eh'lorne cried, throwing his hands up in mock despair. "Your high-thinking philosophy is giving me a headache. All these years I've been trying to convince Eldore of my superior insight and intellect, but it seems that I've been wrong. In future, I'll put my trust in a sharp sword and the strength to wield it. I'll leave this 'wisdom' to those clever enough to make sense of it!"

"Then you've taken your first step on the road to true enlightenment," the old man replied with a knowing smile.

CHAPTER TWENTY

By midday the travellers' good spirits had deteriorated markedly. The sickly red and oppressively unnatural sky bore heavily down on them, draining both their strength and their optimism. It seemed as if the evil in the thick, blood coloured clouds was poisoning their souls as surely as it was staining the snow. Although their progress was relatively good, the very act of lifting their feet out of the cloying snow drained their meagre reserves of energy with every step.

Then, just as their gloom began to slip into despair, the deep covering of snow came to a precipitous end. They looked at each other in surprised wonder. Then, before a single word could be uttered, Eh'lorne leapt over the edge and slid smoothly down the steeply sloping boundary to the rocky ground some twenty cubits below. Bandil shook his head; there seemed no end to his young companion's reckless abandonment. He looked around for a safer, more dignified means of descent; but in the end, there was nothing for it but to follow Eh'lorne's example and slide. This he accomplished with a great deal less grace and crashed awkwardly and painfully onto the rocks below, losing both of his snowshoes in the process.

"Are you alright?" Eh'lorne asked anxiously as he hurried over to the cursing old man.

"No I'm not!" Bandil snapped angrily. "I'm wet, I'm cold, and now I'm covered in bruises. Perhaps if you'd thought to lend me a hand before launching yourself into the abyss, I'd be a little less uncomfortable!"

"Sorry," Eh'lorne replied with a rueful smile.

"Sorry indeed! Instead of just standing there making pointless apologies, perhaps you could help me to my feet."

His young friend obliged and then recovered the old man's snowshoes. They were broken and shapeless, smashed beyond any hope of repair. Once again Bandil shook his head in vexation, then strode angrily away towards the huge, knife-like peak that towered almost directly over them. Eh'lorne watched him for a moment then shrugged, tossed the mangled canvas-bound sticks aside, removed his own snowshoes, and hurried after him.

It wasn't long before the ground began to slope upwards, becoming rapidly steeper with every step they took. Eventually, they had to stop and take stock of their location.

"Where exactly is the entrance?" Eh'lorne asked, carefully searching the area with his eyes.

"Here."

"Where? I don't see it."

"If it were that obvious, it wouldn't be a *secret* entrance would it?"

Puzzled, Eh'lorne scanned the scree-littered slope more scrupulously. He could see nothing that would indicate the whereabouts of the hidden doorway. Suddenly, he stiffened.

"What's that?" he asked in a low, urgent voice as he pointed over to their right, a little further up the incline. "It looks like the ground is scattered with dead children."

"Dead chil...? A look of horrified dread cut the old man short. Then a moment later he was rushing in the direction Eh'lorne had indicated crying, "Please no, please no," as he ran.

The young lord hurried after him, drawing his sword as he went. They arrived together to find the area strewn with the bodies of strange, unearthly creatures. True, they were no larger than an eight-year old child, but their form was anything but childlike. Their hairless skin was dark and leathery, and their evil looking features were sharp and pointed.

Eh'lorne stood watching as the old man went from body to body, carefully examining each one while searching the ground where they lay.

"What are they?" asked Eh'lorne, a distinct note of revulsion creeping into his voice.

"Sellufin," the old man replied absently. "A whole sect if I'm not mistaken."

"I've not heard of them. Are they more of Limnash's twisted creations?"

"No, no," Bandil replied vacantly as he concentrated on his investigations. "Nothing like the lich."

"But they do serve him."

"Considering where they are, I would say so. It looks like they made a bid for the Talisman and died in the attempt. And not a good death by the look on their faces."

"Good riddance to such evil, I say!"

Bandil snapped his head up. "What's that? Evil? What do you know of them? They are no more evil than you or I. They may have been seduced into it, but they have no natural malice in them. They are an ancient race, even older than men, and have as much right to exist as we do."

Eh'lorne looked affronted. "I care nothing for that. If they serve *him*, they deserve to die."

"They serve power and that will be how he's seduced them. They've long envied those who can hold the four fundamentals; so perhaps Limnash lured them into finding the Star of Destiny with the promise that he could wield it. That would explain their presence here; although they've obviously underestimated the mountain's defences. To my eyes they're as much his victims as your people in Sarren. Now stop bothering me and make yourself useful. Count the bodies and tell me how many there are." He turned back to his task so after a moment or two, Eh'lorne emulated him by obediently making a tally of the corpses.

"Fifty-two," he said when he'd finished.

Bandil swung around. "Fifty-two? You're certain?"

"I can count," Eh'lorne replied sullenly.

"Forgive me; the peril has made me sound curt." The old man surveyed the carnage and tugged anxiously at his beard. "I must find it, for if it's not here, our mission has become far more dangerous than I care to contemplate."

"If what's not here?" Eh'lorne demanded, becoming even more impatient with his friend's cryptic answers and unusual behaviour. But once again the old man ignored him and resumed his search with an even greater sense of urgency.

The young warrior gave an exasperated grunt and decided to leave his companion to his eccentric devices while he made a search of his own for the hidden entrance. It was obvious that the sellufin were approaching the slope in a particular direction, so that was where he began his exploration. He sheathed his sword, and taking great care not to send any loose rocks rolling down towards the old man, he began to ascend the steepening slope. There were several promising looking alcoves for him to examine, but before he could reach any of them, Bandil stopped him with an excited shout.

"Look!" he cried, holding up what looked two sticks. "I have it."

"You have what?" Eh'lorne called, sliding back down to his delighted companion.

"Their staff; and look, it's broken in two." He passed the two 'sticks' over to his young friend who examined them closely. They were two halves of a plain ebony staff, each no more than a cubit in length. The snapped ends were ragged and splintered, and even looked a little scorched.

"It's a staff alright but why is it so important?"

"It's not just *a* staff, it's *the* staff belonging to the black sect. This is – or was – their rod of power. Without it, even those sellufin who've escaped can do us no harm. By the grace of Mordan, Limnash has been dealt a blow even more grievous than his defeat at Sirris."

"How can a few bodies and a broken stick compare to the thousands slaughtered by the armshost?"

"Because it's a rod of power!" Bandil repeated, snatching back the two halves and waving them under Eh'lorne's nose. "There are only three, each one serving a separate sect; red, white, and black. And now there's only two. The black sect is finished, for without this staff it can never be reformed!"

"Then let's find the entrance before one of the others catch up and tries to thwart us," Eh'lorne declared firmly. He swung around and began climbing back towards the alcoves he'd spotted earlier leaving the old man standing amid the scattered cadavers. Bandil gave the slaughtered sellufin a final look and as he did, his smile vanished to be replaced by an expression of sad regret. With a mournful shake of his head, he tossed the pieces of the staff aside and followed Eh'lorne up the slope.

In the end it proved remarkably easy to locate the entrance to the labyrinth. By following the exact same direction the sellufin seemed to have been going, they came upon it at the very first try. After kneeling in prayer, the two men squeezed into the black, slit-like opening which after a short distance, widened out into what by its acoustics, sounded to be a chamber of enormous dimensions. The old man ignited his Stone and sure enough, by its light they found themselves to be in a vast, echoing cavern so huge, that even with the Stone at its brightest, the far side was lost in the inky darkness.

In awed silence they made their way across the hallowed hall. When they eventually reached the other side, they found themselves confronted by seven identical tunnels, each one just wide and tall enough for both men to enter at the same time.

"So, which one do we take?" Eh'lorne asked, scratching his head.

"How should I know?" the old man replied helplessly. "My task was to bring you here; it's your task to find the Talisman and claim it as you own."

"But how will I know which tunnel leads to its hiding place?"

"I can't help you with that. Perhaps you could use your Arlien senses and reach out to it with your mind. You are a Starbrow after all, and royal blood flows through your veins. If you're meant to find it, you *will* find it."

Eh'lorne nodded, slipped off his pack and moved to the first of the openings. Standing in front of it he closed his eyes and called out with his mind. After a short while he opened them again, shook his head, and moved on to the next. He repeated the process three more times, but on the fifth attempt, he suddenly cocked his head as if listening intently. With a broad smile he turned to Bandil and nodded.

"This way," he said triumphantly, and trotted off down the tunnel. The old man began to hurry after him but suddenly stopped and looked around the floor. He immediately saw what he wanted and scooped up a small chalky pebble before running after his rapidly disappearing friend.

Running steeply downhill, the tunnel carried on in a straight line for quite some time – although neither man could say exactly how long; for the further on they went, the more time itself became an ephemeral and abstract concept. Eventually though, the slope levelled off, and it became increasingly more difficult to navigate the many twists, turns, and myriads of complex intersections. At each of these, Eh'lorne stopped and 'listened' for the Talisman's call before carrying on at the same loping run. Without this unique ability, they would quickly have become disorientated, and would have found themselves hopelessly and irrevocably lost. As it was, the deeper they went, the stronger the Talisman's call grew, and the more certain Eh'lorne became of which direction they should take.

On and on they went, seemingly forever; but neither one of them became fatigued. It seemed the very power that had slain the sellufin was drawing them along on an effortless wave of energy. Time and distance became a vague confusion for which they had no understanding or interest. With every moment that passed, the air became more charged with the supernatural puissance until it was so strong, the old man's unruly white hair was standing on end. Added to this, his long grey beard – already wild to begin with – seemed to take on a life of its own, giving his face a crazed, fanatical appearance.

Eventually, they saw a light in the distance which grew rapidly brighter until they arrived at a huge, scintillating chamber. The massive cavern blazed with a crystalline brilliance so dazzling, it should have instantly burned out their eyes, but instead, it didn't even make them blink. Unable to stop, the two men careered into the cave; but where Eh'lorne merely skidded to a halt, Bandil was sent crashing backwards as if the cave had judged him unworthy of entry.

S. P. MUIR

He lay where he'd fallen for some time, badly winded but otherwise unhurt. When eventually he did regain control of his breathing, he sat up to see Eh'lorne standing stock-still a few paces inside the supernatural chamber. His tall, slim figure was starkly silhouetted against the blinding silver-white glare. The young warrior-lord was transfixed, staring at something the old man couldn't see from his low vantage point. Wearily, he struggled to his feet. He was acutely aware that the miraculous energy which had enabled him to run so easily had now abandoned him; and in contrast, his thin ancient body felt even more fragile and frail. Cautiously, he tried to re-enter the cave. This time was allowed to take a few steps over the threshold before an unseen pressure told him that this was as far as he would be allowed to go.

As he let his eyes wander around the hallowed cavern, he was filed with a sense of awed wonder so great, he felt sure he was about to burst. The light, far brighter than anything he could have believed possible, had no obvious source, but seemed instead to emanate from everywhere. Every surface, from the sparkling walls and floor to the vast domed roof, burned with the intense argent glow. Even the air itself crackled and sparked with the glittering luminescence. And there, suspended in the middle of the cavern and hanging upon nothing, was the object of their quest – The Talisman of wrath.

To Eh'lorne standing just in front of the old man, it was the most beautiful thing he'd ever seen. It was floating at shoulder height, hilt upward with the razor sharp, rune-engraved blade pointing toward the shining floor. A fantastically sculpted snarling wolf's head formed the pommel, while in keeping with the lupine theme, each quillon of the cross-guard was in the shape of a fierce, leaping wolf. Of course, he knew the sword itself was not the Talisman but was merely a vessel to channel its fury. The actual Talisman of Wrath was the enormous, coldly-glittering diamond-like gem set into the ricasso of the silver-steel blade just below the hilt.

Quite how he could see the talisman in such detail was beyond him though; for surely it was far too distant. Or was it? Although the gleaming blade seemed nothing more than a far-off speck, he could see it as clearly as if he were standing right next to it. Trying to gauge the size of the chamber that held it was pointless, for physical dimensions were as incalculable and elastic as time itself in this seat of divine power.

Instinctively and irresistibly, he began to walk towards the potent artefact, oblivious to the sound of his own footsteps and the tight, expectant sound of his breathing. He couldn't tell if it had taken a mere heartbeat or a whole lifetime, but whether eventually or instantly, the moment came when he found himself standing in front of the Talisman.

Now that he was within touching distance, the scintillating gemstone both fascinated and dismayed him; for deep within its elusive, intangible heart, freezing blue-white flames whirled and writhed in a burning frenzy of ice-cold rage. It seemed as if the powerful jewel held a bitter sentience that was cruelly taunting him, daring him to reach out and touch it.

With a tremendous effort, he tore his eyes away from the shining artefact and looked back over his shoulder. Bandil appeared to be no more than a tiny, indistinct figure in the far distance; yet he could see every line and wrinkle, every spot and blemish on the old man's gaunt, weathered face. The hope and fear in his eyes were as clear as if the ancient theurgist was standing right beside him. Obviously Bandil could see him just as clearly, for he smiled and gave him a barely perceptible nod of encouragement.

Eh'lorne turned back to the Talisman and bit his lip. Was he really the true king, he wondered, or just a pretender to the throne to be instantly destroyed by the holy fire raging within the diamond-like crystal? Either way, he was about to find out.

Steeling himself, he took a deep breath. Then with his ringing battle cry echoing off the vast chamber's walls, he snatched the floating sword from the air.

The moment his hand closed around the hilt, the cave seemed to explode, catapulting him uncontrollably through time and space. A freezing inferno turned his body to ice and seemed to sear the flesh from his bones. Impossibly bright images flashed before his eyes in a frantic kaleidoscope that made coherent thinking all but impossible. But as the glacial, savage anger overwhelmed him, he did retain one clear thought. He knew that he had failed and was about to die.

CHAPTER TWENTY-ONE

Eldore's forge seemed far too modest a building to be the source of such fine, well-crafted weaponry. In the southern kingdom of Mah-Kashia, his handiwork was greatly prized and much sought after – although exactly from where it originated was a closely guarded secret.

The forge obviously belonged in the bustling narrow streets of the southwest quarter of the city, but was in fact incongruously located in a rather well-to-do square near the northern riverbank. It stood slightly apart from the other buildings though, as if the neighbouring, nicely-built homes were far too refined to draw too close. But the residents, if anything, were proud to have it there.

Nothing about the building set it apart from any other forge the world over; an open work area with the usual furnace, anvil, and accompanying hammers and tongs. There was also a large water-butt to quench the red-hot metal and a huge pair of bellows that attested to the immense strength of the smith that usually worked there. Today, however, the furnace was cold and the hammers were stilled. The unfinished farm implements and rows of incomplete blades seemed to stand in mourning for their recently departed creator.

Except Eldore was not dead. Attached to the forge was a substantial shed-like affair that served the same purpose as Eh'lorne's secret cave of solitude; and it was in here, just two days after resigning himself to death, that Eh'lorne was very much alive.

He was sitting at a rudimentary wooden table with his hands behind his head, rocking his chair back on two legs. His face was a study of deep concentration as he stared at the pouch given to him by Bandil as he'd lain stricken on his deathbed. His miraculous cure – so inexplicable to those around him – was obviously down to the Mystic Stone. As a healing agent it was patently a great deal more effective than even the old man had realised; a fact that Eldore had no problem understanding. The Mystic Earth however, was a riddle that was far more difficult to comprehend.

He leant forward, placed his elbows on the table and rested his chin on his clasped hands. There was absolutely no doubt that the red soil was completely inert. Bandil may have underestimated the Stone's effect on his wound but there was not the remotest possibility that the old hermit could be wrong about this. Eldore was also sure that, had there been even the tiniest stirrings of power within the small leather bag, he would have detected it by now. And yet...

He closed his eyes and used his mind to 'see' the room. It was another of the unique abilities his people possessed – and one in which the twins were particularly adept. It was similar to the way that blind people could form a picture of someone's face by running their hands over it. But where fingers could sculpt only a small, incomplete version of reality, the mind painted it in broad, fresh brush strokes, alive with movement and texture. Only colour and light were absent from the remarkably clear vision it revealed. And the picture the twins' minds could paint was far clearer than most.

He could see the shelves on the walls. Even the scrolls and rolled up maps they contained were as plain as if he'd been looking at them with his eyes. Moving around the room he came to the window. Here, the limitations of mind-sight meant that although he could picture the frame and glass, both the midday sun streaming through it and the outside view it provided were invisible to him.

Without hesitation he carried on 'looking'. He noted the tiny ubiquitous stove, the small untidy cot, and then finally, he arrived back at the table in front of him. It was empty. He opened his eyes and sure enough, there was the pouch innocently resting on the rough, uneven surface. He closed them again and once more it disappeared as if it had been instantly erased from reality.

He unclasped his hands and placed them beside where he knew the invisible leather purse to be. How, he wondered, could his hands be so distinct that even the hairs were manifest, yet the soil beside them just didn't seem to exist? He 'watched' as he touched the pouch, feeling the contours of the soft hide and the leather lace that bound it shut. He ran his fingers along the supple thong that hung it around his neck. To his mind-sight, his hands were performing an elaborate mime, yet to the touch it was as solid and as real as he was. Once again, he opened his eyes and thoughtfully returned to tilting his chair back with his hands behind his head.

A sudden hammering on the door jerked him out of his reverie with such a start that he fell backwards and crashed heavily to the floor. Cursing, he struggled to his feet, wincing with pain for although his side was almost completely healed, it was still tender to the touch. He moved quickly to the still shuddering door and angrily threw it open to find the young boy, Yewan, standing in front of him. Both his fists were raised, frozen in the act of assaulting the door with a terrified expression on his face.

"By the four winds lad, you'll have the door off its hinges!" Eldore scolded. "Unless the sky's about to fall, you'd better have a good explanation."

"But my lord," the boy wailed. "Master Rennil sent me with an urgent message."

"Which is?"

Yewan's mouth opened and closed as he struggled to find the right words.

"Well?" Eldore demanded impatiently.

At first the hapless boy seemed to shrink back but then with a helpless shrug said, "The sky *is* about to fall."

"What?" Eldore snapped; then abruptly, he pushed past the frightened child and ran out into the square. There he found a dozen or so people standing transfixed and horrified as they stared up at the western sky. He followed their gaze and gasped. Racing towards them was the same evil, unnatural storm that was soon to assail Eh'lorne and Bandil. For a moment, he too was rooted to the spot, but he quickly recovered and sprinted to the time-repeat bell that stood at the heart of the square. He shouted to the small crowd as he ran, instructing them to seek the shelter of their homes. The bell itself was mounted just above head height on a gallows-like arrangement with a short length of *stencord* dangling from its clapper. Grasping the rope, he began frantically to ring the bell for all he was worth. The strident, high-pitched clanging gave the remaining stragglers all the extra impetus they needed to send them scurrying away to find shelter. He could only hope they had the presence of mind to put up their shutters. A sudden picture of the viltula's huge leaded windows sprang into his head. Any flying glass would cause carnage among the crowded rows of sick and injured.

Out of the corner of his eye he spotted the solitary figure of Yewan standing frightened and uncertain by the forge. Quickly, he made up his mind and waved the boy over with his free hand. Obediently, Yewan trotted across the square until he stood in front of the tall, muscular lord. Eldore let the bell fall silent and placed both hands on the youth's slim, narrow shoulders.

"Listen my boy," he said in an urgent voice. "I know you're probably tired out but I need you to run as fast as you've ever run to the viltula. Tell them I sent you and that they're to put up the shutters at once. Find Aldegar and tell him to prepare for more casualties, then run straight home."

"Yes, my lord." The boy immediately made to run off but Eldore suddenly pulled him short.

"No wait. Don't run home; the Duty Hall is too far away. Do you know Morjeena, the head tender at the viltula?"

"You mean the pretty one?"

In spite of everything, Eldore couldn't help but smile. "Yes, the pretty one. Find her and tell her that I'm placing you in her care and that you're to remain with her until the storm has passed. Is that understood?" The boy nodded. "Good. Then off you go as fast as you can."

As Yewan charged off in the direction of the nearest bridge, Eldore straightened and looked back up at the sky. With every moment that passed, the storm was drawing closer and the air was now deathly still, poised to unleash its violence. Once again, he took hold of the rope then paused. From all around the city he could hear more and more repeat bells taking up the call. Then, to his immense relief, they were joined by the deep, authoritative chiming of the great Time Bell itself. With a grunt of satisfaction, he threw himself into adding his own efforts to the growing cacophony, almost ripping the bell from its mountings in the process.

Not until the boiling, flashing malevolence was directly overhead did he let go of the rope and make his own way through the gathering darkness toward shelter. Before he was even halfway back to his forge, however, the storm struck. Such was the power of the wind, it lifted him from his feet and flung back to where he'd started. He crashed into the bell-gallows so hard that it fractured, leaving the top half held by a few twisted splinters and swaying wildly in the violent hurricane. Eldore lay pinned against its base, badly winded, and with the force of the gale ripping the breath from his lungs, he was completely unable to breathe.

With a huge, desperate effort, he managed to turn his back to the wind and move his head into the lee that his body provided. In this position he was able to suck in great gasps of still air until his head cleared and he regained enough strength to make his move.

He managed to lay flat on his belly and manoeuvre himself round so he was facing into the wind. Raising his head, he was relieved to find that his forge was directly ahead of him, and if he could somehow manage to crawl forward, he might be able to reach it before the unrelenting battering rendered him unconscious. He pushed himself up as though performing a press-up exercise and found himself 'standing' at an insane angle, lying on a cushion of air. Summoning up every last drop of his prodigious strength, with his hands on the ground in front of him, he was able to take one small step at a time. Progress was slow and incredibly dangerous; flying pieces of debris kept careering past, some of it frighteningly close.

Then, to make matters worse, it started to snow. Admittedly, it was but nothing compared to the blinding blizzard and dense fall that was about to imprison Eh'lorne and Bandil, but nonetheless, it stung his face and forced him to close his eyes.

Blinded, deafened, and exhausted, he struggled on, acutely aware that success was becoming less and less certain with each moment that passed. He knew the amount of debris whirling past must be constantly growing and every step he took drained his strength more than he could ever have imagined. Gritting his teeth, he ignored the danger and placed himself in the hands of his god.

Suddenly, the unbearable pressure was gone and he toppled forward, hitting his head on the hard, unforgiving cobbles as he fell. For some time, he lay still, his mind stunned, and a terrible roaring in his ears. Slowly, he regained his senses and managed to raise himself to his knees. To his horror, he found that he was blind. He threw his hands to his face and cursed himself for his stupidity. He'd not been blinded at all but merely rendered sightless by his headband slipping across his eyes. Impatiently, he ripped it off and gingerly felt the large lump over his right eye. His fingers came away sticky with blood but he was fairly sure that he hadn't cut himself too badly. The roaring in his ears told him the unnatural storm was still raging just as ferociously as before, yet incredibly, he was kneeling in calm, tranquil air.

He stood up and shook his head in disbelief. He was standing peacefully a few paces in front of the forge, while less than an arm's length away, the worst storm in living memory was ravaging the city with an evil malice that could surely have only one source. Carefully, he reached out and let his hand cross the boundary that separated him from the onslaught, but he quickly pulled it back again. It felt as though his fingers were about to be torn from his hand. Miraculously, the snow that was being driven so mercilessly around his cocoon of safety was drifting gently to the ground within it.

The illusion of safety however, was rudely shattered when a whirling handcart burst into his protective bubble and hurtled past, narrowly missing his head. Momentum carried the lethal missile all the way to the far side of the preternatural sanctuary, where with a single bounce, it disappeared back into the howling tempest.

Realising the danger he was in, Eldore hurried back inside his shed-like refuge and slammed the door shut behind him. As he leant against it listening to the screaming of the wind and the crashing of the thunder, he started to become angry. And that anger grew from a tiny spark to an unbridled rage that rivalled the storm outside. He could only imagine the damage being done to his beloved city and the terrible injuries its inhabitants must be suffering. He raised his eyes heavenwards and silently railed against his god. Where was he? How could he allow such evil to befall his people – his own children?

He stalked across the room and threw himself into his chair. Angrily, he wiped away the blood that was running down his face and dripping from his chin. The feeling of helplessness was almost too much to bear. A particularly loud crash of thunder only served to heighten his overwhelming sense of impotence. How could their enemy summon up such immense and irresistible forces of nature? Would even the Talisman give them the chance to fight back?

His gaze dropped to the table and fell upon the pouch. A pouch that contained not just earth, but earth from the Mystic Mountains; earth stained red with Mordan's divine blood. It sat there as inert and powerless as ever. Indeed, it seemed so ineffectual, it even failed to occupy time and space; yet surely it was the source of the calm that surrounded the forge.

The truth that dawned on him was so clear and obvious that he couldn't believe he'd not seen it before. Power was not everything. No matter what Limnash threw at them, by their very existence and by trusting in Mordan, they would never be beaten. Once again, he looked to the heavens. He begged forgiveness for his previous outburst and gave thanks for this lesson in trust. Then he picked up the pouch, placed its thong around his neck, and vowed never to take it off again.

CHAPTER TWENTY-TWO

Although the storm that struck Sirris was just a sideshow for the main event further east, it was nonetheless the most destructive in the city's history. It ripped screaming through the streets, smashing any un-shuttered windows and tearing off hundreds of roofs. The indiscriminate nature of the damage was difficult to comprehend, especially in places where a home had completely collapsed while the buildings on either side were ironically untouched. It raged without let-up until the middle of the next day when at first it slackened, then dropped away to an eerie stillness.

Warily, Eldore opened the door and emerged from his shack. His jaw clenched and his eyes burned when he saw the extent of the havoc wrought by the savage wind. Added to that, the thick, blood-coloured clouds overhead had stained the city an unearthly, sickly red, making the damage appear even worse than it undoubtedly was. There was far less snow than he'd imagined, but what there was had been driven into deep drifts and dramatically piled against the wooden walls of the buildings. Many doorways were blocked and would need volunteers to clear an egress for any trapped occupants.

He was relieved to see that all around the square shocked, pale-faced residents were tentatively coming out of their homes. They gawped at each other as if surprised to find that they were still alive. In spite of their dazed confusion, however, they quickly pulled themselves together and instinctively began to gather by the twisted stump that marked where the repeat bell had once stood. Two men in particular seemed to have taken charge and were waving their arms around, organising and directing the survivors with great authority.

He walked over to join them but before he was much more than halfway, a tall, slim man came running into the square. He was dodging around and leaping over the scattered debris with such a degree of agility that it put Eldore in mind of his brother, Eh'lorne. When the newcomer spotted the muscular lord, he immediately changed direction and headed towards him, calling out urgently as he ran.

"My Lord Eldore," he cried. "D'harid Sternhand requests your assistance in the Chanceway. It's devastated and almost every home has collapsed. Scores are trapped or buried."

Eldore glanced around the square. The men were already preparing to attack the blocked entrances and the women were seeing to the injured, none of whom so far seemed too badly hurt. It was obvious that he wouldn't be missed.

"Very well," he said grimly. "Lead on."

D'harid Sternhand's reputation was well known to Eldore. He had served in the armshost until retiring late in the previous year; and he was the source of much frustration for Eldore's brother. Many times, Eh'lorne had spoken of his companion-at-arms, throwing up his hands in despair. "That man could be Prime of the Lord-Guard," he'd rail. "He could be second only to Rennil himself, yet he refuses to rise above division officer. It's a waste!" For some reason known only to himself, the steady and capable warrior had declined every offer of high command that the exasperated Rennil had made. In spite of that reluctance to carry responsibility, Eldore could think of few other people he'd rather have at his side.

As he raced after the fleet-footed messenger, it dawned on him that D'harid must have been out onto the streets even before the storm had completely blown itself out. How else could he have assessed the damage and sent a messenger before Eldore had so much as crossed the square. But then, from what Eh'lorne had told him of the man, it was no surprise he'd been the first to act. Eldore felt a sudden and intense desire to become better acquainted with the resourceful old warrior.

The Chanceway was not as its name suggested a single road, but was instead a small area of narrow streets leading from a central avenue. It huddled close to the western wall and was home to what the uncharitable might label as the 'lost'. Here had gathered the old and the infirm, mothers, who for one reason or another had found themselves without a husband, and – as in D'harid's case – those who had taken it upon themselves to watch over them.

The messenger had not exaggerated; the devastation the storm had inflicted on the Chanceway was almost beyond belief. Less than one in ten homes remained standing and none had escaped unscathed. It was as if the evil tempest had maliciously singled out the tiny district and targeted it for the very worst of its malignant fury. This impression of *deliberate* malevolence however, was in fact a false one. The reason the vulnerable district had suffered such terrible ruination was nothing more than a case of unfortunate geography. Rather than the cliff wall providing a degree of shelter in its lee, an unusual, horseshoe-shaped overhang had instead created a vicious vortex. The very cliff that had protected neighbouring districts had in fact facilitated the Chanceway's destruction.

Eldore's head spun as he turned this way and that, barely able to comprehend the terrible scene unfolding before him. Everywhere, dirty and dishevelled survivors were tearing at the wreckage in a desperate attempt to reach those buried beneath. His heart ached unbearably for the suffering of his people. He slowed to a walk, almost losing his guide until the man noticed the growing gap between them and stopped to wait impatiently for him to catch up.

A short while later they came upon the figure of D'harid. He was standing with his back to them, directing several men toward one particular collapsed home. As they approached the old warrior he became aware of their presence and turned to greet them. His weathered face was far from handsome with its hollow cheeks and broken, misshaped nose. His hair, cut in the cropped military fashion, did nothing to lighten the impression and gave his features a severe and intimidating look. In shocking contrast to that, however, his eyes were deep dark pools of placid serenity; and when he spoke, his voice – although not soft – seemed to both caress and encourage at the same time. His entire countenance exuded a calm confidence that was reassuring to say the least.

"Lord Eldore," he said levelly. "I'm glad Tarryl found you so quickly." Then he looked at Eldore's forehead and added, "You're hurt."

Eldore touched the deep cut and felt the dried, crusted blood.

"I tripped," he replied simply. Then noticing a nasty looking gash on D'harid's neck said, "You look to be in need of a healer yourself."

D'harid grimaced. "The penalty for my own stupidity. I was too eager to leave my home."

"I guessed as much when your messenger arrived so promptly. But tell me, why exactly did you send for me?"

"It's a matter of command and authority," came the steady reply. "You can see from the situation here that we need as many hands as possible to assist us; yet those in less devastated areas are reluctant to come to our aid. I don't blame them for they too have their problems, but our need is greater. If, however, you were to grant me authority over this entire quarter of the city, I could deploy those resources where they're most needed."

"Of course you can have it, and with my blessing."

D'harid smiled with gratitude and then turned to the messenger. "Did you hear that Tarryl?"

"I heard."

"Then you know what to do?"

"Indeed I do. Look to the riverside; I'll go there first." With that he was gone.

The old soldier watched him go and then looked back at Eldore. "Thank you. You may have just saved a great many lives."

"There are no thanks due; I've done nothing except give you what's yours by right. But tell me, is there something more practical I can do to help?"

"Perhaps there is. We have a conundrum I'm at a loss to solve, so maybe a fresh mind can see an answer that I've so far overlooked."

D'harid pointed to the collapsed home where he'd been directing men when Eldore had arrived.

"We have two trapped here," he explained. "A mother and her baby. The woman is pinned by a heavy beam which must be lifted to free her; but there's too much debris to allow access for more than two men at the same time. Although it only needs to be lifted a little, it's proved far too heavy for just two."

"Can't you clear a larger space to allow more access?"

S. P. MUIR

"We have tried but here's the rub: when we attempted to clear space for more men, the area around the baby became unstable and we had to stop. Had we continued, it would have collapsed and his life would have been lost."

"Could you free the child first?" Eldore suggested hopefully.

D'harid shook his head. "The beam sits precariously amongst the debris that imprisons him and to disturb it even a little would crush the woman. Given time we could secure the wreckage but time is something we don't have. Both are bound to have sustained serious injuries – the mother most definitely has – so we must act immediately. If we delay, we'll surely lose them both; but by saving the child we lose the mother and vice-versa. As I say, a conundrum"

"I see," Eldore replied thoughtfully. "Show me."

The old soldier led him to what was left of the small house and pointed to a spot a few strides into the tangled mass of splintered wood. "There, you can just see her."

Eldore followed D'harid's outstretched arm to where he could just make out a head and one hand protruding from the wreckage. He could see the beam that imprisoned her and understood exactly the confines that made her rescue impossible. He scanned the rest of the debris then looked at the men hesitantly waiting for instructions on how to proceed. One man in particular caught his eye. He was sitting on the ground, his broad, powerful shoulders shuddering as he sobbed uncontrollably. He'd covered his face with his massive hands, hiding the desperate despair that had gripped his soul.

"Who is that?" Eldore asked.

"That's Griston," D'harid replied sadly. "He was the closest friend of the woman's late husband. It's a sad tale and not one we have time for now, but suffice it to say that when the husband died, he took responsibility for mother and child. I believe he's fallen for her too. We were expecting an announcement soon, but now..." His voice trailed away poignantly.

Eldore watched the distraught man for a moment then walked resolutely over to him. Kneeling at his side he placed a hand on his shoulder. "My friend," he said softly. "All is not lost. Neither D'harid nor I will rest until they're both safe."

"How?" Griston cried furiously as he raised his head and glared at Eldore. "I've tried so hard but it's too heavy!" As the man's hands dropped from his face his huge forearms became visible revealing a mass of welts and bruises that were already turning an angry red and purple. He had tried very hard indeed. Eldore got to his feet and stared at the tangled mess that had once been a home. His eyes narrowed and his teeth ground until suddenly, he made up his mind. He spun around to face D'harid.

"Do you have any rope?" he asked urgently.

D'harid smiled knowingly. "I've already sent for some. It should arrive at any moment."

Eldore grunted his satisfaction and returned to kneeling beside Griston. Gently he took the man's hands and examined his arms.

"You've done all that you could," he said consolingly. "But do you still have enough strength for one more try?"

Angrily, Griston returned Eldore's look and was about to spit out a barbed reply; but then his expression changed to one of horror as he realised exactly who it was talking to him. He tore his arms away from Eldore's tender grasp and leapt to his feet.

"My lord, forgive me," he cried. "I didn't recognise you."

Eldore stood up and placed both hands on the mortified man's wide muscular shoulders. He peered into the bloodshot eyes and gently but firmly said, "Calm yourself and answer me. Do you still have enough strength?"

Griston stared back into his lord's face then nodded.

"Good. D'harid, where's that rope?"

The old soldier looked around and spotted a youth trotting along the debris-strewn road with a tight coil over his shoulder.

"Here it comes," he said, impatiently waving for the boy to hurry.

When the rope arrived, Eldore took it from the youth and handed one end to Griston. "Here, take this and tie it to her exposed arm – tight mind, it must not slip free. D'harid, can you ready a team to pull her out when I call?"

"Already prepared," came the calm reply.

Inwardly, Eldore smiled. He should have known the capable and resourceful ex-division officer would be ahead of him.

"Alright then. Griston, are you ready?" Griston nodded and Eldore smiled grimly. "Come on then, let's do it."

Trailing the rope behind them, the two powerful men carefully picked their way through the mangled remains. Griston soon reached the ensnarled girl. Whispering encouragement, he tied the rope to her arm and then joined Eldore who was waiting at the beam. It rested at waist height and was just the right thickness to comfortably place their arms under it and grip the far side with their hands. From where the corners met flesh, Eldore could see how Griston's forearms had suffered such heavy bruising. He looked at his companion and for the first time saw a tiny spark of hope in the poor man's eyes.

"We can do this," he said encouragingly. He must have sounded more confident than he felt, for Griston replied with a grim, silent smile.

"Right then," Eldore said settling himself firmly. "On three. One, two, THREE!"

The two men heaved with all their might, their faces turning first red then puce. Veins bulged and sinews strained. The grinding, crushing pain in their forearms was almost unbearable, but neither man would relent. At first their efforts seemed nothing more than futile vanity, but then, with an alarmingly loud snapping sound, the beam lifted. Not much, but enough. To his horror, Eldore found that he'd no breath left to call to D'harid, but he needn't have worried; D'harid didn't need to be told. As soon as the beam moved, he shouted his command and the four men manning the rope hauled on it for all they were worth. The woman screamed in agony as the rope wrenched painfully at her wrist, but she was free at last.

Carefully, so as not to disturb the precarious balance of the rest of the wreckage, Eldore and Griston lowered the beam. Breathless and sweating, they stood grinning at each other until Griston suddenly remembered just who his co-rescuer was. Immediately his face fell and he started to bow, but Eldore stopped him and held out his hand. For a moment Griston hesitated, but then with a broad smile, he grasped it and with shining eyes mouthed a silent, "Thank you."

The rescued woman's peril was far from over though. Her trapped left arm had been broken in more than one place and her breathing was becoming more laboured by the moment. Without urgent care she was plainly going to die. Quickly, D'harid assessed the situation and called for two blankets which miraculously appeared as if from nowhere. She was carefully wrapped in one for warmth and placed on the other so it might be used as a makeshift stretcher. By the time Eldore and Griston re-joined the company, she was ready to be carried to the viltula.

Eldore, amazed at how efficiently the old soldier had organised his volunteers, came to a sudden and momentous decision.

"D'harid Sternhand," he said formally. "You've asked for authority to command the rescue work for this quarter – authority I've already granted you. But now I add to that authority; I charge you with responsibility for the whole city."

D'harid raised an eyebrow. "That is a great responsibility indeed."

"I know that, but in your hands I'm certain that all those who can be saved *will* be saved."

"If it's just for this quarter, I could assure you that would be true, but throughout the whole city? I'm sorry, lord, but with respect, I'm afraid I must decline your request."

"It's not an offer, it's a command," Eldore stated firmly.

"Then command another more capable person. Perhaps Master Rennil would be a more appropriate choice."

"No; no one is more capable than you. You are needed; therefore, I insist."

For several heartbeats the pair locked eyes, Eldore's firm and resolute, D'harid's calm yet questioning. "Very well," the elder man said at last in the same placid and implacable voice. "For the sake of the people, I accept your...*request.*"

CHAPTER TWENTY-THREE

Eldore gripped the knotted corners of the improvised stretcher and tried to shut out the burning pain in his arms and shoulders. He would have taken a short rest some time ago, but the dogged urgency of Griston at the other end of the blanket made such a luxury unthinkable. Although the injured woman wasn't heavy, both men had strained themselves lifting the beam which had pinned her, and were now paying dearly for their heroics – particularly Griston. The poor man should barely have been able to stand, but his deep feelings for the woman gave his exhausted body an energy that defied all reason.

The woman? With a sudden rush of shame and guilt, Eldore realised that he didn't know her name. Nobody had mentioned it and what with all the drama of her rescue, he hadn't thought to ask. Mentally he cursed himself for such unforgivable thoughtlessness. He thought to ask now but speech was an ability which seemed to be beyond both men. It had deserted them not long after beginning their arduous trek through the eerily lit, shattered streets.

There had at first been some conversation, however. Before all their energy had become needed for the task at hand, Griston had explained how he and Tarryl – D'harid's messenger – had come to be in the Chanceway when the storm had stuck. Although the explanation was brief and the words few, Eldore was able to fill in the blanks and form a reasonably accurate picture of how events had unfolded.

It seemed the Arms-Master had sent Tarryl – a team officer who had served alongside D'harid – to ask the old soldier to return to the armshost as a section-leader in charge of the conscripted militia. The newly enlisted men would need training as swiftly and completely as possible and no one was more able to achieve the impossible than D'harid. The Arms-Master had obviously hoped that the citywide call to arms would persuade him to return to the fold at least two ranks above that which he'd held before retiring. To reinforce the urgency of the situation, Rennil had also sent the newly conscripted Griston who was a frequent and familiar visitor to the Chanceway. Perhaps if D'harid could see the peril in which the strong but inexperienced farmhand was being placed, he would relent and take up the commission. By all accounts however, that hope had been in vain. The two men were just taking their leave when they saw the boiling clouds sweeping overhead. There had been just enough time to assist D'harid in closing the shutters before the explosive wind had burst upon the city, forcing all three to dive inside and take shelter together. There they'd stayed until D'harid had made his premature venture outside and had sustained the injury to his neck. Fortunately, Tarryl and Griston had managed to reach the old warrior and pull him back to relative safety.

Despite this brush with disaster, D'harid had still insisted on leaving the house well before the storm had eased enough to be truly safe. It was hard to think of the steady, capable old warrior being foolhardy, but when circumstances demanded that risks be taken, he was obviously not afraid to take them.

Eldore was suddenly brought back to the present when he stumbled over a small piece of detritus, drawing a shrill scream of pain from the injured woman. Carefully he adjusted his grip and resolved to pay more attention to where he was placing his feet. Behind him he heard Griston whisper gentle encouragement to their stricken charge.

"Courage Annisa, we'll soon be at the viltula and D'harid promised to bring Little-Man as soon as he's been freed."

Annisa. She was called Annisa. Eldore couldn't help but wonder if beneath the dirt and the dust, beyond the pain that had distorted her features, she was as pretty as her name. He decided it would only be right to visit her during her convalescence and find out for himself.

Soon after this, they turned a corner to be faced by an uphill slope that Eldore knew to be both a blessing and a curse. A curse because although its incline was not too steep nor its distance too great, in their enervated condition it was going to prove a major obstacle. But a blessing for the reason that at the top of the hill, they would turn another corner and find themselves approaching the courtyard of the viltula itself. He drew a deep breath and led them up the final daunting stage of their journey. Far sooner than he'd feared, this particular nightmare was over.

When the twins and Bandil had arrived at the viltula the day after the battle, the courtyard had been crowded with wounded soldiers. Hard-pressed tenders had been rushed off their feet trying to cope with the sudden influx of wounded men. But despite the scale of their task that day, the overstretched women and girls had coped admirably. The situation now, however, was nothing less than unbridled chaos. The air was again full of moans and sharp cries of pain, but this time not from hardened warriors or the tough labourers who made up the militia; this time the cacophony of misery came from the lips of the pathetic and the innocent.

The sound of so many weeping women and children – some screaming in agony – was one that was almost beyond endurance. Many of the tenders had tears flowing down their cheeks as they hurried from patient to patient, doing whatever they could to ease their suffering.

At the far side of the courtyard a row of bodies had been laid out – the bodies of men, women, and children. Due to the shortage of blankets, only the faces of the dead had been covered – and this only by whatever scrap of material could be found at hand. One body, however, was so small that it was completely enshrouded by a single blouse. The fact that the blouse was a joyous yellow, and was gaily embroidered with bright summer flowers only served to highlight the unimaginable horror of the infant's death.

Eldore called out to one of the tenders. She acknowledged him with no more than a quick glance and a wave of her hand to indicate that she'd get to him in turn. The comic timing of her double-take as she realised who it was she'd just answered so dismissively, would in any other circumstances have been amusing. Her eyes widened in horror and her face flushed as she hurriedly finished binding the young man she was treating. Then sheepishly, she approached the two men who were holding the improvised stretcher.

"My lord," she said apologetically. "I didn't recognise you."

"This woman is in urgent need," Eldore stated curtly, ignoring the apology. "Where shall we put her?"

The tender helplessly waved her arm around the courtyard. "There is nowhere, so wherever you can."

"Good. Griston, gently down." Carefully, they lowered Annisa to the ground. "Here will do just fine. Now, my good tender, make amends for your rudeness and go fetch the healer. Tell him that Lord Eldore's charge has broken bones and is having difficulty breathing. I also need to speak to him about the overall situation, and it would save a great deal of time if we can do both at once."

"Yes, my lord."

"Go on then, hurry!"

The girl scampered away as fast as she could, negotiating the sprawling rows of casualties with amazing finesse.

"Thank you, my lord," came Griston's voice from behind.

Eldore turned and smiled woefully. "I find rank a heavy burden but it does have its compensations."

A low moan came from Annisa and Griston dropped anxiously down beside her. He took hold of her good hand and began whispering encouragement in her ear. Eldore watched for a moment then looked away. Why, he wondered, did love always seem to come at such a cost? He returned his gaze to the crowded courtyard, scanning it for a glimpse of his own particular heartache; but Morjeena was nowhere to be seen. She was obviously working inside the building itself, he decided.

He did catch sight of the animated conversation that was taking place between the tender and Aldegar, however. Although it was difficult to read expressions at this distance, the healer's stiff posture and angry shaking of his head were unmistakably hostile. The tender's desperate pleading was obviously effective though, for after a swift word with another tender, the tall, sharp-featured man nodded and began striding toward them with the flustered tender in tow.

On arriving, and without acknowledging Eldore with so much as a glance, he eased Griston aside and knelt beside the barely conscious Annisa. He put his ear to her mouth and listened to her breathing. He then parted her lips and peered inside her mouth. He was looking for signs of blood, but in the eerie red glow of the unnatural sky, it was impossible to determine. Eventually, he grunted his satisfaction and turned to the smashed arm. It was already swelling and turning a nasty shade of blackish-blue.

"This will need careful manipulation," he said to the hovering tender. "It must be splinted with great attention to detail or she'll be left with an arm that's near useless. It must be done quickly but..." He cast a weary eye over the misery around them, "...we must also prioritise. There are others with more pressing needs."

He put his ear against the girl's chest for a moment then swiftly but gently unbuttoned her blouse exposing her breasts. Griston blushed heavily and turned his head away but Eldore was unembarrassed and continued to watch closely; he found nothing titillating about another's suffering. The left side of Annisa's torso was a livid mass of colours that ranged from yellow, through several shades of red, to an evil-looking purple. With practiced fingers, Aldegar gently probed the area, a look of deep concentration on his sharp, aquiline features. Annisa cried out in pain and tried to move away but the tender knelt at her head and pinned her shoulders down.

Eldore bit his lip. Although he knew the procedure was necessary, it was still unpleasant to watch. Yet somehow, he couldn't look away. It was as if by enduring the discomfort of watching, he was in some strange way helping the poor woman through the pain of the ordeal. At last, Aldegar finished his examination, pulled her blouse closed, and rewrapped her in the blanket. He looked at the tender and gave both his diagnosis and his orders.

"She has at least two broken ribs, perhaps more but it's hard to tell. Thankfully none have yet torn her lungs but I want her strapped tightly at once."

"Yes, healer. I'll go and get some bindings." She jumped up and hurried off in the direction of the building's entrance. Aldegar rose more slowly and looked at Eldore for the first time.

"We have a procedure," he said coldly. "Triage has nothing to do with status. Please don't use your position to influence me again."

"I'm sorry," Eldore replied with a slight nod of contrition. "It won't happen again."

"Good. As it is, she would have been seen to straight away, so no harm has been done. Now, I'm told you want to speak to me about the situation, so be quick, I am after all, a little busy."

"Yes of course. First of all, overall command of rescue and securing damaged buildings is in the hands of D'harid Sternhand; so you'll need to liaise with him with regards to casualty movements and such."

Aldegar raised an eyebrow. "Really? I am surprised, although not displeased. Anything else?"

"Indeed. I was thinking perhaps we could find another building to house the overflow of casualties. I'll be happy to requisition any property that fits the purpose."

"Thank you, but that won't be necessary. A merchant had offered us a warehouse for this very purpose after the battle. We coped without it then but as it's now needed, Morjeena has gone to prepare it. It's not ideal as it's a fair distance from here, but the building itself should suffice."

"And the boy, is he with her?"

Aldegar looked puzzled. "The boy? What boy?"

"Yewan," Eldore replied, his heart sinking to the pit of his stomach. "I sent him to warn you, and as the viltula's shutters are closed, I assumed he'd arrived. I told him he was to place himself in her care until the storm had passed."

"We were warned by the bells. I'm afraid your messenger must have been waylaid for we haven't seen him."

"But he *must* have arrived," Eldore insisted desperately. "We were at my forge when I sent him. That's hardly a great distance from here."

"My friend," the healer said laying a sympathetic hand on the distraught young lord's shoulder. "*I* could not have reached here in such a short time. I'm afraid you must accept that the storm has taken him."

To Eldore it seemed the ground had lurched sideways and only Aldegar's support prevented him from toppling into the gravel.

"What have I done?" he whispered in despair. "What have I done?" He looked into the healer's eyes. "Tell me, Aldegar, how can I bear this responsibility? I've already cost the life of an innocent boy; how many more lives will be destroyed by my decisions?"

"You'll bear it because it's your duty to bear it," Aldegar replied firmly. "Decisions must be made and whatever the consequences, they are yours to make."

"How? I'm not my brother."

Aldegar's expression softened. "No, you're not. You are *Eldore* Starbrow, son of the High-Lord, and the man Mordan has placed at the head of his people at this time of need. Were you worth any less than your brother, would he have laid this burden on you? Were you worth any less, would my daughter have given *you* her heart – against her father's wishes at that?"

"Then tell me, healer, what salves or potions do you have to ease the pain of what I must bear?"

Aldegar smiled sympathetically. "There are no salves or potions, but you'll master the pain. Remember, you're not as alone as you might feel."

Eldore sighed. "And how do I face Sharna, Yewan's mother?"

The healer's smile faded. "In that, I'm afraid, you *are* alone."

CHAPTER TWENTY-FOUR

Two days after the storm's fury had passed, the atmosphere in the Moot Hall was taut and heavy with anxiety. Although it was only mid-afternoon, the eerie red light seeping in through the single window necessitated the lighting of several lamps, the glow of which only added to the dark mood in the room. For the most part, the pale-faced council members sat in strained silence, lost in their own private world of fear as they awaited the arrival of Eldore. The fact that their youthful leader was now very late only added to the tension. The oppressive silence was only broken by the almost inaudible murmur of two conversations; one between Rennil and Gildor near the head of the table, the other between Hevalor and Verryl at the far end. Apprehension was etched deep into every face; every face that is save one. D'harid Sternhand was calmly sitting next to the Spiritual Overseer, his battered features implacable and his large dark eyes as placid and serene as ever. He was watching his colleagues' discomfort with neither compassion nor condemnation, but rather with what appeared to be little more than mild curiosity.

At long last, the door opened and a flustered looking Eldore swept into the room. Without a word to anyone and before the assembly could get even halfway to their feet, he threw himself into the chair beside the High-Lord's place at the table's head. After a moment of confused hesitation and with a great deal of low-toned muttering, the astounded council members retook their own seats.

For a few moments Eldore sat with his hands covering his face; then with a tired sigh, he took them away and looked around the table. "I'm sorry for the delay," he said in a weary and jaded voice. "But there were a great many problems to overcome at the new viltula. Being so far from the main building, establishing it efficiently has proved more complicated than we'd envisaged. It's fortunate that it's only a few streets from here or you'd have been kept waiting even longer than you already have." He sighed heavily before taking a firmer grip of himself.

"But enough of that," he continued in a stronger voice. "Let's get on with the business at hand. Firstly, I'd like to call on our newest member to bring us up to date regarding the city's rescue work. D'harid, if you will."

Deliberately, so as not to scrape his chair on the floor, D'harid got slowly to his feet and addressed the council.

"Honoured members," he began in his soothing, if somewhat gruff voice. "I'm pleased to inform you that every one of the city's citizens is now accounted for, whether alive or dead. I'm also pleased to report that those in the latter category are far fewer than we'd feared. Although there are still many with life threatening injuries, Aldegar tells me that most are expected to live. Those details, however, are outside my sphere of responsibility; but I'm sure when circumstances allow, he'll appear here in person to give you a full account of the situation.

"As you're well aware, the storm left many buildings in an extremely dangerous condition that required immediate repair or demolition. Again, I can report that this work is also complete, thanks in most part to the co-operation of the Arms-Master here. He provided me with all the manpower I requested – most of whom I can now release back to him to continue their training."

"Most?" Rennil queried in a threatening rumble.

D'harid gave him an unperturbed smile. "Most. Many families have been displaced to the refuge and as a great many of their homes can be salvaged, I'd like to retain a workforce adequate enough to carry out the necessary repairs. It would boost morale to see those families return to the city proper."

"The men would be better employed learning how to defend those families."

"Perhaps, but I'm sure a handful of civilians skilled in woodcraft rather than war craft won't make too much of a difference to our strength." Then without taking his eyes from Rennil's defiant, disfigured face, he addressed Eldore. "What do you say my lord?"

"How many men do you want to keep?" Eldore enquired.

"Twenty."

"Ten," Rennil countered in a menacing growl.

"Fifteen it is then," D'harid declared brightly. "Thank you, Master Rennil. I've already instructed the rest of the men to report to the barracks first thing in the morning. I assume that's where you'll be wanting them?"

"I said ten."

"Yes, you did; but then we'd have begun to negotiate and we both know we'd have met in the middle; so fifteen it is."

Rennil's eyes narrowed as he glared up at his one-time subordinate's expressionless face. But then his lips twitched and suddenly curled to form his characteristically twisted grin. With an exasperated shake of his head he held out his hand. "Agreed. Fifteen."

Returning the smile, D'harid shook the proffered hand then turned back to the rest of the council.

"So there you have it; all persons accounted for, all buildings made safe, and reconstruction to continue. Have I missed anything out?" There was no answer. "Very well. Lord Eldore?"

"Thank you D'harid, it's good to hear some good news for a change. Please be seated."

D'harid nodded and carefully did as he was asked.

"Next, I think we should hear from our illustrious Arms-Master. Tell us Rennil, how are our defences coming along, are they adequate?"

Rennil remained in his seat. The unnatural red light coupled with the flickering of the lamps gave his mutilated face an almost evil appearance, and the subterranean gravel of his voice gave his words a terrifying gravity.

"Adequate against what?" he asked rhetorically. "You posed that same question a few days ago in this very chamber and I gave you a qualified 'yes'. As things stand now, however, how can I answer you? If another army of lich were to assault us today, 'adequate' is hardly a word I'm minded to use. Our scouts are gone, swept to their deaths by the force of the storm..." Eldore winced as he was reminded of poor Yewan's fate "...and the conscripted men have been working with D'harid rather than training with the armshost. Nevertheless, whatever the outcome, I'm confident that even now we'd put any aggressor to the severest test. But there is of course, a more difficult problem to take into consideration.

"I'm a soldier – a good one so I'm told – and as a soldier, I understand weapons and tactics, campaigns and strategy. I do not, however, understand sorcery. The red warrior-mage alone was almost too much for us, and his fall came at a price that was far too high to bear. But compared to the black art that summoned such an unnatural storm, he was nothing more than a mere nuisance.

"And what of this sky? What evil purpose does it have? Perhaps the clouds are hiding a horde of flying demons waiting to swoop down on our heads. Maybe it holds a power that as we speak, is slowly draining the life from us, or even filling us with a magical poison. Against such things our defences are not just inadequate, they are useless."

An agitated murmur swept around the table. Eldore studied the Arms-Master's face with sombre scrutiny, unused to hearing such a defeatist attitude from the famous warrior. But Rennil's steady hazel eyes betrayed no sign of defeat or fear, just a bitter and hard-headed pragmatism.

"You're right of course," Eldore replied with grim thoughtfulness. He continued to study the Arms-Master's face for a moment longer then turned his attention to the rest of the council.

"We have no idea as to the threat the red clouds pose; unless any of you have some inspired thoughts you'd care to share. Anyone?" He looked from one blank face to another but was met each time by nothing more than an empty expression and a helpless shake of the head. Last of all, his gaze fell upon the old Lore-Master.

"And what of you, Verryl? Is there anything in the scrolls that can give us guidance on how to counter this threat – or even what that threat might be?"

"Alas no," the ancient scribe said regretfully. "Both I and my apprentice have scoured the archives; but we've found nothing in any writings that are any help at all."

As the old man spoke, Hevalor shifted uneasily at his side and Eldore was quick to spot the Overseer's disquiet.

"Is there something you wish to add?" he asked pointedly. Hevalor's unease grew to a mild agitation. No one had ever seen the caring and confident moral guardian look so unsure of himself. He sat fidgeting uncomfortably, trying hard to avoid Eldore's eye. "Well?" Eldore demanded. "There's obviously something, so speak."

"It's probably nothing, but I've found a..."

"Hevalor!" Verryl warned sharply. "We've talked about this. It is NOT a matter that's open to discussion; so hold your tongue."

The Lore-Master's audacious disrespect drew a shocked gasp from the assembly.

Eldore turned to Verryl and raised an eyebrow. "Since when does your office give you authority over the Spiritual Overseer?" he asked coldly. "Only the Seat of Duty confers such a right; and even then there are circumstances when the Overseer's position outweighs that of the High-Lord. If Hevalor has something to say, he must say it whether you approve or not."

With the Lore-Master suitably chastened he once again addressed Hevalor. "So, my learned friend, what is it that you're so reluctant to tell us?"

"As I say, it's probably nothing but as you know there are certain writings stored in the house of worship. Some of them are articles of prophecy and although I found nothing in these that were any use to us, as I searched the shelves, I came upon a loose section of panelling. Behind it was hidden a parchment that must have been secreted there when the building was constructed some two hundred years ago. The tale the parchment told was one that was not completely new to me, but it does contain details that I've never heard before. Details that have been erased from our history – or at least lost in time."

"Or concoctions of total fiction," Verryl added sourly.

Hevalor ignored the interruption and continued without pause. "It tells of an ancestor of yours that perhaps you've heard of; Murvon, son of High-Lord Marrond?"

Eldore shook his head.

"I'm not surprised, he's barely mentioned in our historical writings. In fact, his name is only of note in that, although heir to the Seat of Duty, he was never High-Lord. The reason for this, so we're told, was that a terrible but unspecified infirmity left him unable to fulfil the duties of office. The Seat therefore passed to his five-year-old nephew, with Murvon's sister standing as Lady Regent until her child came of age. And that, I'm afraid, is all we know about him."

"So how does this Murvon have any bearing on our situation today?" Eldore asked.

"Because he made a prophecy."

"He did nothing of the kind!" Verryl exploded, unable to contain his anger any longer. "The ravings of a dying madman are not prophecy, and to treat them as such is dangerous."

"ENOUGH!" Eldore shouted back. "If we aren't told what this so called 'prophecy' says, how can its veracity be judged? Go on Hevalor, we're all listening. What does the disputed prophecy say?"

"First of all, let me set the scene for you. Have you heard of the *Pilgrimage of Dreams*? No, I thought not. Neither I nor Master Verryl had ever come across it before. But from what the parchment tells us, it was the custom for our people, at least once in their lives, to travel to the shores of the Grey Lake at the very edge of Mordan's Maze. There they would spend the night and experience vivid dreams of what lay beyond the forbidding forest of pillars. Today, such a thing is unthinkable and Murvon's fate is, I believe, the reason why.

"Once, this heir to the Seat was known as Murvon the Bold, and it appears that he was a brave, if somewhat rash hero of the people."

"He sounds like my brother," Eldore commented dryly.

"So I thought; but it seems Murvon had a great deal of two things that Eh'lorne mercifully lacks: stupidity and hubris. When he undertook his own pilgrimage, he decided that – against all laws – he would sleep *between* the pillars. The next morning, he was nowhere to be seen. He had quite simply vanished. For two years the High-Lord searched for his son before he reluctantly declared him dead. Soon after that, despair took hold of the High-Lord, and Marrond died of a broken heart.

"The Lady Regent took the seat, eventually standing aside when the time came for her son – Marrond's grandson – to become High-Lord. From our records we know that he was both wise and just, but he plays no part in my story.

"The secret parchment goes on to tell us that twenty years to the day after he vanished, Murvon reappeared and simply walked into the city. He was naked, his hair had turned white, and he was covered in terrible burns. But apart from those changes to his appearance and despite the passage of time, he seemed not to have aged a single day. He was, however, completely insane and became known to one and all as Murvon the Mad – a detail understandably omitted from the records. All the poor wretch could say over and over was, 'The sky bleeds, the ice burns.'

"He was taken to the viltula where he lay for more than two moons, growing steadily weaker by the day. The Spiritual Overseer, who was also the author of the parchment, spent much of his time at Murvon's bedside. The whole time – even in his sleep – the same litany was repeated without pause: 'The sky bleeds, the ice burns.'

"The time eventually came when the stricken lord was on the edge of death, and the Overseer sat holding the dying man's hand, waiting for the mercy of the long sleep. Suddenly, Murvon sat bolt upright and in a voice which was not his own, declared his 'prophecy'. He then fell back onto the bed and with an unnatural sigh, described as 'a possessive spirit leaving his body,' Murvon died."

For a few moments the chamber was silent. It seemed as though everyone was spellbound and holding their breath. Eventually, it was Hesta that broke the tension in the room.

"I believe Master Verryl is mistaken," she said firmly. "This document must be brought here so we can read Murvon's tale and see his last words for ourselves."

"And so it will be," Eldore agreed. "I'll arrange for it to be fetched at once. Hevalor, where is it? I'll call for a servant to go and get it."

The Overseer looked relieved. "Of course. I gave it to Verryl so he could store it safely at the vil-carrim."

"Good. Verryl, does your apprentice know where it is or will you go yourself?"

"The document is gone," the old scribe declared defiantly.

"Gone? What do you mean, gone?

"Destroyed. Burnt. It was far too dangerous a heresy to be allowed to exist – why else do you think it was hidden. Had that foolish Overseer not concealed it, the council would have burned it as soon as it was written. False prophecy is worse than no prophecy at all!"

"HOW DARE YOU!" Eldore cried, leaping to his feet. "Never has any piece of lore or scripture been harmed by a keeper of the past. You've overstepped your authority beyond words!"

"This ranting was neither!" Verryl shouted back as he too jumped up sending his chair clattering to the floor. "It was the ravings of a madman and deserved nothing less."

"GET OUT!" Eldore roared, apoplectic with rage. "You have no right to be in this chamber nor on this council. Consider yourself banished. And as for your position as Lore-Master, that will be decided in the near future. Now go!"

Verryl looked as if he were about to explode and appeared to be on the verge of physically assaulting the powerfully built lord.

Eventually, however, the futility of such an uneven contest penetrated even the red mists of his fury, and with a loud "HAH!" he stormed out of the chamber, slamming the door behind him so hard that it rattled the window.

Shaking, Eldore sat back down and tried to get his breathing under control

"Was that wise?" Hevalor asked anxiously. "He may be getting cantankerous in his old age but he does have a vast wealth of knowledge. We're sure to need the writings stored in the vil-carrim, and no one knows those scrolls better than he does. He's also my friend," he added quietly.

Eldore shut his eyes and drew a deep breath. When he opened them, he found every face turned toward him with expressions ranging from shock to outright fear.

"You're absolutely right, we can't afford to be without his knowledge. But more importantly, nor can we afford to be baulked in all our deliberations; and he seems to have done little else since this crisis came upon us. As it is, he's ruined any chance we had of determining whether this Murvon spoke prophetically or not."

Hevalor sighed. "If that was his intention he has failed. And that's one of the things that makes me believe it really is an inspired utterance. From the moment I first saw it, I could remember every word as though I'd spent days carefully memorising it. It goes like this:

"A bleeding sky, a freezing fire,
Then comes the time for righteous ire,
An oath's upheld from bygone age,
While hunters prowl and howl with rage.
Because the gift was lost by pride,
What once was whole must then divide,
And law will burn and be undone,
That oil and water mix as one,

*To bring the world new flesh and bone,
United blood, united throne."*

Hevalor shrugged. "To me it sounds prophetic, but how it should be interpreted I don't know. It's certainly very different from every other prophecy in the archives. Perhaps Verryl is right; perhaps we should dismiss it out of hand."

Eldore shook his head. "No, I believe there's something in what you say. I also believe that it *does* apply to us or why else would it turn up now at the very moment of our greatest need? We just need to determine how."

"Could the bleeding sky refer to the red clouds?" Gildor asked hopefully.

"Perhaps the 'righteous ire' it speaks of is the Talisman of Wrath," added Tilmar, the aristocratic-looking trade representative. There then followed a chorus of "What-ifs" and "Could-its" from all around the table but Eldore stilled them all with a raised hand.

"We can speculate till Halgar-come, but without some point of reference, the proph..."

Abruptly, he stopped midsentence. His eyes suddenly widened then rolled back into his head leaving only the whites visible. His body began to shake violently until one massive spasm contorted his frame so aggressively that he was thrown from his chair. Gagging with choked-off screams, Eldore rolled around the floor with his body contorted into impossible, bone-breaking positions. The council members rushed to his side, scattering chairs in their haste to reach the stricken lord. They gathered around him, unsure of how to help. All they could do was to make sure he didn't crack his head as he thrashed helplessly around the floor. Hesta, however, took one look at him and then dashed from the room, muttering a fervent prayer as she ran.

S. P. MUIR

To Eldore himself, it seemed as though the room had exploded in a concussive blast that sent him spinning through time and the fabric of space. He felt that he'd been pitched headlong into a blazing inferno that seemed to freeze the very flesh from his bones. He was deafened by a roaring wind and blinded by a kaleidoscope of images so bright, they seared his brain and turned his mind to ice, rendering coherent thought impossible. In spite of the sensory overload, beyond the screaming pain of the fire that was freezing his flesh, in a distant corner of his mind he was acutely aware that he was sharing his brother's agony. Somewhere, Eh'lorne was dying a terrible death.

In this world of furious torment, time ceased to have any meaning and the torture seemed eternal with no hope of a reprieve. Eventually though, after what seemed centuries of torment, the merciless vortex began to ease, and the pain diminished so as to be almost bearable. The dizzying whirl of images slowed, coalescing to form a clear and terrifying vision. Horrified, he was made to understand exactly what he had to do, and the fear of it appalled him and filled him with dread.

Then the vision faded leaving him emotionally destitute and shivering on the cold hard floor. Instinctively, he clutched at the pouch of earth around his neck and tried desperately to bring his body back under control. He opened his eyes and looked up at the concerned, frightened faces staring down at him. No matter how hard he tried to communicate what he'd seen, the paralysis of his facial muscles allowed nothing more than unintelligible grunts and gasps to pass through his chattering teeth.

Then, with a titanic effort, his trembling lips managed to form one word. Just one; but a word that entailed everything that he'd witnessed:

"Doom."

CHAPTER TWENTY-FIVE

What seemed certain to be the final moments of Eh'lorne's life, were mercifully pain-free. The cold flames had frozen both his flesh and his mind leaving him completely numb and virtually insensate. Then just as the welcome blanket of oblivion was about to envelop him in its dark folds, a brief moment of lucidity flashed through his brain. In it, the full scale of his failure crashed over him like a tidal wave. He'd failed his brother, his people, and of course, he'd failed the old man who'd spent more than two lifetimes preparing for this very moment. But worst of all, he'd failed Morjeena by breaking the vow he'd sworn to her on the night before leaving Sirris. Added to that was a bitter irony; it was the power of the very god he'd served so faithfully that was now killing him. It was all more than he could bear.

But that cruellest of paradoxes struck a spark of resentment in his heart; a spark that touched the dry tinder of his quick temper and lit a tiny flame of indignation. That flame quickly grew until it exploded into an inferno of fury which started melting the ice holding him in its grip of death. But as the heat of that passion began to thaw his body, so the unbearable pain returned with even greater intensity. It was as if his desperate struggling had provoked the Talisman, spurring it into ravaging his body all the more completely.

But this time Eh'lorne welcomed the pain. He nurtured it and demanded more; for each frigid blast that assaulted him fanned the flames of his own fury as surely as the bellows fanned the coals of his brother's furnace.

It was true that Eh'lorne was the greatest swordsman of his age, but it was not just his skill with a blade that made him such a dangerous opponent. There was something else as well; something so fundamental that it went deep into the core of his very being; and it was with that fierce and indomitable 'something' that he now fought back.

In the battlefield of his heart and soul he clawed and kicked and scratched. He screamed out his defiance and refused to die. He demanded the right to be king – to have the power to defend his people and avenge the terrible carnage he'd witnessed at Sarren. Slowly the incandescence of his fury began to push back the arctic onslaught until the pain eased enough for rational thought. And that ability to reason overrode the raw instinct that had saved him. Deliberately, he bent the Talisman's power to his will and took control of the dizzying storm of images that whirled around him. Gradually, he managed to take hold of them, to steady them until they merged together and formed a clear and recognisable picture.

He found himself hovering in mid-air, looking down at the prone figure of a white-clad young man. Despite being unconscious – even comatose – the man held a gleaming slender blade in a tight, vice-like grip. With a start, Eh'lorne realised that he was looking down on his own inert body. It lay just beyond his reach at the centre of the vast chamber which had held the Talisman since the founding of the world. Straining every last scrap of will, he tried to force his ethereal mind back into the physical reality of his body, but to his dismay, no matter how hard he tried, the two remained as separate and distinct as if they'd never been united as one.

Then, with a suddenness that shocked him to the core, he was thrust upwards, rising vertically through the mountain's solid rock at a frightening speed. Like an erupting volcano, he burst from the summit of Mordan's Finger and out into bright, dazzling daylight. The vertiginous ascent continued unabated until at last it seemed that the whole world was spread out before him. Then abruptly, he came to a halt and hung stationary, high in the cold blue sky, bathed in the brilliant afternoon sunshine.

Far below him, the thick, blood-red clouds covered the land like a gigantic scab. Yet despite this, nothing was obscured from his god-empowered, supernatural sight. The evil clouds covered the whole world east of Arl while leaving the royal city shimmering in the sun. Its ancient glory shone majestically – in spite of the malice that now resided there. Eh'lorne marvelled at the way he could distinguish the detail of every brick and stone as if he was close enough to reach out and touch the distant city.

Eagerly he looked to his left where the Mystic Mountains lay behind the protective barrier of the great maze of pillars. He hoped against hope to see the mysterious land which had sustained Bandil so far beyond his natural lifespan. But to his intense disappointment, that holy place was shrouded in a dense mist that remained impervious to his new visual powers. Some secrets it seemed, were not to be revealed.

He turned his attention to Sirris and when he saw the damage and destruction that the storm had wrought upon his home, it reignited the fire of his anger. Just one more injustice to be righted, one more atrocity to be avenged; and now that he had the power to make those responsible pay, he burned to begin the task of meting out that retribution.

The deep snowfield they'd crossed with the aid of Bandil's snowshoes was still a forbidding obstacle that would hamper their return, but he was surprised to see how narrow and localised it was. Its sole purpose was obviously to prevent anyone from Sirris reaching the Talisman – a purpose that had failed miserably.

Away to the northwest stood the strange monastic city of Hornvale with its huge sculpture of a hunting horn carved into the towering cliff which marked the valley's northern boundary. Although he knew the city was a good three-day journey from Sirris, from his elevated position it seemed to be far nearer than that. All the maps he'd seen had placed the two cities much further apart than they now appeared. This distortion in perspective mystified him at first, but then the answer dawned on him. All the mapmakers measured any distance beyond a few stretches in *marches*, and a march was a unit of *time*. The way the path twisted and turned over the difficult terrain between the two cities would obviously make them seem further apart than they actually were.

As he studied Hornvale's unusual architecture, an uncanny feeling began to grow within him. Not with the city itself but instead a perplexing fascination with the secretive, monk-like inhabitants of the extraordinary settlement. He was inexplicably drawn to them, and no matter how he tried, he could not for the life of him work out why.

Puzzled, he returned his focus to the westward view and the full reason why his god was showing him this amazing vision suddenly came into sharp focus. There, on the wide fertile plains of Keshtar, a vast army was marching inexorably towards the Sacred Hills. Within days they would be flooding over the western passes and would come storming across Cor-Peshtar and into Sirris itself. Their numbers were staggering – far greater than the lich horde defeated by Rennil's ambush – but worse than that, every one of these soldiers was human.

The bulk of the force consisted of Keshtari footmen, many of whom were obviously reluctant conscripts; but Eh'lorne could see from the many wide glinting eyes that most were fierce fanatics.

Alongside Limnash's own troops was an eclectic variety of mercenaries: the wild tribesmen of the great forests, Screaming Nomads from beyond the Southern Desert, and most frightening of all, thousands of tall, broad shouldered barbarians from across the sea. They strode bare-chested in spite of the cold; their faces were painted with elaborate patterns of vivid blue and they had human bones braided into their yellow hair. Strapped to their backs they carried huge, double-sided battle-axes, sharp enough and heavy enough to cut a man in two with a single stroke.

Most shocking of all however, against every convention of combat and outlawed by all cultures for more than a thousand years, amongst the ranks of the Keshtari zealots were row upon row of archers. This was a war crime beyond any other and to Eh'lorne's mind, it was worse even than sorcery. He needed to warn his brother of the impending catastrophe but there was no need, for Eldore's mind was already with him, sharing the experience – the intense pain as well as the incredible vision.

A movement from the north caught his eye so he turned towards it and gasped. A huge area of the plain was rippling like an ocean of fur. It was an army of lich; and an army such as the world had never seen before. The hordes of men heading toward Sirris far outnumbered the initial lich attack at the last full moon, but this army dwarfed even that mighty force. Instinctively, Eh'lorne realised their aim. They intended to crush

Hornvale and then sweep down in a surprise attack, taking Sirris from the rear – if, of course, Sirris still existed by then.

Why Limnash felt the need to overcome the reclusive monks was a mystery to him, but despite his puzzlement, he was suddenly and acutely aware of what he had to do. It was a course of action that should have gone against his every instinct, every scrap of his logic and reason; but instead of railing against it, he simply accepted it as if it was the obvious and only thing to do. Somehow, he was sure that his god's purpose would work out for the good.

He felt a momentary and intense pang of sympathy for his brother. Although Eldore had received the same vision and the same instructions, without actually holding the Talisman he could not share in the ecstasy and certainty of its power. All he could feel was the pain, and the horror, and despair.

But Eh'lorne's empathy was only brief, for then the vision began to fade and he was hurtling back down to earth. He braced himself, for it seemed as though he must crash painfully into the mountain's pinnacle summit; but there was no impact. Instead, he found himself descending back through the solid rock until he burst back into the chamber. Then with a concussive thump, he re-entered his body. He lay there for some time feeling small and powerless, shaking with cold and struggling to breathe. It was one thing, he reflected, to know what must be done, but quite another to force one's battered and exhausted body to act. He had maintained his grip on the sword but other than that he seemed to be paralysed. He was completely unable to take control of any other part of his body; but time was precious and there was so much that he needed to do.

He started by moving the fingers of his free hand. When he was satisfied that he'd mastered them, he moved on to his toes and then to his ankles. By methodically concentrating on each body member in turn, he was eventually able to roll onto his side. A few moments later he managed to raise his head from the

THE TALISMAN OF WRATH

floor. In the distance he could see the old man standing at the cavern's entrance. His face was a picture of concern and anxiety as he pulled at his beard mouthing a fervent, silent prayer.

"As one uncrowned king to another," Eh'lorne called out, trying to keep his shaky voice level and jovial. "Would it be too much to ask for a little assistance?"

Bandil let out a whoop of joy and hurried across the chamber to his companion's side.

"Oh, my friend, my friend," he cried, tears of pride and relief leaving clean tracks on his dirty, wrinkled cheeks. "I was convinced that I'd lost you. And to see you suffering so badly, I felt sure that my heart would break!"

"I feel mine already has." Eh'lorne stated wryly as he struggled up into a seated position. He held out his hand so the old man could help him to his feet but Bandil hesitated to take it.

Realising the source of his concern, Eh'lorne smiled encouragingly. "There's no need to be afraid; the Talisman's under control and as long as you don't touch it, you're quite safe."

The old man nodded and then helped his trembling young companion to stand, unsteady but erect. Carefully, so as to avoid contact with the shining sword, he slid an arm around the teetering warrior's slim waist and helped him towards the distant exit.

As they approached the dark, forbidding doorway, Eh'lorne let out a low whistle. "Well now, I didn't see *that* when we came in."

Bandil followed his gaze to see a tall, narrow recess set in the twinkling rock. There, hanging in the alcove was a stunningly beautiful scabbard. To say that it was black would be a dramatic understatement, for it was so dark that it seemed as if a hole had been ripped open in the very fabric of time and space. In spite of this stygian absence of colour, however, it was far from plain; for black against black, it was covered with intricate patterns intertwined around strange runes of arcane power. Its shadowy, exquisite allure made the heart ache with a deep and empty longing.

Eh'lorne took his arm from around the old man's bony shoulders, reached into the alcove and lifted the scabbard from its hanging. It was weightless and seemed to have no substance at all. It was as if it barely registered in the physical reality of this world. It appeared to be nothing more than an ephemeral imprint, stamped into existence from an altogether different dimension.

He shrugged himself free from Bandil's supporting arm and placed the Talisman between his knees. With some difficulty he strapped the scabbard opposite his own weapon and then sheathed the gleaming sword with its scintillating crystal. As it snapped home and its diamond was covered, the abrupt shock and feeling of release was so great, it almost caused Eh'lorne to fall. But he quickly recovered his balance and then turned to Bandil with a look of concerned wonder in his eyes.

"By Mordan, that's a relief. I didn't realise that to possess power would be such a constant burden. How do you bear it?"

The old man looked surprised. "There's nothing to bear. Unless I draw on the Mystic Stone too deeply or too often it has no effect on me. To simply carry it or use it lightly is of no consequence at all."

Eh'lorne frowned. "But they're both artefacts holding one of the four founding forces. Surely they would affect their bearers in the same way."

Bandil shrugged. "I would have thought so; but then again, each one of those forces is very different, so it's not beyond the bounds of credibility that they all carry a different price."

"Then the Talisman's price is expensive indeed," Eh'lorne replied seriously. "Let's hope I don't have to draw on it too often." His face brightened. "But the feeling of strength when its power flowed through me! And the vision I had! Expensive it may be, but it's a price that I'm more than willing to pay."

"You had a vision?" the old man asked eagerly.

"Indeed I did."

"Tell me, what did you see?"

"I'll tell you as we go. Time's short and we need to travel fast." He hesitated. "Except without the Talisman's call to follow, I don't know the way." A look of consternation spread across his face. "How on earth will we find our way out?"

Bandil grinned. "We'll just retrace our steps."

Eh'lorne's eyes widened. "You remember the way?" he asked incredulously.

"Alas no, my memory's never been that good." He held up the chalky pebble he'd collected when they'd first entered the labyrinth. "But I do remember how to follow my own markers."

Eh'lorne shook his head in wonder. "Another example of your great wisdom."

"Hah!" Bandil scoffed. "Now that's a conversation you don't want to revisit." Then chuckling happily, he ignited the Mystic Stone and strode out of the chamber.

With an affectionate smile, Eh'lorne watched his ancient friend's progress along the tunnel. Then after a few moments, he hurried after the receding pool of light.

CHAPTER TWENTY-SIX

As Gildor and Rennil attempted to lift Eldore into a sitting position, he let out an involuntary scream of pain. It felt to the stricken lord as though each of his joints was filled with sharp crystals of ice, and that every one of his huge muscles was so brittle and frozen, the slightest movement would shatter them like glass. Carefully, the two soldiers lowered him back to the floor. The Arms-Master ripped off his jerkin, rolled it up, and slipped it under Eldore's head. He looked up at the shocked, bewildered faces staring down and barked out a command.

"Quickly, one of you go and fetch Aldegar. Gurd, you're the youngest; run!"

With a curt nod, the ruddy faced farming supervisor spun on his heels and dashed for the exit. But just as he reached it, the door crashed open and Hesta burst in, almost colliding with the burly councillor. Nimbly, she managed to avoid him without spilling a drop of the steaming liquid from the large pewter mug she was carrying.

"Careful!" she snapped. "And if you're going to fetch the healer don't bother, I've already sent for him. Now, out of the way."

With an indignant grunt, Gurd stood aside while she swept past and pushed her way through the councillors gathered around the prostrate Eldore. She knelt beside him and gently slid a hand under his head.

Lord Eldore, can you hear me?" she asked in a brisk, efficient voice. There was no coherent reply but she took the strangled moan to be an affirmative. "Good. I know it's difficult but I want you to try and drink some of this. Can you do that please?"

Screwing his eyes shut against the pain, Eldore obediently tried to raise his head, and with Hesta's help, he managed to let a few drops of the warm drink past his lips. He coughed and spluttered, spraying some of the clear liquid into Hesta's face, but swallowed at least some of it. With his eyes watering, he immediately tried another sip.

"What's that?" Rennil queried. "Medicine?"

"In a way. It's hot firebrew with the juice of three flame-berries. Unpleasant but potent."

And it was very unpleasant indeed. The pungent liquid scorched his mouth and burnt his throat like acid. But as the heat of it spread through his chest and down into his stomach, the frost in Eldore's flesh began to thaw and the ice in his joints to melt. Shivering uncontrollably, he nodded his gratitude and with Rennil's assistance, managed to reach a sitting position. At Hesta's insistence, and with his teeth chattering against the metal mug, he managed to swallow a few more mouthfuls. Again, he felt some improvement but his extremities remained numb with cold and his heart remained encased in the ice of despair.

Eh'lorne had been right to feel concern for his brother, for it was true, he'd shared all of his pain but none of the power. Nor had he felt the inspired sense of unassailable certainty; so the vision of the enemy's overwhelming strength, coupled with the folly of Eh'lorne's intentions, had only served to fill him with feelings of hopelessness and misery.

Rennil looked at the tall, graceful woman facing him from across the suffering lord. "He seems a little better but he's still in a bad way. I hope whoever you sent to the viltula is a fast runner."

The mention of a messenger running to the viltula reminded Eldore of poor Yewan's fate; and the guilt he felt over the boy's death drove the final spike of despair into his soul. His will to live was flickering perilously close to extinction.

But then along with the viltula came the thought of Aldegar, and that brought with it a picture of the healer's daughter, Morjeena. *His* Morjeena; his very own Delsheer. Like a shaft of sunlight on a cloudy day, his love for the pretty Keshtari girl halted the fatal descent into black misery and lit a tiny fragile flame of hope deep within him. With Eh'lorne holding the Talisman and therefore now king-designate, the council would be obliged to uphold their agreement and allow the two lovers to marry.

Of all the reasons there were to go on living and fighting, at that moment in time and above everything else, it was the only one that seemed to have any meaning. He grasped at it like a drowning man grabbing hold of a rope.

The pounding of running feet approached from down the corridor, and all eyes turned expectantly to the door. But when it flew open, instead of Aldegar – and to Eldore's delight – it was Morjeena herself. She ran flushed and breathless into the room and was quickly followed by the taller, more buxom figure of Gretya.

Hesta fixed the latter with an icy stare. "I sent you to fetch Aldegar," she scolded. "Not his daughter."

"Aye," Rennil chimed. "We need a healer, not a tender." He glared at Morjeena, barely able to conceal his contempt and hostility.

"And a healer is what you have," she retorted defiantly. "My father appointed me his equal this very morning. The second viltula is now my sole responsibility; so if you don't mind, I'd like to see my patient."

Reluctantly, Hesta shuffled aside allowing Morjeena to take her place. Gretya meanwhile stood hovering behind the small crowd, biting her lip and wringing her hands anxiously.

Swiftly and expertly, the pretty young healer carried out her examination, her face betraying an increasing puzzlement as she progressed. She turned and called to Gretya who pushed her way forward so as to be seen.

"I need you to go and find blankets. Get whatever help you need and warm each blanket in turn. As soon as each is thoroughly heated, have it brought here. Keep them coming until I say it's enough. We must get as much warmth into him as we can."

Without a word, the young maidservant was gone. Morjeena then turned to all those crowding around and spoke in a voice ringing with authority.

"Sit down and give him room to breathe. Master Rennil," she continued, ignoring the resentment disfiguring his face as surely as his terrible scar. "I need you to rub some life back into his limbs; it's imperative that we get some blood flowing back into them. Gildor, can you help him?" The lanky Prime Officer nodded and settle beside her. He took hold of Eldore's left arm and began vigorously massaging it. Rennil, still glowering resentfully, did likewise.

"What did you give him?" she asked Hesta, nodding towards the half empty mug. When Hesta explained she smiled. "Very good. That's probably the best thing you could have done. Thank you."

Hesta studied the young healer's pretty, brown features for a moment then returned the smile. "You're very welcome," she replied in a tone of genuine respect. "Would you like me to assist as well, or shall I also return to my seat?"

"As you like."

"Very well then, I'll assist. What shall I do, rub his legs?"

"That would be perfect."

Hesta nodded and crawled down to Eldore's feet, physically shoving Hevalor aside as she went. The Overseer had remained standing beside Eldore and was determined not to return to the table until he was sure that he'd recover. Swiftly Hesta removed Eldore's boots and began to pummel his calves.

"So what ails him?" the Arms-Master growled.

Morjeena frowned and shook her head. "To be honest I'm mystified but…"

"Then we should have sent for your father." Rennil interrupted, scowling accusingly.

"And he'd have told you exactly the same! If you'll allow me to finish, I recognise the *symptoms*, but how he came by them is what mystifies me."

Hesta looked up. "You've seen them before? Where; when?"

"I've seen the exact same thing in four victims. The first time was when I was newly appointed as a tender. A woman fell into the river. It was midwinter, and although she was pulled from the water, she later died. Two years after that, a young boy suffered the same fate; he also died. Last winter, two men were out hunting white hares and became caught in a sudden blizzard. All four shared the same symptoms. Only one of them survived."

"Snow fever?" Rennil asked incredulously.

Morjeena locked the hard, hazel eyes with her own soft but determined blue. "Snow fever," she replied firmly.

"Shouldn't we move him to the viltula?" Gildor asked anxiously. "The second building's not far away after all."

"N...no," Eldore managed to stutter between his chattering teeth. "N...not...time."

An anxious silence fell on the room broken only by the sound of limbs being massaged, and punctuated by Eldore's responding gasps of pain.

Eventually, there was movement at the door and Gretya re-entered the chamber. There was a faint sheen of sweat on her plain, round face, and she carried a large copper bedpan in each hand. She was closely followed by the same gangling youth that had attended Bandil a few days before. He was struggling heroically with a large pile of blankets.

"The top one's been warmed as you asked," Gretya explained. "But I thought it would be easier to wrap the others around these. It'll save running back and forth at any rate."

"Good girl," Morjeena replied approvingly.

In spite of his condition Eldore couldn't help but smile to himself; Morjeena's tone was one that a mother would use to praise a well-behaved child. Yet Gretya was the elder by more than a year. When she addressed *him* in a similar tone, however, he found it a little less amusing.

"We're going to have to undress you now; it won't be easy but I'm sure you're going to help as much as you can."

Quickly and carefully, the four helpers stripped the muscular lord, who if unable to help, at least did all he could not to hinder the process. In the meantime, Gretya placed the bedpans on the table and took the pre-warmed topmost blanket from the pile in the young lad's arms. With practiced ease she shook it open and prepared to hand it to Morjeena. As she approached, Eldore's attendants removed the last items of his clothes, and the sight of her old friend's naked body made her blush and look away.

Neither Morjeena nor Hesta suffered any such modesty, however, and took their full part in wrapping the muscular lord in the warm, fleecy covering.

As soon as the soft material enveloped him in its folds, Eldore felt as though his body was drinking in its heat as greedily as a man dying of thirst would gulp down cool, refreshing water. Beneath the blanket, he slid his hand up to the pouch of red earth and offered a brief, fervent prayer. He asked to be blessed with the correct words to relate what had to be done; and for the strength to endure the hostile reaction that would surely follow.

He looked over to where Gretya was skilfully wrapping a blanket around each of the bedpans. As she concentrated on the task, her open, friendly features were brushed by an errant wisp of hair – dark golden-blonde in the flickering torch light. It was a strange relationship that he and Eh'lorne shared with her. For a lowly servant to be such close friends with the sons of a High-Lord was unheard of – especially so in Eh'lorne's case, for the two were particularly close. And now that he was king, their relationship was going to have to change forever. Mentally, he shook his head in wonder. Sometimes, for all his self-proclaimed cleverness and sharpness of wit, his brother could be amazingly naïve.

Cora, the only other female on the council, rose to her feet and removed the remaining blankets from the struggling boy.

"Thank you," she said curtly. "We can manage now."

With an awkward half-bow, the relieved lad turned and fled the room. Corah then placed the blankets on the table beside Gretya. "The same goes for you," she said dismissively. "You can go about your normal duties."

"N...no," Eldore managed to force out. "She stays."

Corah's eyes widened in surprise while a low murmur of dissent rippled around the room; but there were no spoken arguments. So Gretya remained where she was, shuffling self-consciously from foot to foot and looking as out of place as she felt. Morjeena glanced up and her expression hardened. She knew what it was to be unwelcome and to feel that you don't belong.

"Gretya, as soon as one of those blankets is good and hot will you pass it to me please?" Deliberately, Morjeena's tone was that of a request to an equal rather than an order to a servant.

Gretya nodded and did as she was asked.

"Thank you, Corah," the healer continued coldly. "I'm sure Gretya is more than capable." The snub was obvious and intended. So, with an affronted look, Corah walked stiffly back to her seat.

With the persistent massage and a constant flow of well heated blankets, the colour slowly returned to Eldore's face and his helpless shivering began to ease. The time eventually came when with the assistance of Rennil and Gildor (and it must be said, the hindrance of Hevalor) he was able to retake his seat at the table.

For a while he sat quietly, breathing deeply and looking from one anxious and expectant face to another. He had so much to tell them that he didn't know where to start. And as much of it seemed to condemn them all to complete and utter destruction, it took all of his courage to even think about beginning his speech. In the end there was nothing for it but to take a leaf from his brother's book and plunge straight in.

"I'm sorry I gave you all such a fright," he said quietly. "I know my apparent seizure seems to have no logical reason, but I can assure that there is real meaning to what just happened.

"As most of you are aware – especially you, Gretya – Eh'lorne and I share a bond in which I'm cursed to share his pain and suffering; and that is exactly what just happened. The Talisman..."

"Don't speak of such matters in front of outsiders," Rennil interrupted with a warning look at the two unwelcome females.

"It concerns them both and that's why I've insisted that Gretya stays. Now, as I was saying, the Talisman is a dangerously powerful artefact, and when Eh'lorne touched it, I shared his terrible suffering to such an extent that it almost killed *me* as well him."

"Eh'lorne is dead?" Morjeena asked, her voice trembling with emotion.

"No!" Gretya screamed, rushing forward and crashing into the table. "He can't be; not Eh'lorne." Then sobbing uncontrollably, she sank to the floor. "I warned him," she wailed. "I told him not to go."

"It's alright Gretya, he isn't dead; he's perfectly safe. I'm so sorry, I should have chosen my words more carefully. Tilmar, help her up, will you?" With great care and consideration, the handsome councillor lifted her to her feet and chivalrously gave her his chair.

"So he's safe?" she sniffed, wiping away her tears.

"Safer than we are."

Corah, still smarting from Morjeena's insult decided it was high time to put the serving girl back in her place.

"Lord Eldore," she said with brittle formality. "Although the girl's concern for her superior is commendable, such an obviously inappropriate relationship is not. Hevalor, as moral guardian it's your duty to ensure such things do not happen. I insist that an end is brought to this improper friendship. If I understand correctly, Lord Eh'lorne is now king. Surely, if I'm right, that makes matters worse."

The Overseer looked intensely uncomfortable at the awkward position he'd been placed in, but Eldore intervened, saving him from his embarrassment.

"The honourable lady is absolutely right," he conceded, addressing the whole chamber. "The relationship *could* be perceived as immoral; she is after all, a mere servant." He glanced at Morjeena and raised a questioning eyebrow. Quick as a flash, she grasped his intention and smiled her consent.

He turned to Gretya and addressed her in a serious, officious voice. "Do you understand what I'm saying?"

She gawped at him uncomprehendingly, and with her eyes full of fear and confusion, she mutely shook her head.

"I'm telling you, that because you have the status of a mere servant, it's impossible for you to have any kind of friendship with either myself or Eh'lorne."

"But we've been friends since we were children," she cried with tears once again flowing down her cheeks. From the corner of his eye Eldore couldn't miss the self-satisfied gloating on Corah's face.

"And now that we're all adults, that friendship is improper. That's why I'm dismissing you from your position here with immediate effect. When you leave this room, you're to pack your things and leave these Halls."

"But...but where will I go?" she wailed with heartrending desolation.

Eldore's voice softened. "You'll report to the new viltula where you're to begin your new career as a tender."

Gretya's eyes widened and she gave Morjeena an enquiring look. "Really?"

"Really. We're desperately short of resourceful girls like you; so the arrangement is perfect for us both. I'm afraid your quarters will be a little basic – we've not yet finished converting the warehouse into a true viltula – but you'll start first thing tomorrow as an apprentice."

"Which means there's no reason we can't continue to be friends," Eldore declared triumphantly. "Am I right Hevalor?"

The Overseer hesitated for a moment as Corah shot him a fierce, challenging look, but he quickly regained his composure. "There's no reason at all," he declared decisively.

"Excellent. Off you go then girl, and don't worry about Freiya, I'll speak to her later."

Gretya's beautiful, characteristic smile lit up her face. "Thank you," she gushed. "Thank you both. But Mistress, who should I report to when I get there?"

"I'll tell you what, wait for me outside and when I'm finished here, we'll walk over together. That way we can get to know each other a little better. It'll also give me a chance to explain what I expect from you."

"Yes, mistress; thank you, thank you." With that she breezed out of the room, her eyes shining with joy and hope.

As soon as she was gone, however, the confident mask on Eldore's face vanished, and with an anguished sigh, he steeled himself to continue.

"At least someone's happy," Tilmar smiled as he sat down.

"Hevalor!" Corah snapped indignantly. "Are you going to allow this sleight of hand?"

"My dear lady," the Overseer replied consolingly. "Your concern for the poor girl's chastity is admirable, as is your worry over the reputations of our noble twins. But Lord Eldore has laid to rest any questions of inappropriateness. Your commendable vigilance regarding their honour is therefore satisfied. Rest assured that you have our deepest gratitude for bringing the matter to our attention." He suddenly frowned. "Unless your motives weren't as virtuous as I've read them to be."

Corah's face fell. "Of course they were," she replied indignantly. A moment later a magnanimous smile softened her features. "How could they be anything else?"

"As I thought. Lord Eldore, please continue."

For a moment or two Eldore sat motionlessly staring down at the exquisite marquetry of the ancient table. Once again, his thoughts were awhirl, but eventually, he picked up the thread of his oratory and forced a smile to his lips.

"So, my friends, there is the good news. Eh'lorne holds the Talisman of Wrath and for the first time since the fall, we have a king – or a king-designate at least. But that, unfortunately, is where the good tidings end. During our seizures, my brother and I shared a vision. An inspired revelation of a vast and terrible foe; one that is marching towards us even as I speak."

He went on to describe the army of fanatics and mercenaries sweeping across the plains of Keshtar. At the mention of archers, a shocked gasp cut the air.

"How long before they reach us?" Rennil enquired when he'd finished.

"A matter of days. Ten at the most, but probably much sooner than that."

The Arms-Master grinned savagely. "And the Talisman can be with us in in two. If it's as potent as we've been told, Limnash will suffer an even greater defeat than before!"

Eldore closed his eyes and sighed. When he opened them again, they were moist with unshed tears.

"The Talisman will not be with us," he said with quiet despair. "Eh'lorne takes another path."

"What do you mean, another path?" Rennil demanded, his deep voice resonating like thunder.

"Hornvale faces an even greater threat than we do; and he's been compelled to go to their aid."

A chorus of frightened voices rent the air but Rennil's deep, rasping boom rose above them all.

"And what of his own people?" he roared. "Without him we're doomed. Even I can't defend us against such a mighty foe; or did your vision provide instructions on how the armshost can perform such a miracle?"

Eldore hung his head and tried to shut out the outraged din assaulting his senses. At last he could put it off no longer. He swallowed hard and looked up at his accusers. He held up a hand in an appeal for silence, and eventually achieved a measure of order. Once the room was still, he forced himself to look into the Arms-Master's eyes. When he spoke, he tried to make his voice sound firm and decisive. "Yes, Master Rennil, Eh'lorne does have instructions for you. Both you and Gildor are to march your men to Hornvale. Eh'lorne will meet you there in no more than four days from tomorrow."

CHAPTER TWENTY-SEVEN

Like an island of serenity amid a raging torrent, D'harid sat quietly watching his colleagues' outraged ranting. Even Hevalor was on his feet, punctuating his furious tirade with an extended index finger. More surprisingly, Hesta's usual sophisticated grace had given way to a terrified, anarchic frenzy.

He looked further up the table to where Eldore sat huddled and diminished, his nakedness hidden only by the tightly wrapped blanket. It was obvious from his deathly pallor and broken expression that he was still suffering the effects of his seizure. Morjeena stood beside him, her arm laid protectively across his shoulders and a fierce, defiant look on her face.

With a gentle sigh, he rose from his seat and strolled nonchalantly behind Rennil and Gildor until he reached the beleaguered couple. He placed a compassionate hand on Morjeena's back and nodded to the High-Lord's chair at the head of the table. Instantly the young healer realised what was being suggested, and between them they heaved Eldore to his feet and eased him into it. Once he was settled D'harid whispered into Morjeena's ear. "Guard his eyes and mind yours as well."

She nodded and pulled Eldore's face to her breast while turning her own head away towards the doorway.

Calmly and casually, D'harid picked up the vacated chair, raised it high above his head, and with all of his might, smashed it down onto the table. As ancient and delicately decorated as the table was, it was immensely sturdy and suffered no real or significant damage. The chair, however, exploded with a loud concussive crash that sent a shower of wooden shards flying amongst the raging councillors. One particularly vicious splinter struck Gildor's face leaving a deep gash on his cheek – ironically, his only wound despite his heroics in the recent battle. He stood shocked and immobile as the blood gathered around his chin before dripping down onto his chest. Fate though, seemed to have retaliated on his behalf, for the effort of smashing the chair had reopened the cut in D'harid's neck, staining the pristine white dressing a bright scarlet.

The effect of his extraordinary violence was as immediate as it was startling. Instantly, everyone stopped as still as if they'd been turned to statues, frozen in time with their mouths open, clearly cut short in midsentence.

With his battered features unruffled and his eyes as tranquil as ever, D'harid looked slowly around at the stunned, frightened faces.

"That's better," he said softly. "In your panic you all seem to have overlooked one very important point; so if you'll permit me, I'd like to bring it to your attention."

"I do not panic," the Arms-Master growled threateningly.

"Of course not," D'harid continued seamlessly. "But both yourself and the Prime are displaying a somewhat overdeveloped sense of...concern, shall we say?"

Rennil merely grunted in reply while Gildor looked distinctly embarrassed.

"The point you've all missed is simple, and I would have thought, obvious. We have a king – admittedly uncrowned but a king nonetheless – and in his absence, Eldore sits as Lord-Regent. As his regent, Eldore speaks with all the authority of the king himself, and must be treated with the respect such a position demands. Only two people in this chamber have behaved as they should." He glanced at the splintered wood lying on the table. "And it appears that I'm not one of them. But ask yourselves this: are you? I think we all know the answer. So, if I may take the liberty, I suggest that we all sit down and continue this meeting with a little more decorum. Oh, and could someone pass along a spare seat for our comely healer," He held up the remains of the smashed chair. "This one appears to be a little worse for wear." He tossed it aside and walked carelessly back to his place.

Slowly, the shamefaced councillors sat back down while the ever-gallant Tilmar obediently brought Morjeena a chair.

"Lord Eldore," Rennil began once the room had settled. "Although I do concede that my outburst was unseemly, the fact remains that without the armshost, Sirris has no defence and every man, woman, and child is condemned to die. I therefore beg you to reconsider. Let us remain here and fight. At least then the people will have a chance, no matter how slight."

Sadly, Eldore shook his head. "I'm sorry but there's no alternative. Eh'lorne was adamant. You *will* go north and meet him at Hornvale. Besides, we'll not be without *any* defensive force. There's still the militia – and of course the conscripts. We still have a few days to whip them into shape."

"And who's going to do that? There's not a single officer I can leave behind capable of the task. And if there was, he'd still have no chance against such a fell foe."

"Be that as it may," Eldore replied in a stern, more confident voice. "I will lead them, whatever the outcome; as Regent the responsibility is mine."

"You!" the Arms-Master laughed scornfully. "With respect, my lord, you are not a soldier, you're a swordsmith. Nobody doubts your courage or resolve, but you have no military training. You can no more lead an army than I can forge a blade!"

"I'll lead them," came a quiet, calm voice from Rennil's right.

The Arms-master turned in astonishment. "D'harid?"

"I said, I'll lead them; and I'll train them too. If there's any way the people can be saved, I will save them." The calm certainty in D'harid's voice left no one in any doubt that if anybody could perform such a miracle, it was him.

Rennil studied his rough, timeworn features, peered into the deep tranquil pools of his dark eyes and smiled. "D'harid Sternhand," he said, his voice full of wonder. "For more than ten years I've waited to hear you speak thus. Welcome back to the armshost. I pronounce you Vice-Master of the host, and equal in rank to Gildor, Prime of the Guard."

D'harid gave a barely perceptible nod. "I'm honoured," he replied in a voice completely devoid of any such emotion.

Rennil pretended not to notice the lack of due respect. "When this meeting is over, I'll speak with you privately and give you your orders."

"You have no orders to give," D'harid replied evenly. "My plans for the city's defence are not your concern"

"Of course they're my concern," Rennil replied angrily. "I am the Arms-Master."

"You are a soldier," D'harid countered in his serene, level tone. "And as such your only concern is to obey your orders; and your orders are to lead your men to Hornvale. My orders are to defend the city's inhabitants. How I carry out those orders is my responsibility alone."

"By Mordan you're a contrary soul. Perhaps it's as well you never accepted promotion. You'd probably have taken my place if you'd been so minded!"

D'harid grinned. "No one could ever think to take your place, Master Rennil."

"Do you have a plan to save Sirris?" Eldore asked hopefully.

"My lord, you misunderstand me. Although I don't yet have a real plan, and have nothing more than a kernel of an idea, I do at least know that Sirris is lost; it cannot be saved. My task is to protect the people, not the city."

Eldore studied him for a moment and then nodded. "If it must be so, it must be so. If all we have left is the Refuge, then we're no worse off than our ancestors. They lived there for two centuries before building the city we know today."

He paused reflectively than addressed the whole assembly.

"So that, my friends, is it. I've told you all I can. All that remains unsolved is Murvon's prophecy. Hevalor, have you had any more thoughts on it?"

"What prophecy is this?" Morjeena asked curiously.

"One that doesn't concern the likes of you," Rennil snapped contemptuously.

"Please, I'd like to hear it. Doesn't the old proverb say that '*new ears bring new wisdom*'?"

Hesta nodded sagely. "That is the proverb; and let's all be honest, this girl's mind is far from slow."

The Arms-Master snorted derisively, but Hevalor gave him a reproving look. "I think you're a little too quick in your judgement, Master Rennil. True, the girl is not a member of the council, but that doesn't mean she has nothing to contribute."

He looked to the head of the table. "With your permission, Lord Eldore, I'm willing to recite it to her."

"Please do. We need all the help we can get."

"Very well then, it goes like this." The Overseer cleared his throat and then somewhat theatrically, began his recital.

"A bleeding sky, a freezing fire,
Then comes the time for righteous ire,
An oath's upheld from bygone age,
While hunters prowl and howl with rage.
Because the gift was lost by pride,
What once was whole must then divide,
And law must burn and be undone,
That oil and water mix as one,
To bring the world new flesh and bone,
United blood, united throne."

For a few moments the words hung heavily in the air, but then suddenly and shockingly, the mood was broken when Morjeena burst out laughing.

Rennil looked down and shook his head in disgust while Corah half rose from her chair and glared indignantly at the still chuckling young healer.

"This is not a joke!" she snapped. "It's plainly beyond your intellect so kindly keep yourself to yourself in future."

"I'm sorry," Morjeena replied trying to bring herself back under control. "But in a way it *is* a joke. Or at least very like the ones that drove me mad with frustration when I was a child. It's a valdekter."

Rennil's head snapped up and he stared at her in surprise.

"And what's that?" Corah asked derisively.

"It's a kind of riddle. Valdekter means 'backwards'. It's the language of a foreign ambassador who was once a patient at the viltula."

THE TALISMAN OF WRATH

"Tell us about him," Hesta prompted encouragingly.

"There's not much to tell. I don't know a great deal about him other than that he was very important – something to do with trade, I think. He'd fallen very ill while staying at the Duty Halls. I was only about seven or eight when he was brought in. He was so weak that he had to stay there for a whole moon.

"He was a lovely man, quite jolly once his fever subsided; and during his long convalescence, he became like a well-loved uncle to me. And he used to continually tease me with riddles – these valdekters. The joke of them is that they're unsolvable, but when you know the answer, it seems so obvious that you can't understand how you didn't get it in the first place. He had hundreds of the damned things, and by the time he left, I was beside myself with frustration. If this is one of those, it's not warning of something that's *going* to happen, but explaining it when it does."

"It's pronounced *'Varl-dekteer'*, Rennil said softly as he gazed at Morjeena with a strange, almost distant look in his eyes. It translates as 'truth in hindsight'; and the ambassador you speak of was my fa..."

He checked himself; then after a brief pause, he continued, still staring at her in the same odd way.

"He became a very dear friend of mine while I lived in Mah-Kashia; and yes, he also drove me to insanity with those infernal riddles of his. But I do believe you're right; this prophecy *is* a *varl-dekteer*, and when the time comes, Mordan's plans for us will become clear. And my lady," he added in an abnormally gentle tone.

"Yes?" she asked warily.

"Thank you."

Wordlessly, Morjeena opened and closed her mouth, unsure of how to respond to Rennil's strange new warmth towards her.

Eldore breathed a sigh of relief. "That's that taken care of then. If everyone's agreed, that concludes the main business of the council and I can get some rest. I'm afraid the seizure and the vision have left me rather exhausted. I would like to address one last thing though.

"It was agreed by this council that should Eh'lorne be successful in his quest, I would have the right to marry Morjeena. Do I take it this agreement still stands?" A murmur of consent rippled around the table, and although some of it was noticeably reluctant, there was no real dissent from anyone.

"Good. Hevalor, if you'd be good enough to perform the ceremony later this evening, we'd be more than grateful."

The Overseer looked shocked. "But Lord Eldore, this is too soon. There are preparations to be made, official announcements to be posted. Convention states that a forthcoming marriage of the royal bloodline should be declared at least one full moon before the event – preferably two. Surely you can't be serious?"

"Very serious indeed."

Corah, unable to contain her resentment any longer jumped furiously to her feet.

"This has gone too far!" she shouted, her voice reaching a near hysterical crescendo. She pointed an accusing finger at Morjeena who was sitting looking up at her, perplexed and stunned. "It's not enough that you want to marry an Arlien noble, but now you want to do it in a cheap, sordid charade. You're nothing but...but... Nothing but a Keshtari peasant!" she finally spat.

Morjeena flinched as though she'd been slapped in the face, and while most in the chamber displayed varying degrees of shocked anger, Tarth, the quiet and unassuming cooper glared at Corah and shouted, "Shame on you!"

To the casual observer, D'harid betrayed not a trace emotion as he rocked his chair nonchalantly back on two legs. However, closer scrutiny would have revealed a minute tightening of his jaw and a slight narrowing of his eyes.

THE TALISMAN OF WRATH

But there was nothing subtle or slight about Rennil's reaction. His chair clattered across the room as he exploded to his feet and drew his sword. He pointed it threateningly at Corah's throat as once again the room became deathly still.

When the Arms-Master spoke, the subterranean rumble of his voice was quiet and menacing. "You will take back that insult and grovel at my lady's feet," he growled. No one had ever seen Rennil act with such terrifyingly controlled fury.

Instantly, Corah's anger vanished to be replaced by horrified, abject terror. "You'd stoop to threaten a lady so?" she asked shakily, ashen faced and trembling.

"Do not think you can hide behind your skirts after making such a monstrous slander; and neither should you dare to call yourself a lady. But believe me, madam, were you a man I would not now be acting with such restraint. Now apologise and beg for forgiveness."

"I...I'm sorry."

"Not to me, to the Lady Morjeena."

"I'm sorry my dear, I meant no harm. Please forgive me." Tears of anguish were now coursing freely down her cheeks and her eyes were filled with desperate pleading.

"Of course. I... erm... Rennil is this really necessary?"

"My lady it is. Never while I live and breathe will I allow anyone to give you such slight or slander. That must be made plain."

Morjeena stood up and gently pressed the Arms-Mater's blade down to the table. "It *is* understood and I forgive *Lady* Corah completely."

Rennil looked into the diminutive healer's blue eyes – startlingly bright against her dusky brown skin – then bowed his head. "As you wish." He sheathed his sword but remained standing with his arms folded, glaring at the unfortunate woman across the table.

The whole assembly gawped at him, unable to comprehend the sudden and complete change in his attitude. He'd gone from scornful mistrust to deep and unquestionable loyalty in the blink of an eye. Of all the things they'd seen and heard that day, nothing had caused such bewildered and confused expressions to appear on their faces.

All faces that is, save one. D'harid still sat with his chair rocking back on two legs; but his eyes, now placid again, also carried a faint look of mild amusement.

"I hope I'm invited to the wedding," he said brightly. "I've nothing else planned for this evening."

CHAPTER TWENTY-EIGHT

The further they travelled from the bright, supernatural cavern, the less its effect distorted the two travellers' perception of time and distance. Within little more than a stretch, the full weight of their recent exertions crashed down on them as the power that had buoyed them up finally vanished completely. It was bad enough for Bandil but at least he had the Mystic Stone to draw upon; whereas Eh'lorne had nothing but his resolve. And prodigious as his determination was, it wasn't enough to overcome the overwhelming consequences of his exhausting trial. He was soon staggering along like a drunkard on a dark night. When at last he tripped and fell, his pitiful attempts to regain his feet made it obvious they could no longer continue.

"I didn't realise we'd come so far from the entrance," Eh'lorne groaned bitterly as he sat propped against the tunnel wall. "It seemed barely a few moments from entering the labyrinth to reaching the Talisman."

"To you maybe, but I assure you it was a great deal longer than that. We entered the tunnels in the afternoon, I'd guess at what your people call the 'fifth turn of the time-glass'. Although it's hard to be sure, by my reckoning we used up another half-turn at least before we reached the cavern."

"As long as that?" Eh'lorne asked, his eyes wide with surprise. He rested his head back against the wall and sighed. "Then it's no wonder I'm tired. It must be gone sixth turn and we've not stopped all day. And that first touch of the Talisman drained me more than I'd have believed possible."

He suddenly sat bolt-upright. "If your calculation is correct, it should have been dark when I had my vision."

"Which you still haven't describe to me."

"No, I haven't, have I. Well let me describe it to you now and perhaps you can explain the discrepancy."

He went on to tell the old man of his rise through the mountain, the clarity of his sight, and the enemy hordes sweeping towards Sirris and Hornvale. As he spoke Bandil sat with his eyes closed, stroking his beard and muttering the occasional, "I see," or "Go on." When Eh'lorne told him of their new destination, however, his eyes flicked open and he fixed his companion with an intense, penetrating look.

"This is a perverse road to take," he said warily. "Are you certain of it?"

"Absolutely," Eh'lorne replied firmly. Then after a momentary pause added, "Or at least I was."

"Was? What makes you doubt yourself now?"

"Firstly, because the path *is* so perverse."

"That's understandable but no reason to lose faith. And secondly?"

"As I say, the discrepancy in time. When I was looking down on myself, I was in the 'here and now', yet when I surveyed the world just moments later it was mid-afternoon. By your reckoning it should have been well past sundown. So, unless the sun moved backwards across the sky, we've either been under the mountain all night and most of the next day, or I wasn't seeing what was there at that moment in time. I can't believe so much time has passed, so the vision must therefore have been unreal. If that is so, how can I trust it?"

Bandil shook his head in exasperated wonder. "Eh'lorne Starbrow, for all your quick wit you haven't a tenth of your brother's capacity to reason. Consider this: when the Talisman's power flowed through you, you were gifted with Mordan's spirit. He elevated you with it and he spoke to you with it. Now, however, you examine what you saw with you own mind – your own *mortal* mind with all its frailties and imperfections. Tell me, who is the more reliable source of wisdom, you or the great god himself?"

"Mordan obviously; although I resent your assertion that I'm in any way inferior to Eldore!"

"I thought you might; but putting that aside, why do you think you were shown your body? Could it be specifically to establish that you *were* in the present and not in the future or the past?"

"That would make sense; but then how do you account for the time of day being so out of kilter?"

"You yourself said that there are only two possible explanations; and we've already discounted one, so that leaves us with the answer: it took far longer to reach the Talisman than we thought possible."

Eh'lorne sighed. "Then that would also explain why my stomach's grumbling like a nagging wife. If I'd have known, I would have brought my pack; at least then we could have a meal."

"Your stomach's not the only thing that's grumbling too much. A belt can be tightened, but we need to rest. So stop complaining, have a sip of firebrew, and get some sleep!"

Muttering bitterly that he'd never be able to sleep on the cold, hard ground without so much as a blanket, Eh'lorne took a long pull from one of Bandil's flasks and then stretched out on the smooth rock of the tunnel floor. Immediately, he fell into a deep slumber.

Bandil looked across at him and smiled. "Goodnight my young king," he said softly. Then after extinguishing the Stone, he joined his companion and almost as quickly, drifted off into the dark velvet of his dreams.

* * *

Eh'lorne awoke to find Bandil standing over him wearing a broad grin on his wrinkled, dusky face. His blue-grey eyes were twinkling merrily in the Stone's bright, milky-white light.

"Good morning!" the old man chirped in a bright, singsong voice.

"How do you know it's morning?" Eh'lorne replied grumpily, rubbing the sleep from his eyes.

"Because whatever the time of day outside, in here it's breakfast time, and breakfast time means morning."

"If we had any breakfast, I'd be more inclined to agree with you."

"Oh, but we do."

"What?" Eh'lorne demanded, rapidly rising into a sitting position.

Bandil pointed to a large pile of flat, brown and black mushrooms. "You see, Mordan has provided. He has done so for me ever since I awoke in the Mystic Mountains."

"Where on earth did you find them?"

THE TALISMAN OF WRATH

"They were growing all around us from the very walls. I simply picked them. Try one, they're quite delicious."

Eh'lorne took one and sniffed it warily. "Are they safe?"

"Of course they are," Bandil replied sinking to the floor and picking out a particularly plump mushroom. He took a large bite and closed his eyes in appreciation.

Eh'lorne watched him for a moment then shrugged and took a large mouthful himself. The old man was right; it was delicious. It had a firm, meaty texture and an earthy, fragrant taste. Greedily he finished it off and took another, then another.

"I see breakfast meets with your approval," the old man chuckled.

"Indeed it does. At least I'll not waste away before we can retrieve our supplies."

"Perish the thought. Speaking of which, I think we should make a start. After all, we've no idea how far we need to go before we reach the entrance."

Eh'lorne nodded and climbed to his feet. He gathered up a handful of the remaining mushrooms and carefully stuffed them inside his tunic.

"Lead on then, old man; the weight of the rock above us oppresses me, and I long to breathe fresh air once more."

So on they went, following the chalky marks Bandil had left at each fork or junction in the long, twisting and bewildering maze. At first they were hardly aware they were climbing, but gradually the gradient became more acute and their pace began to slow. Once again, they began to tire until eventually, they had to concede that they'd need to sleep once more.

"Can we really say that we've spent another day down here?" Eh'lorne asked incredulously. "Surely, we must be going around in circles."

"Have no fear, we're on the right path; but it does seem beyond comprehension that it's taking so long."

"Aye, it's a strange place alright. And have you noticed that there's no echo down here?"

"A long time ago. In any other place it would be terrifying, but here..." The old man left the sentence hanging poignantly.

Eh'lorne grunted and lay himself down. "Terrifying or not, let's pray that we find the exit soon after we wake. I gave instructions for Rennil to meet us at Hornvale in four days from when I touched the Talisman and it'll take us at least that to get there from where we entered. We're going to be late as it is. Much longer in these tunnels and we'll be too late."

And find the exit they did, but not soon after they awoke. In fact, they were forced to spend what seemed another whole day trudging relentlessly up the disorientating myriad of twists and turns.

They'd been greeted by another crop of mushrooms, which although they ate just as gratefully, had by now become a somewhat monotonous diet. It did sustain them however, and even seemed to give them an energy beyond their natural means. Because of that they managed to keep plodding on not stopping once until at the end of another 'day', they emerged into the vast echoing cavern that marked the end of their ordeal.

Eh'lorne gave a whoop of delight and rushed off to find his pack, but as the impetuous young warrior disappeared into the gloom, Bandil heard a muffled crash along with a sharp cry of pain. He hurried after his friend and found him lying face down on the ground, cursing in a most ignoble manner.

"Are you alright? What happened?" he asked anxiously.

"I tripped!" Eh'lorne snapped back. He rolled around to see the cause of his misfortune and the anger immediately vanished from his grime smeared face.

"My pack," he declared brightly. "I tripped over my own pack. Now we can have real food as well as firebrew. Luxury!"

Bandil burst out laughing. He laughed so hard that tears ran down his cheeks leaving smudged tracks that were ploughed by the deep, ancient wrinkles.

"And what, pray, is so funny?" Eh'lorne demanded seriously.

"Oh my, oh my," the old man wheezed, clutching at his aching sides.

"Well?"

"I'm sorry," Bandil replied, struggling to get himself back under control. "But it's just too perfect. The fate of the world rests in the hands of a warrior so adept in his craft that he's brought to his knees by a carelessly placed bag; a king so resolute that any thoughts of duty are cast aside in preference for a full belly!"

Eh'lorne's eyes narrowed and his cheeks flushed angrily, but the withering look he shot the old man only provoked more gales of wild laughter. Gradually, the infectiousness of Bandil's mirth caused the young king's face to soften and then to split into a broad grin.

"I'm glad I've managed to entertain you, but be careful you don't laugh too hard, you might hurt yourself; and I'd hate to have your injury on my conscience." He held out his hand. "Here; be useful and help me up."

Still laughing heartily, Bandil grabbed his companion's hand and heaved him to his feet. "Oh, my friend," he chuckled, wiping away the tears and smearing the dirt even further across his gaunt face. "Since the day we first met I've marvelled at your lithe agility, but the sight of you sprawled there with all the grace of a drunken ox? Oh, it's a memory I'll treasure for all eternity."

"Then remember it and take pleasure in it with my blessing," Eh'lorne said with a smile. "But speak of it to anyone and you'll feel my displeasure." He scooped up the pack, slapped his friend on the shoulder, and strode off towards the exit on the far side of the massive cave. Still grinning widely, Bandil followed on, holding the Stone high so as to better light their way.

When they finally squeezed through the narrow exit, they emerged to find that it was late in the day and the sickly red light was fast fading into a dark, chill night. For some time, they stood quietly, breathing deeply and savouring the cool breeze that was ruffling their lank, dusty hair. It was obvious that they'd be unable to continue before morning, so they re-entered the cavern to shelter for the night. They ate and drank their fill, wrapped themselves in their warm blankets, and settled into a fitful, restive sleep, unaware that it was a full three days since they'd first entered the labyrinth.

CHAPTER TWENTY-NINE

They left the cave at first light, sliding down the precarious, scree-scattered slope in the dim red glow of dawn. The lack of light made the descent a great deal more hazardous than they'd expected; but where Bandil repeatedly and painfully fell back onto his rump, Eh'lorne somehow managed to descend serenely and gracefully as if he were performing a carefully choreographed and well-rehearsed dance. When they reached the bottom, they turned to their right and began to make their way northward. They'd taken no more than a dozen paces however, when Bandil suddenly cried out, "Wait!"

Eh'lorne turned to him and raised a questioning eyebrow. "What is it, have we forgotten something?"

"They're gone," the old man replied urgently. "Vanished."

"What have?"

"The sellufin. Their bodies have disappeared. Something or someone has removed them."

Eh'lorne scanned the area where the cadavers had lain when they'd entered the tunnels. "So they have," he said indifferently. "I can't say that I'm surprised. There's a lot of carrion in these mountains and it wouldn't take long for the buzzards to find them – not to mention foxes and wolves. I'd be far more surprised to find them undisturbed."

"Undisturbed is one thing, but for every last trace of them to disappear is not natural – especially as there were so many. No, they must have been deliberately removed. We must search for the remains of the staff. If that's also missing it'll be proof of the fact and will warn us of the danger we'll be facing."

"The young warrior shrugged. "Why should we care? We know there's danger to be faced and that'll not change whether we find the staff or not. And besides, we've no time to spare. As it is, we may be too late. So come my friend, leave this puzzle and we'll confront our fate as *it* confronts *us*."

The old man cast a regretful eye behind them and then with a nod of consent, he reluctantly followed his companion's lead.

They travelled due north in order to avoid the precipitous edge of the snowfield, and had gone little more than a stretch or so when they came upon what appeared to be the remains of a large bonfire. Cautiously, they approached it, warily watching every rock and shrub that could conceal a hostile presence. On closer inspection it became clear that it wasn't just a bonfire, but was instead a huge funeral pyre.

"Well at least we know where the bodies went," Eh'lorne stated brightly.

"But who carried them here and who set the flame? And more to the point, where are they now?"

Eh'lorne stretched out a hand towards the charred, twisted pile that were once bodies.

"Whoever they are they can't be too far away; it's still hot. Let's hope we don't meet them; we can't afford the delay."

The two men continued on their way, both of them taut with anxiety, half expecting to be ambushed with every step they took. Thankfully, the lay of the land made such a surprise attack unlikely. The terrain was relatively flat with mostly low, sparse scrub and only a very few large rocks that could conceal an ambush.

At around midday, they altered course, swinging more to the west until they came upon the chasm that had so confounded then a march or so to the south. Although here it was a less daunting obstacle, it was still wide enough to bar their way.

"This is awkward again," Eh'lorne commented dryly. "I didn't notice it in my vision so now I'm going to have to rethink our course. Unless perhaps we can find a crossing point further along."

"Well it's certainly not as wide or as deep," Bandil said hopefully as he peered over the edge. "Perhaps it'll continue to diminish as we go."

"Perhaps. It does slow us down again though. We need to head northwest and the longer we go due north, the more we're delayed."

"At least the going looks easy enough."

"For now. This side of the fissure soon turns to steep hills and deep valleys; they'll be hard to negotiate and will slow us down even further. But let's stay positive and hope we can cross soon."

Bandil smiled and laid a hand on his companion's shoulder. "I'll pray for it," he said cheerfully.

As Eh'lorne had predicted, the going soon became far more difficult and did indeed change from flat scrubland to steeply undulating hills and valleys. It also became impossible to keep to the chasm's edge, and they found themselves forced to travel even further to the east.

S. P. MUIR

It was as they were scrambling up one particularly steep slope that Bandil noticed a strange confluence in the sky almost directly over their heads. The blood-red clouds were starting to flow together and swirl in a disturbing, circular motion. With mounting apprehension they watched the building vortex, puzzled as to its cause until they crested the rise. There, Eh'lorne suddenly threw himself to the ground, dragging the old man with him. Bandil gave a sharp cry of pain and surprise as he was flung to the ground so hard, it knocked the breath from his body.

"Shush!" Eh'lorne hissed urgently. "We're not alone. Now carefully, take a look below."

After a pause to compose himself, Bandil crawled up to the summit and peered over the edge. The ground sloped down for less than a hundred strides before levelling off into a wide, flat, valley floor. There, little more than a good stone's throw away, a group of fifty or so lich were gathered in a circle around three sellufs. The small, grotesque trio were standing in a triangular formation with the foremost of the creatures holding something in each of his outstretched hands. The remaining two sellufs stood behind him with one hand on each of his shoulders and their free hands stretched up towards the seething sky. The gentle breeze carried the creatures' faint chanting across to where the two companions were lying prone in the dirt just a matter of strides away.

"What are they doing?" Eh'lorne asked as he crawled alongside the ancient theurgist.

"Nothing good; of that we can be sure. But exactly what mischief they are performing, I can't quite see." The old man screwed up his eyes and peered intently at the three sellufs. Suddenly, he stiffened. "Mordan preserve us," he breathed. "They're remaking the black staff!"

It was true. The lead selluf was holding the two broken halves of the ebony rod and was slowly bringing the fractured

THE TALISMAN OF WRATH

ends together. The closer they came, the faster the vortex in the clouds spun and the more the air became charged with a terrifying energy; an energy that gave the two companions goose-bumps all over their bodies.

"We must stop them," Bandil hissed urgently. "But I need a few moments to raise the power of the Stone. Give thanks that there's just three of them as who knows what strength they're drawing from the blood-sky."

"Then be quick, time is short."

Bandil slithered away from the skyline and rose to his knees. He took out the Mystic Stone, gripped it firmly between his hands and began to chant.

Eh'lorne looked around at him sharply; never before had he heard the old man use such a harsh tone. The very sound of it made his blood run cold – it certainly boded ill for their unsuspecting enemies.

He returned his attention to the events in the vale. When the two pieces of the staff finally came together, everything changed. With a blinding scarlet flash and a deafening thunderclap, rain as red and as thick as blood began to poor from the sky. The whirling vortex funnelled down in a miniature tornado until it reached the trio of sellufin. As soon as it touched the upraised hands of the two hindmost creatures, the staff burst into life. It burned with tongues of red flame, crackling and sparking with power as the two halves melded into one.

"We can't wait!" Eh'lorne cried, jumping to his feet. "Follow me."

Before Bandil could stop him, he was gone, storming down the blood-lashed hillside with his sword flashing in his hand.

"No!" the old man shouted after him. "I need time to harmonise the Stone with the Talisman." But it was far too late; his impetuous friend's charge had taken him far beyond the point of no return.

"Damn fool!" he snapped angrily as he jumped to feet. He was not even close to being ready, and would need more time to be of even a little help. He took a deep breath and continued his incantation.

Eh'lorne had now reached his quarry, and leaping high into the air, he fell upon them like a bolt from the blue. "*MORDAN!*" he roared as he sliced through the startled lich, scattering them in confusion as he cut his way towards the sellufin.

But now the staff was whole, and while the two sellufs continued to draw power from the sky, their leader pointed it at the charging warrior and uttered a single guttural word of command. The flickering, sanguineous flames gathered for a moment, then burst from the staff's tip, striking Eh'lorne full in the chest. The force from the puissant shaft sent the sword spinning from his hand and threw him violently backwards, pinning him to the ground. He lay on his back, paralysed by the crimson flames that were ravaging his body. Although his eyes were open, he was blinded by the torrential blood-rain that was turning his white shastin tunic bright red. Glutinous puddles were forming around him and beginning to run across the valley in tiny rivulets.

Fortunately for the helpless warrior, the embattled lich were so terrified of the staff's emanation that they backed away and were more likely to turn and run than to deliver a mortal blow. Even so, Eh'lorne had but moments left to live.

But then Bandil appeared. He came sprinting down the slope, splashing through the slick puddles and looking for all the world like a crazed, gore-soaked barbarian. He held the shining Stone in his right hand and his hunting knife in his left. He'd not had time to build the crescendo of power he needed to counter the sellufin, but neither could he sit back while Eh'lorne's life was scorched into extinction.

"*Mordarnish-carr!*" he roared as he approached his stricken friend. The Stone flashed with a dazzling, silver-white light that

THE TALISMAN OF WRATH

scattered the lich but had little effect on the sellufin. It did, however, cause the briefest moment of distraction; the tiniest instant of hesitation in the flow of power from the staff's tip. The interruption of its energy was almost imperceptible but was enough to save the life of his companion.

Taking advantage of the fractional pause and using every last atom of his strength, Eh'lorne managed to close his hand around the lupine hilt of the Talisman. The feel of the wolf's-head pommel beneath his fingers seemed to give his arm enough impetus to draw the potent artefact. At first it was no more than a minute movement, but as a tiny sliver of blade became visible, its cold fury coursed through his veins giving him the strength to expose some more of the shining sword. Once the crystal itself was revealed, the full force of its power raged through him and he whipped the rest of the blade clear with a mighty flourish. Although still forced to the ground by the sheer weight of the sellufin's beam, he was no longer being ravaged by it. With a huge effort, he managed to raise himself onto one elbow.

The sickly clouds overhead boiled more widely and whirled more violently as the two hindmost sellufs desperately drew more and more power from the evil sky. But it seemed that the more they tried to crush their foe, the stronger he became. Slowly he gained his knees, then his feet, until at last he stood, leaning forward and resting against the crimson beam. His face was a grotesque, blood-soaked grimace of rage.

To Bandil, standing no more than ten strides away, it seemed as though the air was about to burst and rupture the very fabric of existence. The valley became so charged with energy that his blood-rain soaked hair was standing on end, and his skin pricked painfully as though he was being stung by a whole nest of hornets. He had to use all the Mystic Stone's power just to remain standing and sane. The fleeing lich had yet to escape the valley and were rolling in the puddles, screaming in agony.

Suddenly, the ground beneath the old man's feet bucked wildly as behind them, hidden above the thick clouds, the towering pinnacle of Mordan's Finger exploded into a terrifying volcano. But where a volcano erupts with ash and magma, the sacred peak spewed out cold white flames of unbridled fury. Silver lightning spread through the clouds as far as the eye could see; and wherever the bolts touched the clouds, they simply evaporated revealing a clear blue sky.

When the shockwave hit, the intensity of it threw the old man to the ground where he lay winded and ravaged by the cold. The blood in his hair and clothes turned instantly to ice, while all around the valley the last of the raindrops were frozen into twinkling rubies that tinkled melodiously as they fell to the red-frosted ground. Of all those in the valley, only Eh'lorne kept his footing. He stood like a statue with the Talisman of Wrath thrust high into the air, and his grimace transformed to an even more grotesque, savage grin.

As the terrible power eased and the mountain's roar quietened to a deep and distant rumble, the old man struggled to his feet and surveyed the aftermath of the titanic struggle. The lich were all dead, so deeply frozen that many of them had simply shattered like glass, while the three sellufin lay in a huddled heap, their staff smashed into a thousand splinters. Unsteadily he walked over to his motionless companion and laid a gentle hand on his shoulder.

"Relax, my friend," he said quietly. "It's all over. The Talisman called and the mountain answered. Look around you; the sun shines and the sky is blue from horizon to horizon. You've declared yourself to the world and Limnash now knows that the heir to throne has arisen. The Talisman of Wrath has been claimed and all his plans are now in jeopardy; we have a victory."

Slowly, Eh'lorne turned to look at him and the savage wildness left his face. With a nod and a tenuous smile, the young warrior-king sheathed the Talisman then retrieved his own sword from where he'd dropped it.

Bandil drew a deep breath and grinned; it was indeed a great victory. Perhaps now Limnash would think again and recall his dread armies. Star or not, in these Sacred Hills the Talisman's power was overwhelming – even more so than he'd dared to hope. So surely the sorcerer king would realise that he couldn't win here. Unfortunately, they had no way of knowing whether Sirris or Hornvale were now safe – unless of course Mordan were to give either of them a vision. He considered it for a moment then grunted. Yes, he was sure they'd soon receive a sign of some kind.

He was brought back to reality by a low gurgling moan from behind. He spun around to discover that the lead selluf was still alive and was struggling to raise its head from the ground. He called to Eh'lorne and hurried over to the stricken creature with the tall Arlien following behind. To Eh'lorne's amazement, the old man knelt beside the selluf and gently placed its head in his lap. It tried to speak but instead broke into a gasping, rattling cough that brought dark, blackish-red blood frothing to its lips.

"Easy now," Bandil said softly. "Your lungs are ruptured so breathe lightly and stay still; I'll do what I can to ease your pain."

The creature looked gratefully up into the old man's face but then its large sad eyes widened in surprise.

"You?" it croaked.

Bandil frowned. "You know me?"

"The missing prince. My sect sought you for many years until we were certain you were dead."

"And yet here I am," the old man smiled.

The selluf began to cough again, its entire body convulsing painfully.

Eh'lorne stared at the selluf distastefully. "You pity this filth?" he asked coldly.

Bandil ignored him and continued speaking to the strange looking, child-like creature. "So, you know who I am; that is good; but tell me *your* name and why you sought me with such determination for so many years."

"My name is Mylock, master servant of the Black Staff. We sought you so that we might kill you and put an end to the Keshtari royal line." It broke into another fit of coughing causing a fresh flow of blood to bubble from its mouth.

"Then it's as well you failed or I wouldn't be here to help you now. As it is, I can't save your life but I can at least take away your pain and ease your passing."

Mylock tried to shake his head. "No prince, withhold your mercy. I'll take my pain as penance for the murder of your parents and your brother. And for those descendants that we tracked down over the years."

Bandil looked puzzled. "You must be mistaken for I had no living brother; he died when I was a small child not long after he was born. He was frail and weak and certainly not a victim of murder."

"There is no mistake. You were not the only escapee from Arl before it fell. Your mother also fled the city and when she did, she was with child – your brother."

Bandil's expression hardened slightly. "And what happened to them?"

"Your mother..." Again, the dying selluf was wracked by coughing, this time each gurgling gasp becoming weaker than the last. So pitiable was the creature's distress that the old man couldn't help but feel compassion, in spite of the terrible tale it was telling.

"Gently, Mylock, gently," he said softly as he cradled the selluf in his lap. "Go on when you're ready."

Behind him, Eh'lorne snorted with disgust.

Eventually, the selluf grew still again and lay so motionless that it appeared to have passed away. But then its eyes flicked open and after a few shallow, wavering breaths, it continued its story.

"Your mother was found several years later and at my master's behest, was slain. Your brother escaped and was taken in by another family who brought him up as their own. He went on to have children of his own before he too was tracked down and killed. It took many decades to trace every one of his descendants but eventually, all were found and sent to their graves."

"All murdered," Bandil sighed, shaking his head in sad disbelief.

"All of them. I myself tracked down the last survivor to a village close to the foothills of these very mountains. She got word of me as I entered the village and fled into the night. She climbed into the foothills where she perished."

"You found her body?"

"No, not even we were strong enough to enter these Sacred Hills at that time. But as it was deep winter and she was wearing nothing but her night clothes, I had no need to find her. She was also heavily pregnant, so how far could she get in the snow? No, prince, I'm ashamed to say that she couldn't have lasted to see the dawn."

"I'll wager she lasted longer than that!" Eh'lorne laughed scornfully. Bandil appeared not to hear him.

"Nevertheless, Mylock, no matter what crimes you've committed under the evil one's influence, you're of a noble race once greatly favoured by Mordan himself. I will give you mercy."

"No, I don't need your kindness, I have my own contentment to help me bear the pain"

"Contentment?"

"Contentment." Mylock reached out and reverently stroked the Mystic Stone then pointedly looked over at the sheathed Talisman. "I die in the knowledge..."

This time the cough was little more than a weak, choking gurgle that left the creature hanging onto life by only the narrowest of threads. When finally it was able to continue, its voice was nothing more than a croaking whisper. "I die in the knowledge that I'm the only one in all creation to have seen all four of the founding forces."

"Then you're fortunate indeed," Bandil conceded. Suddenly, his eyes widened with horror.

"Four?" he cried, furiously shaking the stricken selluf. "It can't be four; you mean three. Tell me you mean three. Tell me!"

But it was too late. With a final rattling sigh, the creature's soft, sad eyes glazed over and its tiny child-like body went limp.

For some time, the old man sat in silence staring down at the dead creature. His mind was awhirl and his body was trembling. Then he gently lowered the selluf to the ground and climbed unsteadily to his feet.

Eh'lorne laughed and slapped Bandil's shoulder. "Cheer up old man, you won't believe the irony of the accursed creature's failure..." He stopped short as he caught sight of the old man's expression.

"What's wrong?" he asked cautiously.

Bandil looked at him, his perilous blue-grey eyes clouded with fear.

"Spite!" he said in a voice laden with dread.

CHAPTER THIRTY

The remains of the armshost stood stiffly to attention on the northern bank of the High River. The sickly midmorning light was staining their hauberks and polished helms a ghastly shade of red. It was as if every last man had been dipped in a vast vat of blood, but Rennil did his best to ignore the ominous portent. He walked along their ranks and inspected their readiness for the rigorous trials that lay ahead. He couldn't help feeling a huge sense of pride in the men under his command – and there was no doubt that they were *his* men, for he'd planned and built this army himself.

Before his return from Mah-Kashia, the Arlien forces had been nothing more than a handful of regulars and a hundred or so militiamen whose main purpose was to patrol the hills and scare away any trespassers. True, they were capable of thwarting the fierce bandits who were sometimes foolish enough to venture into the mountains, but the terrible battles he'd fought against the Screaming Nomads of the south had opened his eyes to the realities of war. When he'd finally come home to Sirris, he'd felt the need to create a force capable of defending the city from such formidable adversaries. More than that, he'd felt as though he was being *driven*. It was as if some outside influence was compelling him to do it, while leaving him with no choice in the matter.

Of course, it hadn't been easy at first as there'd been a great deal of opposition. High-Lord Larryl himself, although not exactly hostile to the proposal had certainly not been enthusiastic. His belief that since the fall, the Arlien people had no right to fight wars meant he was constantly trying to impose restrictions on Rennil's bold ideas. After his untimely death however, his son had taken the Seat of Duty, and Lorne had very much shared Rennil's visionary concerns. The resulting force, although still small, was perhaps the most disciplined and highly trained army the world had yet seen.

The Arms-Master's persistence had been vindicated a few years later when several of the nomadic eastern tribes had banded together and had marched on the young settlement of Sarren. An intangible feeling of deep unease had been growing in Rennil's heart which had caused him to send out an intricate network of patrols; one of which had spotted the approaching danger. The Arms-Master had learned the Screaming Nomad's trick of using mirrors to send messages, and by this means the alarm had been relayed back to the city almost instantly. That warning had enabled Rennil to lead his men south in good time to intercept the incursion. The victory had been total and emphatic, reinforcing the fear and superstition that had helped keep the outside world at bay. The Arms-Master had suddenly found himself elevated to the status of a living legend. Never

THE TALISMAN OF WRATH

before had the exiled Arlien people felt so safe; never before had their existence been so secure. But now?

Just nine days ago the armshost had numbered twelve hundred men, but now half of those were either dead or severely injured. He was left with just six hundred warriors to face an army that numbered scores of thousands; and every one of those six hundred already carried some kind of injurious token of battle. Despite that however, all of them to a man stood solidly resolute; confident in both themselves and their leader.

A little apart from the main body of men, Gildor was waiting patiently at the head of the Lord-Guard. The small elite force had been ready to move for some time, proud of the speed and efficiency of their preparations. Only thirty of the original fifty men were truly fit for battle, but five of the more seriously wounded had also reported for duty that morning.

"You're supposed to be convalescing," Gildor had growled.

"Yes Prime!" the five had snapped in unison.

He'd eyed them thoughtfully. "You realise that if you fall behind, you'll be left behind."

"Yes Prime!"

Unable to deny such dedication he'd shrugged and reluctantly allowed them to take their place. Secretly, he'd felt a stinging pang of guilt. These five men had risen from their sickbeds and shrugged off their wounds while he alone stood unhurt and unmarked. At least the deep cut in his cheek – courtesy of D'harid's dramatics – mitigated that appearance slightly.

At last Rennil was satisfied, and catching Gildor's eye, he indicated that the Lord-Guard should lead the way.

With a sharp, "Guard ho!" Gildor's men marched off, accompanied by much clapping and cheering from the small crowd of mainly women and children who had come to watch. Inwardly, Rennil grimaced. If they knew our destination, he thought grimly, they wouldn't be quite so enthusiastic.

Seamlessly, the armshost fell in behind the Lord-Guard, and the tiny but potent army marched along the bankside path before climbing the winding road that Eh'lorne and Bandil had used when they'd set out on their quest. Instead of following their predecessors, however, Rennil's men immediately turned to the left and onto the rough, broken moorland that the trodden road avoided. Although the normal path added a fair distance to the journey, this shorter route was arguably more time consuming and definitely more exhausting. However, both Rennil and Gildor were certain that the well trained, hardened warriors of the host would make nothing of the moorland's hardships, and could travel just as quickly without a smooth road to follow.

"Rough-march!" bellowed one of the eight remaining division officers out of the original twenty low-ranked officer corp. This man had been designated as pacesetter; and as that name implied, he was responsible for ensuring that the host's momentum remained steady. With hardly a break in step, the men separated into informal and haphazard-looking small groups that were in fact a well-practised and proven method of moving a large body of men across rough ground as quickly as possible.

Rennil caught up with Gildor and slapped his lanky second in command on the back.

"Well, Prime," he said with a rare cheer in his rumbling voice. "We're on our way. When Eh'lorne gave us four days to reach Hornvale, I'll wager he didn't reckon on us being ready to move the very next morning."

"Aye, and with fair chance we should be there by the morning of the third day. That'll give us time to prepare a few surprises of our own before our royal lord arrives to take all the glory."

"It will indeed." A mischievous twinkle appeared in the Arms-Master's eye. "But just imagine, if we could make it before noon on the *second* day, we could set our defences and

THE TALISMAN OF WRATH

then kick our heels and rest before the battle starts. What do you say, Prime, are you up for the game?"

Gildor thought for a moment and then grinned. "I am, but are you? I know the Lord-Guard are up to the challenge but whether your slovenly crew can keep up with us remains to be seen."

Rennil laughed scornfully then called to the pacesetter.

"Master?" the division office responded questioningly.

"Speed-march, four hundred both."

"Yes master!" The pacesetter turned, and trotting backwards, he called out the new instructions in a clear, loud voice. "Speed-march; on my count and my mark!" He faced the front again, drew a deep breath, and while simultaneously pumping his fist into the air cried out: "MARK!"

As one, close to six-hundred-and-fifty men broke into a fast trot and pounded across the sharply undulating terrain of low scrub and bare rock. As he ran, the pacesetter counted off the paces to himself until on the four hundredth footfall, he once again called out, "MARK!" The troops returned to their normal marching speed for another four hundred paces. Then once again, the pacesetter ordered them to run.

The speed-march continued unabated – trot, march, and trot again – until well after midday when Rennil decided to call for a rest. The host sank gratefully to the ground, breathing hard but far from spent. Even the five unfit Lord-Guard, although certainly pale and strained, still had more to give. Everyone drank some firebrew, ate some of their rations, and rested their aching legs as best they could. Then all too soon, the order came to resume the journey.

The gruelling, repetitive slog continued without another break until the unearthly red daylight had faded to a deep and gloomy twilight. Even then, Rennil only allowed a halt when the dark shadows had grown so impenetrable that the tangled shrubs and loose rocks were turned into treacherous mantraps.

At the order to "Halt and encamp!" the grateful, enervated men sank to the ground and sat with heads bowed and knees drawn up, desperately trying to catch their breath. Worst affected of all – worse even than the five injured Lord-Guard – was the Arms-Master himself. He was after all, the oldest man in the company and although he followed a rigorous fitness regime, he was well past his prime. Gildor was also suffering, for in spite of his youthful appearance, he too was no youngster. He sat next to Rennil with sweat running down his ashen face and his breathing heavy and laboured. He looked at the Arms-Master's face, barely distinguishable in the gathering darkness and smiled ruefully.

"I think perhaps we overrated ourselves when we began this game. You look even worse than I feel."

Rennil gave him no more than a fleeting glance. "Don't be deceived by my looks," he replied dryly. "You may *appear* to be in better condition but remember, your face started the day with an unfair advantage. Were I to possess your unnaturally boyish features, I swear I'd look the better by far."

Gildor didn't reply but hugged his knees and scanned the gloom trying to make out the dark silhouettes of the spent warriors.

"Can we keep pushing them like this and still expect them to fight a desperate battle?" he asked soberly.

"The sooner we arrive, the sooner we can set our defences and improve our chance of victory."

"Is that in any doubt? If *Koreen* Bandil is to be believed, the Talisman guarantees our success; and I can see no reason to doubt him."

With his arms braced behind him, Rennil leant back and looked up at the blackened-red overcast of the unseen evil sky. "And if Eh'lorne is delayed?" he growled quietly. "Or if the weapon isn't as potent as Bandil believes, what then?"

For some time, the Prime didn't reply. He sat thoughtfully chewing his lip as he mulled over Rennil's chillingly baleful words.

"We'll continue to make haste whatever the cost," he eventually murmured. Then he pulled a honey cake from his pack and picked at it dolefully.

Rennil, far too exhausted to eat, merely grunted his reply and spread out his bedroll. Within moments of laying down his head, he fell into a fitful and troubled sleep. Gildor finished his frugal supper then followed suit. He drifted off to the sound of the group-hands barking out their orders for the placement of sentries. The night was dark and still, and it wasn't long before the whole camp settled down for a restless and uncomfortable sleep. Soon the only sounds were the soft snoring of the soldiers, the faint rustling of nocturnal animals, and the occasional sharp cry of distant night birds.

Suddenly, not long after midnight, a deafening cacophony of howling wolves broke out around them, waking the whole camp with a terrified start. The men leapt to their feet, desperately fumbling for their weapons as the nightmarish baying grew closer and louder as more and more lupine voices took up the cry. Never before had anyone seen or heard a gathering of so many wolves in one place.

Despite their sleep-fuddled minds and soul wrenching fear, not for a single instant did the host's discipline and training leave them. Blindly and instinctively they formed into groups of three, standing back to back with their swords drawn, poised for either defence or attack. The howling went on and on, growing to the point where it seemed the whole land was filled with the unseen, wild and savage creatures.

Then, as abruptly as it had begun, the nerve-shredding dissonance ceased. For a long time, the men stood anxiously listening to the eerie silence, straining their ears for any sign of the preternatural packs that had surrounded them. There was nothing to be heard. Even the normal nocturnal rustling seemed to have been shocked into silence. Gradually the men started to relax and a fretful murmuring began to spread through the ranks, threatening to interrupt the tight discipline that had been ingrained into their very being.

"Stand to!" Rennil bellowed, quickly regaining the cohesive obedience that he'd instilled into his troops. "Section officers, double the sentries. Division officers, I want every group in order with all provisions packed except bedrolls. Men, get some sleep while you can; you'll need all your strength tomorrow. But sleep with weapons drawn mind, for who knows what threat is waiting for us out there.

"Prime, form up the Guard and scout the perimeter. I want a full report on any wolf-sign – or whatever else might have been out there."

"Yes Master!" Gildor snapped. The informal banter of their earlier conversations had vanished completely and was now replaced by a stern tone of strict military discipline. Abruptly, he spun around and disappeared into the darkness with only his voice to mark his passing as he called his men to order,

Rennil sheathed his sword, and with a weary sigh, he rubbed his tired eyes. There seemed to be no end to the troubles that assailed them. Not content with hordes of vicious beast-men and their huge magi commanders; as well as unnatural storms and evil blood-clouds, they were now threatened by pack upon pack of wild, savage wolves. It seemed that Limnash had harnessed nature itself in his determination to eradicate the Arlien race.

He bowed his head and waited for the accustomed dark emotions to rise up and attack him. Years of practice had given him an unparalleled mastery at repelling the black despair and violent rage that dwelt poised within his soul. He steeled himself for the inevitable internal conflict to come; a struggle that made the most savage battles he'd ever fought seem nothing more than petty squabbles. But this time, the emotional assault remained at bay, and the terrible thirst for bloody revenge didn't come.

Like a man probing a problem tooth, he cautiously peeked around the door that he'd kept firmly closed for so long. He found to his surprise that he could now face the buried memories which haunted his dreams. Instead of the boiling cauldron of anguished fury, he found a stillness that was like a pool of cool, calm water. He knew this was in part due to D'harid's willingness to lift the burden of Sirris' defence from his shoulders – but only partly. The main source of his new spiritual serenity was the Lady Morjeena. His hostile suspicion of the tiny Keshtari healer had been miraculously transformed into a deep respect that bordered on love.

It was when she'd mentioned the *varl-dekteer.* Then he'd realised the foreign dignitary of whom she'd spoken was in fact Xarish-Shah, his own father-in-law. At that moment he'd looked at her anew. He found it was as though he was looking on the face of his long-dead, beloved wife. Not literally of course, for the two women were very different in so many ways, but they also had much in common. The same slight build and smooth brown complexion; the same apparent vulnerability hiding a steely determination that shone out through the eyes – eyes that were paradoxically both identical and opposite. They shared the same shape and the same passion – concealed as it was by a cool firmness. But where Morjeena's eyes were bright blue against her dark skin, Kharyn's had been a brown so dark as to be almost black.

It was as a volunteer in the militia that he'd travelled to Mah-Kashia. He'd been part of the armed escort for a consignment of shastin. It had been a great privilege for one so young to leave the city and have contact with another race. Perhaps even then his potential had been recognised – or perhaps Mordan himself had inspired his superiors to allow it.

After all, if he hadn't gone and hadn't suffered so terribly, would there ever have been an armshost at all? An image of Eldore flashed into his mind. "There's a lesson in everything for all to see, but only the wise will learn." He smiled ruefully. Perhaps the old proverb was right. But that particular lesson had come at an impossibly high price; and it seemed that he'd had to pay all of the cost himself.

Kharyn had been the only daughter of a rich merchant who'd had great influence in the court of King Xyron. Xarish-Shah had entertained high hopes for Kharyn. He'd hoped to marry her into one of the great houses or even to one of King Xyron's four sons. But from the moment Kharyn had first laid eyes on the handsome, fair-skinned soldier, those hopes had vanished like the morning mist. Many fathers would have stood firm and banned the two from ever meeting again. But something had softened Xarish-Shah's heart, and soon the two were inseparable.

The Arlien traders had left without him and the two lovers had been married within a moon. They'd set up home in one of Kharyn's father's many houses in a small town close to the Southern Desert. There they'd intended to stay for just one year before returning to Sirris with the first trade caravan of spring. But then war had broken out and as fate would have it, the first of the Screaming Nomads' raids had fallen on that very town. The recently wed couple had been caught in their sleep.

As he stood alone in the darkness listening to the bustle of his men with the occasional shouted command, he stroked the terrible scar on his face. It was not the only token he had to show for the injuries he'd sustained that night. Beneath his hauberk he carried even more horrific reminders of the desert people's sadistic cruelty. They'd left him for dead while Kharyn had been...

He slammed the door shut again. He was not ready to relive *that* particular memory – at least not yet. Perhaps one day, if civilisation survived, that story would be told and maybe even recorded for posterity; but not now, not yet.

Mercifully, at that moment Gildor returned. His slim towering figure was unmistakable even in the deep shadows of the dark night.

"We've made an initial sweep and found nothing," he reported. "I've instructed the Guard to make a more thorough search then to relieve the sentries. We'll take the remaining watches. The host can sleep soundly knowing the Lord-Guard are awake and watchful."

"It'll be a long night," Rennil warned. "And tomorrow will be a hard day. Can you and your men go without rest and still keep up the pace?"

"We are the Lord-Guard!" Gildor replied stiffly. Then without another word he turned and strode indignantly away.

The Arms-Master stood for a while longer, listening to the sounds of the camp resettling. Then as all became still once more, he too lay back down and tried unsuccessfully to sleep.

CHAPTER THIRTY-ONE

The gleaming white marble temple snuggled neatly against the precipitous cliff that marked Hornvale's northern boundary. It was a huge and impressive edifice, architecturally unlike any other in the whole land. The severity of its angular design was strangely at odds with the purity of the bright, twinkling stone and the colossal, ornately arched windows. Most of the expansive leaded glass was clean and clear but much of it was stained with radiant colours. They depicted scenes that Bandil would have recognised from the magnificent murals of the throne room in Arl. It was surrounded and protected by a high, deep wall resplendent with battlements that turned the whole structure into something more akin to a fortress than a place of worship. A river of water cascaded over the cliff and formed a large pool just beyond the

THE TALISMAN OF WRATH

temple's eastern wall. This small but deep lake then drained away as a fast flowing, chattering brook that disappeared into the impenetrable forest at the valley's eastern border.

Although often referred to as a city, the rest of the settlement was nothing as grand as that name would imply. It was actually nothing more than an expansive collection of drab, drystone hovels that spread out from the southern gates of the monastic fortress and surrounded its eastern side right up to the deep pool at the foot of the waterfall. The stark contrast between these humble dwellings and the harsh but opulent temple made the apparent poverty of its inhabitants all the more shocking. The streets – if indeed the rough dirt pathways could be called streets – were wide enough but impossibly tangled. If any thought had been given to designing the city's layout, the planner's mind would have to have been a study of twisted psychoses. But the reason for the 'city's' lack of order was due to the fact that the hundreds of squalid-looking homes were nothing more than an afterthought to the temple itself.

The rest of the long, wide valley was mostly turned over to pasture or to the fenced, circular vegetable plots peculiar to the northern regions of the land. Usually, a small army of men in dreary brown habits could be seen caring for the plots or tending to the goats that roamed free across the grassy vale. It was a pleasant and tranquil scene that made a wonderful, contrasting backdrop to the gleaming white temple edifice which should have been the focal point of the whole vale.

Rivalling the stunning temple's demand for attention, however, was the gigantic and improbable feature that gave the valley its name. Five hundred strides west of the temple and carved into the cliff face itself, stood the huge sculpture that was fashioned into the shape of an enormous hunting horn. Either side of the massive horn, steep stone steps led up to the polished silver mouthpiece a full eighty cubits from the ground. Although fashioned from solid stone, every last detail was a perfect, if massively scaled up replica of a regular instrument. The only noticeable difference was that the bands that encompassed a regular sized horn were made of iron, whereas the Great Horn's were instead fashioned from pure, rune-engraved silver. The sculpture was so well crafted, it appeared as if a giant huntsman or some titanic warrior had rested it there, waiting for the right moment to return and claim it. A strong, shoulder-height wall surrounded the sacred object, turning the enclosure into a restful, garden-like area which instead of grass, was covered with glistening chips of emerald-green jade gravel. Delicately wrought cast iron gates gave the monks and priests the access they required to tend the hallowed monument.

Although the proportions of the valley were substantial to say the least, it was in fact a very private place. Apart from a steep, zigzagging path cut into the vertical rock face above the temple, there were only two other ways of entering Hornvale. High in the foothills of the mountains, at the northeast borders of Keshtar, there existed a long, treacherously narrow gorge that finally opened out into the valley a full march west of the city. The other entrance was from the south. Here, between the impenetrable Dark Shadow Forest and the blasted, knife-like crags of the impassable 'Ravages', was the narrow approach that the Arlien people called 'The Choke'. This passage, although only fifty strides wide, ran for a full stretch before widening out and sloping down into the valley opposite the Great Horn. It was through this channel that the road from Sirris ran, and it was along this road that the armshost finally arrived, breathless and sweating, late on the morning of the second day.

They'd awoken at dawn on Eh'lorne's 'first' day (their second day of travel) and had immediately set off on another 'speed march'. This time however, Rennil had called for "Five by three," – five hundred paces at the run followed by just three hundred paces of walking. This extreme rate of progress was cruel and agonising, but none of the men had complained. The previous night's experience had lent wings to their heels and they would happily have run all the way to Hornvale if their bodies had been capable. Even the five injured Lord-Guard had kept up – albeit aided by their comrades. Some of their helpers had shared the burden of their equipment while others had taken it in turns to half carry and half drag them along. Although Gildor had warned the five men that they'd have to keep up or be left behind, he'd pretended not to notice this illicit assistance. It was impossible to allow such a profound and flagrant breach of code, but rather than confront it, he'd tactfully managed to keep out of the way. After all, it would be one thing to leave the men to follow at their own pace or to return to Sirris where they belonged, but it would be quite another to leave them at the mercy of countless savage and spectral wolves.

The second night had passed quietly and uneventfully so the pace on the second day had been mercifully dropped to a more comfortable, "Two by six." At around midmorning they'd reached the road at which point they'd reformed their ranks and continued the march in normal formation – although still at a somewhat quicker pace than was usual.

They'd entered the 'Choke' full of cheer, knowing their ordeal was about to end, but were brought to an abrupt halt when their path was blocked by fifty or so of the priest-like Hornvalers.

They were not as tall as the Arliens – although certainly not short as counted by other races – but were broad and powerful with grim, expressionless faces. Their hair was close-cropped and like the Arliens, they were beardless. The shadow on their chins, however, revealed that this was due to a razor's edge rather than the nature of their race. Their long robes were actually of a pale blue but were given a deeper, lilac tint by the unnatural red light of the evil sky. In their right hands they held short wooden staffs that were of an unusual and complicated design. Planted into the compacted dirt of the road, the bottom end of the shafts held a small but heavy iron ball, while at the other end they were tipped with a large, wicked-looking wolf's paw. The silver paws appeared to be of polished, hardened steel while their claws were long and razor sharp.

One of the priests stepped forward and approached the Arms-Master. Around his neck he was wearing a thick heavy chain that held a silver, horn-shaped medallion which was obviously a mark of high rank. For a moment or two he studied Rennil's scarred, mutilated face then spoke to him in a flat, expressionless voice.

"Greetings, *Dithkar-Geer*. Although it is not yet your time, it is an honour to meet you. Your reputation precedes you."

Rennil frowned. "I'm afraid you've mistaken me for another. I'm not this *Dithkar-Geer* of whom you speak. My name is..."

"Your name is Rennil, son of Raul," the Hornvaler interrupted. "You are the Arms-Master of Sirris and the one the Screaming Nomads of the desert name *Dithkar-Geer* – the 'Deadly Ghost'. A dreaded name that they'll not utter above a whisper lest he once again rise from the grave and wreak bloody vengeance on their heads. It is a fitting title, is it not?"

"Perhaps," Rennil growled sourly. "You certainly know more about me than I know about you."

"Then allow me to rectify that a little. My name is Nirsuk, *First of the Watch* and *Chief Guardian of the Pledge*. For now, that is all you need to know except that, as the *First*, it is my duty to prevent your entry into Hornvale. As respected as your name may be, there is no welcome for you here. As I've already said, it is not yet your time."

"Then Nirsuk, in this duty you must fail. We've come with a dire warning and an offer of help and friendship in these dark times."

Pointedly, the *First* looked at the armshost behind Rennil and raised an eyebrow. "Friends do not usually arrive with an army at their backs," he commented dryly.

"Nor do they treat their allies with contempt!" Gildor snapped, unable to keep quiet any longer.

Nirsuk seemed not to have heard the Prime's outburst and continued scrutinising the Arms-Master's scarred face, patiently waiting for a reply. Rennil returned his gaze, unsure of the Hornvaler's meaning or how to handle his rebuff. He knew that he'd have to choose his words prudently and that he'd have to tread softly.

"We seem to have started with a misunderstanding," he eventually said with great care. "We've come here to prevent your destruction by a vast army which as we speak is marching ever closer towards you. I'm told that we worship the same god, and it is that god himself who has sent us to you. Perhaps if I can speak to your High Priest, we can put this matter straight."

"There is no need for that," Nirsuk replied in the same firm, expressionless tone. "He already knows of your coming; how else would he have sent us here to meet you. And as for the vast army that you say threatens us, if it were true then he would know of that as well – he is after all, the High Priest. Were we about to face such destruction, Mordan himself would have revealed it to him."

While the *First* was speaking it began to rain. The first few crimson drops splashed to the ground almost unnoticed, but within moments, the blood-rain was falling thick and heavy.

"This is ridiculous!" Gildor cried angrily. "Look around you; look at the sky; look at the rain. Does your High Priest in all his wisdom know the cause of it? Does he know that Sarren is gone or that Sirris has been attacked?"

Again, the *First* ignored him and aimed his reply solely at Rennil. "I understand your concerns, *Dithkar-Geer*, but I cannot turn my back on my duty."

"Then the world is lost," Rennil growled softly. "And Mordan will hold you and your people accountable. I hope for all your sakes he shares the view that *your* duty is more important than *his* creation."

"You use Mordan's name too lightly, *Dithkar-Geer*. If the great god had intended you to enter here, he would have given us a sign."

"And what do you call this?" Gildor shouted angrily, thrusting his cupped hand under the priest's nose and letting the blood-rain overflow through his fingers.

For the first time Nirsuk acknowledged Gildor's existence. He looked at the outstretched hand, at the Prime's furious, blood-streaked face, and then raised his eyes to the sky. "This is... unexplained," he said without inflection. He turned back to Rennil and with a smile so brief and slight that the Arms-Master wondered if he'd imagined it, said: "It is *not* the sign; but as the High Priest gave me no word of blood from the sky, I'll grant you time for one to be given. We'll wait until nightfall and if no sign appears by then you must leave... or fight," he added ominously.

"Then either we fight amongst ourselves and save Limnash the trouble, or we'll leave you to your bloody fate. Either way he wins."

"Mordan will not abandon us," Nirsuk replied stoically. "We serve the Pledge at his bidding, and any that interfere with that service are our foes – even you, *Dithkar-Geer*. Until your time comes, you are not our friend and neither are you welcome."

"You keep talking of my 'time' but I have no idea what you mean. All I do know is that you're *wasting* time – both yours and mine. I just pray that Mordan teaches you to distinguish your friends from your enemies before it's too late."

Nirsuk remained unmoved. "If Mordan has a lesson to teach, I'm listening to him. As I've said, we'll wait until nightfall."

With that he turned and re-joined his fellows leaving Rennil and Gildor standing open mouthed and frustrated.

"What now?" the Prime asked, his voice tight with exasperation.

Rennil shrugged. "Now we wait. We have no other choice."

The two groups stood facing each other in the narrow confines of the Choke while the thick, sticky rain fell steadily down. It wasn't long before it suddenly became torrential, hammering and rattling against the metal of the host's helmets and mail hauberks. Deep, glutinous pools began to form around their feet, and the men began to stir and murmur uneasily.

"The sky bleeds, Rennil!" Gildor shouted above the pounding of the rain. "The sky bleeds!"

Before the Arms-Master could reply an impossibly bright flash rent the air from the south. It was as though a thousand lightning bolts had struck at once; yet in spite of the intensity of the light, not one of the men was blinded. Everyone looked to see the source of the flash and gasped in wonder. Far in the distance they could see Mordan's Finger erupting with its cold, white fire. The silver bolts of lightning were streaking towards them, evaporating the red clouds as they came. First the ground shook, then a fraction of a heartbeat later, the arctic blast hit them. Everyone – warrior and priest alike – were thrown to the ground, their blood-soaked clothes instantly becoming stiff with hard, crimson frost. Every man felt the cold flames of fury searing his flesh and scorching his bones to the very core of his soul. Then, just as they all felt they'd breathed their last, it was over. The last of the raindrops tinkled down as frozen, shimmering rubies, and the sun was shining high and warm in the clear azure sky.

Shakily, the armshost climbed to their feet. Their fear-struck eyes were wide with surprise, shocked that the terrifying, frigid inferno had left them, after all, whole and unharmed. Rennil drew a deep, quivering breath and surveyed his men. They were cold, tired, and shaken, but to his relief and pride, they were still soldiers.

Gildor pulled at his arm, demanding his attention. He turned toward his slim, towering lieutenant and saw that his face, burnished red by the cold blast, was agitated and intense.

"The ice burns!" he cried excitedly. "The sky bleeds and the ice burns. It's Murvon the Mad's insane litany."

Rennil studied him and then nodded soberly. "Aye, the *varl-dekteer* begins to unfold. We must be watchful so as not to miss its meaning." He looked over his shoulder at the Hornvalers. They'd already regained their feet and were calmly brushing the frost and dirt from their robes.

Nirsuk caught his eye and spoke to him in a curt, implacable monotone. "It is the sign. Follow me."

The priests led them out of the Choke and down the hill towards the temple. The red ice cracked on their clothing and crunched loudly beneath their feet as they marched. They passed many of the dourly dressed monks, who in spite of the unnatural rain and the fierce arctic blast of power, remained as impassive and expressionless as the blue-clad priests. They eyed the newcomers with such a remote indifference that it seemed to border on disdain. Upon reaching the gates in the temple wall, Nirsuk brought the column to a halt and spoke to Rennil in a loud voice that was clearly for the benefit of all to hear.

"Your soldiers cannot enter this place, so my priests will find billets for them amongst our workers. The accommodation will be simple and sparse, but they will be warm and fed – although perhaps not to the standard of which they're accustomed. *Dithkar-Geer*, you will come with me."

Rennil nodded in agreement but Gildor pushed his way forward and laid his hand on the *First's* arm. There was a sharp intake of breath from the other priests but Nirsuk merely looked at the offending hand with an expression of mild distaste. Slowly he let his gaze wander up until it reached the lofty Arlien's face. He then raised an enquiring eyebrow.

"Is this arrangement unsatisfactory?"

Rennil winced. He'd have never believed that such a level, expressionless voice could convey so much scorn, but Gildor remained unmoved and determined.

"The arrangement is fine for most, but I have five men in need of care. They were injured in battle only days before we left Sirris, and the journey has been particularly hard for them."

"Then they should complain to you, not us. If *you* gave no consideration to their plight before you left, then why should *we* give them that consideration now you've arrived?"

Gildor's cheeks flushed angrily. "They make no complaint; they are Lord-Guard! But they refused to be left behind and would rather have walked here barefoot on broken glass than forsake their comrades at a time of great peril. They ask nothing from you; it is *I* that plead their case for your mercy."

Without replying to the incensed Prime, Nirsuk turned to one of the priests and spoke to him in a harsh, complicated language. Strangely, the pitch of the *First's* native tongue rose and fell sharply, while each syllable seemed loaded with passion and meaning. The contrast to the Hornvaler's normal flat monotone was startling.

Once he'd finished speaking, he returned his focus to the Arms-Master. "Those five men are *tsorechny* and will therefore be allowed to enter the temple. They will be given the best care possible and will be treated with the respect they deserve. I believe that takes care of the matter to your Prime Officer's contentment; so now lets you and I continue. Follow me." He strode quickly off and seemed oblivious to Gildor's call of "Thank you."

Rennil looked at the Prime and shrugged helplessly. Then without another word he hurried after the *First*.

"What was that you called those men?" he asked curiously when he caught up. "They're what?"

"They are *tsorechny*."

"Which means?"

Nirsuk frowned. "I do not think I can translate it. It is not something I've had cause to explain before, and there is no word like it in the common tongue. 'Fool' is the nearest word I can think of, but that is a derogatory term and '*tsorechny*' carries a meaning that is quite the opposite. In my language, words often have many different meanings that all apply simultaneously. It is a concept that outsiders are incapable of comprehending."

"I think I understand," Rennil replied, amazed at his intuitive grasp of the idea. "It seems to make perfect sense."

Nirsuk stopped abruptly and pulled the Arms-Master round to face him. He peered intently into his eyes then gave a rare smile. "Of course; you would understand. It must be nearer to your time than we thought."

Without giving Rennil an opportunity to question him further, he marched off again leaving the remark hanging cryptically in the air. The puzzled Arms-Master hurried after him, determined to discover exactly what the *First* meant by his constant reference to Rennil's 'time'. But as they entered the temple, its opulent grandeur pushed all other thoughts from his mind.

He found himself in a vast, airy atrium that bustled with the silent, blue-clad priests. The warm midday sun streamed brightly in through two enormous clear glass windows that arched up high on either side of the double doors. The clean, radiant light – so welcome after the days of sickly red – set the speckled marble floor twinkling and sparkling delightfully. Intricate angular patterns were carved into the walls – patterns so fantastically complex that to spend too long trying to comprehend their form sent the mind spinning into a hypnotic trance.

THE TALISMAN OF WRATH

Directly ahead of him, a beautifully fashioned grand staircase climbed gently up to a wide mezzanine floor that ran all the way around the three internal walls of the huge chamber. Everywhere he looked, myriads of corridors led away to places with purposes that Rennil could hardly begin to imagine. Never in all his broad experience had he seen anything approaching such startlingly unusual, angular beauty. In spite of the incomprehensibly alien design of the architecture, it gave him a strange feeling of familiarity and a sense of security that he'd not known since he was a child. He couldn't stop himself from just standing still and gazing around in awed wonder.

It took a moment or two for Nirsuk to realise he was no longer being followed, but once he noticed, he came striding back to the gawping Arms-Master with a faint but tangible air of impatience.

"If you have urgent business with the High Priest it would be wise for you to make haste. Arbenak will know of your arrival and will wish to interview you as soon as possible. It would not be wise to keep him waiting."

"Of course not; I'm sorry. Lead me straight to him and maybe I can marvel at your wonderful temple later."

"Straight to him?" the *First* asked flatly. Somehow, he managed to convey a heavy note of shocked surprise in his neutral voice. "Is it the custom of your people to enter a hallowed place covered in bloody filth and stinking like a pig? I'd have thought Mordan's children would have more respect."

Rennil looked down at his stained hauberk and dirt-ingrained hands and grimaced. "My apologies, Nirsuk; you're absolutely right. We would never enter our own House of Worship in such an unclean condition. Is there somewhere I can go to wash?"

"That is where I am taking you – if you'll do me the courtesy of following."

"Of course, lead the way."

Nirsuk gave the slightest bow of acknowledgement and then took him down the first corridor on their left. It was long and wide and was brightly lit by a series of large windows that were set into the marble wall on the left-hand side. In stark contrast, the right-hand wall was constructed of nothing more exotic than drab, grey stone. The wall was plain and unadorned, broken only by small wooden doors that were spaced at intervals of exactly ten strides. Many unlit lamps were hung on chains from the high ceiling, all carefully placed at regular, efficient intervals.

The corridor seemed to go on for an eternity but eventually it opened out into what appeared to be a well-proportioned communal bath area. Twenty large copper basins stood against one wall, each one supported on its own wooden tripod. Beside each basin, a low pine table held a huge pitcher of water and a basket full of dry, greenish-brown moss. At the far end of the stone chamber a wide, circular pool was filled with clean, clear water that reflected the light from the high-set windows and sent it shimmering around the walls of the room. The air was kept comfortably warm by a huge, matt-black, wood burning stove in the centre of the room.

Nirsuk pointed to one of the tables. "Poor the water into the basin and use the moss from the basket to scrub yourself clean. There is a drainage grate over there. If you stand over it you can rinse the dirt away. Once you are completely clean, you must immerse yourself fully in the pool. Only then will you be pure enough to meet the High Priest. In the meantime, I will take your clothes away to be cleaned. I will bring you something more appropriate to wear and something to dry yourself with. Please undress."

Obediently, Rennil began to strip while Nirsuk respectfully turned his back. He laid his clothes on the floor beside the *First* then walked over to the basins and filled one from its accompanying pitcher.

THE TALISMAN OF WRATH

"This water's freezing," he complained, shooting the *First* a disgusted look.

"Cold water hardens the body," Nirsuk intoned absently as he gathered up the Arms-Master's hauberk and undergarments.

"Does my body appear to need hardening?" Rennil asked dryly.

Nirsuk turned around and looked at the naked Arms-Master. When he saw the mass of scars that covered his torso and registered the savagery of the wounds that had so disfigured it, his eyes widened in horror. For the first time, Rennil saw clear and genuine emotion on the face of a Hornvaler.

"Well?" he insisted.

"No, it does not."

"Then would some hot water be too much to ask for?"

Nirsuk stood looking at Rennil's mangled body for a moment longer, then finished collecting the clothes. "Hot water softens the mind," he said quietly; then he walked quickly out of the room.

Rennil shook his head and sighed resignedly. "Cold water it is then." He picked a good handful of moss from its basket, sniffed it and grunted appreciatively. It had a clean, sharp fragrance and a tough, firm texture. He dipped it in the water and began diligently to scrub away the filth. When he was satisfied that he'd reached all of the dirt and blood, he picked up the half empty pitcher and walked over to the drain. Standing astride the grate he took a deep breath, then emptied the last of the water over his head. It felt as though his brain had been suddenly gripped by a tight, mind-numbing vice. Once he'd recovered from the shock, he trotted over to the shimmering pool and squatted at its edge. He tested the water with his fingers and let out a cry of dismay. If anything, it was even colder than the water in the basin! Carefully, he sat on the edge and gingerly lowered his feet into the freezing water until it reached up to his knees. If his eyes hadn't told him differently, he'd have sworn that his legs were being amputated by a jagged saw of solid ice.

"So cold water hardens the body does it?" he muttered dubiously. "I hope they're right." He braced himself, gritted his teeth, then thrust himself away from the edge and plunged into the huge, freezing bath. The water came up to his chin and left him fighting for air. He knew he'd have to be quick or he'd be in danger of succumbing to the cold. He forced some air into his protesting lungs, gripped his nose, and submerged himself completely. Almost immediately he resurfaced. Then, coughing and spluttering alarmingly, he struggled over to the side and heaved himself out of the pool. He hurried across to the hot stove where dripping and shivering, he stood hugging his torso, desperately trying to absorb some of its life-giving warmth.

A short time later Nirsuk returned. Somehow, he'd found time to wash and dress himself in clean, well-pressed robes. He no longer carried his staff but instead was holding a small pile of clean, pure white towels and a new set of clothes for his guest. Keeping his eyes averted from the Arms-Master's nakedness, he handed him one of the towels.

To Rennil's delight it was pre-warmed and wonderfully soft. "Surely soft towels weaken the soul?" he commented sarcastically.

"Are they not to your liking?" the *First* asked seriously, completely missing the heavy irony in Rennil's tone. Rennil shot him an incredulous look, shook his head in disbelief, and then vigorously began to rub himself dry.

When he was finished, Nirsuk held out the robes he'd brought for him. They were of a similar design to the priest's but instead of pale blue, they were a deep and luxuriant purple. Quickly, Rennil pulled them on. He marvelled at the quality and the craftsmanship of the tailor.

"They fit you well do they not?"

"Indeed they do," Rennil replied appreciatively. "They could have been made for me."

"They were."

"Don't be ridiculous," the Arms-Master scoffed. "You can't expect me to believe that you've cut and sewn the cloth in the time it's taken me to wash. I haven't even been measured for them."

"*Dithkar-Geer*, you must understand, these robes were made for you more than a decade ago and have been kept in a sacred store awaiting your arrival."

It took a moment or two for the implications of Nirsuk's words to sink in, but once they did, along with the incredulity, Rennil felt a sudden burst of anger. "Then why in Mordan's name did you try and turn me away?" he asked sharply.

"Because it is not your time," the *First* replied calmly. It was as though he considered that the oft-repeated statement explained everything. "Now, if you are ready, I'll take you to the High Priest. If Arbenak feels it right to tell you more, he will; but I fear you will get more questions from him than you'll get answers."

Rennil closed his eyes and tried to bring his frustration under control. These damned Hornvalers were infuriating beyond belief. He'd never before met such a race of men that were so...

His eyes flicked open. Men! Of course; they were all men. There was not a single woman to be seen in the whole city. It's no wonder they're so miserable, he thought with a wicked grin.

"Come on then," he said with a hint of sympathy. "I'm ready."

The *First* led him back to the great atrium and up the stairs to the mezzanine. Directly in front of them at the top of the grand staircase, Rennil could see a pair of ornate double doors. Each one bore a large, detailed engraving of a leaping wolf. They passed through these doors and into what seemed to be a small but luxurious waiting room. Several comfortable looking upholstered chairs were arranged along one wall, and at the far end, two stone-faced priests stood stiffly guarding another set of doors identical to the first. In their hands they held the same wolf-paw staffs that Nirsuk and his men had carried when they'd met the armshost at the Choke.

As they approached the guarded doors, Nirsuk stopped and faced Rennil. He then spoke to him in a low, unexpectedly urgent voice. "Behind these doors, High Priest Arbenak awaits you. He is a remarkable man with great prescience and boundless wisdom, but he has little patience. You are highly respected *Dithkar-Geer*, but that will be of little benefit should you cause affront. I can offer you no help other than this advice: be yourself and be completely honest. Any deceit – no matter how innocent in motive – will be clear to him. If you speak the slightest falsehood, however good your intentions, it will not go well for you."

"I understand," Rennil replied seriously.

"Good. I am unable to enter with you so you will be alone under his gaze." Surprisingly, he laid a hand on the Arms-Master's shoulder and gave him a small but encouraging smile. "May Mordan bless you, Rennil, son of Raul. I will wait for you here until your trial is over. Rest assured, I will be here when you return." He nodded to the two guards who immediately threw open the doors and stood aside.

Rennil took a deep breath, squared his shoulders, and then marched in to learn of his fate.

CHAPTER THIRTY-TWO

As the cold, dark night crept slowly towards the unnatural red glow of dawn, the newlywed couple lay warm and content in their bed. As Eldore had requested, the wedding had taken place the previous evening as soon as possible after the council had ended. It had been a small, quiet affair and few of the city's citizens had been able to witness the ceremony. News of the union had quickly spread however, bringing a welcome note of cheer to the beleaguered population. Although most had been a little shocked at the mixing of race in the royal line, none had felt cause to complain. Speculation had already been rife since the two had appeared together at the High-Lord's funeral.

The official celebrations at the Duty Hall has been somewhat low-key and the happy couple had escaped to their bedchamber long before the last toast had been drunk. Their lovemaking had been tender and passionate and the two had then drifted off to a contented sleep, wrapped in each other's arms. Such was the weight of their impending trials however, they'd woken well before sunrise. They now lay bathed in the soft glow of the remains of the fire, reluctant to leave the sanctuary of their embrace.

Eldore lay on his back with Morjeena's head resting on his deep, powerful chest. His huge right arm, capable of such unimaginable feats of strength, now held her with the gentle delicacy of a child holding a butterfly. His hard, calloused hand was lightly stroking her silky, long dark hair. Never before had the tiny Keshtari girl felt so safe and so secure. The bitter irony of that feeling weighed against the reality of what they now faced was not entirely lost on her.

"Is Mordan teasing us?" she asked dreamily. "After all these years apart, we're finally united only to face the possibility of a terrible end."

"Mordan does not tease," Eldore replied firmly. "Everything he does has a purpose and if we are now part of that purpose – whatever the outcome – we should count ourselves blessed."

"I wonder if there's any hope that we can grow old together."

Softly, her new husband kissed the top of her head. "Of course there's hope or why else would we fight? And as you yourself said, there's always Eh'lorne. As long as he has a sword in his hand, Limnash can never entirely conquer us. And don't forget, he now holds the Talisman of wrath. Then of course there's *Koreen* Bandil. I'll wager there's far more to that old hermit than we could ever imagine."

"I know you're right but they're not coming to us here are they."

THE TALISMAN OF WRATH

Eldore sighed. "No, they're not; but even so, we mustn't give up hope. We must have faith." In spite of the strength of his words, his voice betrayed his doubt.

After a long moment of silence, Morjeena spoke again. "Why hasn't Eh'lorne contacted you? He used the Talisman's power to do it once, can't he do it again?"

"I don't know," Eldore replied heavily. "It's possible that the Talisman doesn't work that way. Maybe it was only his pain and peril that joined us together when he touched it." His voice then took on a note of bitterness. "Although it's more likely that it just hasn't occurred to him to try. For one who genuinely cares so much about others, his arrogance is such that he gives little thought to their concerns or their feelings."

Morjeena raised her head. "I've never heard you speak of him so. You were so close when I first met you both. Has something changed since then?"

He shook his head. "No, nothing's changed. I still love my brother more than life itself. We've shared everything since we were born; and even before then we shared our mother's womb. Sometimes we're so close that we seem to be two halves of the same person – albeit opposite halves." He frowned angrily. "But his impulsive, reckless behaviour frustrates me beyond measure! His complete disregard for danger is selfish beyond belief – especially as I'm forced to share the pain of his foolishness!" His voice then softened wistfully. "Yet I envy him as well. He's always so certain, so sure of himself. I'm jealous of his boldness and his fearlessness. If I possessed half his courage..."

"How dare you!" Morjeena cried shooting bolt upright. "How dare you say such a thing. You are the most courageous man I've ever met." She sat staring furiously down at him, her naked body tantalisingly indistinct in the soft warm glow of the fire's embers.

Eldore laughed sourly. "Then you know me less well than you think. No man alive is more afraid than I am. I'm afraid for my people, I'm afraid for you, and yes, I'm afraid for myself too. The thought of the battles to come terrifies me, and I long to run and hide from my responsibilities. Already the guilt of the lives lost crushes…"

She silenced him by placing a finger against his lips. "And yet you do fight," she said tenderly. "And against all your instincts, no matter how reluctantly, you carry the weight of your obligations."

Eldore snorted his disagreement.

"Tell me my love," she continued, changing tack. "Would you consider me a coward if I told you I was afraid to work in your forge? Or if I told you that the furnace there terrifies me, and the thought of carrying red hot metal to the anvil makes my blood run cold? And as for hammering it into shape with all the sparks that causes… Well, that's something I could never bring myself to do! So tell me, am I a coward?"

"Of course not. I'd not even allow you near me while I was doing it. It's dangerous work and you could be hurt."

"And yet you carry on that work unafraid. How I envy your courage."

"What courage? It's my trade; it's what I do. Why should I be in fear of that?"

"Exactly! She declared triumphantly. "What you perceive to be courage in your brother is merely that same lack of fear. And all those things you envy in him are also the wellspring of all those things that frustrate you. Likewise, it's your fears and your doubts that are the wellspring of your thoughtfulness and your caring. Courage is not the lack of fear but the willingness to overcome that fear; and the greater the fear, the greater the courage. Never for a single instant have you given in to your doubts. Why else did I choose you and not him? Be proud of yourself as I am proud of you."

He stared up at her for a moment then broke into a grin. "So, I'm to be lectured and chastised by a mere woman, am I?"

"No, by a wife."

His smile widened and he reached up and stroked her cheek. "*My* wife." Slowly, he let his hand move down her neck and over her body.

"*My* husband," she replied huskily. Then she lay back down and pulled him to her.

✷ ✷ ✷

It was midmorning before they finally emerged from their bedchamber. They hurried along the corridor, ashamed that they'd let their duty slip. As they started to descend the long staircase, they became aware of a commotion coming from below in the direction of the servants' quarters. The disturbance grew louder as it approached, until its cause became apparent when a small number of the Halls' household came into view. Two of them – red faced, agitated women – were trying to force their way in, while several others, including Bishtar and Freiya, were trying to prevent them. Eldore's heart sank when he recognised one of the distraught women as Yewan's mother, Sharna.

"What's going on?" he asked as he and Morjeena reached the foot of the stairs.

At the sight of him, Sharna's face lit up. "Lord Eldore," she cried. "I must speak to you urgently." She made a desperate lunge to break free but Bishtar caught her arm. "You must help me please!" she implored helplessly.

"Of course; if I can," Eldore replied, trying to emulate his father's firm but compassionate tone. "Bishtar, let them through."

Reluctantly, Bishtar stood aside and allowed the two women to push past. They rushed up to the muscular young lord – Sharna even going so far as to take hold of his jerkin – and both began speaking at once. The words came tumbling out in such a rush that neither Eldore nor Morjeena could understand the reason for the women's distress.

"One at a time please," Eldore retorted, holding up his hands. The two women fell silent "Now, Sharna, what's the problem; how can I help?"

"Oh, my lord, they're saying we must all leave the city and go to the Refuge. Is it true? Please tell me it isn't."

Eldore placed his hands on her shoulders and spoke with gentle reassurance. "I'm afraid it is but there's no need to worry; Vice-Master D'harid has everything in hand and I'm sure you'll be well taken care of."

"That's not the point," Sharna's friend interrupted impatiently.

"So what is the point? Please explain; what do you want me to do?"

"It's my son!" Sharna wailed, her eyes brimming with tears. "We've not found him yet. Please, my lord, they've stopped the search and if we don't find him before we abandon the city, he'll be left to the mercy of the enemy."

"Oh, my dear Sharna," Eldore groaned mournfully as the barbed blade of guilt twisted agonisingly in his heart. Beside him, Morjeena sensed his pain and silently placed a comforting hand on his arm. "If I thought for a single moment that he could be found, I'd personally scour every rock, every crevice, and every blade of grass until he was. But hard as it is to bear, we must face the fact that he's gone."

"But gone where? Please, I can't rest until I have him back. I'm begging you; restart the search. Use the militia or the conscripts. Please, my lord, I know you care for him too." She stared up at him with such desperate pleading that he almost gave in – almost.

"I'm sorry Sharna but it's just not possible. I have to think of the whole city, and you must face the truth: Yewan is dead."

THE TALISMAN OF WRATH

For a moment she seemed not to comprehend his words; but then a look of horrified betrayal spread across her face. She let go of his jerkin and in one fluid movement shrugged off his hands and slapped his face so hard that the sound of it reverberated around the hall. The assembled servants gasped at the outrage but Eldore just stood quietly staring down at her with an unbearable pity in his eyes.

"HE IS ALIVE!" she screamed. Then, turning on her heels, she fled wailing from hall with her friend in tow.

Eldore, his cheek burning bright red, groaned with anguish and made to follow but Morjeena held him back.

"Leave her," she said gently. "I'll see to it; I'll make sure she's all right."

Her husband drew a deep breath then nodded gratefully. Morjeena kissed his crimson cheek then hurried after the two fleeing women.

"I'm sorry, my lord," Bishtar called, wary of coming too close. "We tried to stop her but she was insistent. If it's your wish, I'll dismiss her from the household; it won't happen again."

"You'll do nothing of the sort. I hold no ill will towards her at all; the poor woman is mad with grief. Perhaps if we'd found Yewan's body it would be easier for her to find closure, but as it is..."

"Is there no hope at all?" Freiya asked, wringing her hands.

"None!" Eldore replied firmly. "Now, I'm sure you've all got better things to do – I know I have; so if you'll excuse me, I'm going to find D'harid."

Without waiting for a reply, he strode quickly out of the Halls and instinctively made his way towards the river. The red gloomy daylight reflected his mood – dark, dreary, and full ominous portent. The day had started so joyously, but now his feelings of guilt and inadequacy had returned all the stronger, making it difficult to concentrate on what needed to be done.

His suffering was alleviated slightly when he came upon six militiamen who were struggling heroically with a huge beam. They were attempting, without success, to place it between two houses in order to form the basis of a barricade. Their cheery greeting and heartfelt congratulations brought a smile to his lips; and with the help of his prodigious strength, their task was completed in no time at all.

His instincts to head for the river were proved right when they indicated that D'harid could be found at the stone bridge that was the second crossing from the waterfall. With their calls of thanks ringing in his ears and with a somewhat lighter step, he made his way through the city. As he went, he felt even more encouraged, for in spite of the upheaval of the move to the Refuge, the people he met still managed a smile and a congratulatory word.

He arrived at the bridge to find the newly appointed Vice-Master standing mid-span and surrounded by a dozen or so militiamen. He had a large parchment spread out on top of the bridge's wall and was scanning the city while making wide, descriptive gestures with one arm. When he caught sight of Eldore's approach, he rolled up the parchment and turned to greet him.

"Good morning," he called cheerfully. "I'm glad you've found me. I'm in the process of deciding which bridge best suits our purpose and could really use your advice."

Eldore grimaced apologetically. "I know, I'm sorry to be so late."

"On the contrary; I hadn't expected to see you much before noon bell. I'm sure you had far more pressing matters before you... or under you," he added mischievously. Then he caught sight of the angry handprint on Eldore's cheek. "Although perhaps things didn't go quite as well as you'd hoped."

"Which bridges are you looking at?" Eldore asked tight-lipped, ignoring the innuendos.

"We've only two that are suitable," D'harid replied, suddenly serious. He unrolled the parchment and laid it on the wall again. It was a detailed map of the city with the High River shown snaking through its centre and every one of the seven bridges clearly marked. "We could use either The Walker's Bridge here…" he pointed to the fourth of the crossings on the map, "…or this very bridge where we stand. Both have their own advantages and disadvantages."

"Which are?"

"The Walker's Bridge is narrow and therefore the easiest to defend; and the northern bank has an area of grass that lends itself well to the construction of a strong wooden wall. However, the city to the south of the bridge is not so helpful. The streets are wide and straight making it far more difficult to prepare the surprise I have in mind. And of course, we need to destroy every other bridge, and this one…" he stamped his foot on the cobbled roadway, "…will prove difficult to pull down.

"Alternatively, the city to the south of here is almost perfectly laid out. The streets are narrow and lined with workshops and warehouses making it easy to channel our enemies to where we want them. But then this bridge is wide and open to a large body of men to force the passage. Added to that, the northern bank is paved, which means it'll take more time to erect a decent stockade.

"So, Lord Eldore, once again I present you with a dichotomy. Which do you advise we use, Walker's Bridge or Stonebridge?"

Eldore studied the map then raised his head and surveyed the city both sides of the stone bridge. Carefully, he deliberated on the options before them. Eventually he spoke both slowly and thoughtfully.

"If I understand your plan correctly, the initial phase is the most important and any victory hangs almost entirely on its success. Am I right?"

"You are."

"Then I'd utilise this bridge and tear down all the others."

"My thoughts exactly!" D'harid declared emphatically. He handed the map to one of his men and smiled his crooked, enigmatic smile. "I'll make a soldier of you yet, Eldore."

He turned to the rest of his men. "Did you hear that? Lord Eldore has made his decision, so let's get on with it."

As the entourage left the bridge and headed into the city's southwestern quarter, D'harid paused and gave Eldore a wink. "Coming?" he asked in his calm, reassuring voice.

It suddenly dawned on Eldore that the Vice-Master had already decided on which of the bridges to use, and had merely put on a charade to boost the young lord's confidence and to inspire the men to place their trust in him.

Shaking his head in wonder, he followed his new friend to begin what would turn out to be the most exhausting few days of his life.

CHAPTER THIRTY-THREE

The city's preparations for the coming onslaught were proceeding at an unimaginable speed – a speed that was born out of fear and desperation. It was only the morning of the third day and already many of the barricades, fences, and screens were in place. It seemed that every one of the city's inhabitants had their own specific task to perform, and they had thrown themselves into those tasks with an unbridled zeal. The men were providing the muscle for the heavy construction while the women were employed in painting the buildings with pitch or supplying food and drink to the labourers. Even the children had a part to play, running errands or fetching and distributing necessities such as nails and tools.

In one street, heavy wooden screens were being erected between the lines of houses in order to separate the southeast quarter from the rest of the city. Each screen was laid flat on the ground then pulled and pushed upright by a team of four men. One of the teams however, consisted of just two: Eldore and Griston. D'harid had cleverly put the pair together for two reasons: firstly, it demonstrated that the Lord-Regent did not consider himself as being *above* the people but as *one* of them. And secondly, he knew the sight of the two powerful men performing such amazing feats of strength would encourage the others to push themselves beyond their own perceived limitations.

When the two had finished lifting and nailing their fourth screen into place, they looked at each other and grinned. Their red faces – exaggerated by the unnatural daylight – were running with sweat and their breathing was heavy from their exertions.

"Griston, my friend," Eldore panted. "What would you think if I were to suggest a short break?"

"My dear Eldore, I'd likely shake your hand so hard I'd be in danger of tearing it from your arm!"

"I thought as much. Come along then, a drink and a bite."

They sauntered off down the street until they reached a long, low table, laden with plates of food and huge flasks of a clear, yellow-tinged liquid. Several women and children were serving the lines of exhausted men who were queuing for a welcome mug of the salted, honey-infused firebrew.

As Eldore and Griston waited their turn, they chatted and laughed as though they'd been the best of friends their entire lives. Gone was the sober formality that had at first marked the difference in their rank. Not once was there a single "my lord."

"How is Annisa?" Eldore asked as they drew close to the table.

"Did I not tell you? She's at home now. She left the viltula last night, and although Aldegar says she must stay in bed, she is doing much better."

"Home?"

Griston blushed. "She's staying with me at the moment," he said quietly, then defiantly added, "After all, she has nowhere else to go."

Eldore burst out laughing and slapped his companion on the back. "Don't worry, I'm sure Hevalor's far too busy to come and lecture you on morality. Anyway, you'll be moving to the Refuge soon, so who knows who'll be staying with whom. In fact, most people have already gone."

Griston tried to cover his discomfort with a smile. "Aye, as soon as she's a little stronger we'll be joining them."

"And Little Man?"

The smile grew broader. "Oh, he's fine; no ill effects at all. And such a pair of lungs! I'm surprised you haven't heard him all the way over at the Duty Hall."

"Good, I'm glad for you all. And the future?"

"Marriage. And of course, I'll adopt Little Man; but we'll always tell him about his real father; he was a good man."

Before their conversation could go any further a young boy came rushing up to Eldore with an anxious, terrified look on his face.

"Lord Eldore," he cried. "You must come quickly; Master Verryl has gone mad!"

Eldore frowned. "What do you mean mad? Mad in what way?"

"He's locked himself inside the vil-carrim with the apprentice and he says he's going to burn it down!" The frantic child grabbed hold of Eldore's hand and tried dragging him away. "Come on, Hevalor says you must come right away."

"Alright, alright, I'm coming. But I'm sure G'harvil is quite capable of handling an old man like Verryl without my help." Indeed, the Lore-Master's apprentice was a big, burly, thirty-year-old, and the thought of him being overpowered by the thin shrivelled ancient seemed frankly preposterous.

"Not G'harvil, he's got Corrin!"

Eldore's expression hardened. Corrin was G'harvil's eleven-year-old assistant, sometimes referred to as the second apprentice.

"Corrin!" he thundered. "He would dare...?"

He started to run. Faster and faster he went, pounding recklessly through the streets, heedless of the people that had to throw themselves out of his way. In his mind, the fate of the shy, intelligent young scribe had somehow become intertwined with the death of poor Yewan. It was unthinkable that he could allow another child to die needlessly. He was completely oblivious to the presence of Griston, sprinting after him only a few paces behind. The young messenger, unable to match the speed of the two powerful men, soon gave up the chase and came to a panting, breathless halt. He gazed after them and allowed himself a little smile of relief. Whatever the outcome, he knew that he'd done his duty.

It wasn't long before they arrived at the low, white painted building that was the vil-carrim – the house of scrolls. They turned into the short, gravelled drive just as the evil blood-rain began to fall and found four men – including Hevalor – wielding a short but heavy beam to try and batter down the door. G'harvil was standing at one of the tiny windows trying to see exactly what was going on inside.

"It's no use," Hevalor cried as Eldore arrived. "The door's enchanted; it won't open!"

Sure enough, no matter how hard they hit the door with the ram, it remained undented and unmoving. They might as well have been slapping it with a damp rag. To make matters worse, the sticky blood-fall was now making the beam slippery and difficult to hold.

"I see him!" G'harvil shouted with anxious excitement. "He has the boy tied to a chair with scrolls piled around his feet." He raised himself up onto his toes to try and get a better look. "He...

THE TALISMAN OF WRATH

he's pouring something over his head. I can't quite see what... Oh Mordan help us; it's lamp oil! He intends to burn him alive!"

"Out of the way!" Eldore thundered as he pushed his way through to the door. He braced himself then threw himself at it, striking it heavily with his shoulder. Whatever sorcery was protecting the building from Hevalor's party, for some reason it was powerless against the broad, muscular lord. The strong, metal-banded oak door shuddered promisingly under the weight of his assault. His second charge was accompanied by the encouraging sound of splintering wood. On his third attempt he was aided by the welcome assistance of Griston. As they simultaneously crashed against the door, it burst open and the two men stumbled into the sacred library.

Verryl, a dozen strides away from the entrance, turned to them in surprise. But then with an evil laugh he shouted: "Too late!" In his hand he was holding a lighted taper and with a theatrical flourish, he threw it onto the oil-soaked scrolls at Corrin's bound feet. Instantly, they burst into flames – flames that immediately leapt up the screaming boy's legs, threatening to engulf his entire body.

Eldore charged forward and picked up the blazing boy – chair and all – and dashed for the exit. At the same time, Griston threw himself at Verryl, intent on subduing him and dragging him out of the building. To his surprise, the skinny, withered old man resisted his efforts with a superhuman strength that was beyond all reason. Only when Hevalor and G'harvil arrived to assist him was the ancient Lore-Master overwhelmed and forced outside.

Eldore had hoped the sticky red rain would extinguish the boy's flames, but even though it had now turned torrential, the fire seemed to burn all the hotter. Desperately, he tried to beat it out with his bare hands but it seemed that despite his best efforts, another child was going to die.

But then the sky flashed silver as Mordan's Finger erupted. A moment later the frigid blast struck throwing everyone to the ground. The chair-bound boy was sent spinning away to be pinned against the low wall that surrounded the building. But for Corrin, trussed and trapped though he was, the furious arctic gale was a blessed mercy. It turned his blood-soaked clothes to ice, instantly killing the fire while at the same time both numbing the pain and healing his burns. For the men however, the mountain's fury was anything but benevolent. It sliced their flesh and ate into their bones with an agony that made death seem a welcome option. Nor were they given the release of crying out against the pain, for the torture had paralysed their lungs, preventing them from screaming.

But not Eldore. He'd felt this power before when Eh'lorne had first touched the Talisman; and because of Eldore's unique link with his brother, it had almost killed them both. But that time he'd had no direct control and had been at the mercy of Eh'lorne's weaknesses – although admittedly, he'd also been saved by his brother's strengths. This time however, the trial was his alone and he welcomed it.

He found himself on his hands and knees with his back to the vil-carrim. He could hear the roaring inferno even above the howling, supernatural gale. It seemed that the freezing wind was fanning the flames of the burning building the way the bellows at his forge fanned the fire of the furnace.

The mountain's frigid blast was as fierce and as cutting for him as for anyone else, but instead of paralysing his body, it energised it. To his surprise he found he had the strength to crawl round and face into the puissant hurricane and use its force to heave himself to his feet. He stood leaning into it at a crazy angle with his arms spread wide and a savage grimace of ecstasy on his face. The cold fire ripped deep into his soul, incinerating his doubts and shrivelling his fear. He welcomed the searing pain as penance for Yewan's death, absolving that sin and assuaging his guilt. When finally the ordeal ended, he fell back to his knees and gave thanks. There was indeed a lesson in everything and he'd been granted the wisdom to learn from it.

The groans from the stricken men behind him brought his mind back to the plight of the young boy. He jumped up and rushed over, almost crashing into him as he slipped on the treacherous red ice. He was still tied to the chair that lay on its side with its back against the low wall. Eldore crouched down beside him and fumbled at the rope. He intended to untie the knots but there was no need. At his first touch, the tightly wound cords crumbled away to dust.

"Corrin," he called, gently shaking the stunned boy. The boy shifted his gaze to focus on his rescuer's concerned face. "Are you alright, are you hurt?" Corrin didn't reply but attempted to sit up and with Eldore's help, he succeeded. "Are you hurt?" Eldore repeated more gently. The boy looked down at his scorched, ice-stiffened clothes and felt his legs. He raised his eyes again and mutely shook his head.

"Good. Are you alright to sit here for a few moments? It won't be for long." Corrin nodded but something in his manner caused Eldore to pause. He studied the poor boy's face and frowned. His complexion was deathly white and his eyes were blank. The experience had understandably shocked him to the core. "I'll be as quick as I can," he said, laying a compassionate hand on his shoulder. He then hurried back to the others.

They were now all on their feet apart from Verryl who lay curled in a ball on the ground with Griston standing guard over him. The miserable wretch was rocking to-and-fro, his arms tightly wrapped around his head and crying out: "The ice burns – you all must burn! The ice burns – you all must burn!" The jarring litany went on and on without pause.

G'harvil was standing as close to the holocaust as he dared. He held his hands to his distraught face, completely transfixed by the sight of the blazing vil-carrim. Hevalor, equally horrified, stood at his side with a consoling arm around the apprentice's broad shoulders. The three other men whose identities the young lord didn't know, were staring around them in shock and wonder, blinking in the bright, welcome sunshine.

Eldore joined the Overseer at G'harvil's side. The vil-carrim itself was hardly visible among the roaring inferno of flames that were consuming it. It seemed inconceivable that such a solid, strongly constructed building could be destroyed so quickly.

"How did it happen?" he asked, raising his voice so as to be heard above the roaring fire.

G'harvil shook his head despairingly. "It's gone, all gone. Hundreds of years just wiped out in a few moments – all gone; lost forever."

"But what happened, what made Verryl do it?"

G'harvil seemed not to hear him. "All gone," he repeated hopelessly.

Eldore placed himself in front of the apprentice, pulled his hands away from his face, and forced him to look into his eyes. "What happened to Verryl?" he pressed firmly.

"He...he went mad... No, not mad exactly, more... possessed."

"Possessed! How could he have been possessed?"

"It's true," Hevalor interjected supportively. "He's been behaving strangely for some time – even before you ejected him from the council. He hasn't been himself since the battle and I have to take some of the blame. As Overseer, I should have noticed – even more so as his friend."

"But why do you say 'possessed'?"

"It's his eyes," G'harvil continued. "They're no longer his own; and after he was dismissed from the council, he couldn't hide it any longer. He was always difficult to get on with but he was never cruel or spiteful. Since then though... he frightened me."

THE TALISMAN OF WRATH

"He frightened *you*?" Eldore exclaimed incredulously. The thought of the brawny thirty-year-old being frightened of the ancient Lore-Master seemed ridiculous.

"He did. There was something...monstrous about him."

Eldore looked behind them at the pathetic figure curled up on the ground at Griston's feet. "Well there's nothing monstrous about him now," he said with a faint note of disgust.

"True," Hevalor replied with a degree of sympathy for his old friend. "But the damage is done."

"Damage!" G'harvil wailed pointing at the burning building. "This is more than damage; it's the destruction of our past, our laws – our whole way of life!"

"Then it's up to you and Hevalor to make sure our laws and culture remain intact. You are, after all, the new Lore-Master – Verryl can no longer hold the position."

"Lore-Master! There is no Lore to be Master of. It's all gone. All that's left for me are ashes!"

"Then between the two you, you must rewrite whatever can be recalled. Before we abandon the city you must scour it for any books or scrolls that might help you; and in the end, you must start anew. We will begin a new lore, a new history, and perhaps even create new laws. This is your task, and Corrin will be your apprentice."

"We're both too young," G'harvil protested.

"All the better. Young minds for a new way."

The new Lore-Master stared thoughtfully at the inferno in front of him and then drew a deep, shuddering breath. "Very well then. Come along Hevalor, we have our instructions."

"We do, and we must begin at once; time is very short."

All three men turned their backs on the past and walked over to where Griston stood guard over G'harvil's disgraced predecessor. Verryl's position had not changed and nor had his crazed litany of "The ice burns – you all must burn!"

Hevalor looked at his old friend with compassionate eyes. "What shall we do with him?" he asked quietly. "There's no doubt that he's still dangerous, but I'm reluctant to punish him; after all, his mind is not his own."

"You didn't see the look in his eyes as he set fire to Corrin," Eldore stated coldly. "Whatever the damage to book and building, he tried to murder a child, and that is something I struggle to forgive. The law says that the punishment for such an act is death."

"And you yourself have just said that G'harvil and I are to write new laws," Hevalor countered. "What do you say, G'harvil, should we show mercy?"

The new Lore-Master stared thoughtfully down at Verryl. The conflict raging in his heart was clearly reflected on his face. After a long while he sighed reluctantly. "I say withhold the axe; but he must be held securely somewhere."

"We could put him in the oil-store at the Refuge," Griston suggested. "It's almost empty now D'harid has requisitioned the supplies. It's a strong cage and plenty big enough for a bed and a table. It's got a good lock too, which judging by the strength he showed when I tried to apprehend him is no bad thing."

"Very well," agreed Eldore. "Feed him and keep him warm, but never forget what he's done."

G'harvil snorted derisively. "There's no fear of that. I'll always remember the sight of the burning vil-carrim and my poor Corrin bound and aflame."

Griston poked Verryl with his foot. "Do you think he'll remember?"

Hevalor sighed. "I hope not. If ever he regains his senses, he'll suffer more punishment from his own guilt than we could ever impose. I'm going to pray for him."

"You do that," Eldore replied coldly, sounding more like his brother than he'd care to admit. "But I, for my part, shall save my prayers for those more deserving!"

With that he turned and strode stiffly away.

Hevalor watched him go with sad eyes. "Then I shall pray for you as well, my friend," he said softly. He then walked over to assist poor Corrin.

CHAPTER THIRTY-FOUR

Eh'lorne and Bandil sat beneath the star-studded velvet sky and drank in the warmth from their meagre campfire. Although the fire was small, and being only built from rough scrub would be short in duration, it was still a huge risk to light it. The decision to do so had been Eh'lorne's and Eh'lorne's alone. When he'd tried to discuss the danger of it with Bandil, the old man had just given him an empty look and an indifferent shrug. Since the encounter with the sellufin earlier that day, he seemed to have withdrawn into a private world that was full of despair and devoid of hope. His bright perilous eyes were now dim and defeated, and his whole demeanour was somehow shrunken and diminished. Several times as they'd walked on, Eh'lorne had tried to engage with the old recluse; to pass on the news that would lift his spirits and relight the fire in his eyes. But despite the glorious early-spring sunshine, every attempt had fallen on deaf ears or had been met with a disinterested grunt. Now the old man just sat staring sightlessly into the dancing yellow flames, heedless to his companion's very existence.

Abruptly, Eh'lorne got to his feet. "Ah well," he said resignedly. "It was good while it lasted. I'd have been more use if I'd stayed in Sirris but at least I've had some excitement over the past few days."

Bandil's eyes lifted from the fire then widened in surprise as Eh'lorne unbuckled the Talisman and threw it at his feet. The young warrior-king then picked up his pack and made off in the direction of his home.

"So long, my friend," he said in his uniquely cheerful yet unnerving voice. "Although I doubt it, I do hope we'll meet again someday."

"Where are you going?" the old man asked in puzzled alarm.

Eh'lorne paused and turned back to face his ancient companion. "I would have thought that was obvious. I'm returning to Sirris where I belong."

"But the Talisman?"

"What of it? Without your guidance it's of no use to me. My skills lie in swordplay, and in spite of its appearance, that isn't its role. It's a thing of magic and sorcery and that's your speciality, so I'm leaving it with you."

The old man looked horrified. "So you're just going to give up?"

"To the contrary – but it's plain that you have. I'm merely going to where my abilities can be best utilised. I'm of no use to anyone here if you've given up hope."

"What do you know of my hope?" Bandil asked bitterly.

"I know that you should have more than any man alive. No one has ever seen or felt more of Mordan's power than you; yet all afternoon I've watched as dark despair has blackened your soul."

"You heard what the selluf said. If he speaks truly – and the sellufin do not lie – there is no hope. But then, you can't be expected to understand the importance of his words."

Eh'lorne walked back to the fire and knelt beside the old man. "Then *make* me understand," he beseeched softly as he put his arm around his thin, bony shoulders.

Bandil shook his head despondently and returned to gazing into the fire; but Eh'lorne remained where he was, silently compelling him to continue. Eventually, with a heavy sigh the old man gave in.

"Do you recall at the council when I told you of the four great forces at the founding of the world?"

"I do, but you would only tell us about three of them. Of the fourth you were strangely reticent."

"I was; and with good reason. I described three of the Stones of Power – one of which was the Star of Destiny which is already known to you. The second is the Mystic Stone, which although it had been hidden since the dawn of time, both you and your brother recognised the moment you saw it."

"We did, but how that's possible is beyond me."

Bandil looked at his friend in surprise. "Really? Surely it's obvious. It's Mordan's bone, overflowing with his spirit, and you're known as Mordan's children. How could a child not recognise his own father?" He peered questioningly into Eh'lorne's eyes then went back to staring into the flames.

"The third of course, is the Talisman, the gemstone set into the blade of that sword." He glanced at the scabbard lying near his feet. "All of these three – Dignity, Hope, and yes, even Anger, are forces for good. They could be turned to evil of course – as indeed the Star of Destiny has – but they are not intrinsically destructive in their nature."

"That's not my experience with the Talisman," Eh'lorne snorted wryly.

Bandil shook his head sadly. "I knew you wouldn't understand," he sighed.

"I'm sorry." The young Arlien settled himself more comfortably and peered intently at the old man's face. "Go on, I'm still listening."

For a while it seemed the conversation was over, but eventually Bandil resumed his narrative. This time however, his voice was even more morose, more dejected.

"When Mordan founded all things, somehow, somewhere, there was a rebellion. Its cause or nature has never been revealed to me, but the result was a fourth, unintended force. Hatred and malice began to spread throughout the earth, corrupting all the races of men. To prevent the total ruination of his creation, Mordan took hold of this evil force and imprisoned it in another Stone. Sadly, a little of that evil remained in all men's hearts, save for the Arlien race. And for that reason, he named your people as his children.

"The new Stone posed a terrible threat; for should anyone be strong enough to take hold of it and wield it, the malice within it would be unleashed in an unstoppable tide of malevolence. To prevent this, it was hidden beyond the reach of any man, and even the memory of it was erased.

"But from what the selluf said, and from the way the weather has been manipulated against us, it's evident that Limnash holds the Spite Stone and has unlocked its evil power."

There was silence. Only the crackling of the fire and the distant, unearthly howling of wolves disturbed the ominous stillness. These sounds only added weight to the oppressive atmosphere that hung menacingly over their heads. After a while, Eh'lorne leant over and picked up the Talisman. He held it up and studied the intricate black-on-black patterning of the scabbard. He ran his fingers over the hilt and traced the shape of the leaping wolves that made up the cross-guard.

"Are you saying that even with the Talisman of Wrath in the hands of the rightful king, this Limnash is too powerful to be defeated?"

"He has the Spite Stone," Bandil stated emphatically.

Eh'lorne drew the sword just enough to reveal the Talisman itself. The gem sparkled with a cold, arcane beauty. "But surely," he said thoughtfully. "In a world created by good, evil can never be truly triumphant?"

"Perhaps in the fullness of time you're right; but in the span of eternity, the lifetime of a hundred generations is but the blink of an eye. If Limnash were victorious now, his evil reign could last a thousand years before the power of good could bring it down. Think of this: it takes many men many days to build a house, yet one madman could destroy it in just one turn of the time-glass. The power that built the house is stronger than the power that demolished it, but it takes time for good to restore what evil has destroyed."

"I see your point," Eh'lorne conceded gloomily. Absently, he twisted the Talisman this way and that, catching the light of the fire in the scintillating diamond. Abruptly, he stopped as a new thought struck him.

"But you are saying that the many men shouldn't try to stop the madman, or that they shouldn't rebuild the house because it takes too long. To my way of thinking, that is evil in itself."

Bandil looked at him with an expression of surprised admiration. "And when did you become so wise?" he asked with a minute trace of his old humour.

Eh'lorne grinned. "Perhaps I've always possessed such wisdom but *you've* not been wise enough to see it."

The old man shook his head in mock disgust. "Your arrogance is truly breath-taking, and your own actions betray you. Sagacity strikes a discordant note on your lips, my reckless young friend!"

Eh'lorne roared with laughter and slapped the old man hard on the back. "You see, there's another lesson you've taught me. You truly are a good tutor – no, a master tutor! With you to guide me, I'll make a fine king, yes?"

So infectious was his companion's mirth that Bandil couldn't help but smile himself. "Yes, I believe you will."

"Good! In that case I'll stay, and together we'll stand side by side and fight on – whatever the odds. Even if he has the Star and the Stone, win or lose he'll come to rue the day that he crossed us."

"Don't forget there are still two sects of sellufin at large."

"And what if there are?" Eh'lorne cried defiantly. "We'll fight them too; with sword and Stone we'll make them pay for their crimes." His dark eyes flashed passionately in the firelight and his strong, clear voice rang out into the night. "And if weapons should fail, I'll carry on the fight with my fists and my teeth. I'll fight with all my strength for my family, for my friends, and for my people." He knelt in front of the old man and put his hands on his shoulders. "And I have something that's worth more than all the sorcery in all the world. I have Bandil, son of Bail beside me!"

The light of excitement that was growing in the old man's eyes suddenly faded again. "And what does Bandil fight for?" he asked dejectedly.

"He fights for his family!" Eh'lorne declared, punching the air with a clenched fist.

"I have no family," Bandil replied bitterly.

"But you do! I've been trying to tell you all afternoon but in your self-pity you wouldn't listen. You have a relative living here in these very mountains."

"How is that possible? Mylock said he'd personally killed my last living relative himself."

"Ah, but he didn't. You have a great, great...I have no idea how many 'greats', but she is your niece nonetheless. You've even met her."

Bandil's eyes widened as the truth finally dawned on him. "The young tender, Morjeena!"

.

"Morjeena," Eh'lorne confirmed. "As soon as that creature spoke of the pregnant woman fleeing into the mountains, I knew. So, Bandil, son of Bail; prince of Keshtar and emissary of the great god himself, now do you have something to fight for?"

The perilous light behind the old man's eyes burst into life and a look of untamed joy spread across his wrinkled brown face.

"To my last breath!" he growled fiercely.

CHAPTER THIRTY-FIVE

The High Priest's sanctum was far smaller than Rennil had expected – smaller in fact than the room he'd just left. What it lacked in size however, it more than made up for in grandeur. The walls and floor were of the purest marble; gleaming white, and veined with a rich, deep blue. It glistened and sparkled in the bright light of a dozen beautifully cast wall-lamps.

In the centre of the room was a square-cut, waist-high, black granite column. It was plain and unadorned but highly polished to achieve a shining, mirror finish. Taking pride of place on top of the stone pillar and cradled in a finely crafted framework of solid gold, was a horn. Not a sculpture or a representation, but a genuine hunting horn; identical in every way to the massively scaled-up replica that dominated the valley.

Beyond the low column, against the curtained far wall of the chamber was what could only be described as a throne. It stood on a low marble plinth and was carved from the same lustrous black stone as the horn's pillar. It was without doubt the most gloriously imposing seat that Rennil had ever seen. Even King Xyron's golden throne in Mah-Kashia paled in comparison. Its true shape was difficult to comprehend, so complicated was its design. Every one of its multi-faceted surfaces was covered with intricate patterns – those same patterns that had so captivated the Arm-Master in the great atrium. The shape of the armrests, however, was easy to determine. Each one was sculpted into the perfect semblance of a huge wolf, poised ready to pounce.

Sitting comfortably amongst the seat's plush, red-velvet cushions, was the orgulous figure of the High Priest himself. He too was dressed in the now familiar style of robes, but to Rennil's surprise, instead of pale blue, they were the same rich purple colour as his own. The High Priest's however, were edged with gold braid and were tied at the waist with a gold-coloured rope belt. Around his neck he wore a gold chain that held a horn-shaped medallion, similar to Nirsuk's but made of gold rather than silver.

Although his posture made it difficult to be sure of his stature, Rennil had the distinct impression that he was taller than the other priests he had so far encountered. His features were chiselled and refined, while his intense green eyes were somehow both aloof and compassionate. His age was unclear, for although his cropped hair was the colour of tarnished silver, his pale skin was smooth and unblemished. Apart from the crow's feet around his eyes and a slight wrinkling of his forehead, his face was as fresh and as tight as a young man in his twenties.

Rennil advanced confidently towards the throne, carefully skirting the granite pillar. Then, keeping his eyes fixed firmly on the High Priest's, he performed a small but formal bow. He then stood comfortably at ease, patiently waiting for his audience to begin.

For a long time Arbenak said nothing. He sat motionless, scrupulously scrutinising every detail of the Arms-Master's face. He examined his brow and hairline, the deep scratches that Rennil had received in the recent battle, and then traced the full course of the hideous, disfiguring scar.

When at last he spoke, his voice was as deep in tone as Rennil's, but instead of the Arms-Master's gruff, rumbling timbre, it was as rich and as smooth as cream.

"By what right do you come to this valley unasked and unwelcome?"

Rennil raised a questioning eyebrow. "Unwelcome?"

"And unasked."

"Does a man need an invitation to defend a friend from a violent attack? And why would his aid be so displeasing to his friend?"

"If such an attack were imminent, I would agree; but if it were, I would know of it. Mordan has always protected us here; the High Priest is given insight and revelation in his name, and he has given me no such warning in either dream or prophecy."

Rennil shrugged. "What would I know of such matters as dreams? But I do know that an army – the largest ever to march – will fall upon you within days. That threat is as real as the ground beneath my feet and I've willingly led my men here to fight for you, and if need be, to die for you."

For a while there was silence as Arbenak considered the Arms-Master's words. He peered intently into Rennil's eyes, searching out every nuance of meaning and motive.

"Your voice carries the weight of truth," he said at last. "But there is some falsehood too. You claim to have come here

S. P. MUIR

willingly, but that is a lie. I can see that you were pressed into it against what you consider to be your better judgement."

"You're very perceptive," Rennil replied with a conciliatory smile. "It is true, my own instincts would compel me to stay in Sirris, for it too faces a terrible foe. But as I've recently been reminded, I am just a soldier and therefore must go where I'm sent."

"Then tell me, Rennil, son of Raul, who is it that's able to force the mighty *Dithkar-Geer* to abandon both his duty and his people?" But before Rennil could reply, Arbenak smiled knowingly and answered his own question. "Of course, High-Lord Lorne. I know how close you are to him and your fates are as intertwined as the wind and the rain. There, you see, even here in the confines of this temple I know what happens in the world."

"Then you know less than you think. High-Lord Lorne is gone. He fell into the long sleep some ten days ago when Sirris was attacked by the same army that annihilated Sarren." Rennil's voice then became heavy with remorse as he added: "He was slain by the great warrior-mage that commanded them."

Arbenak jerked forward in his seat. "Lorne is dead?" he asked incredulously. "That cannot be true or I would have foreseen it. And the Lord-Guard, where were they?"

"At his side; but even they could not protect him when he threw himself against that evil, enchanted general."

"If I could not read the truth in your voice, I'd not for a moment believe your words; after all, the High-Lord is prohibited from using a weapon by law. Believe me, no one is more aware of the Oath of Duty than I – and all it entails." He paused a moment and thoughtfully stroked his freshly shaved chin. "But I have no other choice than to believe that Lorne fell in battle." Then he smiled and sat back into the throne's cushions. "In a way I'm glad. It's a fitting end for one so noble, and I'm certain it's the manner of passing that he would have chosen.

"So then, *Dithkar-Geer*, which of his sons was it that sent you here? Which one of them is the new High-Lord?"

"We no longer have a High-Lord; the Seat of Duty has been abolished."

Arbenak frowned. "I don't understand; how can it be abolished? Your people must be governed and someone must have sent you here. Who now has the Authority if not the High-Lord?"

Rennil drew himself erect and in a bold voice declared: "King Eh'lorne Starbrow, first of the exiled second line, and by Mordan's will, the rightful ruler of all Keshtar."

The High Priest leapt to his feet. "*King* Eh'lorne!" he shouted angrily. "*King* Eh'lorne? Impossible! I've had no dreams and been given no signs. If Eh'lorne held the Star of Destiny he'd be here himself instead of you. If the Star had been found, I would know of it!"

Astonished by the outburst, Rennil knew he'd have to choose his words more carefully than ever.

"The Star *has* been found," he began cautiously. "But it's not yet in his possession."

"Then he has no right to call himself king!"

"Under normal circumstances, I would agree; but circumstances are far from normal. Evil has possessed the Star and Mordan's emissary has come forward and declared the right of Gorand's heir to be king."

"What emissary?" Arbenak scoffed. "I've seen no emissary in my dreams and neither has one ever been prophesied."

"Be that as it may, it's nonetheless true. He has proved his fidelity to the High Council, and the whole land has witnessed the great power that he unleashed this very day – or were you also blind to the eruption of Mordan's Finger?"

"Be careful, *Dithkar-Geer*," the High Priest warned "Don't presume to test my patience too far." Rennil bowed in apology – an apology that the High Priest acknowledged with a minute nod before continuing with his questions. "So, are you saying that this emissary and Eh'lorne unleashed the mountain's power together?"

"They did," Rennil confirmed confidently, hoping that he was right.

"And am I correct to assume that this is part of Eh'lorne's right to be king?"

"It is."

Arbenak retook his seat and with a look of hope and wonder in his eyes breathed: "Then you have a king at last." His gaze then snapped sharply back to focus on Rennil. "Does he come here, are we finally to fulfil the pledge?"

Rennil looked confused. "Yes, but he comes here to do battle. I know nothing of any pledge or how it should be fulfilled."

"What?" Arbenak cried, turning puce with rage. "For all these centuries we've served the pledge and kept watch; for hundreds of years we've eschewed the company of women, forsaking comfort and family to guard the integrity of that promise. And your people..." He pointed an accusing finger at the startled Arms-Master, "...could not even do us the honour of remembering it!"

Rennil was stunned. He'd never have believed that these stoical people could display such emotion, and he'd no idea of what he'd said to cause it. Frantically, he searched his memory but nowhere could he recall anything relating to the Hornvalers' history, nor to any promise. It flashed into his mind that the world's fate hung precariously on his ability to choose his words with care and tact. He was also acutely aware that, whatever the gifts his creator had given him, diplomacy was not among them. Perversely, he decided to turn that weakness into an asset. Feigning a cold, barely controlled anger, he fixed the raging

THE TALISMAN OF WRATH

High Priest with a contemptuous stare and quietly growled his reply.

"I thought I'd already made it clear to you that I'm just a soldier. I leave policy and politics to High-Lords, and history to the Lore-Masters and Keepers of the Past. I have no interest in such things; but I'm sure when the king arrives, all your questions will be answered. Until then, I strongly suggest that we join together and prepare to defend this temple of yours against the hordes that threaten you!"

The High Priest glared at the Arms-Master with indignant fury, his angry green eyes boring deep into Rennil's mind. Never before had the hardened warrior felt so threatened and defenceless. But firmly he stood his ground and defiantly returned Arbenak's intense gaze.

Eventually, with a supreme effort, the high Priest regained his dignity. "My apologies, *Dithkar-Geer*," he said tightly. "You are right of course; a royal pledge is a matter for royal blood. I shall look forward to discussing the Oath's end with the 'king' when he arrives. In the meantime, I'll allow you to work with the *First of the Watch* to ensure that our defences are adequate. Now, if there's nothing else, there's much upon which I need to ponder and to pray."

Rennil frowned. "There is one thing that's puzzling me. Ever since I arrived here, I keep hearing that it's not yet 'my time'; but exactly what and when is 'my time'? And how could you have been preparing for it for so many years?"

Once again Arbenak coldly scrutinised the old warrior's scarred, determined face. But when he eventually spoke, his voice was surprisingly gentle.

"There are many reasons why you shouldn't have that knowledge – not least because there is a danger of the prophecy becoming self-fulfilled." There was another long pause. It seemed to Rennil that Arbenak was debating with himself on whether or not to continue. Eventually, he gave a deep sigh of resignation. "But it does appear that prophecy has completely failed us in this case. Destiny has become warped and somehow the timescales have been reset. I'll try to tell you what little I can without jeopardising the future any further. But first you must tell me how much you know of my order and of our lives and our purpose."

Rennil shrugged. "I know very little about you I'm afraid. I know that you live here in this temple-city, that you shun the outside world, and that you worship the Great Horn. Other than that, I know nothing."

Arbenak's eyes widened incredulously. "You really believe we worship that stone sculpture?"

"That is what I've heard and nothing I've seen has led me to believe differently."

"But you know that we worship Mordan, and his laws prohibit such idolatry."

"And yet wherever I look I see the Horn's image. You wear it around your neck as does the *First*. And even here..." he gestured towards the stone column behind him, "...its form is venerated."

Arbenak shook his head in disbelief. "How could you know so little of your own people's past? Ah well," he sighed. "It appears that I'm to give you a little lesson in history first." He settled himself more comfortably among the cushions. Then, while gazing sightlessly over the Arms-Master's head, he began to speak in a level, tutorial tone.

"Many centuries ago, King Gorand's grandfather, Eh'zoar, sent a small army against the wild men of the western wilds. He seriously underestimated them, for they were cannibalistic savages; murderous heathens without pity or fear. The Arlien force was well trained and valiant, but they were in danger of being overwhelmed. But the wild men had another enemy; the mountain tribes of the north. And when these good people – my people – saw Eh'zoar's plight, they quickly gathered an army of their own and swooped down to rescue the beleaguered Arliens.

THE TALISMAN OF WRATH

In the following respite, a message was sent to Arl calling for reinforcements and when they came, the allied armies decimated the wild men and drove them out of the western wilds completely. Eh'zoar was so grateful that he presented those lands to my people for all time.

"We in turn gave up our many gods and learned the ways of Mordan. Our queen, Shakra the Great, then swore an oath on the Star that should ever the Arlien kings be in need, her people would once again come to their aid. A hunting horn was infused with the Star's power and kept in the palace at Arl, waiting for the time when it would be necessary to sound it.

"When the Star was lost, we left the wilds and Gorand led your people into exile. The Covenant Horn was entrusted to my ancestors and a new oath was sworn. We vowed to keep the Horn safe and pure until such time as the Star might be found again. If it was, then the king would return to reclaim the Horn and free us from our bondage. Thus, we built this temple to preserve the Horn until the Oath's end."

"But what of the Great Horn? Where are the women and children? Where do I fit...?"

Arbenak silenced him with a curt wave of his hand. "Your ignorance is breath-taking, *Dithkar-Geer*," he snapped. "You insult me with your lack of understanding. Nevertheless, I'll continue the tale. Queen Hashka, Shakra's granddaughter, chose two thousand and one men to serve the Covenant. They were all ordained as priests of the Pledge and Guardians of the Watch. Over time, the terms of that service were refined until each man – chosen and trained from a child – comes here at the age of nineteen and serves for exactly ten years – not a day more nor a day less." A wistful look came into his eyes. "All that is save the High Priest," he added sadly.

"And how long does he serve?" Rennil asked softly, his gruff voice laden with sympathy and awe.

Arbenak smiled ruefully. "Until Mordan sees fit to release him."

A strange tingle of fear and excitement flooded the Arms-Master's body as he asked: "Who chooses the High Priest?"

"Mordan makes that choice. The name is passed on to the current High Priest in either dream or vision, often many years in advance. It is the power of the Star contained in the Horn behind you that gives the High Priest his abilities; and it was that power that revealed to me the name of my successor. It was not a pleasant experience for never has a High Priest been chosen more emphatically!"

Rennil spun around and stared at the horn sitting innocently on the square stone pillar. "This is *the* Horn?" he asked in an awed voice.

"It is."

Rennil turned back to face Arbenak. "Then when King Eh'lorne comes, he can reclaim it and put an end to your servitude. Then when we're strong enough, he can sound it and together our peoples will march on Arl and destroy the evil one that rules there."

The High Priest shook his head. "Therein lies the problem. Nothing of this has been prophesied. Without possessing the Star, the king cannot return, and worst of all, *you should not be here*!"

"But I've already told you, Mordan's emissary has come forward. His warning prevented Sirris' destruction – although sadly, he was too late to save Sarren."

"Sarren was an abomination!" Arbenak declared coldly. "Although I grieve for its people, it was a heresy that should never have been built."

Dismayed by the callous outburst, Rennil opened his mouth to object but was unable to think of anything to say.

"Do I shock you?"

"You appal me! Would you have preferred that I let Sarren be destroyed and its people slaughtered ten years ago? Is that really what you're saying?"

"Not at all. They were not destined for destruction at that time. But that attack was a warning – and a warning that the people ignored to their cost. They should have abandoned Sarren and returned to Sirris – the City of Shame – where they belonged. If Mordan had wanted to save them now, his emissary would have arrived sooner."

Rennil shook his head emphatically. "No, you're wrong! I can't believe that a merciful god would make such a harsh judgement against his own people."

"It matters little what you believe," Arbenak replied flatly. "And remember, Mordan did not destroy Sarren, he merely restrained his hand. Don't make the mistake of judging his actions, *Dithkar-Geer*; he may in turn decide to judge yours."

Rennil remained tight lipped but he glared at the High Priest with outraged fury. Arbenak ignored the disrespect and continued in a calm, inquisitive tone.

"But we must return to this emissary of yours. You say he has declared the second line and that Eh'lorne has proved his right to the crown; so again I ask, how is that possible if he does not hold the Star of Destiny?"

"Your ignorance is breath-taking!" Rennil snapped sarcastically, echoing the High Priest's own words. "Don't make the mistake of judging the king lest he in turn decides to judge you."

Arbenak's eyes narrowed and his cheeks flushed with anger but he kept his voice remarkably cool.

"I've already warned you not to overstep the mark; I'll not do so again. My question is just, so please answer it. I ask again, by what right does he claim the throne?"

"By the power of the Mystic Stone that Mordan's emissary has used to place the Talisman of Wrath in his hand!" Rennil took a defiant step forward. "Does that satisfy you, High Priest Arbenak?"

"The Talisman?" Arbenak sat eagerly forward, his voice tense with excitement. "He comes here with the Talisman of Wrath?" Rennil nodded, amazed that the High Priest knew of the Talisman's existence. "And the Mystic Stone accompanies it?"

"It does. So if that satisfies your doubts about the king, perhaps you can finish telling me about your prophecy concerning 'my time'. Or would you rather prevaricate until the enemy is tearing down your walls!"

Again, Arbenak's face flushed with anger and this time the peril in his voice could be clearly heard. "I've cautioned you about your insolent tone twice already. I WILL NOT TOLERATE IT, no matter who you are!"

"AND WHO AM I?" Rennil demanded loudly.

For the third time Arbenak studied the Arms-Master's disfigured face. Then with a resigned sigh, he sat back in his throne. "Do you really not know, even now?"

"Tell me."

The High Priest allowed himself a gentle smile. "Very well," he conceded softly. "You are Rennil, son of Raul; you are *Dithkar-Geer* – the Deadly Ghost; and when 'your time' comes, you will be High Priest of the Pledge and Guardian of the Watch."

CHAPTER THIRTY-SIX

The smouldering remains of the vil-carrim had been damped down late in the morning of the following day. Thick clouds had rolled in from the south delivering a brief but heavy downpour of rain. Real rain. Proper rain. A torrential shower of fresh, clean water. Under normal circumstances the black sky would have been oppressive, but after the evil red overcast of the past few days, it had felt gloriously natural. Many of the city's citizens had rushed out into the downpour and watched it rinse away the last vestiges of the glutinous blood. They'd revelled in the cold deluge that had left them drenched and shivering but refreshed and cleansed. The storm had then rolled away to the north, relentlessly growing and spreading as if their god was purifying the sacred, mountainous lands by washing away the evil filth that had contaminated it.

With elevated spirits, the Arlien people had then thrown themselves back into their work with an even greater enthusiasm. They'd performed superhuman feats of strength and endurance as they'd constructed the defences for their city. By the end of the sixth day, they were close to completion; and although there was still a pervading sense of fear and apprehension, it was at least tempered by feelings of achievement and hope.

The morning of the seventh day – the fourth since Verryl's insane act of arson – had dawned shrouded in a thick, impenetrable mist that had threatened to delay the final details of the preparations. There'd been no need for concern, however, for by third turn of the glass, the bright spring sun had burnt away the dense fog to leave the day unseasonably warm and pleasant. Indeed, were it not for the impending calamity, it would have been the most promising start to the growing season for over a decade. Gurd, the burly farming supervisor, was beside himself with frustration at the thought that such good fortune being put to waste. But even he had given his all to the work, drawing sly, amused looks from those observing his ruddy, round face, flushed and dripping with sweat.

And so it was that at midday, D'harid and the Council members (including G'harvil as Verryl's replacement) were standing at the city outskirts during a brief tour of the finished fortifications. Every road into the city had been sealed with strong, high barricades – all that is, save the southwestern approaches. The whole of the industrial quarter had been left separated and defenceless – apart from a long row of stout, curved wicker shields, each just large enough to hide a man.

"Your plan is of course insane," Hesta stated dryly.

D'harid smiled. "I hope so, for without the unpredictability of such madness, we have no hope of survival."

THE TALISMAN OF WRATH

Tilmar frowned. "Are you saying that if your plan fails, we have no hope?"

"What else would you have me say?" D'harid replied with a shrug. "If I told you that a few civilians with no military training could defeat a huge and merciless army, would you believe me? Of course not! But the situation is what it is. We stick to the plan and pray for deliverance."

G'harvil looked puzzled. "Vice-Master, there's still too much I don't understand. Could you explain them to me one more time?"

"Of course," D'harid replied in his calm, steady voice. "What would you like to know?"

While the new Lore-Master asked his questions, Eldore found himself looking out over the great valley-plain that he'd called home for his whole life. The fields and pastures seemed as tranquil as ever, but at the same time they were somehow now strange and alien. A great deal of blood had already been spilled there; he wondered how much more the fertile soil would have to absorb before the struggle was finally over.

A faint, distant cry was carried on the breeze from the southwest. He strained his ears, hoping against hope it had been nothing more than the plaintive call of a bird seeking a mate; or perhaps even, the bleating of a goat. But there it was again, nearer this time. Then again, and again; closer and louder each time. It was the chain of sentry horns calling the warning of the enemy's approach.

"D'harid," he called.

The Vice-Master turned and nodded. "I hear it," he said coolly. Then in the same calm, unflustered voice he addressed the others. "Well, it seems we'll have to finish our little tour here; our guests look as though they're going to be fastidiously punctual. Lord Eldore, if you wouldn't mind, will you escort these good people back to the Refuge? Then once our men have taken their places, perhaps you'd like to join me at the watchtower."

Eldore nodded and made as if to lead the Council members back into the city, but at Hesta's insistence, they refused to follow him.

"If I may," she said with stiff indignation. "We are not children that need to be shepherded back to our mother's aprons. We are more than capable of finding our own way to the caves and do not need a chaperone."

"My apologies," D'harid replied sincerely. "I'm afraid my concern for you outstripped my manners. Please forgive me, I meant no insult."

"Then none is taken," she replied graciously. "Come then, 'good people', we'll leave the soldiers to wage war while we in turn support and reassure the citizens in our charge." She turned and walked gracefully away, radiating a proud, courage-inspiring dignity.

D'harid watched her go with an admiring smile playing on his lips. As Eldore came to his side he gave the young lord a mischievous wink. "Now there's a woman I could easily lose my heart to." Then with an exaggerated sigh he playfully added: "But she's a high-born lady and I'm nothing but a common soldier..."

* * *

It was mid-afternoon when the massed hordes of Limnash's army swept across the plain towards Sirris. D'harid and Eldore stood atop a tall, makeshift watchtower in the northern half of the city close to the river at Stonebridge. From that lofty vantage point they could just make out the distant enemy coming towards them like a dark stain spreading across Cor-Peshtar's sacred earth. Despite having shared his brother's vision, their

THE TALISMAN OF WRATH

numbers were so unimaginably vast that just seeing them here in the flesh caused him to sag helplessly against the wooden guardrail. "Mordan help us," he breathed despairingly.

Even the implacable Vice-Master seemed perturbed. He stood stiffly at Eldore's side, his jaw clenched and his eyes hard and narrowed. "My plan will fail," he stated with a flat chill in his voice.

"What do you mean, it'll fail?"

"Just that. Their numbers are too great; I'd never have dreamt such an army was possible."

"Then all is lost!"

D'harid drew a deep breath and stared at the advancing hordes. A moment later his taut frame relaxed and he turned to his disconsolate companion. The steady calm returned to his eyes and his voice regained its reassuring note of competence.

"Perhaps not. If all goes well, we'll kill half of them; and although I doubt that'll send them scurrying away in fear, it might at least buy us some time." He placed a hand on Eldore's shoulder and smiled consolingly. "Take courage, my friend; we must have faith and fight well. We are Mordan's children and if he so desires it, we *will* prevail."

Back at the city's edge, just three hundred men barred the enemy's way. Each man stood beside the wicker shields with a powerful bow notched in his hand and the ground at his feet bristling with planted arrows. They wore no mail or helm and their feet were only lightly shod. Even to call them men was greatly stretching the truth, for most were yet to see their twentieth summer. Their fresh young faces were pale and anxious, and the closer their foes came, the greater the fear in their eyes grew. As a first line of defence they looked pathetically inadequate, to say the least.

Pacing up and down behind the line of archers was their commanding officer. He was dressed in the same inappropriate manner as his men but was a little older and seemed far more experienced. He was in fact a regular soldier of the armshost, but the clean white head-bandage that completely covered his left eye attested to the reason why he'd been excluded from the expedition to Hornvale.

"Steady boys," he called out as he paced. "I'll tell you when." Every ten steps he stopped and peered out towards the enemy, gauging their progress and trying to judge the most opportune moment to act.

Soon, it was possible to make out individual figures amongst the solid mass of bodies, and this caused even more consternation amongst his youthful charges. It wasn't just their numbers, for as daunting as they were, the young Arliens had been warned to expect such a vast onslaught. No, it was the sheer animal ferocity of their adversaries that was so shocking; for at the forefront of the attack marched the bare-chested barbarians. As soon as they caught sight of the small force barring their way, they screamed out their bloodcurdling battle cries and began to charge. Their blue-painted faces were twisted with raging bloodlust as they rushed forward, effortlessly whirling their massive battle-axes around their heads.

As they came into range of the Arlien bows, the one-eyed officer stopped, drew himself erect, and then shouted out his instructions.

"Set your arrows; draw; loose!" At his command, three hundred arrows flew and without so much as an instant's pause, he repeated the refrain. His voice was soon drowned out by the howls of the approaching barbarians but by now the archers were well into their rhythm. In rapid succession, their barbed missiles flew, and by the time the attackers were halfway towards their quarry, almost two thousand had fallen to be trampled underfoot by their comrades.

But then, from the massed ranks behind the yellow haired tsunami, a dark cloud rose into the air almost blocking out the sun. The Keshtari archers had made their reply, launching ten arrows for every one shot by the Arliens. Instinctively, the defenders ducked behind their wicker shelters, safe from the deadly hail that rained down around them. But the damage had been done; their commander had no shelter to protect him from the raining arrows and had been pierced at least a dozen times. He lay on his back with his one dead eye staring sightlessly towards the heavens. With no one to pull them back together and with their rhythm broken, the Arlien resistance quickly wavered and then crumbled completely. After one or two half-hearted volleys, they threw away their bows and fled back into the city with the frustrated, baying mob close on their heels.

But against all appearances, this was no rout. Each man had been carefully chosen, not for his proficiency with a bow – most Arlien men were equally as skilled – but for his fleetness of foot. Their light clothing and soft shoes gave them a speed and agility that left their aggressors struggling in their wake. These men were not warriors – they were bait. With extraordinary dexterity they sprinted through the streets, ducking under or leaping over the ropes that were strung across the roads from ground to rooftop. They eventually dashed over the stone bridge and raced the final fifty strides or so to the semi-circular stockade on the north bank of the river. There, dozens of hands reached down to haul them up and over the parapet to safety. Apart from their unfortunate officer, not one life had been lost.

As soon as the last man had reached sanctuary, the first of the barbarians appeared. Their blonde hair was now slick and wet while their naked torsos glistened in the bright afternoon sunlight. In their blind eagerness to kill, they'd blundered straight into D'harid's trap. As they'd charged recklessly through the streets, they'd caught the ropes that the Arliens had so skilfully avoided, pulling buckets of lamp oil down onto their heads. They were completely soaked with it, and those following along behind were splashing through great puddles of the reeking, slippery liquid.

"Fire your arrows!" came the order from behind the barricade. Hundreds of archers dipped their flame-pitched arrowheads into the dozens of braziers that were strategically scattered along the defensive line. At the command, "Loose!" the flaming missiles poured into the packed bodies of the barbarians on the bridge. Instantly, they burst into flames, screaming and flailing wildly in their terrible agony. Many threw themselves over the wall into the river, only to be swept away by the fast, freezing current.

The burning arrows flew again, this time igniting the men on the far bank. The next volley climbed high into the air and then dropped down onto the flame-pitch painted mills and workshops that made up that sector of the city. Great fires began to spring up in one place after another and as they did, the disparate factions of the endangered army became aware of their peril and turned to escape the city before it could become their fiery tomb. Desperately they tried to force their way back to safety but were hampered by the great crush of the thousands at the city outskirts trying to force their way in. Even so, it seemed inevitable that most would escape unscathed.

But D'harid wasn't finished yet. The burning arrows and blazing buildings were not an end in themselves. They were also a signal to the seven-hundred conscripts waiting in the untouched eastern sector. These men – including Griston – were just farmers and labourers. They'd not even been given the most basic training that Rennil had hoped to give them; but none were unacquainted with archery. At exactly the right moment, they joined the battle and launched their own fiery salvoes over the protective barricades. Although lacking any kind of disciplined co-ordination, their volleys were no less effective. Deliberately they targeted the south causing a conflagration that immediately trapped any soldier that had been foolish enough to enter the city. If the size of the invading force had been even twice the size of the preceding lich army, it would have been completely annihilated. But as it was, little more than half of its warriors had become ensnared in D'harid's fiery trap.

The Keshtarim and the Screaming Nomads that made up the bulk of the forces outside the city, were cunning and experienced warriors, and it didn't take them long to assess and evaluate the situation. As wave after wave of the fiery arrows fell onto the western city, they tore down the barriers on the outskirts and flooded into the quarantined eastern quarter. Dozens of the Arliens were caught before they could react but those warned by the spreading commotion fled towards the small wooden footbridge that had been left standing to facilitate their escape.

Once again, a deadly race ensued but this time the defenders had no advantage. As fast as they ran, the enemy was faster – particularly the dark-skinned Nomads with their fierce eyes, golden earrings, and long, curved swords. Few of the makeshift Arlien force had managed to cross the rickety wooden footbridge before their attackers fell on them. They were caught as they waited their turn to step onto the narrow causeway, and although they tried valiantly to form a perimeter, they were no match for the Nomads with their sharp, savage blades and their nerve-shattering, ear-piercing screams.

Griston was the last to fall. He stood barring the bridge's approach while the final few survivors made their way across behind him. His face was grim and covered in the blood that flowed from a gaping wound in his head. When the last escapee leapt to freedom behind him, he began to back onto the wooden walkway. But before he was even halfway across, the Nomad he was facing aimed a vicious blow that was intended to remove his head. Although Griston managed to block the heavy scimitar with his own sword, such was the power of the strike that it knocked him from his feet. The Screaming Nomad stood over him and grinned savagely. With his white teeth flashing against his dark skin, the fierce desert warrior raised his scimitar high over his head and prepared to cut Griston in half.

But before he could deliver the dolorous stroke, he staggered and fell against the rail as the bridge suddenly lurched beneath his feet. On the far bank, whips cracked and the oxen that were roped to the bridge's buttresses began to pull. With loud, splintering creaks, the whole structure began to give way and as it fell, Griston reached up and gripped the lowest rungs of the railings. He looked up into the mocking, clear blue sky and wept.

"Annisa," he whispered as the bridge collapsed into the rushing water below.

High up on the rickety watchtower, D'harid and Eldore had witnessed the entire battle. From the chase to Stonebridge, right through to the catastrophe at the walkway where they'd watched in horror as that tragedy had unfolded. And even after the bridge was finally torn down, the Vice-Master continued to stare at the site of the massacre, transfixed by the overwhelming horror of it. Of the seven hundred civilian conscripts he'd deployed there, barely a hundred had escaped to safety. Eldore could feel the sense of guilt and culpability radiating from the man like the heat from a stove. In a sudden flash of insight, he understood the true reason for D'harid's lack of ambition.

When at last he spoke, D'harid's voice was as cool as ever, but the contrast between his calm tone and the chilling resolve of his words sent a shiver running down Eldore's spine.

"I don't know how, and I don't when, but I swear by all that's holy, I will live to see those men avenged a hundredfold."

Eldore looked out over the blazing inferno that was the city's western quarter and shuddered. The screams of the burning enemy soldiers had thankfully now stopped; but whether that was because they were all dead or because the roaring fire was simply drowning them out, there was no way of telling. With almost no men with any military training, D'harid had managed to slaughter more than twice as many as Rennil had killed with the full armshost.

He placed a consoling hand on his companion's shoulder and felt almost sorry for the remainder of the enemy. He didn't know how, and he didn't know when, but he knew that D'harid *would* fulfil his promise.

CHAPTER THIRTY-SEVEN

However high the esteem in which Rennil was held, it certainly wasn't reflected in the accommodation the Hornvalers had provided for him. His sleeping chamber was small and sparse in comforts. Although clean and bright with its whitewashed stone walls and polished wooden floor, the furnishings consisted of nothing more than a cramped, lumpy bed and a single, crudely made table. It was pleasantly warm however, for a small but efficient wood-burner sat in one corner of the room with its smoke stack disappearing straight into the wall. The Arms-Master had been reliably informed that it then joined a vast, complex system of ducts that linked every stove and fire in the temple to one great chimney. Nirsuk had almost sounded proud when he'd explained that this provided a draw that was stronger than any other arrangement in the world! All very ingenious but hardly comforting.

Not that Rennil now cared or even noticed. He was sitting on the bed, tightly hugging his legs with his chin resting thoughtfully on his knees. He was staring intently at the purple robes lying carefully folded on the bare wooden table. A single ray of the morning sun streamed in through the slit-like window, illuminating them as if to highlight their importance. He'd only worn them until his own clothes had been cleaned and returned that first evening, but he'd then been strangely reluctant to surrender the odd, priest-like garments. It was now his fifth morning at Hornvale, and although he was already dressed, the pull of the sacred garments had grown so strong, it was almost irresistible.

What in the name of the great god was he to do? He was a seasoned warrior, a hardened soldier – a killer, not a holy man. Every fibre of his being was dedicated to the art of war; to the most efficient method of slaughtering his enemies while at the same time preserving as many of his own men's lives as possible. Avenging the innocent and defending the helpless had been the driving force behind his actions for most of his adult life; but now...?

The dreams had started on his very first night at the temple, but in the morning, he'd put them down to his strange conversation with Arbenak. But with each successive night, the visions had grown more vivid and more troubling until now, he could deceive himself no longer; this was not just a revelation, it was a command. And that was his dilemma. To obey that command would mean abandoning his sworn duty and sacrificing his own life and the lives scores of others for what seemed nothing more than a pointless and futile gesture. For the hundredth time he wished that Eh'lorne was there with him. He and Bandil should have arrived at least three days ago but there was no sign of the charismatic king-designate or his ancient, enigmatic companion. Nor had he seen either of them in his dreams – and that troubled him. He now knew a great many things; and not just from what he'd seen in the clear, intense visions of the night, but also from the intuition that had seemingly come from nowhere.

Sirris for instance. He'd had no idea of what D'harid's plan had entailed when he'd left the city, yet for no discernible reason, he was now intimately acquainted with its every nuance. Last night, when Gildor had called him to the Choke and had shown him the red glow in the southern sky, he'd merely smiled. The Prime, of course, had been understandably outraged by his apparent indifference.

"Sirris burns and you find it amusing?" he'd cried.

Rennil had then tried to explain that there was no cause for concern and that the huge fire reflected in the sky was just part of the plan.

"And you know this how?" the perplexed Prime had snapped.

But Rennil could only shrug. "I just do," he'd replied lamely.

So, what to do now? He bit his lip and stroked the long deep scar on his cheek. In the end it came down to a clear choice between obeying his sworn duty and obeying his god – and he'd never been the most conscientious follower of his religion. Although his belief in Mordan was as strong as any other Arlien, his years abroad had taken their toll on the time he now spent in prayer and meditation. But now his new insight could not be ignored; and last night's dreams...

Abruptly, he made his decision. He got to his feet, stripped off his own clothes and pulled on the sacred purple robes. Once re-clothed, there was a moment's hesitation before he drew a deep breath, and then strode out of the chamber.

A short time later he emerged into the temple's huge, bright central atrium. Normally this area was bustling with activity but Rennil knew that at this time of day most of the priests were occupied elsewhere. There were still a few blue-robed men scurrying through the vast chamber though, and the Arms-Master wasted no time in attracting the attention of one of them. Without a word the stone-faced, important-looking priest approached Rennil and stood patiently waiting for him to speak. The old warrior gave a polite nod of greeting and then inquired of the priest's name. The puzzled Hornvaler tilted his head inquisitively, failing to see why the question was relevant. Nevertheless, he gave his reply.

"My name is Reeshuk," he said flatly.

"Excellent. Tell me, my good Reeshuk, do you know Nirsuk, the *First of the Watch*?"

The priest raised an eyebrow, which for these most implacable of people signified the height of incredulity. This disbelief was not wasted on Rennil who suddenly realised that he might just as well have asked a great scholar if he knew the colour of grass, or in which direction the sky could be found.

"My apologies, Reeshuk," he said contritely. "I didn't mean to insult your intellect." The priest accepted the apology with an almost imperceptible bow. "But I do need you to run an important errand for me. I want you to find the *First* and instruct him to meet me at the city gate immediately. Tell him that it's most urgent."

"That is impossible," Reeshuk replied stoically. "None have the authority to instruct the *First* save the High Priest himself; and besides, he will be at morning devotions and cannot be disturbed."

"It is *Dithkar-Geer* that gives the instruction," Rennil insisted. "And as for disturbing him, if he fails to do as I say, there'll be no need for devotions. By tomorrow there will be no temple and your centuries of service will have counted for nothing!"

For a few heartbeats the priest didn't move but stared into Rennil's face as he considered the Arms-Master's words. Then with a curt, "As you wish," he hurried away.

Rennil sighed and closed his eyes. That was it then. Events had been set in motion and there was no going back. After several deep breaths he left the temple building and made his way through the courtyard to the gate out into the ramshackle city. The settlement itself was far busier than the temple. Brown-robed monks were hurrying here and there as they prepared for a long, hard day's work. He caught the arm of one passer-by who stopped and looked at him with the now familiar implacable expression.

"I need someone to take a message for me, can you do that?" The monk thought for a moment then nodded. "Good, I want you to find the Prime of the Lord-Guard and tell him to meet me at the Great Horn. Do you know who he is and where to find him?"

"Is he the soaring elder with the face of a boy?"

"That's him," Rennil smiled, amused by the monk's apt description.

"Then I will find him at the King's Gate. He stands there watching the road as if waiting for someone to arrive. I'll go at once." With that he disappeared into the city.

Immediately, Rennil turned his attention back to the temple. He hoped against hope that Reeshuk had managed to convey the urgency of his instruction. He needn't have worried though, for far sooner than he'd expected, Nirsuk came scurrying across the courtyard towards him.

"You have need of me?" In spite of the exertion of running, the *First's* breathing was as level and controlled as his expression.

"Beyond question!" Rennil replied emphatically. "We must go to the Great Horn at once. I'll explain why as we walk."

"In that case, I will fetch my staff."

"No you won't; there's no time for that. We have to go at once!"

"Of course," Nirsuk replied in the same even tone. "But first I will fetch my staff."

Before the exasperated Arms-Master could protest any further, Nirsuk was gone. Rennil put his hands to his head and choked off a cry of frustration. These people were unbearably stubborn and obdurate. He wondered if it was going to be possible not to throttle at least one of them before the day was out! His vexation was short lived however, for almost immediately the *First* returned with not one but two of the unusually ornate staffs.

"This is yours," he said, holding one of them out to the startled Arms-Master. "May it guard you well."

"Guard me?" Rennil muttered questioningly as he took it from Nirsuk's hand. But as soon as his fist closed around the wooden shaft he understood. It was far heavier than he'd expected and although a little biased towards the heel, was almost perfectly balanced. This, he realised, was far more than a support. With its razor-sharp wolf's claws at one end, and a weighty club at the other, this was in fact a formidable weapon. And although Rennil had never seen one before arriving at Hornvale, it felt completely familiar to him. It was as though he'd been practising with it for all of his life.

Strangely moved he stood rooted to the spot, staring at the beautifully forged wolf's paw, marvelling at its intricate detail. For the first time he noticed an incongruous threaded hole in the centre of the paw. It was as though the screw that bolted it to the shaft had been removed. Despite the missing bolt though, the wickedly lupine metal tip seemed as tightly secure as it ever could be.

An impatient cough brought him out of his daze.

"You mentioned that time was short," Nirsuk said with just the trace of a question in his tone.

"Yes, of course. I'm sorry, I was just taken back by your gift."

"As well you might be. But come, let us go to the Horn and you can tell me why it's so important that I must forgo my devotions to attend your side."

The two men walked briskly towards the huge monument with Rennil talking animatedly the whole way. As he related his revelations and explained his plans, Nirsuk's normally expressionless face grew more and more agitated. By the time they reached the gate to the Horn's enclosure, he was visibly shaken. Shocked and wide-eyed, he was completely dumbstruck.

"Well?" Rennil asked, studying his companion's distraught, ashen features. The *First's* lips moved but his mind was so stunned that he couldn't find a single word with which to reply.

"You must tell me what you think," Rennil pressed. "Without your assistance I can't proceed with what I have to do."

"I... I think... I think this is madness!" he exploded at last. "Do you really believe that any sane man would suggest such a thing?"

"Perhaps not," Rennil replied steadily. "But sane or not, this is what I've been commanded to do."

"Then you *are* mad!" Nirsuk shouted, drawing surprised looks from the nearby priests who were cleaning the sculpture. "It is not your time! It is not for you to receive divine revelation or to endanger the lives of the servants of the Oath. They are not yours to command!"

"No, they are not; and that is why I need your co-operation. Only you have that authority."

"And only the High Priest himself has the right to ask me to do so."

Rennil laid a huge gnarled hand gently on the *First's* shoulder. "My dear loyal and devoted Nirsuk," he said sadly. "Arbenak has been a wise and noble Guardian of the Oath, but his eyes are now closed, and the vision – if not the authority – has passed to me. I wish it were not so, but how can I deny our god? All I can do is ask for your trust; and if you cannot find it in your heart to give it to me, then I'll have no choice but to stand here alone. Mordan has given me no other option."

"Then risk the lives of your own men," Nirsuk snapped contemptuously.

Rennil sighed. "That, my friend, is the hardest part of the revelation to bear. They are no longer my men. In fact, I have no one to command at all. Your men are still yours and the armshost are to be led by Gildor – at least for now. So all I can do is beg you: if you value the Oath, if you value your service, trust me and stand here with me. And if you can't find it within yourself to trust me, then trust Mordan; for I swear by all that's holy, he speaks to you through me."

Nirsuk stared into Rennil's steady hazel eyes and then scrutinised every detail of his earnest, beseeching face. Every line and wrinkle seemed to cry out to the *First*, begging him for his help. Even the terrible scar seemed to add weight to his pleading. For a long time, the two men stood gazing at each other with Rennil's hand still resting on the *First's* shoulder. Gradually the calm returned to Nirsuk's face and his expression regained its flat, emotionless implacability.

"You are *Dithkar-Geer*," he said at last. "How can I deny you?" Relief flooded across Rennil's face until Nirsuk added: "Although how I explain it all to Arbenak is beyond me."

Rennil swallowed hard. "And somehow I've got to explain it all to Gildor," he said uneasily.

CHAPTER THIRTY-EIGHT

The stars sparkled like a myriad of twinkling diamonds set against the deep void of the moonless sky. Magnificent as their beauty was however, they did little to dispel the impenetrable shadows that filled the long deep valley of Hornvale. It was, Rennil reflected, as dark a night as any he could remember. He was standing inside the hastily fortified compound of the Great Horn, peering blindly into the darkness as he waited for the imminent onslaught.

Nirsuk's priests had worked a small miracle by reinforcing the garden-like sanctuary in an amazingly short time. For the whole of the day and without a moment's rest they'd dug, chopped, dragged, and hammered. Somehow, they'd turned Rennil's imagined plan into a solid reality before the sun had even dipped behind the western edge of the vale. The brown-robed monks had also joined in with the construction work, throwing themselves into the task and swarming around the compound like ants. The Great Horn was now as secure as it could possibly be. The decoratively cast gates had been reinforced with thick timbers and the whole compound was now surrounded by a deep trench that encompassed it from cliff-wall to cliff-wall. The night air was filled with the pungent reek of pitch and oil. His visions of D'harid's success at Sirris had taught him well. Not that he was under any illusions that the position could be held; he was acutely aware that neither he nor any of the three hundred priests standing with him would live to see the dawn.

At least the armshost hadn't joined this futile, suicidal venture. Gildor, his voice angry and embittered, had held nothing back when Rennil had informed him of his intentions. The Prime's parting comment had struck him like a knife to his heart.

"If you wish to have a pointless death," he'd spat. "Throw yourself from the cliff. At least then you'd die alone!" The memory caused a soft sigh to escape Rennil's lips.

"This waiting is a curse, is it not?" came Nirsuk's voice out of the darkness beside him.

"Aye," Rennil replied heavily. "But unlike other soldiers, I thought I'd grown accustomed to it. I was wrong!"

There was silence for a while but then the *First* spoke again on a different tack. "How do you like your staff?" he enquired in a surprisingly light tone.

Rennil hefted the cunningly designed weapon and gave an appreciative grunt. It had been potent enough already, but in preparation for war, each staff now had a short sharp blade tightly screwed into the wolf's paw. Far from missing a bolt, this had been the purpose of the incongruous threaded hole all along. It could now club, grip, tear, slice, and stab.

"I could have made good use of this at Cor-Peshtar," he growled admiringly.

"That would not have been allowed," Nirsuk stated firmly. "And besides, I've heard that you personally slew hundreds of these lich with just your sword. Surely that is a tally to satisfy even the mighty *Dithkar-Geer*?"

"Then you heard wrong. My tally was no higher than any other man in the battle; but numbers mean nothing. Victory was secured by means of a single man who took only one life. The thousands of lich slaughtered that night died mostly at their own hands."

For a while they fell silent and there was no sound to be heard other than the faint stirring of the breeze and the shuffling of impatient feet. Then Nirsuk spoke again.

"I've heard it said that these lich were once human and that the god-king reduced them to animals with his dark arts."

"That is what the emissary said and my new intuition only confirms his story."

"Then I am at a loss. If thousands died at the battle of Sirris, and many times that number march on us now, how can there be a single Keshtari man left in the whole land?"

Unseen in the darkness, Rennil's lips twisted into a grim, wry smile. He'd asked himself that same question, but his new perception had provided him with the answer. "He actually turned no more than a few hundred; but he began that corruption two hundred years ago when he carried away the inhabitants of entire villages – women and children as well as men. He then began breeding these abominations, increasing their numbers generation after generation until now we face the culmination of that vile agenda. He now throws almost every last one of his disgusting soldiers against us."

"Then we are fortunate!" the *First* cried out for all the priests to hear. "Before we are overrun, we have the opportunity to slaughter more of these execrations than any men who ever lived!"

From all around the compound came a solid and dispassionate, "In Mordan's name."

To Rennil's ears, the flat monotone of the priest's response was more chilling than the fiercest war cry he'd ever heard. Yes, he thought to himself as he tested the weight of his weapon; they would definitely take a great many of the creatures with them before being finally overwhelmed. Quietly, he offered up a prayer. He asked not for victory but for a good death. Then silence reigned once more.

It was almost midnight when a wave of excitement rippled through the ranks of priests. The men standing lookout on the stairs either side of the Horn had spotted a wide shadow – darker even than the black night – spreading remorselessly across the valley towards them. Rennil screwed up his eyes and peered out into the gloom. At first, he could see nothing, but then he too glimpsed the dark stain drawing inexorably closer with every heartbeat. He felt the familiar flutter of fear in his stomach, but almost immediately it was replaced by a surge of tingling anticipation. It brought a fierce smile of joy to his disfigured face and once again he tried the weight of his deadly staff. The original slight bias to the heel had been corrected by the addition of the blade at its tip. The weapon was now perfectly balanced and in spite of the inevitability of his death, he was looking forward to putting it to the test.

Any hopes that the lich army would ignore the compound and launch their main attack on the temple city itself were short lived. A sudden red flash illuminated the whole valley, and by its light the small garrison could see that they were to bear the entire brunt of the initial onslaught. The flash was immediately followed by three more – each consecutive burst emanating from further down the valley and revealing the true extent of the numbers they faced. As far as the eye could see, the valley floor was alive with an undulating mass of feral hatred.

Rennil fought back the panic that came with the evil red flashes. He'd felt their effect before and used that familiarity to overcome the blind terror they inflicted; but what of the priests?

"What does the red light signify?" Nirsuk enquired in a voice that carried no more than a trace of nervous excitement. To Rennil's delight, he realised that the Hornvalers were immune to the warrior-magi's enchantment.

"It's a form of devilry that Limnash's commanders use. It confounds their enemies while emboldening and controlling the lich."

"I see," the *First* replied dispassionately. "Sorcery then."

Before Rennil could respond, dozens of the foul creatures came vaulting into the compound, landing among and behind the startled defenders. They'd crept unseen and unheard right up to the edge of the hastily thrown up defences. Silently, they'd crawled through the ditch and then with astonishing agility, had leapt right over the wall. Pandemonium ensued as the defenders blindly tried to battle the savage, dark-enshrouded interlopers. It seemed the battle would be lost before any meaningful defence could be mounted. As the priests desperately fought this initial surprise attack, the main body of the enemy force reached the compound and began throwing themselves into the fray.

But Rennil was nothing if not prepared. Either side of the Horn a trail of pitch and oil was set alight, the flames of which streaked across the ground, tracked over the wall and down into the ditch. A raging fire sprang up on both sides of the enclosure, each racing along the ditch until they joined together thus encircling the compound. The flames jumped to the last few lich to make the assault, turning them into living torches, covered as they were in oil after their scramble through the ditch. Screaming and writhing they landed in the midst of the fight and immediately set fire to those lich that had preceded them.

THE TALISMAN OF WRATH

Soon, every one of the man-beasts in the enclosure was ablaze. All that was left for the defenders to do was use their staffs to keep the unfortunate creatures at bay until their death-throes finally ceased. The smouldering bodies were then dragged into the centre of the compound where they formed a foul-smelling bonfire. The thick, acrid smoke caused many a priest to retch helplessly until they grew accustomed to the cloying stench. The few dead Hornvalers were reverently laid out in front of the huge monument while the wounded were treated where they stood or where they lay.

With the immediate danger over, the defenders returned to the wall and gazed out at the protective inferno.

"What now?" Nirsuk asked, his bloody, sweat-streaked face glistening in the bright firelight.

"Now?" Rennil replied grimly. "Now we wait for the fire to burn itself out."

"And then?"

"And then we fight; and then we die."

"Ah yes," said the *First*, his eyes bright and his voice fiercely exultant. "But it will be a magnificent death!"

Rennil stared at him in disbelief. He'd thought these most stoical of people incapable of such passionate emotions. The absurdity of it caused him to suddenly throw back his head and roar with laughter. Nirsuk looked at him with a puzzled expression; but then a smile began to spread slowly across his face. Then the smile turned to a chuckle, then a guffaw until soon, he too was clutching his sides with tears rolling down his face. Their laughter was so infectious that it began to spread around the enclosure as surely as the fire had spread along the ditch beyond the wall.

Beyond the moat of flame, the sound of such loud defiant mirth sent a ripple of consternation through the massed ranks of lich. As their confusion grew, they began to back away from the compound until suddenly, they panicked and turned to run.

Order was only restored when all four magi simultaneously slammed the heels of their staffs down causing their crystals to erupt with the brightest flash yet seen. The fell generals then roared out their orders in deep, chillingly powerful voices.

Slowly and reluctantly, the revolting beast-men crept back to the burning ditch and once again waited to resume their assault.

CHAPTER THIRTY-NINE

Gildor watched the events at the Great Horn from a vantage point high up on the temple wall. He was completely alone, standing on the battlements close to where they met the cliff and invisible in the deep shadow it provided. Inside he seethed with anger and a sense of betrayal. The man he had most admired and respected – even more so than the High-Lord himself – had turned his back on his own men and everything he stood for. Who'd have believed that the great Rennil, son of Raul, the architect and driving force behind the armshost itself, would lay down his sword in what amounted to no more than a pointless, suicidal gesture. True, he still intended to fight but with what – that idiotic staff?

When the flames had leapt up around the compound and had revealed the true magnitude of the tiny garrison's peril, he'd gripped the parapet in horror, hardly daring to breathe. Once the immediate danger had passed, he'd heaved a great sigh of relief, grateful that no one had been with him to witness his intense agitation. He now stood brooding, helplessly waiting for the inevitable conclusion when the protective fire finally died.

He was startled by a rich, deep voice that spoke to him out of the darkness at his side.

"Your Arms-Master seems to have made a strange choice in the defence of our temple," the voice said in the characteristically expressionless tone of a Hornvaler.

Gildor snorted bitterly. "He is no longer my Arms-Master. No officer of the host would sacrifice so many lives so needlessly – not to mention his own!"

"You feel he should be here in the temple with us?"

"Of course he should. Every inhabitant of the city is now within these walls where they can be protected. But even more importantly, the true Covenant Horn rests here; and that is what must be preserved; not a worthless ornament – no matter how impressive it may appear."

"You speak wisely," the unseen stranger said quietly. "What you say is undoubtedly true; but before you condemn *Dithkar-Geer* entirely, ask yourself one question: how is it that he and the *First* are in such desperate peril when we stand here and watch while the enemy ignores us?"

The Prime frowned and peered into the darkness at his side. He tried to make out the owner of the low, strangely demulcent voice beside him; but the shadow was too deep. "What exactly are you trying to tell me?" he asked suspiciously.

"I am *telling* you nothing. I am merely suggesting that perhaps the situation is not quite as it appears. In these uncertain times, even the greatest of us have had to accept that what we once perceived to be undeniable truth, cannot in fact be relied upon."

THE TALISMAN OF WRATH

Gildor returned his gaze to the Great Horn. The brightly flickering light of the flames made the huge sculpture appear to dance against the precipitous cliff face. He let his eyes drift down across the compound and then out to the dense hordes of lich pressing as close to the inferno as they dared. With his mind racing and his heart pounding in his chest, he realised that if what the priest was inferring was true, then the betrayal had been his all along and not Rennil's.

"Do you really believe that...?

His voice trailed off as somehow he realised he was once again alone. The priest had set off along the narrow walkway that ran along the cliff-side and back to the temple. As he looked in that direction, a series of evil flashes rent the shadows and illuminated the walkway for a whole heartbeat. The magi's bursts of power revealed the back of the priest as he was about to pass through the open portal that led back into the building. Somehow the blinding red light had turned his pale blue robes a deep shade of purple...

Once again, he looked over to where Rennil's men waited precariously for their inevitable end and bit his lip – hard! As the conflict within him grew to a crescendo, he pounded the stone rampart with his fists, oblivious to the salty, iron taste of blood in his mouth. Then, as if a light as bright as the magi's crystals had burst in his mind, he knew exactly what he had to do.

He raced along the wall, passed through a softly lit arch in a wide buttress, and careered into the men manning the parapet on the other side. Although most of the defenders were priests, there were a few Arlien soldiers among them. They were gathered together in small, tight cliques. They all looked at him with surprised curiosity but he'd no time to stop and explain. Without pause or apology, the slim, towering Prime pushed his way past them, calling for the Arliens to follow as he went. Without a word they hurried after him as he led them down a flight of stone stairs and across the dim temple courtyard. Once they reached the huge main gate he stopped, put his horn to his lips, and sounded the summoning.

Impatiently, he paced to-and-fro while he waited for the rest of the armshost to respond. The small group of soldiers with him watched on anxiously, fearing the Prime had gone as mad as the Arms-Master. Or was it that he'd become aware of some new and unforeseen threat that was about to befall the Temple? Fortunately, it wasn't long before the well trained men of the host began streaming towards them from where they'd been placed. A small group of the implacable blue-robed Hornvalers were amongst them, war staffs in their hands. Gildor looked at the priests questioningly.

"I'd thought to see the five Lord-Guard you've been caring for. Are they still not fit for battle?"

They are well," one of the priests replied. "But they are *tsorechny* and now have another destiny. They need take no part in your own *tsorechnikar*. We five will take their place at your side."

"My what?" the Prime started to ask; but there was no time for questions. With an exasperated shake of his head he turned his attention to the armshost.

"Fighting men of Sirris," he cried. "You are well aware of the Arms-Master's recent behaviour. It seems he has forsaken his duty for a suicidal delusion. That may well be true, but look at the great army that assails him. Have no doubt that when they're finished at the Horn, they will turn their attention to this temple. Can any of you be certain that you'll live to see another sunset? Is he really more suicidal than anyone of us?

"I've had the privilege of serving under Rennil for many years now. He is without doubt the greatest warrior of our time, and no matter how insane he now appears, I know for my part, that if I must die in this valley, I'd rather die at his side than anywhere else." He paused and tried to read the faces of his men but they were too indistinct and appeared nothing more than pale, ghost-like balloons, floating in the gloom. "That is why," he continued. "I've decided to lead the Lord-Guard in a strike and make an attempt to reach the compound." His statement was greeted with a chorus of surprised muttering. He took a deep breath before resuming his speech. "Now I can't order the rest of you to join us in this venture – I'm not the Arms-Master – but if any of you feel as I do, then I urge you to follow me. If, however, you'd rather stay here and defend the temple, then do so with my blessing – that is why we originally came here after all. If that is your choice, then walk away now and go with your heads held high."

He stopped and scrutinised the crowd giving anyone who wished to, the opportunity to leave. His heart swelled with pride when not a single man turned and left.

"Very well then; first section."

"Prime!" snapped that section officer, jumping smartly to attention.

"Your men will go first. You're to clear the way through the city then form a perimeter at the outskirts to make room for us to form a wedge. The Lord-Guard will then form the tip with the rest of the host arranged behind. As we pass through, you will fall into line behind us. Is that clear?"

"Yes Prime!"

"Good. Then take your positions but don't open the gates until I give the order."

The five priests approached and stood in front of him. "And what of us, where shall we go?"

Gildor looked at them appraisingly. "We fight in a particular way and although I don't doubt your courage, I'm not certain that I can use you."

One of the five stepped forward. "Prime Gildor," he said firmly. "The *tsorechny* have fully acquainted us with your methods. They are Lord-Guard and we five will take their place.

Therefore, it is our responsibility to join you at the tip of the wedge." The priest was close enough for Gildor to see him grin with uncharacteristic savagery. "I'm sure our staffs will teach these lich an unwelcome lesson in etiquette."

"Very well," the Prime agreed after a moment's thought. "But make sure you don't get in the way of my men."

The priest bowed. "It shall be so."

In a remarkably short time, the well-trained soldiers of the host had taken up their positions and were ready to go. Gildor faced them and addressed them one last time. His voice – loud, clear, and defiant – was strangely at odds with the apparent defeatism of his words.

"Hostmen," he cried. "Do not be misled; there is no hope of victory for us here. When we march out of these gates, we march to our doom; but we march with pride. So forward now in Mordan's name; to death and to glory!"

"Death and glory!" echoed the men as the gates were flung open and they charged through. The first section led them through the city meeting little resistance. Almost none of the lich had dared defy their masters' command to concentrate on destroying the Great Horn; and those that did met a swift and bloody death. The situation was very different at the edge of the city, however. The lich were packed shoulder to shoulder every step of the way to the Horn; but fortunately, so intent was their desire to push forward and reach the compound that none noticed the danger at their backs until it was too late.

Swiftly, the armshost formed the fighting wedge and charged at their unsuspecting foes. Almost unopposed they cut through the shadowy ranks of the savage man-animals leaving bloody carnage in their wake. Gildor's reservations about the priests' abilities soon proved unfounded. Their skill with their staffs was astounding and more than a little frightening to see. The ruthless relish with which they wielded the lethal, unusual weapons was truly shocking. Many a lich met a terrible end at the hands of the five priests. The staffs' wolf-paws were soon dripping with blood and gore. Even the most hardened warrior shuddered at the sight of the hapless creatures having their faces ripped off by the razor-sharp claws.

The spear-like wedge was more than halfway to its destination before one of the magi spotted the danger. Striding towards them he roared out his orders and sent another flash of light from the red crystal atop his staff. But the Lord-Guard and hostmen barely faltered, for like Rennil, they too had felt the effects before. But now the lich were being driven against them by the warrior mage's cruel, relentless will. Screaming ferociously, they hurled themselves at the Arlien swordsmen, quickly transforming an effective, determined attack into a desperate, futile defence.

Gildor realised the situation was now hopeless – as hopeless as it had been at the battle of Cor-Peshtar. Had that really only been a few days ago, he wondered. But that thought brought with it the memory of how the High-Lord had snatched victory from the jaws of certain defeat.

He barked out his orders and once more the wedge began to surge forward. But to reach the mage, the unwieldy formation had to swing to the left and this move proved to be disastrous. Under the immense weight of the swords, teeth, and claws assaulting it, the wedge began to break apart. Soon, the disciplined cohesion the armshost prided itself on was gone. Several scattered circles of no more than fifty or sixty warriors in each, were all that was left of Gildor's once proud formation. The fact that these pockets of resistance were slowly diminishing in size bore witness to the fact that the battle was now in vain. But there could be no surrender.

The prime stood amidst the largest of the circles, shielded by the potent weapons of the five priests, the blades on their whirling staffs glinting red in the light of the dying fire around the nearby compound. He'd suffered much embarrassment for escaping the battle at Sirris unscathed, but there was no danger of that here. Although much of the blood covering his face and body belonged to the enemy, too much of it was his own. His left arm was hanging uselessly at his side from where a terrible gash had cut the bicep to the bone. Blood ran down his youthful face, flowing freely from a deep cut beneath his split and dented helmet.

He did his best to carry on the fight but were it not for the protection of the Hornvalers, he would have been slain long ago. As he laboriously tried to cut and parry, he caught a glimpse of the compound at the Great Horn. The flames had now died to a point where the lich were able to resume their attack. He had just time to register the loathsome creatures vaulting the wall before his vision exploded in a violent flash that along with the loud ringing in his ears, quickly faded into cold, dark oblivion. He didn't even see the lich that had struck the final blow.

CHAPTER FORTY

Desperately, Eh'lorne tried to return to the cosseting, numb luxury of deep, exhausted sleep; but a nerve-shredding, high-pitched, screeching sound made it impossible. Reluctantly, he opened his bleary eyes and discovered the source of his discomfort. The irritating, ear-piercing racket was in fact Bandil's sorry attempt at a cheery whistle as he happily pottered around the camp, preparing to make an early start. Obviously, the news of his relationship to Morjeena had completely dispelled the previous day's bleak despair.

"Do you have to make such an infernal din so early in the morning?" Eh'lorne grumbled.

"Ah, you're awake," the old man said brightly.

"I didn't have much choice with that dreadful cacophony ringing in my ears."

"And a good morning to you too! Tell me, your majesty, what's happened to your usual good humour? You normally bounce out of bed with unnatural exuberance." The twinkle in the old man's eye did nothing to improve his companion's disposition.

"I'm tired," came the sulky reply.

"Perhaps some breakfast will raise your flagging spirits."

"Breakfast?" Eh'lorne enquired eagerly. They'd not eaten since leaving the cave at Mordan's finger where they'd finished off the last of their provisions. The thought of that place brought back greedy memories of the miraculous mushrooms they'd found in the tunnels.

"Breakfast," Bandil replied mischievously, holding out his large water bottle.

Eh'lorne groaned. "Can't you leave it until later in the day before tormenting me; it's far too early for such torture."

"Why wait? Time's short and I've a great deal of teasing to do before I redress the balance between us."

With a resigned sigh, Eh'lorne took the flask and shook it. "It's almost empty," he said uneasily.

Bandil laughed. "You complain like an old woman. Fine company you'll be if you don't cheer up."

Eh'lorne climbed indignantly to his feet and winced as his stiff muscles complained at the sudden movement. "I'm cold, I'm hungry, and I stink like an old goat-pen."

"And have I made a single complaint about the odour?"

At last a smile crept across the slim Arlien's grime-streaked face. "I should think not; you smell even worse than I do!"

Bandil tried to look hurt but such was his newly found good humour, it was impossible. Chuckling quietly, he continued making ready to leave. For several moments Eh'lorne watched affectionately then joined him by stamping out the remnants of the previous night's fire.

They were well on their way before the sun cleared the jagged eastern horizon, casting the men's long shadows to their immediate left.

"Shouldn't we strike more to the west?" Bandil asked. "Surely we're well clear of the chasm by now."

"Perhaps, but the land is harsh in that direction now. We'll travel much faster if we keep heading north until we reach the Dark Shadow Forest. We can then follow its border all the way to Hornvale. It'll still be a hard journey though, for there's no water between here and the temple – and we've no food left."

Bandil frowned. "'Dark Shadow' is a name that has an ominous feel to it. Is it safe to draw close to such a dangerous sounding place?"

"It *is* well named," Eh'lorne conceded. "But as long as we don't venture beyond its fringes, we should be safe. If we were foolish enough to go more than a few strides inside the treeline however, we'd soon find ourselves totally lost – and fell things are said to lurk in the darkness there."

"Very well," the old man agreed dubiously. "But for my part, I'd prefer to avoid it; I've a bad feeling about it and I've learned to trust my instincts over the years"

The two men trudged relentlessly on through the long morning and into the afternoon. Apart from having to negotiate the occasional steep gully, their progress across the bare and bleakly rolling landscape was surprisingly good. The most disturbing aspect of the journey was the large number of foul-smelling puddles of blood-rain polluting the ground. As careful as they were, they frequently found themselves splashing through one of the sickening pools and in spite of their growing thirst, if they had come across a source water, they'd have refused it due to the danger of contamination from the evil filth.

The thought of drinking even a tiny amount of it made them feel physically sick.

Not too long after midday, the old man started to lag behind so Eh'lorne called a halt. He studied the old hermit anxiously. The natural brown of his Keshtari complexion was deathly pale beneath the dirt, and his eyes were now sunken and dark-ringed. Were it not for the mass of deep wrinkles, his face would have looked nothing more than a bearded skull. His breathing was fast and shallow and the cheery good humour of the early morning was now well and truly gone. He noticed Eh'lorne's concerned look and tried to smile reassuringly but managed only a macabre grimace.

"I've pushed you too hard," Eh'lorne said with quiet regret. "I'm sorry."

"For what? It's I that should apologise; my ancient bones are slowing you down and endangering the quest. Already the destruction of Sarren weighs heavily on my soul because I was too slow. So push on as hard as you please my young friend. I'll keep up – somehow."

Eh'lorne nodded soberly and got to his feet. "In that case, onwards and..." He broke off as he spotted the dark clouds rushing towards them from the south.

Bandil followed his gaze. "It seems we're in for rain," he commented wryly.

"Is it more sorcery?"

"Bless you, no. it comes from the direction of my home in the Mystic Mountains. No evil can originate in that holy place so if it rains, it will be rain and nothing more than rain."

"Then let's press on and not rest until sundown; I'd prefer to walk as far as possible in dry clothes; but tell me if I'm setting too fast a pace."

And press on they did. Eh'lorne marvelled at the way the rapidly approaching rainstorm had galvanised the old man and filled him with cheerful energy. It seemed as though the imminent downpour had somehow provided a link to the power that had preserved him so far beyond his natural span.

Just as the sky grew dark and heavy with the threatening clouds, Bandil let out a sudden whoop of joy and ran over to a small patch of knee-high plants. He took hold of a good handful close to the ground and tried unsuccessfully to pull them up by their roots. Eh'lorne stood watching in amazement until the old man straightened and with his hand on his hips, gave him an indignant look.

"A little help wouldn't go amiss," he said sarcastically. "But of course, if you'd rather starve..."

Eh'lorne needed no further encouragement and sprinted over to his ancient friend's side. With the aid of the old man's knife to loosen the hard, compacted soil, the combined strength of the oddly matched pair soon pulled the tough plants up by their roots.

"This is food?" the young Arlien asked doubtfully as he peered at the dirty, egg-sized, tuberous bulbs.

"You'll see," the old man chuckled as the first raindrops began to fall. "You'll see."

The rain quickly changed from a heavy shower to a torrential downpour. It lashed relentlessly down, soaking them both to the skin and penetrating even their shastin clothes. For a while they splashed miserably on with their heads down, hunched against the icy deluge. But then Bandil came to a sudden stop. He stood looking around at the ankle-deep water then down at his clothes. Finally, he held up the large bunch of broad-leaved plants and watched the dirt being washed away from their tuberous roots.

"What is it?" Eh'lorne called, raising his voice so as to be heard above the sound of the rain. "Why have you stopped?"

"Can't you feel it?" Bandil shouted back.

"Feel what?"

S. P. MUIR

The old man didn't reply but lifted his face to the heavens and with his eyes shut, opened his mouth wide so as to drink the fresh clean water splattering his face. He appeared to be lost in some kind of deep religious ecstasy.

Eh'lorne scanned their surroundings, searching in vain for the source of his friend's rapture. In despair he returned his gaze to the transfixed, frail-looking hermit.

"I don't see..." he began to say, but even as the words left his lips, realization burst upon him as surely as the sun breaking through the clouds on an overcast day. He looked down at his clothes, at his arms, then at his hands.

"We're being cleansed!" he cried delightedly.

"As is the land!" the old man replied at the top of his voice.

Eh'lorne tore off his headband and vigorously rubbed his scalp, rinsing the filth from his hair in the process. Then, laughing like a madman, he spread his arms wide and spun around and around until he was so dizzy that he collapsed to the ground. He sat in the water trying to catch the rain in his cupped hands in order to slake his thirst. His drunkard-like efforts, however, were in the main thwarted by the way the world seemed to spin crazily around him. This unaccustomed lack of co-ordination only served to increase his amusement and his ridiculous chuckling hampered his efforts even further.

"There, you see," the old man declared triumphantly as he flopped down beside his merry companion. "Only this morning you complained of being hungry and dirty; and then Mordan provides you with both food and a bath!"

"Ha!" Eh'lorne snorted with mock scorn. "I've yet to taste your so-called food; and as I recall, I also complained about being cold. Now, if anything, I'm colder than ever; and marching in soaking wet clothes won't make me any warmer!"

"Do you ever show your god any gratitude?" Bandil chastised. "Soon, we'll set up camp for the night and a good fire

THE TALISMAN OF WRATH

will both warm your bones and cook these *asportas*. I assure you, they taste far better than they look."

Eh'lorne was suddenly serious again. "Then you're going to be disappointed. If you haven't noticed, apart from a few shrubs, this land is now nothing more than rocky waste and patchy grass – and all of it just as saturated as we are. There'll be no fire tonight."

Bandil shook his head in dismay. "You've still not learned to have faith, have you. We are doing Mordan's will so our needs will be met. You just need to have patience – if such a quality can exist in one as impetuous as you."

Eh'lorne grinned. "Oh, I have a great deal of patience," he said mischievously. "But I need all of it just to put up with your incessant lecturing; I've none left to spare for anything else."

The old man tried to look angry. "You're an impudent young pup who needs to have some respect for his elders."

"Oh, I save that for my betters," laughed Eh'lorne as he pulled back his wet hair and replaced his headband. He stood up and held out his hand to his ancient colleague.

"Come on then, let's go and find this cheery fire of yours."

"I need no help from an insolent whelp like you," Bandil replied stiffly. Ignoring the outstretched hand, he climbed to his feet and strode indignantly away to the north, once more leaving his friend to smile fondly after him.

Fortunately, the pounding deluge didn't last too long, and the dark clouds soon rolled away to leave the unseasonably warm sun shining down from a clear azure sky. Although its rays certainly helped take the worst of the chill from the two shivering travellers, they were still frighteningly cold. But then, well before the sun touched the western peaks, they crested a steep rise and spied the obscenely twisted shape of a distant and solitary bare tree. They hurried down the gentle slope as fast as their tired limbs would carry them, covering the five or six hundred strides far quicker than they'd dared hope.

The tree itself was a dark, long dead skeleton, killed off by decade upon decade of repeated lightning strikes. Eh'lorne was easily able to break off more than enough branches for the promised "cheery fire".

Although, as he'd predicted, they were still far to damp to burn, within the split heart of the blasted trunk was a cavity from which he was able to kick and prise a great deal of dry, dead wood to serve as kindling. Once started, it didn't take long for the fire to take hold enough to dry out the larger branches and the flames were soon dancing and leaping with satisfying merriment.

While his young companion fashioned a couple of basic frames, Bandil separated the *asporta* roots from their stems and wrapped them individually in the broad, tough leaves. Then, with the aid of a long stick, he poked them deep into the base of the fire to cook. Once that was done, he opened out their blankets and examined them closely. Although damp, they were not nearly as wet as he'd feared and it took no time at all to dry them off by holding them up to the flames. When Eh'lorne's frames were completed, they both stripped off their clothes and hung them on the simple constructions, close enough to the fire to make them steam but not so close as to scorch the fabric. They then sat huddled and naked, each wrapped in the delicious heat of their warm bedrolls.

They made an incongruous pair, so different were their physical appearances and attributes. The young Arlien king-designate was tall and improbably slim but his muscles, although lacking in bulk, were toned and well defined. The ancient Keshtari hermit on the other hand, was more than a head shorter in stature, and so emaciated that his body looked nothing more than a thin, frail skeleton, loosely swathed in a dusky-brown, wrinkled hide. Eh'lorne couldn't help marvelling at how such a gaunt, cadaverous form could be pushed to such extremes of endurance.

As they soaked up the substantial fire's life affirming warmth, Eh'lorne tried to press the old man into relating more details of the reclusive decades of his life. Bandil, however, insisted that the younger man regale him with anecdotes of his childhood exploits with his twin brother. Soon, the old man was rocking with laughter as Eh'lorne – with expert comic timing – told stories of broken windows, flour bombs, and egg attacks. He thought his sides must surely split at the mental picture of the foul-tempered 'Cookie', smothered in flour and milk, chasing the unfortunate brothers through the streets with her huge meat cleaver in one hand, and a wildly brandished rolling pin in the other. Small wonder she was now so belligerent and tetchy. The two men shared such a happy evening, they almost forgot the impending doom and terrible tragedy of recent events. Almost.

When at last the old man dragged the charred *asporta* parcels from the depths of the fire, Eh'lorne, at first eager, soon snorted derisively. The smoking, leafy wrappings were crisp and black; and when Bandil passed him one using the corner of his blanket to protect his fingers, the charred leaf crumbled to ash revealing a very unappetising, wrinkled brown lump. Eh'lorne looked at it, sniffed it, and then sneered disgustedly.

"This is surely another attempt to trick me," he said warily. "There's no way in creation that this can possibly be edible."

"Try it," Bandil urged, his eyes shining in the firelight. "Mind your mouth though, it'll be hot."

Reluctantly, and with great care so as not to burn his lips and tongue, Eh'lorne bit into the ugly, shrivelled vegetable. The crisp brown skin burst open to reveal a soft, fluffy white interior that was far from unpleasant. Under normal circumstances the flavour would have been a little bland, but hunger turned the plain staple into a gastronomic delight.

"Well?" the old man demanded eagerly. "Is it good?"

Eh'lorne smiled and nodded. "It is good," he conceded.

"There!" Bandil cried, delightedly slapping his thighs. "You are clean, warm, and fed. What more could you want?"

"An end to our troubles?"

"Ah," the old hermit replied sagely. "For that we must pray even harder."

CHAPTER FORTY-ONE

The third day of their journey from Mordan's finger should have been easier for Eh'lorne and Bandil. The landscape had gradually become less severe with the harsh, rocky wastes giving way to gently rolling moorland that was covered with springy moss and patchy grass. The two men were now so enervated, however, that their progress was as difficult and as taxing as ever. Eh'lorne was surprisingly close to the end of his endurance, while the old man needed every last drop of the fierce determination in his soul just to stay upright and place one foot in front of the other. He shambled doggedly along, leaning heavily on a staff his tall companion had fashioned for him from a branch of the dead tree. But in spite of his physical condition, the eyes that were fixed determinedly on his young friend's back held no trace of defeat or despair. His body may have been on the brink of collapse, but his spirit burned as brightly as ever.

As had become their custom, they stopped to rest at around noon. The old man sat hugging his knees with his eyes closed, whispering a quiet prayer. Eh'lorne, sitting at his side, studied the terrain, carefully plotting a route that held as few obstacles as possible. In other circumstances, it would have been a pleasant place to sit and rest; the mossy grass was a lush green and here and there some of the hardier early wildflowers were pushing tentatively up into the warm spring sunshine. Amazingly warm weather considering the altitude and the fact that it had been so cold and snowy just a few short days ago.

"Be careful what you wish for," Eh'lorne muttered to himself bitterly. For although he'd complained so loudly about being cold, without water this pleasant balmy weather would dehydrate them all the faster. As it was, their mouths had been too dry to force down the remaining *asportas* that morning.

Without food or water there seemed little point in delaying too long and it wasn't much later when they climbed wearily to their feet and continued their laborious trek. They travelled in silence, each man locked in his own private world of seemingly eternal torture. Their usual playful banter was gone as if it had never been.

As the day wore on and their shadows began to lengthen, they came to a particular slope that was far steeper than any they had encountered since arriving in this more agreeable region of the mountains. Although normally they'd have shrugged off the obstacle with hardly a thought, in their present decrepit state, the hill seemed to stretch on forever forming a daunting and impenetrable barrier to their progress. They stared at it in dismay, horrified at the prospect of forcing themselves to perform so impossible an undertaking.

THE TALISMAN OF WRATH

"Perhaps we should camp here for the night," Bandil said hopefully. "The climb will seem a lot less difficult after a good night's sleep."

Eh'lorne gauged the sun's position in the sky and judged that it would be quite some time before dusk fell. "We'd be wasting too much daylight, and we've lost too much time already. We've no choice but to keep going."

"I feared as much," sighed the old man. "You're right of course. My heart tells me the same with each step I take but..." he shrugged despairingly, "...my body tells me that this task is beyond me."

Eh'lorne put an arm around Bandil's thin, bony shoulders. "I understand what I'm asking of you," he said regretfully. "But what choice do I have?"

"You have none," the old man said heavily. "But nor do I, and that's why you must go on without me. I'll follow you as best I can but the quest is too important to be jeopardised by my feeble dotage."

"Can't you use the stone, if only for this one hill?"

"I daren't. I've told you the price I have to pay for its usage, and to use it even one more time could leave me insensate for days."

Eh'lorne nodded; he'd guessed as much. "Then I'll help you. Put your arm around me and lean as heavily as you need. With your staff to your left and a son of Starbrow to your right, how can we fail?"

Bandil laughed scornfully. "You can barely hold yourself upright without me to burden you further. I say again, leave me."

Eh'lorne turned the frail old theurgist to face him and peered deep into his eyes. "My dear ancient friend," he said with gentle conviction. "On the day we first met I swore a solemn oath that I would never leave you and that I'd give my life to protect you should the need arise. That oath is unbreakable and will stand till Halgar-come. And even after that, when the world is made anew and the dead wake from the long sleep, for the rest of eternity I'll still be at your side. If I must carry you all the way to Hornvale, then that is exactly what I shall do."

As the two men stood staring into each other's eyes, tears began to course down the old man's brown, withered cheeks. "Eh'lorne Starbrow," he said in a voice choked with emotion. "No man has ever had a better friend. If I'd ever been blessed with a son, for all your impetuous arrogance, I could not have wanted better."

"Then since you have no son – no *arrin* in the Arlien tongue – and since I've lost my father – my *veldar*; you shall be my *Eh'veldar* and I will be your *eh'arrin*; if you'll have me."

"I would be most honoured, my son."

After a long embrace, the oddly matched pair set about the daunting task of climbing the hill. It proved even more difficult for the old man than they'd feared, but with his newly adopted son's support on one side and the crudely fashioned staff on the other, he didn't falter and at last they reached the summit. Both men collapsed gratefully to their knees and surveyed the vista that was spread out before them like a map.

The grassy moorland sloped gently away to where, little more than a stretch in the distance, a dense forest sprawled across the rolling hills as far as the eye could see. The sweeping panorama glowed with the golden radiance of the late afternoon sunshine that seemed to set the trees ablaze with a fire of heart-aching beauty.

"Magnificent!" Bandil breathed, his eyes shining with joy. "I would never have thought such glory could exist outside the Mystic Mountains."

"Magnificent indeed, "Eh'lorne agreed. "But don't forget that it's the Dark Shadow Forest; a perilous name for a perilous place. Only a fool would enter there and expect to come out alive."

"It doesn't look so evil or forbidding to my eyes."

Eh'lorne laughed. "That's a rich comment for you to make! To my eyes nothing could look more sinister than those sellufin creatures, and yet you claim they're not evil. They've murdered your family and seek to destroy my people, but you insist that they're merely misunderstood. Perhaps we should revisit our conversation on the meaning of wisdom, my friend."

"Can we reach the forest before dark?" Bandil asked, ignoring the jibe.

"I should think so – if you're up to it. The going looks favourable and it's downhill all the way."

"Very well then; help me to my feet and let's finish this day with a successful conclusion."

Obediently, Eh'lorne stood up and reached a hand down to the old hermit. With the aid of his young friend and his own staff, he clambered upright and continued the journey with an easier, lighter step.

The speed with which they covered that last stretch surprised and delighted them both. The sun was only just beginning to dip below the western horizon when they arrived at the densely packed treeline and began to set up camp. Bandil unpacked their provisions and unrolled their blankets while Eh'lorne scavenged for what firewood could be found without venturing more than a few paces beneath the forbidding canopy. The old man's doubts about the supernatural nature of the forest were soon dispelled when he realised that the trees, far from being the evergreens that these altitudes dictated, were not only broad-leafed and similar to maple and sycamore, but had kept those leaves throughout the long, cold winter.

Suddenly, Eh'lorne came running out of the forest, his eyes bright with excitement and his arms full of brushwood.

"Eh'veldar!" he called wildly. "Eh'veldar!"

"What now?" Bandil asked. His voice sounded wearily impatient although he was secretly pleased with his new name.

"Water!" Eh'lorne cried as he ran up and dropped the firewood at the old man's feet. "I can hear water."

Bandil shook his head sadly. "I'm sure you *think* you can but you're parched; and a thirsty man can imagine water at every turn. Some are even tricked into seeing a lake in the middle of a dry desert."

Eh'lorne's smile faded and a note of anger entered his voice. "I'm not a fool that can be easily tricked. My hearing is excellent and I tell you I can hear running water."

"Where, in the forest?"

"In the forest."

The old man shrugged. "Then even if you're right it's of no use to us. It may as well be in the sky for all the hope we have of reaching it. Didn't you say that no man could enter that accursed place and emerge alive? Stop tormenting yourself with that which you cannot have. Put the thought of it out of your mind and help me with the fire."

Eh'lorne turned and stared thoughtfully back into the deep darkness that lay beyond the forest's eaves – a darkness that was becoming more and more threatening in the deepening twilight gloom.

"I fear no harm from any living creature," he mused quietly. "The only peril would be the loss of direction. If I could overcome that danger then we would have water; without which I fear we'll not reach our goal in time – if at all."

"My son," Bandil said gently while laying a consoling hand on the tall Arlien's shoulder. "I don't doubt your conviction or your bravery, but this is an unnecessary torture. Perhaps there is water in the forest, but you could never find it. And have you considered there might be an evil in there that's trying to lure you into its clutches?"

For a few moments it seemed as though the old man's advice would go unheeded, but then with a deep sigh, Eh'lorne turned away from the trees and gave his ancient companion a dejected smile. "Once again, you're right; I'll try and put it out of my mind."

In despondent silence they built a good-sized fire and soon its flames were capering merrily in a bright, cheerful dance. As the cold, dark night closed in around the warmly lit circle of their camp, Eh'lorne stared glumly into the fire. In spite of his assertion that he'd put the thought out of his mind, the tantalising babble of the brook or stream that was so near yet so far wouldn't let him lay it to rest. Then, as if the flickering tongues had ignited the flame of his imagination, he suddenly leapt to his feet, his eyes bright in the reflected fire.

"Of course!" he cried, startling the old man and making him choke on the cold *asporta* he was trying to force down his parched throat. "What fools we are! Without water our mission will fail and there is water nearby. I have no choice but to find it; and find it I will!"

"How?" Bandil demanded, his voice growing shrill with exasperation. "And if you do, how will you find your way back?"

Eh'lorne made no reply; instead he swept up Bandil's water bottle and strode purposefully toward the trees. The old man hurried after him, grabbed him by the arm and swung the impetuous young Arlien round to face him.

"Answer me!" he shouted. "How will you find your way without a lamp or a torch to give you light?"

"I am an Arlien!" came the fierce reply. "I need no light to find my way. My eyes will be blind but my mind will not. I'll use it to feel my way as only my people can."

"And the confusion, the loss of direction in so dense a maze? Even if it were as bright as day, you'd be lost for all time."

"Did I not lead us through the labyrinth beneath Mordan's Finger? Have no fear old man, I'll not get lost."

"Yes, you led us *to* the Talisman, but were it not for the trail of marks I left on the walls, we'd have never found our way out. We'd be wandering there still – if we hadn't succumbed to hunger and thirst by now. Is your mind sharp enough to distinguish any marks you might leave on the trees?"

"Perhaps, perhaps not; but I'll need no marks to guide me; I'll have a beacon!"

With that, he drew the Talisman; and then holding the lupine hilt in both hands, he raised it high above his head, and drove the glinting blade deep into the ground.

"I'll be back!" he declared and then plunged into the trees.

"Eh'lorne!" Bandil bellowed. "Eh'lorne!" But there was no reply save the faint rustle of leaves in the gentle breeze and the distant hoot of an owl. He put his hands to his head and let out a strangled cry of frustration. "You stupid, impetuous, rash, thoughtless..." His voice trailed off impotently. Then slowly and tiredly, he trudged back to the fire and flopped down beside it, once again praying as he'd never prayed before.

CHAPTER FORTY-TWO

The Dark Shadow forest was even more daunting than Eh'lorne had expected. The inexplicable darkness was absolute. Only once had Eh'lorne experienced such a solid absence of light. But beneath Mordan's Finger the darkness had been pure and natural – even benign. Here however, it was oppressive, frightening, and bewildering. It was all he could do to force down the overwhelming sense of panic that threatened to rise up and disorientate him even further. Within a hundred strides from his entry into the unnervingly black world, the sense of claustrophobia became too much for him.

Deliberately, he stopped, shut his eyes, and concentrated on the three things that could see him through the terrible ordeal he'd taken upon himself. First, he strained his ears to locate the direction of the faint, tantalising sound of running water; then he reached out with his mind to feel his surroundings. His Arlien gift seemed to illuminate the trees as though he was standing in an ordinary, if extremely dense wood in deep twilight. But above all else and overriding all other senses, he could feel the Talisman at his back. It was radiating a powerful but muted glow that sent a cold chill running up his spine.

Once he had himself back under control and was sure of his bearings, he started off again. He squeezed between the thick trunks and held his hands out before him to confirm what his mind was telling him. He soon found it impossible to use the sound of the water as a guide, for sometimes it appeared to be on his left then as if by magic, it would suddenly be on his right. Once, it seemed as though he was surrounded by a myriad of fast-flowing, babbling streams. Without the reassuring presence of the Talisman's power at his back, he would have quickly become totally and irrevocably lost. Even so, in spite of that solid point of reference, his progress was painfully slow.

Then there were the strange noises. From all around came the sound of rustling and scampering punctuated by distant (and not so distant) growls and grunts. As much as he told himself that they were nothing more than the natural music of woodland fauna, the eerie dissonance grew steadily more and more unnerving. The sudden sound of something large crashing through the undergrowth close by made him almost jump out of his skin. He wiped the cold sweat from his brow and quietly drew his sword.

At first, he wasn't sure if it was his imagination but eventually there could be no doubt; the sound of running water was definitely growing louder. Even so, it was still a shock when he stumbled out of the trees into a gloriously open space. He found himself bent double, sucking in huge lungsful of fresh, cold air as if he'd been holding his breath since he'd entered the dark folds of the ancient forest.

THE TALISMAN OF WRATH

He opened his eyes and surveyed the scene around him. He marvelled at his breadth of vision, for although it was a dark and moonless night, compared to the absolute pitch-black that had gone before, it seemed to Eh'lorne to be as bright as an overcast day. He was standing a few paces outside the treeline, at least fifteen strides from the bank of the rushing, gurgling river that sparkled gently in the dim light of the stars. It was as though the oppressive and brooding forest was afraid to draw too close to the happy chattering of the water lest it became infected by its contagious merriment. The river itself was little more than five strides wide and was more of a fast-flowing, boulder strewn stream than anything else. But in Eh'lorne's desperately parched state, it was the most wonderful body of water he'd ever seen.

He sheathed his sword, unhooked the straps of the water bottles from his shoulders, and carefully approached the riverbank. Kneeling beside the rushing water, he scooped some up to his parched lips and cautiously took a sip. It was cold, clean, and refreshing with no trace of contamination or evil. Greedily, he slaked his thirst then filled Bandil's voluminous leather bottle before filling his own more modest container.

All too soon his task was complete and he had to turn his back on the cheerful, gurgling brook and face the grim menace of the threatening, tightly packed trees. Reluctantly, he walked back to the edge of the wood, drew both his sword and a deep breath, and then plunged once more into the deep, forbidding darkness.

Although the return journey was just as unnerving, it was at least easier in one way. Before, he'd had to concentrate on the unreliable, ever-changing sound of the river while using the Talisman as a guiding anchor; but this time the powerful artefact acted as a beacon, drawing him on towards safety.

He'd been going for some time when he gradually became aware that something was wrong. For a few moments he couldn't quite put his finger on what had changed, but then it hit him; the forest had grown quiet. But not just quiet, it was deathly still. The rustling and occasionally louder sounds of movement that had so rattled his composure before, were now completely absent. The noise of his own clumsy progress amid the aberrant stillness made him feel exposed and vulnerable. His anxiety mounted to the point where the blood was pounding in his ears and the sweat was pouring coldly down his face.

Deliberately, he forced himself to a standstill and took several deep, slow breaths. This was ridiculous. He was Eh'lorne Starbrow, the great and fearless warrior. He had no equal with a sword and more than that, he was king-designate of all Keshtar. He scolded himself fiercely, demanding that he pull himself together and act accordingly.

Once he had himself back under control, he continued on his way. He tried to allay his fears by concentrating on the reassuring beacon of power that grew steadily colder and stronger with each step he took. Eventually though, he could deceive himself no longer; something ominous and malevolent was fast approaching from behind.

It took every last drop of his resolve to remain calm and maintain an even, steady pace. But soon, the mysterious evil had drawn so overpoweringly close that he unwittingly began to run. And once he'd given in to the temptation, any pretence of control was gone. In a blind panic he charged forward, careering into trees and branches with only the Talisman's call to keep him from losing his mind completely.

Eventually – inevitably – he was brought crashing to the ground when a thick branch smashed into his forehead, knocking him backwards with great force. For a few moments he lay there, dazed and confused, unsure of where he was or how he'd got there. But then the growing malice brought him back to his senses. Urgently he climbed to his feet, wincing at the throbbing pain in his head and blinking against the bright flashing lights that danced before his eyes. Horrified, he realised that he was no longer holding his sword and there was no time to search for it in the undergrowth. He had no option but to flee before the pursuing, nameless evil finally overtook him.

He raced through the trees as fast as he dared, his hands thrust protectively before him and his eyes closed as he felt his path with his mind. It was a desperate balancing act between speed and safety, made all the more terrifying by the rate at which the strange presence was gaining on him.

Then, sobbing with relief, he exploded into the open air and sprinted to where the Talisman impaled the earth. He couldn't see the startled old man jump to his feet by the fire, for his eyes were blinded by blood and by the long hair hanging loosely across his face. But he didn't need eyes to focus on the Talisman; never had he felt it so keenly. His hand closed around its wolf's-head hilt and in one fluid movement, he snatched it from the earth, spun around to face the forest, and thrust it towards the stars.

"*Mordarnish carr d'sharn!*" he roared at the top of his voice. The sword's crystal heart erupted in a fierce blaze so cold that the grass and trees immediately turned white with frost. Bandil threw himself down beside the fire in the vain hope that its warmth would shield him from the vicious fangs of the frigid blast. But the fire's flames seemed to shrink away in fear leaving the old man's flesh and bones seared by the glacial tempest.

Eh'lorne stood there like a statue, the blazing Talisman held aloft and his teeth bared in a vicious snarl. His face was twisted and distorted by his fury and his chest rose and fell as though every breath was articulating his bitter anger.

But then at last, to the old man's immense relief, the blinding light began to diminish and the tall Arlien's arm began to fall. Then as the last glimmer faded and died, he fell to his knees and sat back on his heels with his head bowed and his shoulders slumped. His long fair hair, unfettered by his lost headband, cascaded forward hiding his face. He held the

Talisman loosely at his side with the blade flat on the ground. Even though the crystal now appeared dormant, the powerful sword's blade glinted ominously in the reflected firelight.

Bandil struggled painfully to his feet, wincing as his frozen joints creaked and popped alarmingly. He was covered in frost and his hair and beard were stiff with ice. Forcing his protesting legs to move, he staggered over to where his young companion knelt at the very edge of the camp's warm circle of light. He peered into the darkness to where he could just make out the black line that marked the forest's boundary.

"What happened?" he asked, his voice full of both alarm and concern. "Was something in there? Were you attacked?"

Eh'lorne showed no sign of having heard the question and remained slouched at the old man's feet. Bandil looked down at his friend and a pang of pity stabbed his heart. Never had he thought to see this fearless and flamboyant warrior-lord so crushed and broken. He laid a reassuring hand on Eh'lorne's shoulder.

"My son," he said softly. "You have to speak to me. Whatever happened in there I must know, for if you don't tell me, how can I help?"

For a long while Eh'lorne didn't move; but then he gave a great heaving sigh that seemed to shake his whole body.

"Something came after me," he said flatly. "It sought to overtake me and..." His voice trailed off as he seemed to fall back into his dark reverie.

"And what?" Bandil pressed gently.

Eh'lorne shrugged. "How should I know? But it meant to harm me, of that much I'm certain."

"What was it, did you see it?"

"No, I didn't see it but I felt its presence. It was dark and malevolent and immensely powerful. I barely escaped its clutches; a few more heartbeats and it would have had me."

THE TALISMAN OF WRATH

The old man returned his gaze to the unseen, threatening mass of trees. Thoughtfully, he stroked his damp, defrosting beard. Beneath the shadows, his expression was full of concern and apprehension.

Suddenly he laughed and slapped the kneeling Arlien on the back. "Well whatever it was, it's gone now. And however powerful it seemed, it was no match for the rightful king with the Talisman of Wrath in his hand!" Carefully, he pushed the long hair away from the young lord's pale, blood-soaked features.

"Look at you," he scolded with soft cheerfulness. "You're tired, unkempt, and hurt. And more to the point, I'm frozen stiff; so if you care for me at all, you'll accompany me back to the fireside and eat the last morsels of your food. It would also be prudent for you to allow me to clean your wound."

Eh'lorne sighed dejectedly, climbed to his feet, and sheathed the Talisman. Without a word he shuffled over to the warmth of the fire with the old man holding his arm supportively.

"So tell me," Bandil asked, forcing his tone to be light and jovial. "After all this did you actually manage to find some water?"

Eh'lorne managed a wan smile. "Would I dare to return and face your wrath had I failed?"

"What!" Bandil exclaimed feigning shock and surprise. "Am I so intimidating a figure that I inspire such fear and trepidation?"

Eh'lorne chuckled, at last breaking free from his dark mood. "Verily! My knees are sore from knocking at the very thought of you."

"Good. Then do as I say; sit down and eat your *asportas* and let me see to the cut on your head."

Eh'lorne pulled the water bottles from around his shoulders and handed them to the old man before obediently sinking to the ground as close to the fire as he dared. The supernatural frost had melted away leaving the grass unpleasantly damp, but he barely noticed. Bandil passed him the last three *asportas* which he devoured with great relish while the old man slaked his thirst. Bandil then cut two strips from his blanket, one of which he wetted to clean his friend's forehead and face. The other he fashioned into a bandage-cum-headband that he carefully tied into place. When all was done, they sat next to each other staring reflectively into the burning branches, both watching the hypnotic dance of the orangey-yellow flames.

"Eh'veldar," Eh'lorne asked quietly. "Have you any idea of what pursued me in the forest?"

Bandil frowned. "You've told me next to nothing about what happened; so you'll need to elaborate on what you experienced and what you felt."

Eh'lorne was silent for a while as he gathered his thoughts, and then at last, he made an attempt to describe the terrible presence that had assailed him.

"It felt huge and shapeless like a vast kind of shadow. But not like a shadow for at its core was something solid – no, not exactly solid but more...tangible."

"Was it a creature of some kind?"

Eh'lorne thought for a moment then shook his head. "No, it was something new yet at the same time something very old. Very different to anything I've come across before; neither spirit nor flesh. It was..." He hesitated as he searched for the right word. "It was something primal."

Bandil nodded seriously and glanced anxiously towards the forest. But then he forced another smile and nudged his companion's leg. "Well whatever it was, it's gone. So put it behind you; we've got far more important things to deal with and you're in need of rest. I must therefore insist that you settle down and get some sleep."

"Yes, my Eh'veldar," grinned Eh'lorne. He then rolled himself up in his blanket, lay himself down on the grass and immediately fell into a deep slumber.

Bandil watched him for a while. Then, when he was certain that he was well and truly asleep, he got up and walked a few paces toward the brooding wood. There he sat down and stared fearfully into the darkness while absent-mindedly toying with Mystic Stone. From Eh'lorne's description, the malevolent presence *was* something he recognised, but it was impossible. That being had slept since the founding of the world and could not be woken. Unless...

Could it be that when Eh'lorne had impaled the ground, the Talisman had disturbed its slumber? If that were so, the young king-designate had been in no immediate danger at all – in fact the presence wouldn't even have been aware of his existence. But if the creature had reached the Talisman first, then the world would have been in more peril than any threat Limnash could pose. If he was right, all they could do now was to hope it would return to the deep places of the earth and go back to sleep. But even better than that, he hoped and prayed that he was wrong.

CHAPTER FORTY-THREE

The next morning found the two travellers in much better spirits. Although physically they were in no better shape – particularly Bandil who'd barely slept – they had water and just as importantly, a sense that they were making genuine progress. The lay of the land also helped, for although they were travelling slightly uphill for most of the day, the grassy moorland was at least smooth and totally devoid of anything that could be describe as an obstacle.

The old man watched his companion carefully, scrutinising him for any lingering signs of the distress he'd displayed after the previous night's disturbance. Eh'lorne, however, was back to his annoyingly cheerful, extrovert self with no visible ill effects at all. Even so, Bandil understood exactly why the experience in the forest had so affected the young warrior. For the first time in his life he'd known not just fear, but outright terror. Although he was glad to see that his young friend had recovered, the old man hoped that the lesson would not be forgotten. Perhaps Eh'lorne would now be a little less judgemental of his brother.

The forest edge led them unerringly toward their goal, even if a little more northerly than was ideal. They followed its fringes but maintained a more respectful distance from the dense treeline, unwilling to risk another encounter with whatever had been disturbed the previous night. On and on they trudged, covering so much ground that their exhaustion became almost irrelevant. They stopped occasionally for a brief rest and a sip of water, but such was their sense of purpose, they were unwilling to pause for too long.

The sun had sunk well below the western horizon before they finally stopped to make camp. Eh'lorne gathered the firewood as usual but Bandil noted that the tall, slim warrior was unwilling to take more than a single step beyond the first line of trees. His dangerously impetuous nature had obviously been tempered somewhat, which was, the old man reflected, no bad thing.

Both men were now far beyond any level of exhaustion they'd experienced before; and hunger was a constant and unwelcome companion. But in spite of this unprecedented degree of fatigue, their mood remained amazingly positive – although conversation was more effort than it was worth. This, along with the lack of any kind of a meal, meant that they soon wrapped themselves in their blankets and settled down to sleep.

They awoke just before dawn, then immediately broke camp and set off on their way. Initially, their mood was cheerfully confident, but it wasn't long before their steps began to falter. Even the slightest of inclines was now beyond their abilities, and in order to avoid the few slopes that they met, they found themselves pushed ever closer to the forest. It was painfully obvious that they were drawing on reserves they no longer possessed, and their brief respites became more and more frequent.

At one of these rest stops, not long after midday, the pair sat quietly gazing in the direction of their respective homes. The sky overhead was a rich, deep blue while far away to the southwest, a thin translucent veil of cloud was drifting imperceptibly towards them. It had a uniquely ethereal beauty that looked to Eh'lorne as though Mordan himself had spread a soft, delicate lace across the highest reaches of the heavens. He glanced at the old man with the intention of commenting on its exquisite loveliness, but the parlous state of his frail, ancient companion stopped him short. Already little more than a wrinkled bag of bones when they'd met, the old hermit-cum-theurgist was now shockingly emaciated. Mushrooms and *asportas* aside, the privations and ordeals of the past few days had left him close to the point of starvation. And if Eh'lorne was honest with himself, he wasn't too far behind. Their earlier high hopes had proved as ephemeral as the morning mist, and the truth of it was, they were beaten.

"Eh'veldar," he called softly. But Bandil was lost in his reminiscing and didn't hear him.

"Bandil," he persisted more sharply.

"Eh, what?" the old man replied absently as he returned to the present.

"Eh'veldar," Eh'lorne continued, his voice soft again. "We have to face facts; we're finished. Without a substantial meal and a good rest, we'll be lucky to live more than a day or two, let alone cover the distance from here to Hornvale. If we were on a good road it would still be beyond us, and we don't even have that small luxury."

"Is it much further?"

Eh'lorne bit his lip as he tried to picture the maps his brother had spent so much time poring over.

"I can't be certain but I believe if we were as strong as we were when we left Sirris, we could arrive tomorrow morning – at the latest by the afternoon. But look at us; we have as much chance of reaching Hornvale as we have of making it all the way to Arl!"

Bandil sighed. "As much as I'd like to argue, I can't deny the truth. You're right, we are finished."

"So what now?"

Bandil gave the young Arlien an incredulous look. "Why, we pray of course," he replied as if any other action was unthinkable.

"Pray!" Eh'lorne exclaimed bitterly. "I've done nothing but pray with every step I've taken. I've nothing left; I have no more prayers within me!"

"Then I will pray for us both. Here, place your hand in mine. That's it. Now relax, let go of your frustration and your anxiety. Open up your mind and your heart; let Mordan speak to you."

"Why should he?" Eh'lorne asked sceptically. "He's never spoken to me before."

"Ah, but he has; you just didn't know how to listen. So now, as I pray, consider my words and let yourself be lifted by them – without thought or reason. Just let yourself go."

Eh'lorne looked unconvinced but dutifully, he closed his eyes and tried to follow the old man's instructions. Bandil settled himself more comfortably, gave his young friend's hand a reassuring squeeze, and then began to petition their god in a soft, beseeching tone.

At first the exhausted young warrior tried to concentrate on the content of the old man's supplications, but gradually, the hypnotic, soothing cadence of the prayer lifted him far beyond mere words. Soon he was floating, riding the breeze along a plane that was far above the pressures and privations that assailed the two travellers. He felt a growing sense of warmth and security such as a young child might feel in the firm, safe

S. P. MUIR

embrace of their father. Whirling images began to form moving pictures in his mind; remembered scenes portraying his many blessings and everything he held dear.

There was his brother, gentle and thoughtful but as strong as an ox. And there was Rennil, his beloved mentor who'd taught him so much. He found himself looking at the whole of Sirris and at his home in the Halls of Duty. For a moment there was a terrible pang of sorrow as he beheld the face of his lost father; but then, as if a comforting hand had stroked his brow, he realised just how blessed he'd been to have had such a loving relationship at all. His childhood flashed before him and along with it, all those who had helped to bring the twins up, taking the place of their long dead mother. He smiled to himself as a rosy-cheeked Freiya came into view, fussing and clucking over them like a mother hen. And of course, there was Bishtar, her husband. The head servant's strict, officious bearing could hardly conceal his true caring nature and his prodigious loyalty.

Then at last, there was his oldest and closest friend, Gretya. She was standing in the Duty Hall's small, formal garden where they'd played since she'd first arrived as a small child. The sun was shining through her fine, brown-blonde hair as a gentle breeze lifted it from her shoulders. She was smiling happily – a smile he'd seen so many times over the years. A smile that illuminated her plain round face with a beauty that eclipsed even the prettiest, most sophisticated young ladies in all the land. It radiated a gloriously infectious, effervescent joy.

He suddenly felt an empty ache in his heart; a longing to be reunited with his dearest companion. He remembered the unexpected embrace she'd given him when he and Bandil had left Sirris. How shocked Bishtar had been at such an inappropriate display of affection! He'd been somewhat taken back himself, but now he yearned to feel those arms around his neck again; but this time he'd return the embrace; he'd put his own arms around her waist and pull her to him, and...

His eyes flicked open in surprise. He turned to the old man, his jaw slack in amazement and his eyes wide with shock. Bandil immediately stopped praying and gave him an enquiring look.

"Something has come to you?" he asked soberly.

Eh'lorne's mouth moved dumbly as he struggled to find the words to articulate what he'd seen and felt.

"Well?" the old man pressed.

Still Eh'lorne couldn't find the right words until eventually he blurted out, "It's Gretya!"

"Ah," Bandil replied sagely. "The maidservant who bade you such a fond farewell. What about her?"

"I...I love her."

"Of course you do," the old man laughed. "I knew it the moment I saw you both in the same room."

Eh'lorne blushed, deeply embarrassed by the old man's mirth. "Does everyone know except me?" he asked quietly.

Bandil squeezed his hand again. "Bless you, no. I'm sure your brother knows and your father would have guessed, but apart from me, your secret is safe – at least until you decide to reveal it to the world."

Eh'lorne hung his head. "What would be the point? I'm sure she doesn't hold the same affection for me."

"Really?" Bandil exclaimed incredulously. "You're closer to her than anyone alive and still you can't see what's in front of your nose? My dear boy, a blind man could see that she adores you. Why else do you think Bishtar disapproves of your friendship so? Have no fear in that regard, your union is only a matter of time – if you wish it of course." The look on Eh'lorne's face revealed that he wished it very much indeed. "So apart from your improper feelings for a mere serving girl..." the serious reproof of his words was belied by the twinkle in his eye "...what else did Mordan's voice reveal to you?"

"Nothing."

"Nothing?"

"That's right. I only had memories – unless of course... perhaps a sort of feeling? No, feeling is the wrong word; it was more a faint sense of certainty."

"That's usually the way of it. Go on."

Eh'lorne thought for a moment as he tried to recall what he'd experienced. Then he gave a faint smile as he became more certain of the message he'd been given.

"I was 'told' that as long as I put all I had into something and it was in his name, no matter how impossible the task or how feeble my effort, he would provide me with the means to succeed."

Bandil returned the smile and nodded. "There you see; you listened properly and you heard. And within Mordan's words to you, there's also reproof for me. I was starting to forget the lessons I learned in my long exile. So come then, my son, let's stand upright and attempt the impossible. If we truly have faith in Mordan, with his help, we will succeed."

They helped each other to their feet and prepared to continue the seemingly hopeless, gruelling slog. But before they could take a single step, they were startled by a sudden and crashing commotion behind them. They whirled around to face the source of the alarming racket that was growing louder with each heartbeat. Bandil whipped out the Mystic Stone while Eh'lorne's hand flashed across his body to draw his sword. He cursed furiously as his fingers met nothing but an empty scabbard. Then before he could react any further, the cause of the uproar burst from the forest not thirty strides from where they stood.

It was a large deer that was frantically trying to escape from the pack of five wolves that were seeking to bring it down. The leading predator – a huge, silver-grey creature with rippling, powerful muscles – flanked its terrified prey, running almost level with its head. The chase had gone no more than a few strides beyond the treeline when the massive hunter threw itself at the deer's neck, twisting as it leapt so as to clamp its

THE TALISMAN OF WRATH

fearsome jaws around the doomed creature's throat. Such was the wolf's grip that as the deer stumbled and fell, its throat was torn out by its own impetus.

The deer made one feeble attempt to rise before slumping to the ground with blood pouring from the gaping wound in its neck. The panting, triumphant pack gathered protectively around the twitching carcass, the great silver-grey with its back to the two startled travellers.

Bandil touched Eh'lorne's arm and motioned that they should make a stealthy withdrawal. Slowly, the two men crept backwards, hardly daring to breathe lest they attract the attention of the five formidable hunters.

The old man found himself overwhelmed by conflicting emotions. He was almost within touching distance of the creatures he'd longed to meet for all of his unnaturally long life; but he was realistic enough to realise that this was not the Mystic Mountains, and that the wolves would defend their kill from any perceived threat with savage ferocity.

Cautiously, they backed away taking one tiny step at a time; but the situation was hopeless. The two wolves on the far side of the carcass lifted their heads as they simultaneously spotted the traveller's slow, discreet movements. The huge grey spun around, studied them for a fraction of a heartbeat, and then bared its teeth. With a low growl it began to slink threateningly towards them.

Eh'lorne started to reach for the Talisman but Bandil placed a hand on his arm and shook his head.

"That weapon was forged to combat evil," he whispered reprovingly. "It wasn't created to slay wildlife."

Reluctantly, Eh'lorne dropped his hand to his side. Not since his encounter in the forest had he felt so exposed and defenceless.

Relentlessly, the huge grey stalked towards them with its head held low, its ears flat, and its sharp white teeth flashing menacingly.

"Bandil?" Eh'lorne hissed urgently.

The old man made no reply until the terrifying threat was almost upon them. "Hold fast," he whispered. "And have faith!"

Fine words, Eh'lorne thought sarcastically when the wolf singled him out and came right up to him. He felt a cold shiver of alarm as it sniffed first the sheathed Talisman then the man who carried it. He took an involuntary step backwards as the massive creature's low warning growl suddenly changed to a loud baying snarl and its muscles bunched ready to pounce.

Quickly, Bandil pushed himself between them and thrust the gently glowing stone under the beast's nose.

"Peace noble friend," he said in a hurried yet reassuring voice. "We carry Mordan's blessing and mean you no harm."

The wolf paused only to sniff the Stone before throwing itself at the old man, sending his thin, frail body crashing into Eh'lorne and knocking them both to the ground. As Bandil hit the floor, the Stone flew out of this hand, its soft light fading as it rolled away to leave the old man helpless and pinned beneath the creature's great weight.

Eh'lorne was equally powerless, for as he fell, he was not only badly winded, but he struck his head against a hidden rock so hard that it left him only semi-conscious. He lay gasping for air, desperately fighting against the dark mists of oblivion that threatened to overwhelm him as the old man's screams of pain and terror echoed in his ears.

CHAPTER FORTY-FOUR

Eh'lorne fought back against the dark oblivion that was seeking to drag him down into its inky depths. It called seductively to him, softly whispering promises of blessed relief from the sharp pounding in his head and the terrifying panic of suffocation. Any other man would have surrendered to the temptation but surrender was a concept that was absent from every fibre of his being.

With a fierce snarl on his lips and a blazing fire in his eyes, he forced his unyielding body to obey his commands. Twisting onto his side, he raised himself up onto one elbow while at the same time drawing the Talisman. He didn't care what Bandil had said; it may be wrong to use the powerful artefact on dumb wildlife and it was obviously too late to save the old man, but he had no other weapon with which to defend himself. If he didn't

S. P. MUIR

use the Talisman, the mission would fail and the whole world would be lost. But before the gleaming blade was even halfway clear of its black-on-black sheath, he stopped, frozen with slack jawed, wide eyed, disbelief.

Amazingly, Bandil was still very much alive. Pinned to the ground by the great weight of the huge wolf, he was frantically twisting his head from side to side in a vain attempt to avoid the large pink tongue that was eagerly licking his face. What Eh'lorne had taken to be anguished screams of pain, were in reality nothing more than helpless shrieks of uncontrollable laughter. Eventually, Bandil summoned up enough strength for one tremendous heave and managed to throw the enormous beast off and struggle up onto his knees. The creature rolled once then sprang up to face him with its head close to the ground, its rump in the air, and its tail wagging happily. It looked, to Eh'lorne's amazement, nothing more dangerous than a gigantic, playful puppy.

"Enough!" Bandil laughed. "As much as I'd like to tarry here and frolic, I'm on a quest that can't be delayed." He sighed wistfully. "If only you'd come to me before this burden was laid on my shoulders. But then your brethren have never wanted to befriend me. Alas that they didn't if they were all as magnificent as you."

The wolf sat up with its pink tongue lolling from the side of its mouth, panting happily as it stared into the old man's ancient, wrinkled face. Its savage, noble eyes followed the old man's movements as he climbed to his feet and retrieved the Mystic Stone from where it had fallen. Then with a wide grin, Bandil helped his dumbstruck companion to his feet before once more turning to face the patiently waiting wolf.

"I'm sorry, my friend," he said in a voice heavy with regret. "But we must be on our way. I bid you farewell and enjoy your meal."

THE TALISMAN OF WRATH

The huge beast stood up and made a strange noise that was somewhere between a yelp and a growling bark. It stood staring at the old man with an intense, unwavering gaze. The two men started to turn away but something about the wolf's unusual behaviour made Bandil hesitate.

"Wait," he said catching his companion's arm.

"For what?" Eh'lorne replied testily. "Another game of rough-and-tumble?" He was tired, starving, and once again his head felt as though his brother was using it as an anvil. Gingerly he touched the large lump where he'd hit his head on the rock and sourly noted that his fingers were sticky with blood. That, compounded by the nasty gash on his forehead, was not going to improve his mood one bit.

Bandil didn't answer but took a few steps towards the huge, silver-grey predator. As he approached it, the wolf turned and walked away, then after a few paces it looked back. Once again it made the strange, unearthly yips and growls.

Bandil frowned and cocked his head enquiringly.

"What is it?" he asked. "What do you want me to do?"

As if in answer, the wolf walked a few more paces towards the fallen deer then turned and pointedly met the old man's eyes.

"You want me to follow you, is that it?"

The wolf yapped sharply then trotted towards the rest of the pack who were standing protectively guarding their kill.

"Ah, I see, you *do* want me to follow you." He shook his head in wonder then started after the savagely graceful beast.

"Eh'veldar!" Eh'lorne cried out in alarm, but the old man seemed oblivious to his friend's concerned warning.

As Bandil approached the carcass, one of the wolves growled threateningly but the huge grey lunged at it, furiously snapping its jaws. The unfortunate creature backed obsequiously away, its head low and its tail between its legs. The grey then stood patiently looking at the old man.

"So what now?" Bandil asked with a questioning shrug.

The wolf sat down, looked at the body of the deer then back at the baffled theurgist.

A sudden wave of understanding swept over Bandil, a realisation that once again he'd been blessed just as he had been for the many decades he'd spent in the Mystic Mountains.

"By Mordan," he whispered. "You wish to share your food."

The wolf made no sound but continued to gaze at him, its intelligent, untamed eyes somehow appearing both feral and benign.

Without another word the old man knelt beside the carcass, took out his knife, and with a fair degree of difficulty, cut a large area of skin from the dead creature's ample rump. He then carved away several generous slices of the exposed meat which he carefully wrapped in the piece of hide. Still on his knees he then turned and faced his lupine benefactor with a grateful smile.

"I know Mordan's spirit has moved you to make this generous gift," he said softly. "And I'm not sure you're able to understand why, or how important it may prove to be; but rest assured that my appreciation – *our* appreciation – is beyond measure."

The wolf gave his face another huge, wet lick. Bandil threw his arms around the creature's powerful neck and hugged it tightly before climbing back to his feet.

"Fare-you-well, my friend," he said in a voice choked with emotion. "May Mordan bless both you and your pack; and perhaps when the world is once more put to rights, he'll permit us to meet again."

He turned and hurried away, not daring to allow himself a backward glance. At his approach, Eh'lorne opened his mouth to speak but on seeing the look on the old man's face, he thought better of it. Without a word he fell into step and the two men continued their journey in silence.

THE TALISMAN OF WRATH

They'd not gone far, however, when it became clear that they could go no further. Eh'lorne was spent beyond belief, but Bandil was staggering along like an old drunk on the point of collapse. The young Arlien motioned for his companion to rest and looked up at the sky. It was barely mid-afternoon but in spite of the heavy weight of urgency bearing down on them, he knew they had no choice but to stop and make camp. Laboriously, he set about gathering firewood while the old man sat hugging his knees with his eyes closed in silent, exhausted prayer.

Once the fire was well and truly alight, however, he roused himself enough to skewer two good-sized venison steaks onto green sticks. He handed one to Eh'lorne and the pair then sat holding them carefully over the flames, both lost in their own private world of reflection. The meat when cooked was delicious and they devoured it ravenously, washing the meal down with large refreshing mouthfuls of water. After slaking his thirst, Eh'lorne shook his flask to gauge its contents; it was perilously close to empty again, as indeed was Bandil's. He decided not to make a point of it but the old man was watching him closely.

"We're running short again, aren't we," he stated wearily.

"It would seem so. Perhaps we should have been more frugal."

"The old man nodded. "Have we much further to travel though?"

Eh'lorne closed his eyes and tried to think. The forest edge was running a little more to the west than before, and they were drawing ever closer to the distant jagged peaks of the Ravages that marked the far boundary of this central moorland. Surely Hornvale was not much more than a day's journey away.

He drew a deep breath and looked at his ancient friend with an exhausted smile on his lips. "I think we should have enough left to see us there. If all goes well and we set off at first light, we may arrive before nightfall – or at least, not long after."

Bandil nodded again. "Then if you've no objection, I'm going to try and get some sleep. The sun may still be high but I don't think I can stay awake and talk."

"How could I object when I'm of the same mind? Sleep well, my friend, for tomorrow's a busy day."

With an appreciative grunt, Bandil wrapped himself in his blanket and lay down on the soft, mossy ground. Within moments he was fast asleep, closely followed by his young companion.

Bandil's dreams were to prove unremembered but nonetheless comforting until a mounting unease roused him well into the darkest reaches of the night. He opened his eyes to see Eh'lorne's crumpled blanket empty and the tall young warrior-king nowhere in sight. He leapt up in alarm and scanned the darkness beyond the edge of the dying firelight. At first, he could see nothing, but then he breathed a huge sigh of relief when he made out the motionless figure of his companion dimly silhouetted against the dull red glow in the night sky.

Then it hit him. Why was there a red glow in the sky? He hurried over to Eh'lorne's side and stared in horror at the delicate lace of the high, ephemeral clouds now shimmering with an ominous, warm radiance. It seemed Eh'lorne was unaware of the old man's presence as they both stood gazing at the distant, beautiful horror. But then the Arlien spoke in a tone so cold and flat, it sent a chill running down Bandil's spine.

"Sirris burns and my people die. I deserted them for a fool's errand and stripped them of the only men that could protect them. Was this part of Mordan's great plan for his children? To see them all slaughtered just as they were in Sarren?"

Bandil laid a hand on Eh'lorne's shoulder. In spite of his expressionless voice, the young warrior-king's body was tense and he was shaking with impotent fury.

"My son," the old man said consolingly. "Do you really believe that the great god would allow your people – *his* people –

to be destroyed? Would you blaspheme and call him a fool? No, I think better of you than that. Search your feelings; surely, if your brother was dead, you'd know it?"

"He lives," Eh'lorne replied bitterly. "For now, at least."

"Then take heart in that and have faith. It was you that lectured me just a few days ago on having the courage and the will to fight on. However wrong it may seem that we aren't where we feel we should be, we don't have Mordan's wisdom. Wherever he commands us to fight, we can trust that it will be the most effective place to strike."

"Fight with what?" Eh'lorne scoffed. "I've lost my sword and I've no idea how to use the Talisman. I'm a warrior, not a theurgist or a sorcerer; my name is not Bandil! I say again, I have no effective weapon."

"You're wrong, "Bandil stated firmly. "Come back to the fire with me and I'll show you what you have."

Although he shook his head, after a last lingering look at the luminous sky, Eh'lorne reluctantly followed the old man's lead.

Bandil wrapped himself in his blanket, sat down beside the glowing embers, and motioned for the tall Arlien to do the same. Eh'lorne ignored him and continued to stand, stiff with suppressed anger. The old man shrugged, then gathered his thoughts for a few moments before speaking.

"You really believe you don't know how to use the Talisman?"

"Of course I don't; I'm not a sorcerer. I can't wield magic."

"And yet you've used it twice already."

"Have I? It's true that when we confronted the sellufin it gave me the strength to stand against their power, but it was the mountain that slew them. And when I faced the entity of the forest, I merely called for light in Mordan's name. Although the crystal answered that call, I had no control over its power. I can't wield it as you wield your Stone."

"What!" Bandil exclaimed. "Can I believe my own ears? How many times must I tell you to have faith? Draw the Talisman; look at it."

Eh'lorne glared back at him defiantly but something about the burning light in the old man's eyes convinced him to obey. Slowly, he pulled the potent artefact from its sheath and held it up to the firelight. The diamond-like Talisman sparkled silver-red in the fire's glow while the blade glinted coldly, its engraved runes standing out in sharp relief.

"That's it," Bandil continued sternly. "So tell me, what are you holding, what form does it take? Is it not a sword with an edge so keen it could cut the very wind? And are you not the most accomplished swordsman in the land? Now tell me again that you have no weapon!"

Eh'lorne studied the Talisman thoughtfully. Then with a well-practiced flourish, he spun a full circle, cutting the air skilfully as he turned. Then he held the Talisman out in front of him and grinned.

"I do have a weapon," he conceded.

"Good. So let's have no more of your nonsense; trust in our god and go back to sleep!"

Eh'lorne's smile faded. "Eh'veldar," he said sombrely. "Even with this blade I can't defeat the enormous multitudes that swarm against us. No matter how many I take with me, eventually I'm bound to be overwhelmed."

"Then we will fall together and our deaths will be glorious!"

Eh'lorne grinned again. "Aye, and what a song it would make if only someone was there to see it."

Bandil laughed, relieved to see the passion returning to his friend's soul. "Mordan will see it and the very stars will sing of it. I'd wager that the sky itself would blaze forth and declare that the king has come and gone in glory!"

Eh'lorne's smile grew broader. "Then, my friend, let's cook the last of the meat and tomorrow we'll eat as we walk; there'll be no pause and no rest until we reach Hornvale."

* * *

They set off as soon as the pre-dawn light was bright enough to see the ground. The food and rest had worked wonders for their energy reserves, and they carried on their journey with a grimly determined spring in their step. The thin, lacy clouds had dissipated as though the distant inferno had burned them away to nothing. Once again the sun rose clear and bright, adding to their purposeful mood. It wasn't long, however, before Eh'lorne became increasingly uneasy. Repeatedly, he glanced at the brooding forest fifty strides to their right. Eventually, he stopped dead and peered apprehensively into the darkness between the densely packed trees.

"It's back," he said simply.

"Are you sure?" the old man asked, hoping that his young friend was mistaken.

"I'm sure. It hasn't spotted us yet but it is searching for us."

Bandil frowned. If he was right about the entity in the forest, it wasn't searching for them, it was searching for the Talisman – but how? Eh'lorne had said that when it was in its sheath it was invisible even to his intensely acute Arlien senses. Unless...

His hand went to his pocket where the Mystic Stone nestled safely in his tunic. Could it be that now the Talisman had woken it, the entity could feel the Stone's power as well?

"We must get as far away from the forest as possible," he said urgently.

"If you insist but we can't go too far."

Bandil placed his hands on Eh'lorne's shoulders and looked intently into his face. "I said as far as possible," he said earnestly. "That means directly away from it and as far from it as we're able to run!"

Eh'lorne shook his head. "That can't happen; we'll be going southwest and moving further from our destination with every step we take. We'll be delayed for far too long and we know that we might already be too late."

"Better late than not at all," Bandil replied ominously. They locked eyes, each determined to hold their ground. But such was the Arlien's respect for the old man that, contrary to his arrogant nature, he yielded once again.

"Very well," he said resignedly. "But I hope 'running' was an exaggeration; although if you insist, we'll up the pace. I hope you're prepared for it though."

"I'll manage – I'll have to."

They set off without another word, the old man pushing them on at a merciless speed. Eh'lorne's mind was awhirl with questions but the look on Bandil's face persuaded him to keep them to himself. Not until well past midday did the old man begin to relax a little and allow them to slow down and curve more to the north. Eh'lorne kept glancing at his companion's face in an effort to gauge his mood. When he was sure it was safe to pursue the matter, he tentatively raised the subject.

"Eh'veldar," he began carefully. "You seem to have some idea of what it was that threatened us. Whatever it is, surely it can't be more powerful than both the Stone and the Talisman united against it?"

The old man's expression hardened and at first it seemed he was refusing to answer. But then, without a sideways glance he spoke, his voice clipped and tense.

"I've reason to believe that it's the *Kamarill* – the Earthsoul. I pray that I'm wrong but..." He trailed off poignantly.

"The *Kamarill*? I've not heard of it before, and although I've not exactly studied our scrolls, I'm sure if it was in those writings it would have been mentioned by someone at some time."

"There's no reason why you should have heard of it; I only learned of it from my visions of the Earth's founding. It has slept since that ancient time and I hope that if it's left alone, it'll simply return to its slumber and cause no harm to the world. And as for the Stone and the Talisman, at best we could drive it off again but I can't even be certain of that. No, it's best to give it a wide berth and let it go back to its rest."

"But tell me..."

"Enough!" Bandil snapped tersely. "I've said all that I'm going to say. Save your energy for walking and forget it ever happened. With good fortune, that's the last we'll ever hear of it."

For a man of Eh'lorne's temperament this was hardly a satisfactory answer, but he decided to bide his time before pressing the old man any further.

As the sun arced across the sky and began to sink towards the western horizon, the two men rested for the first time since setting off that morning. Eh'lorne sat lost in thought, absently tapping the side of his face with his fingertips. Abruptly, he turned and looked at the old man as though he'd suddenly come to a decision. Bandil raise his eyebrows questioningly, waiting for his young companion to speak.

"We have to keep going," Eh'lorne said firmly. "Somehow, we *must* arrive today for I know in my bones that tomorrow will be too late."

"And travel in darkness? If you haven't noticed, the ground is becoming more and more treacherous the further west we go. How do you suggest we find our way with no moon to guide our footsteps?"

"You'll have to use the Stone just as you did in the tunnels."

"I've already told you that I can't. If I do, I'll be fit for nothing when we arrive – that is if I have the strength to get that far!"

Eh'lorne was adamant. "That's as may be," he persisted firmly. "But unless we do as I say, I know for certain that all our efforts will have been in vain."

Bandil studied him for a few moments then sighed. "So be it then," he said reluctantly. "Let's get started and go as far as we can in whatever daylight is left."

They got to their feet and with renewed urgency continued on their way. Bandil delayed using the Stone for as long as possible, but as twilight began to dwindle into night, it became obvious that he couldn't put it off any longer. Soon they found themselves stumbling along in its shadowy ghostly light with only their ragged breathing and the occasional screech of an owl to disturb the oppressive silence of the night.

As Bandil had predicted, the ground continued to grow more and more hazardous; and in spite of the Stone it began to look as though they'd be forced to stop and wait for dawn after all. But then, to the relief of both men, they stumbled upon the road. They permitted themselves the luxury of drinking the last few drops of their water before carrying on, confident that they were indeed drawing close to their destination.

They'd lost all sense of time as they trudged on and on, for the swaying light of the Stone was growing more and more hypnotic as it moved to-and-fro in time with the old man's stride. Their minds held no other thought than the need to keep taking another step. Neither of them had any idea of exactly how far they'd come. But then a distant flash of lightning revealed that they were near to the point where the forest and the Ravages came together to form the tight, narrow passage that was the Choke.

The lightning was followed in quick succession by three more flashes, each seeming a little more distant than the last;

but none were accompanied by thunder. Eh'lorne had seen such lightning before and knew exactly what it heralded – battle!

They broke into a shambling, stumbling run that was particularly hard on the old man. His shrivelled, emaciated body had exceeded its natural extremities long ago, and he was only able to continue by drawing ever more heavily on the power of the Stone. But even that was beginning to fail him as he lost the strength to channel its might.

As they entered the confines of the Choke they peered warily at the dark mass of trees to their right; trees that seemed to float in an eerie, macabre dance in the unsteady light of the Stone. Their fears were unfounded though, for the terrifying *Kamarill* – if such it was – had obviously lost track of them. Also, this part of the forest was far less dangerous and forbidding; it was possible that whatever it might be was just loath to tread between the more cheerful and widely spaced trees.

The dark, claustrophobic corridor seemed to run on for an eternity, an impression made all the more real when another flash split the night. For as far as they could see there was nothing but the press of trees to their right, and the towering jagged rocks of the Ravages to their left. But eventually, the two exhausted men emerged onto the long slope that led down into the great valley itself. The sight that greeted them there brought them both to a shuddering and horrified halt.

The compound of the Horn was illuminated by a dying ring of fire that surrounded it from cliff face to cliff face. A seething, undulating mass of lich pressed tightly against it, waiting their chance to overwhelm the small band of men within its walls. The great, white marble temple was only dimly visible in the light of the torches that were sparsely spread along its surrounding battlements.

Then there came another flash, and in its light, between the temple and the Horn, they saw the remains of the armshost's fighting wedge as Gildor's desperate attempt to reach Rennil's men faltered and began to break apart.

But in that burst of scarlet lightning, Eh'lorne saw something else – something that set his soul aflame with the delicious anticipation of exquisite revenge. The blinding flash had emanated from the staff of a red-armoured warrior, tiny in the distance but standing almost twice the height of the stooped, man-like beasts it commanded. It had been just such a giant warrior that had slain his father at Cor-Peshtar, and here were three – no four of them, all waiting ripe and ready to feel the keen edge of his vengeance.

With a savage laugh he began to sprint down the hillside but from behind him, Bandil's loud cry of anguished pain immediately brought him up short. He turned to see the frail old man sprawled face down on the dirt road with the Stone held out in a desperate grip before him.

"Eh'veldar!" he cried anxiously as he ran back to his stricken comrade. Bandil made a feeble attempt to rise but it was to no avail; he was finished.

"Oh, my friend, my dear friend," Eh'lorne lamented as he lifted his companion into a sitting position. "What have I done to you? I've pushed you too hard again and now you're hurt."

"No, my son," the old man croaked. "I've twisted my ankle, that's all. And we both knew that I'd be too exhausted to help when we arrived; so you go on and leave me here. It's for you alone to finish what we began together; my part in this adventure is over now."

Eh'lorne shook his head. "You're wrong, Eh'veldar; I need you for one more task. This filth must know exactly who it is that now falls on them. So I beg of you, if it's in your power, raise up a banner of light across the valley. Let the standard of the old kings blaze over their heads and strike fear into their hearts."

Bandil gave a weak smile. "That would be a grand sight indeed, but I don't think I have it left in me." He held up the Stone. Its light had now diminished to the point where it barely illuminated the old man's face. "You see; I can barely call up enough power to light my own hand."

Eh'lorne nodded sombrely. "I understand. But if you can find it in you..."

"Then you will see it reflected in the eyes of your enemies. Now go, and I promise you that I'll try my best."

Eh'lorne kissed the old man's head and stood up.

"No man could ask for more," he said before turning away and sprinting down the hill to meet his destiny.

CHAPTER FORTY-FIVE

Bandil watched Eh'lorne disappear into the darkness and sighed. He could see the terrible catastrophe unfolding in the valley below and knew there was nothing he could do to assist his gallant young companion. It was as much as he could do just to remain conscious. He held up the stone and sighed again. Its radiance was now so weak as to be nothing more than a tiny glimmer. It was only the depth of the night's darkness that made it visible at all, and had there been any kind of a moon, the Stone's light would have been completely overwhelmed. But Eh'lorne had asked for a royal banner in the sky – for the king's standard to be raised in fire and light for the whole valley to see.

Ah well; he'd promised to do his best, so he at least had to try. He attempted to move from his sitting position to the required kneeling posture of supplication, but the intense sharp pain in his ankle made him stop and cry out in agony. There was nothing for it but to remain sitting where he was, although that was going to make the task even more difficult. Ignoring the throbbing pain in his ankle, he settled himself down, closed his eyes, and began to chant.

As he intoned the words of power, he pictured in his mind the standard of the old kings; the great flowing banner he'd seen depicted on the murals in the ancient ruined temple in Arl. Despite the passage of so many years, he remembered it as clearly as if it had been only yesterday. As a child he'd stared enthralled at the painting of a tall, fair-haired king, proudly holding aloft the streaming pennant with its plain, pale blue background and white seven-pointed star emblazoned in its centre. He now tried to visualise that star-adorned banner etched across the sky, shining and burning with silver light. But his efforts were in vain, for no matter how hard he tried, he no longer possessed the strength.

Even so, he refused to give up; he'd made a promise to try his best and to give anything less would be to admit defeat. And if there was one thing he'd learned from the impetuous, flamboyant young Arlien, it was that defeat was never an option. But despite that, he knew in his heart of hearts that the task Eh'lorne had given him was an impossible one – probably beyond his capability even when he was at his strongest – but now?

But then below him in the valley, Eh'lorne drew the talisman and roaring his mighty battle cry, he fell upon the hapless lich like a thunderbolt. The gleaming blade flashed as it bit into flesh and the moment it tasted blood, the crystal at its heart erupted in a bright silver fire of cold, unbridled fury. It devastated every one of the revolting creatures within a stone's throw, hurling them to the ground and leaving them as smoking, frozen corpses. The Talisman's arctic rage crackled in the air with such potency, the old man only needed to grasp it and shape it into the form he desired.

So as Eh'lorne stormed through the massed ranks of the enemy's deformed foot soldiers, Bandil took hold of the Talisman's raging storm, drew energy from it, and then used the Mystic Stone to mould it to his will. The air above the valley began to shimmer and shine with a radiance that rapidly grew until finally, it formed the unmistakable shape of a fluttering banner emblazoned with a single star – a star so bright, it lit up the whole valley like the full moon on a clear night.

At the very moment the king's standard blazed across the valley, the gates of the temple burst open and a thousand warrior-priests flooded out led by none other than the High Priest himself. They poured out through the city and fought their way on towards the Horn. They were followed by hundreds of the brown-robed worker monks – each one a willing volunteer. These humble labourers were armed with anything that might serve as a weapon: shovels, picks, and clubs; and one brave soul – a simple cook – carried nothing more potent than a kitchen knife.

From the moment Gildor's men had left the temple, Arbenak had begun marshalling his forces, gathering them together in order to join the valorous but doomed attempt to reach the Horn. They now charged out of the city, confounding the startled lich to such an extent that their progress toward the decimated armshost was as swift as it was bloody.

What was left of that small valiant force was now gathered in three tight groups with the men in the largest of these desperate circles standing protectively around the inert body of the Prime. The five priests had managed to save his body from being trampled by dragging it behind them and were now fighting with suicidal extravagance to keep the bestial lich from taking the corpse and mutilating it – something the foul creatures were performing with great relish on every other body they could lay their claws on. But as the circle grew ever smaller, it became clear that Gildor's body would soon become exposed again. So at the very moment that Bandil cast the dazzling banner across the sky, one of the few remaining Lord-Guard ducked behind the whirling blades and staffs to pull it back to safety. In the banner's cold light, the soldier could clearly see the extent of the horrific injuries that had cut Gildor down, but it revealed something else as well.

"The Prime lives!" the soldier cried. "Fight for the Prime!" Somehow, the battered and exhausted remnants of the armshost found both the strength and the will to fight on with even greater ferocity. The lich, unsure of what the fiery banner heralded, were now starting to waver, and the tiny force of men began to push the savage beasts back.

Rennil's priests however, were still in serious trouble. The flames that had kept the lich at bay were now low enough for the agile, loathsome creatures to leap over the trench and clear the compound wall. Even so, their attack was not as devastating or as co-ordinated as it should have been, for the attention of the nearest warrior-mage had been drawn by Gildor's doomed attempt to come to Rennil's aid. In truth, the armshost's terrible sacrifice had not been completely in vain; and although the price had been appallingly high, they had purchased the precious extra moments that Eh'lorne and Bandil needed to arrive before it was entirely too late.

When the royal standard ignited above the battlefield, all the priests in the compound cried out in joyous triumph. "It's the king; the king has come!"

"Eh'lorne!" Rennil breathed in fervent relief before setting about slaughtering the hated lich with renewed savagery.

Eh'lorne appeared to be unstoppable as he cut a swathe through the dense ranks of Limnash's army. Like an arrow he drove on towards the giant red-armoured general that stood commanding the lich army in front of the compound. Again and again the mage's staff flashed as he threw more and more of his bestial troops against the charging Arlien. Effortlessly, Eh'lorne brushed them aside, hacking their flesh and incinerating them with flames as cold as ice. Then the two deadly warriors met.

When his father had faced the great warrior-mage at Cor-Peshtar, it had laughed scornfully at the High-Lord's efforts – as skilful as they were. This one however, did not laugh. In a macabre replay of the earlier combat, the mage roared its defiance and wielded its massive sword for a mighty, death-dealing blow. In the plains of Sirris, Lorne had parried just such a stroke before spinning around and striking his opponent with an expert cut to its side. But Lorne had been armed with a common sword, and although he'd executed the manoeuvre faultlessly, he'd been but the pupil. This monster faced the master, and the master held the Talisman of Wrath.

In a single movement performed with more fluidity and grace than the most elegant of dancers, Eh'lorne parried, pirouetted, and struck the giant with a fearsome, powerful blow. Where his father's blade had merely glanced off the supernatural red armour, the Talisman cut through it as if it were made of butter. A hideous scream split the air as a dazzling silver light exploded within the creature's plate mail. It glared from every chink in the enchanted metal suit while the massive warrior's staff splintered and the huge ruby at its tip shattered with an ear-piercing crack.

And now Eh'lorne knew exactly why he was here and not at Sirris. Without breaking step, he skipped past the falling hulk and hurtled on towards the Great Horn. Lifted by the boundless power of the blazing Talisman, he vaulted the burning trench, cleared the wall, and landed lightly amid the besieged defenders. He then sprinted across the compound, and taking the stone steps beside the Horn two at a time, he raced up to the topmost platform. There, he pressed his lips to the huge silver mouthpiece and blew.

THE TALISMAN OF WRATH

Even if the massive sculpture had been a real horn, no mortal man could possess the capacity to sound so vast an instrument. But Eh'lorne blew not with air, he blew with power. And not just any power, he winded the Great Horn with the raging, freezing wrath of the great god himself; and the sound of it was beyond all imagination. It was deep and terrifying and although so loud it stunned the senses, it was at the same time completely silent – heard not with the ears but with the heart and the mind, shaking the very soul as it resonated through the body.

All the moisture in the air turned instantly to ice, shimmering in the light of the fiery banner and floating down as delicately as the softest of snowflakes.

The three-remaining warrior-magi suffered the same fate as the first with silver light bursting out from beneath their red armour. The lich screamed in pain and terror as they burst into flames of raw, freezing fire. A few turned instantly to ice, shattering like glass as they hit the ground. Never in all the history of the world had so many lives been extinguished in a single moment.

The royal banner shining over the valley dissolved into a shapeless, shimmering haze that hovered for a few heartbeats before rocketing up to the highest reaches of the sky. There it exploded in a huge soundless burst that momentarily blinded all the survivors and seemed to shake the earth to its very foundations. When the stunned priests and hostmen regained their sight, they looked up to see the king's standard emblazoned across every corner of the heavens for the whole world to see.

Eh'lorne blew and blew and when he was finished, he looked out across the battlefield, eagerly surveying the carnage he'd brought down upon his enemies. Then he threw back his head and laughed, drunk on victory and power.

CHAPTER FORTY-SIX

There were many miraculous events that had helped to preserve the Arlien people after the fall of Gorand's kingship. But that incredible exodus is a saga in its own right, and one that would now need to be retold and rewritten after Verryl's wilful destruction of the vil-carrim. The heavy responsibility of accurately retelling that account – and many others – now fell on Lore-Master G'harvil's young but capable shoulders. He would need to do careful research, listen to the old songs, and seek out whatever scraps of parchment or books that had survived. But there was no need to read or hear ancient folksongs about the most amazing miracle of that fateful relocation. It was there to be seen every time the people of Sirris set foot inside the huge cave system that was the Refuge.

THE TALISMAN OF WRATH

More than five hundred years previously, the Arlien people had arrived at Cor-Peshtar, guided to the remote sanctuary by Gorand's dreams and visions. It had been late summer and the need to find shelter for the thousands of people before the onset of winter had been paramount – especially as the summer was comparatively short at such high altitudes. But the Refuge had provided a wondrous and ready-made solution.

The system consisted of a vast, wide entrance set thirty cubits up in the northern most cliff face of the valley-plain's rim wall. A wooden staircase had been constructed over the years to provide safe, easy access for the population – a staircase that could be quickly thrown down in the event of siege. A small river flowed through the enormous main atrium providing the people with both fresh water and sewerage. The labyrinth of tunnels and myriads of room-like caves furnished the exiled Arlien nation with a huge underground city. That such providential accommodation was there to be found was amazing enough, but that was not the real miracle of the Refuge. No, the greatest marvel of all was sunstone.

The Refuge's walls, roofs, and floors were veined with the white crystalline rock – rock that shone brightly, reflecting whatever light existed in the world outside. It carried the warm yellow brilliance of summer deep underground, and even the dim light of an overcast or rainy day was reflected through the miraculous stone. By night the caves were dark, but not the tangible, disconcerting pitch black that was normal for such deep recesses. Rather, it was the natural darkness of the night, whether it be moonlit, starlit, or overcast. Far from being the dank, oppressive dungeon one would imagine, the Refuge was bright, warm, and airy. And although not exactly luxurious, it had been home to the Arlien people for almost two hundred years before the city of Sirris was finally completed. During that time the tunnels and caves had been expanded and refined, and it was during these excavations that another feature of sunstone became apparent. Once separated from its place in the mother-rock, its ability to transmit light ceased. This caused some disappointment, for a generous handful of sunshine would have been more than useful in exploring the dark recesses in other areas of the rim-wall.

One of the hundreds of rooms contained within the Refuge was almost an exact replica of the viltula – except of course for the massive windows. Even the private quarters attached to the huge ward-room were a flawless facsimile of those at the large wooden house of healing. The huge stone ward-room was now filled with relocated patients transferred from both the old viltula and the new one set up under Morjeena's care. The overcrowding was as bad as ever – in spite of the fact that D'harid had stolen away as many of the wounded as could still hold a sword.

It was now mid-afternoon of the day after D'harid's defensive inferno, and the sunstone in the wall was filling the vast ward-room with the warm brilliance of a bright sunny day. An exhausted Aldegar was squeezing between the beds and mattresses as he went about his rounds with half a dozen uniformed tenders in tow. They were listening intently as he gave them his instructions for the care of those in their charge. Several more tenders were scattered around the huge chamber, going about their duties either singly or in pairs depending on the task required of them. Among these pairs were Morjeena – now un-uniformed as befitting a healer – and the newly recruited Gretya. The latter was concentrating intently as Morjeena demonstrated how best to clean and re-dress a wound while causing as little discomfort to the patient as possible. Her wrinkled brow and narrowed eyes accentuated her plain round features, completely hiding the infectious light that lurked beneath the surface.

But then the door opened and both girls smiled as they saw who'd entered. Morjeena, easily the prettiest girl in the room seemed suddenly to fade into obscurity as Gretya's hidden beauty burst forth.

"Eldore," she cried happily.

"Hush!" Morjeena admonished. "Have respect for the patients." Her tone was not too severe however, and Gretya merely responded with a meekly apologetic grin.

Eldore was followed into the room by a tired and strained looking D'harid who whispered something to the young lord and then made his way over to Aldegar. Eldore stood patiently by the door, waiting for the two women to finish dressing the soldier's wound. Not until Morjeena was satisfied that Gretya had fully understood the lesson did they pick their way through the crowded ward to where he stood. As they approached, Morjeena's welcoming smile faded a little. Her husband's face was deathly pale and his bloodshot eyes were deep-set within large dark circles. She knew he'd not slept the previous night and had hardly eaten all day. Even so, he managed to greet them both with a warm, if exhausted grin.

"And how are my two favourite girls today?" he said trying to sound jovial.

"Better than you, my love," Morjeena replied. Gently she brushed his pale cheek. "You're exhausted. Why not go and rest for a while; I'm sure the war can manage without you for a turn or two."

He shook his head and sighed. "I'm afraid that's not possible; there's far too much to be done; and anyway, there's many a man in a far worse state than I am."

His wife looked unconvinced so he turned his attention to Gretya. "And how are you getting on? Are you enjoying your new position?"

"Oh yes, very much," she gushed; but then her brow wrinkled a little. "Although I'm not altogether sure I'm suited to it. It's far more complicated than I'd ever imagined."

"Don't listen to her," Morjeena countered laying a proprietary hand on the taller girl's shoulder. "I've yet to have a more dedicated pupil, and she's far from the slowest learner I've ever had."

"There," Eldore said giving his old friend a playful punch on the arm. "I knew you could do it. Eh'lorne will be proud of you."

Hope flashed into Gretya's eyes. "Have you had word from him? Is he coming home?"

"No, you know that's not the case. But I can assure you he's in good health though."

"You're sure?"

"Of course I'm sure. You know full well I'd know if it were otherwise; and you'd be the first person I'd tell. Rest easy, he's fine."

He hoped he sounded more convinced than he felt, for twice now he'd suffered intense, un-attributable pains in his head – pains that he must have had from his brother. The first time was three night ago. He'd been walking through the dark streets close to his forge when he'd suddenly been knocked from his feet by a sharp concussion to his forehead. It had felt as though the cut he'd sustained during the storm had burst open, even though by then that injury was no more than a rapidly fading scar. Despite having healed at the same unnatural speed as the wound in his side, he'd still expected to feel blood flowing down his face. In reality, just as had happened so many times in his life, there'd been nothing; not a cut, not a scratch, not even a tiny mark to explain his discomfort. Then yesterday afternoon, he'd felt something similar but this time on the back of his head. Wherever he was, Eh'lorne was not having the easiest of times; of that much he was certain.

Morjeena reached out and squeezed his hand; she at least knew of his concerns. "Well we must be grateful for small mercies," she said reassuringly. "And at least we have you here.

It's nice of you to take the time to come and see us, busy though you are."

Eldore sighed. "Aye, but as good as it is to see you both, I'm afraid it's not a social call. D'harid and I are on our rounds taking stock of our resources and bolstering our defences. I'm afraid I can't stay long. As soon as D'harid's finished talking to your father we'll be off."

Morjeena glanced over to where the Vice-Master and her father were in earnest and somewhat heated discussion.

"Well whatever he's saying to him, my father seems to be getting rather upset."

Again, Eldore sighed. "I'm not surprised," he said tiredly. "D'harid's asking him to release more of those wounded in the first battle. Many of them are regular hostmen which is an asset we're in desperate need of."

His wife flushed angrily. "Look around you," she snapped. "Do you see one single man fit to lift a weapon? There's not one here well enough to carry himself, let alone a sword. Of those already taken, most should still be here; and yet D'harid has the nerve to ask for more? I thought better of him than that!"

Eldore wearily shook his head. "You judge him too harshly – he has eyes and a heart. He knows that what he asks is impossible, yet he has no choice but to try. Even one extra hostman, no matter how injured, is of greater value than you could possibly imagine."

Morjeena studied his face. The strain and the fear were obvious to her; and the sight of his internal conflict was like a knife to her heart.

"Is the situation that desperate?" she asked softly.

He closed his eyes for a moment then looked from one girl to the other. His gaze finally settled on his pretty Keshtari wife. "I can't lie to you, Delsheer. And Gretya, I know you see yourself as just a humble servant, but your future is far, far more than that. So I feel the truth is yours to know as well. Our situation is more than desperate. The fires on the far bank are dying down and our enemies will soon attack again. And when they do, we won't be able to hold them back for long before we're overrun."

"But we'll be safe here in the refuge, surely," Morjeena replied. It was half question, half statement.

"On the face of it, yes. Against any other army it would take a long siege to dislodge us from this underground fortress; but this is no ordinary army. D'harid has a bad feeling about what we may have to face and frankly, I share his concerns – I've grown to trust our reluctant Vice-Master implicitly."

"Eh'lorne will save us!" Gretya declared so firmly and vehemently that her two colleagues could do nothing but stare at her in surprise. "He will," she repeated more quietly before turning away and going back to her duties.

"I hope she's right, Delsheer," Eldore said flatly.

"So do I," she replied a little absently. Then she spotted D'harid making his way back to them leaving the dismayed Aldegar staring after him and shaking his head in disbelief.

"Ah, it looks like I'm about to lose you," she said regretfully.

"Aye, it's back to reality for..."

He was cut short by a loud, explosive crash as the door burst open, almost ripping the wooden frame away from the rock wall. A frightened, agitated militiaman rushed into the room, his face white and his eyes wide with fear. Relief spread across his features as he spied both Eldore and D'harid in the same room.

"Vice-Master, Lord Eldore," he cried in a strangled, high-pitched tone. "You must come at once, Hevalor needs you."

"Calm yourself man," D'harid replied firmly as he approached the door. Though tired and strained, his voice was as serene as ever. "What's so urgent that Hevalor should be in such desperate need of us; has the attack started?"

"No sir, but there's...there's a ghost in the city."

"Don't be ridiculous," Eldore scoffed. "The dead are dead and sleep until Halgar comes. It must be some sort of devilry from the enemy – a trick to undermine our resolve."

"No, my lord," the terrified man wailed. "It *is* a ghost. The spirits of the dead must be rising from their graves."

D'harid laid a comforting hand on the man's shoulder. "Now come on lad, Lord Eldore's right; the dead sleep the long sleep and hold no power over us. I'm surprised that Hevalor of all people would say otherwise."

"But it's true!" the man insisted. "It's the boy, Yewan. His Shade is in Pump Square. He's come back to hold us all to account for his death!"

In a single fraction of a heartbeat the blood drained from Eldore's face and his stomach seemed to perform a sickening somersault. But then like an arrow from a bow, he shot from the room, barrelling the unfortunate militiaman aside as he went. He raced along the wide corridors that mirrored streets until he reached the huge atrium that marked the Refuge's entrance. The news of the apparition had spread like wildfire and the massive entranceway was crowded with the panicked and the curious. Eldore barged through the pandemonium shouting, "MOVE!" at the top of his voice as he went. Morjeena followed in his wake with D'harid at her side, desperately trying to shield the diminutive Keshtari healer from being crushed in the crowd.

Eldore threw himself down the stairs, his boots thumping a staccato rhythm on the wooden steps as he hurtled recklessly down them and into the city. He raced through the seven long streets that led to Pump Square (paradoxically a circle) where the terrified messenger had said the ghost had appeared. He arrived to find the approach choked with a great throng of the most curious (and bravest) of Sirris's inhabitants. With some difficulty, he elbowed his way through to the front of the pack where he was met with a spectacle that sent a maelstrom of wildly conflicting emotions through his soul.

There, standing motionless beside the large water-pump in the centre of the square, was a spectral apparition that had taken the form of a naked ten-year-old boy. It was without doubt poor dead Yewan's double, but this creature was glowing so brightly that its radiance outshone the afternoon sun. Standing uneasily before the shade and trying to engage it in some kind of conversation was the Spiritual Overseer himself. The atmosphere around the square was tense and electric, the silence only broken by one voice that rose up in a loud, heartrending wail of distress. Eldore looked along the crowd and discovered the owner of the voice was none other than Sharna, Yewan's mother. She was desperately trying to break free from the many hands that restrained her, preventing her from rushing to sweep the ghost of her son into her arms.

As he watched the tragic scene unfolding before him, he was only dimly aware of his wife, panting and breathless, arriving at his side. She clutched his arm in a tight grip, sensing the terrible conflict boiling within him.

Time and time again Hevalor addressed the spectre. He tried to reason with it, pleaded with it, and even commanded it to depart; but the phantom seemed oblivious to the overseer's very presence. Instead, it continued to stand like a bright, luminous statue, its unseeing eyes fixed in a distant, unearthly stare.

Completely at a loss, Hevalor looked over his shoulder and upon seeing Eldore, turned and shrugged helplessly.

"Lord Eldore," he called in an uncharacteristically nervous and trembling voice. "I don't know what else to do. The shade is unresponsive but we can't just leave it here – who knows what evil threat it poses."

"It's not evil," shrieked the boy's mother. "HE IS MY SON!"

"Let me try," Eldore replied walking tentatively forward. He attempted to shake Morjeena's hand from his arm but she held on tightly, determined not to leave her husband to face the boy's ghost alone.

With a grateful nod, Hevalor wasted no time in retreating back to the ring of people crowding around the edge of the square. Eldore took his place, but to the consternation of the crowd, he went much closer to the spectre than the Overseer – close enough even to put out a hand to touch it. He knelt down and peered into the creature's eerily glowing eyes. Morjeena stood over him with a hand laid protectively on his shoulder. He scrutinised the boy's perfectly replicated features, searching for any signs of the life-spark that had once made the young servant who he was.

"Yewan?" he whispered softly. "Is it you?"

At the sound of his voice the shining apparition fixed Eldore with a penetrating stare, then looked up into Morjeena's eyes and did the same. Eldore staggered to his feet and took an involuntary half-step backwards. The couple both felt as though the spectre's gaze had reached deep into their souls, illuminating their deepest emotions and leaving them both feeling naked and violated.

Then the creature spoke; but not in the light, childish voice they both knew, but rather in the full deep voice of a grown man. The voice was rich and sonorous, of a tone and timbre that resonated around the square and hung in the air for all to hear – if not to understand. For it spoke in a language that although sounding like an obscure dialect of old Arlien, no one could comprehend save for one or two words by the most educated among the throng.

"*Id erran id Reshgar reshi ar Sirarl, I tam ish-dor kalar urr.*"

As it spoke, the creature pointed at the startled pair; at Eldore with its left hand and at Morjeena with its right. Then to the crowd's horror, as soon as it fell silent it took a step forward and touched them both on the left breast over their hearts.

The instant the spectre's fingers touched them, there was a blinding, silent flash and all three – man, woman, and child – were thrown to the floor where they lay unconscious and unmoving. The shining luminescence had gone from the boy, leaving only the real and tangible figure of Yewan himself, naked and supine on the ground.

With a scream of horror, Sharna broke free from the stunned onlookers and rushed to her son's side. Sinking down beside him she pulled him towards her and listened for his heart. She then cradled him tightly in her arms and with tears of joy cascading down her cheeks, she called out to those who'd restrained her.

"I told you he was alive," she cried. "I told you but you wouldn't listen. Oh, my boy's alive, my boy's alive." Sobbing happily, she rested her wet cheek on his fair head and rocked his unconscious body to-and-fro.

D'harid had reacted almost as quickly as the boy's mother, coming to Morjeena and Eldore's aid before anyone else had even registered what had happened. But despite his best efforts to rouse them, the Lord Regent and his Lady lay side by side, barely breathing and comatose.

CHAPTER FORTY-SEVEN

At first, Eldore felt as though his mind was floating untethered and adrift in a black void – a disembodied spirit bereft of any physical sensation or connection. He knew that at some point he'd been unconscious, or at the very least unknowing, and that now, he was awake and aware. But aware of what? Was he in fact dead? Was his soul now drifting in a spirit world, waiting to be elevated to some unexplainable, ethereal paradise where it would be rewarded with eternal ecstasy? Or if found unworthy, if he hadn't donated enough of his wealth to the myriads of gods and their many temples, was he about to be abandoned to the merciless tortures of the under-gods and their attendant demons? Such were the teachings of the Keshtari heathens and their avaricious priests; yet Arlien scripture declared that the dead slept in a dreamless and peaceful sleep. Was his deeply held faith, in truth, based on a lie? With that thought came a sudden rush of panic, but he quickly regained control of his emotions. He employed the same reasoned argument that had served him so well all his life – apart from the times when that logic had been overwhelmed by his brother's impetuous nature of course.

He relaxed and concentrated on his surroundings. Could he see anything, feel anything, or hear anything? Was there anything at all, no matter how remote or slight? For a long while there was nothing; no sensations of touch or sight, no sounds or smells.

But wait! There *was* a sound. It was distant and remote, so quiet as to be almost inaudible; but it was there. It was a soft and rhythmic sighing like the gentlest of breezes tenderly brushing the leaves of a far-off tree. But it was doing so with a slow, metronomic cadence. It was puzzling in its familiarity but what was it?

Then it came to him; it was his own breathing. He was alive! Amid a wave of intense relief, he grasped at the sound, clinging to it as though it was an anchor, a cord that reconnected him with reality. Using all of his will, he took hold of that chord and heaved himself toward the sound; towards wherever it was that his physical body continued its existence. Slowly, mental-hand over mental-hand, he drew the sound towards him. Gradually, the rhythm of his life grew stronger and louder, until with one final superhuman effort, he opened his eyes.

There was nothing to see but a disconcerting yellowish grey fog. Slowly, however, the mist solidified to reveal a white-veined, smooth stone surface, warmly lit by the yellow glow of innumerable flickering lamps. As his vision cleared, he found he could move his eyes but he also realised that the rest of his body was completely numb and paralysed. Again, a wave of panic threatened to rise up and overwhelm him, but he forced it down by returning his focus to his breathing. The regular, hypnotic passage of air through his lungs calmed his nerves, allowing him to bide his time and patiently wait for life and sensation to reappear. Gradually, that patience was rewarded by the incremental return of feeling to his face. He soon found that he could blink at will and even move his lips a little. Eventually, his neck muscles were able to move and instinctively he turned his head to the left.

He was lying on a bed in the stone viltula, and lying in the very next bed was Morjeena. Her bright blue eyes were wide open and gazing lovingly into his. Somehow, he knew that they'd both awoken at the exact same moment, and that they'd shared the exact same experience. Somehow, he knew that this linked them with a new and magical, unbreakable bond. He tried to give her a warm, reassuring smile. But he quickly realised that if his own smile was anything like the twisted grimace his wife managed in return, his effort was far from a spectacular success. But however inadequate the couple's smiles may have been, the immeasurable and mutual adoration in their eyes more than made amends.

With Eldore's growing perception came the sound of happy tears from the bed on his right. He turned his head to see who was crying and discovered it to be Yewan's mother, Sharna. She was kneeling on the far side of the bed, clutching her son's hand while sobbing a joyous prayer of thanks for the return of her only child.

Yewan turned to look at him exactly as Morjeena had done – except the boy's eyes held only bewilderment and an inexplicable shame. But what could he possibly be ashamed of? Eldore was about to put the lad at ease with a reassuring smile but he quickly thought better of it. With his lack of control over his facial muscles, he was far more likely to frighten the boy than to encourage him. Instead he gave him a slow, deliberate wink. Yewan made a valiant attempt to return the gesture, but could only manage what amounted to a clumsy, lopsided blink.

Inwardly, Eldore smiled to himself. He'd recently witnessed an exasperated Gretya trying without success to teach the boy to wink properly; but that was another time and another world; one that had been full of certainty and security – unlike today. Could it really have been only two moons ago?

He returned his gaze to the ceiling and once more waited patiently for the feeling to return to his numb, dislocated body. Slowly and steadily, life was returning to his limbs but to what extent he would eventually regain control over his movements remained to be seen. He closed his eyes and concentrated, willing his fingers to flex and his toes to curl. He opened and closed his mouth, clenching his jaw then stretching it apart as far as possible. Gradually, the slow drip of improvement increased until it became a steady dribble. Then, as though the sluice gates of his soul were opening, it became a rush, then a torrent, and then a flood. Energy cascaded through his body, filling it with a puissance that crackled and sparkled as it coursed through his limbs and tingled on his skin. And still it came!

Simultaneously, all three victims of the strange, supernatural malady sat bolt upright. Eldore and Morjeena threw off their covers and swung themselves around to face each other, their flushed, excited faces shining with health and vitality. Fortunately, their modesty was preserved as they found themselves to be fully clothed, while a simple bed gown covered Yewan's former nakedness. His mother pulled the poor boy into so tight an embrace, he was fortunate not to have his new lease of life immediately crushed from his body. From close behind Eldore, at the head of his bed there came a sudden squeal of delight. It was Gretya. Just how long his friend had sat watching over him he couldn't guess, but now she jumped to her feet and beaming radiantly, rushed off to fetch Aldegar.

The healer was sitting at a low bench in the far corner of the wardroom, grinding dried wild herbs for the preparation of an infusion. Gretya called out loudly as she approached and Aldegar responded by jumping to his feet so quickly that he scattered the contents of his mortar and pestle across the bench and onto the floor. Without a word he rushed around the bench and followed Gretya back to his daughter and son-in-law. Gently, one in each hand, he took hold of their chins and turned their faces from side to side, noting every detail of their skin tone and colour. He peered into their eyes, felt their pulses, then put an ear to each of their chests in turn. With a disbelieving grunt he got to his feet, moved across to Yewan and gave him the same examination. Eventually, he stood up and scratched his balding head.

"I don't understand it," he said in a puzzled voice. "Just moments ago, all three of you were barely alive, yet now you're all fit as fiddles and bursting with health. By all rights you should be dead."

"Well father, I'm sorry to disappoint you but I for one feel as right as rain."

Aldegar grinned at his daughter's gentle reproof. Her razor-edged tongue had obviously recovered as completely as the rest of her.

"Believe me child, it's not a disappointment." He turned to Gretya. "I know you're off-duty my girl, but D'harid asked to be informed of any change; could you send word to him for me please?"

Gretya's happy smile faded and for a single moment she hesitated. But then with a reluctant nod, she agreed and started for the door.

"Oh, and could you also inform Hevalor," Aldegar added. "I expect he'll have some questions for the boy." He watched her leave then cheerfully addressed his three miraculously recovered patients.

"There now, that's all in hand. I expect you're hungry so I'll go and organise some food; I suggest you relax while I'm gone. Sharna, I imagine you could eat something as well, yes?"

Sharna nodded gratefully. Once again, she was clutching her son close to her breast; but mercifully for Yewan, not quite as tightly as before.

"Aldegar," Eldore asked cautiously. "How long have we been lying here?"

"Too long. It's well past seventh turn and young Gretya hasn't moved from your side since she came off duty. She seems to be devoted to all three of you."

"Then perhaps she could have some food as well?"

Aldegar pretended to be shocked. "What's this? Me, a healer, pandering to one of the tenders as though I was no more than a common servant – and she a novice at that! Ah well, war is war." He walked away shaking his head indignantly; but the spring in his step betrayed the relief in his heart at his daughter's recovery.

Meanwhile, Yewan managed to free himself from his mother's smothering embrace. Timidly, he addressed Eldore.

"My lord," he began shakily.

Eldore turned and beamed at him. "Yes, my boy?"

Yewan hung his head, his eyes full of uncried tears. "I'm sorry my lord, I let you down. Please forgive me, I won't fail you again"

Eldore looked mystified. "Fail me? How in the world do you think you've failed me?" Gently, he put a hand under the boy's chin, lifted his head and peered compassionately into his welling eyes. "When could you possibly have let me down?"

The floodgates opened and the boy began to sob helplessly. "This morning," he wailed with tears flowing freely down his cheeks. "You told me to run straight to the viltula but I didn't. I saw two of my friends playing in the street so I stopped to warn them. At first they wouldn't listen and it took me ages to persuade them to go indoors. Then before I could deliver your message, the wind came and knocked me off my feet. I must have really hit my head because the next thing I remember is waking up here."

The pain and distress reflected in the boy's face brought a sympathetic lump to Eldore's throat. "Oh, my boy," he said tenderly. "There's not a single man, woman, or child in this whole city with more courage and loyalty than you've displayed to me every day that I've known you. So don't ever think that you could possibly let me down – ever."

"But this morning I did!" Yewan persisted.

"How? By saving the lives of two friends? If that's not loyalty, I don't know what is."

"But, my lord..."

"That's enough," Eldore said firmly; then more softly he added, "And from now on there's to be no more formality between us, or between you and my lady here for that matter. From this moment on, you must call us by our names, not our titles. After all, that's the way it is between friends, is it not?"

The boy's face brightened a little and he sniffed back his tears. "Yes, my lord."

"What did I just say?"

Yewan managed a little smile. "I'm sorry; I mean Eldore."

"That's better. Anyway, the storm was ten – no, eleven days ago now, so as far as I'm concerned, the whole incident is over and done with."

"Eleven days?!" the boy cried incredulously. "I've lain here all that time? I must have hit my head *very* hard!"

"No, my lad, you've not been lying here, you've been missing. In fact, we'd all given you up for dead."

"*I* didn't!" Sharna declared defiantly.

"All except for your devoted mother," Eldore conceded with a guilty smile.

"So where have I been?"

"Nobody knows, but earlier today you…"

"No, my lord, I beg of you!" Sharna cried, her eyes full of pleading.

Eldore gave her a considered look. "Very well," he agreed. Then returning to the boy he explained: "Earlier today we found you wandering around the city. You were dazed and confused so I'm not surprised you don't remember anything. But then you collapsed and were brought here."

"Oh," Yewan replied simply, apparently satisfied with the explanation. But then a moment later his brow wrinkled. "But what happened to you and Lady Morjeena?"

"Just call me Morjeena." she interrupted.

Yewan turned and grinned at her sheepishly. "I mean Morjeena."

"You needn't concern yourself with us," Eldore continued briskly. "We're as right as rain and more concerned about your welfare."

The boy frowned. "That's funny because I feel sort of… sort of… fit."

"And hungry?"

Yewan thought for a moment then shook his head. "No, not really, I just want to go home; and I'd like to go back to my duties tomorrow. Can I do that please mother?"

"We'll see," Sharna replied, exchanging a glance with Eldore. "I'll decide later; but only if you eat something first."

"Oh, all right," he agreed reluctantly. But for all his protestations to the contrary, when Aldegar arrived with five steaming bowls of thick broth and two good sized loaves of bread, he set about the food with the gusto of a starving man. Both Eldore and Morjeena also found themselves to be far hungrier than they'd realised; and for some strange reason, the food tasted better than anything they'd ever tried before. Yet Morjeena knew for a fact that the broth was no more than leftovers, thrown together from whatever had gone unused throughout the day. And the bread was also far from fresh yet it tasted better than if it had come straight from the oven.

Aldegar stood watching them and once again shook his head in disbelief. It seemed impossible that they could be sitting up and devouring food with so much relish so soon after being in such deep comas.

A movement by the door caught his eye and he looked up expecting to see Gretya returning with the Vice-Master. Sure enough, it was the girl but rather than D'harid, she was accompanied by Hevalor and G'harvil. The former looked tired and pale but the new Lore-Master's face shone and he seemed to have an excited spring in his step.

As they approached, Aldegar handed Gretya her food then gave the two men a warning look.

"Please don't interrupt their meal too much," he cautioned. "I'm sure they need their nourishment far more than they need your questions."

With a final smile at his three patients, he turned and went back to his bench.

"Good evening, Lord Eldore," Hevalor said, then shot Yewan a wary look. "It's good to see you all awake and looking well." His tone was weary and careworn, but the exhaustion couldn't hide the note of suspicion in his voice.

"Thank you," Eldore replied. "And by the look of it, we're in better health than you. Perhaps you should get some rest; you look as though you're on the point of collapse."

The Overseer ran a hand through his thick mane of light brown hair and drew a resigned breath. "You're probably right but it's far more important that I speak to the boy here. We must establish exactly who or what spoke through him and discover the meaning of what he – or it – said."

"Exactly!" G'harvil agreed, his face bright with enthusiasm. "It's similar to old Arlien but almost completely indecipherable. The dialect seems to predate anything we've seen before and unless the boy can shine some light on the matter, it could take many moons to accurately translate."

"Leave the lad alone," Eldore warned. "He remembers nothing."

"What do they mean?" Yewan asked sounding more than a little frightened. "What have I done?"

Sharna put her bowl on the floor and pulled her son close. She glared fiercely at the two newcomers, almost daring them to interrogate him.

Morjeena stood up and placed herself defiantly in front of the Overseer.

"Eldore is right," she said firmly. "The last thing Yewan remembers is being caught in the storm. It'll serve no purpose to quiz him. All you're doing is causing him distress – and his mother too for that matter. Haven't they both suffered enough?"

"You're forgetting that he almost killed you both."

Eldore's bowl clattered across the stone floor as he leapt to his feet.

"No!" he cried angrily. "Whatever touched us meant no malice, of that much I'm certain. I'm also sure the words that it spoke were prophecy, and the meaning of that prophecy will be found in scripture or scroll, not in the interrogation of an innocent child!"

Hevalor sighed heavily and sadly shook his head. "Perhaps you're right, but with the vil-carrim gone and our library of writings turned to ash, what other choice do I have?"

"I don't care, I won't allow it."

"My lord," Hevalor persisted with quiet determination. "You don't seem to realise that although you rule here in your brother's stead, you have authority over me in all things save one: the spiritual welfare of our people. And without doubt, this matter comes within *my* jurisdiction."

"Then we are at odds," Eldore declared grimly.

"No, wait," G'harvil interjected. "Perhaps Eldore is right. Not every book or scrap of parchment was lost. We may have only a tiny fraction of the works we once possessed, but that may actually be to our advantage. It would have taken years to trawl through the contents of the vil-carrim but it'll take only days to scour the remaining works. If Mordan intends us to understand this prophecy, he'll have preserved the relevant texts for us to find."

"*If* the words are from Mordan," Hevalor countered.

"What of Verryl?" Eldore asked hopefully. "If he could regain his senses he'd be of immense value; there's no man on earth with more knowledge of language and dialect."

G'harvil's expression turned cold. "My old master is gone. His body sits locked in the oil store, but his mind and soul are absent."

"So there's no change?"

"Hah!" G'harvil snorted derisively, but Hevalor laid a placating hand on his arm.

"Peace, my friend," the Overseer soothed. "Let me explain. Yes, there is a change but not for the better. He sits on his bed, unmoving and unspeaking, but he glares at those who come near his cage with such hatred and malice..." He closed his eyes and drew a deep breath. "Such is the evil in his eyes it makes the blood run cold and sends a shiver of fear down the spine. Even the bravest are reluctant to bring him his food and remove his waste bucket. I dread to say it, Lord Eldore, but perhaps I should have listened to you and we should have ended his life as the law prescribes."

Morjeena placed a gentle hand on the Overseers cheek. "My dear Hevalor," she said softly. "Could you really have lived with your conscience if you'd condoned such a sentence?"

"I doubt it, my lady, but you've yet to see the venom in his eyes. Perhaps if you saw it for yourself, you would understand."

"Then I'll take you at your word; but if we're delivered from our current plight, I'll go to him and see for myself – I am after all a healer."

Hevalor peered into her bright, compassionate eyes and smiled. "My lady, I'd be most grateful if you would; he was once my closest friend and a great support to me when I was first appointed as shepherd of our people."

Throughout the conversation Gretya had been sitting on the end of Morjeena's bed, carefully following each word as she slowly ate her broth. Every now and then she stole a glance at Yewan who seemed to be growing more frightened with every moment that passed. During her time at the Duty Hall she'd drawn quite close to the boy and his discomfort was beginning rankle with her. At last she could take no more. Deliberately, she placed her bowl on the floor and got indignantly to her feet.

"I think that's quite enough!" she declared with tight anger. "If the four of you want to pursue this topic then I must insist you take the conversation elsewhere!"

They all turned to look at her in astonishment. But where Eldore and Morjeena's expressions were full of surprised admiration, Hevalor's was far from impressed. Although by no means a proud or arrogant man, the Spiritual Overseer had no intentions of being ordered away from his perceived duty by a novice tender – especially one that had been a lowly serving girl just a few short days ago.

"Do you always allow your tenders speak to those in authority with such indiscipline?" he asked Morjeena coldly.

Morjeena studied Gretya for a moment before answering the Overseer. The apprentice tender was standing her ground, her face flushed with embarrassment, but defiant nonetheless. Morjeena gave her new assistant an encouraging smile then turned back to face Hevalor. "Under normal circumstances I'd take firm action against such insubordination, but in this case, that would not be appropriate. One day you may come to realise that she hasn't spoken out of turn at all! And anyway, she's right; this is the house of healing and not a debating hall."

Hevalor's jaw dropped but he quickly regained his composure and gave the Keshtari healer a small, gracious bow, "So be it, my lady. G'harvil and I will leave you in peace and gather together whatever texts remain to us. We'll not rest until every line and paragraph has been digested in our search for a translation. We already know three of the words so we at least have a start."

"Four words," G'harvil corrected.

"*Three* words for sure, plus one that's debatable."

"And they are?" Eldore asked.

"Oh, this is where it gets interesting," G'harvil gushed enthusiastically. "In the common tongue the old Arlien word *ed* translates as *the*; so we can be pretty sure that the *id* in the 'prophecy' carries the same meaning. Likewise, we can be confident that *Sirarl* corresponds with the word-phrase *Alsirarl* or 'the City of Arl'. In the old dialect, *ish* means 'must' and *dor* means 'very'. It would therefore seem logical that *ish-dor* could be translated as an emphatic 'must'; that is a 'must' that cannot be gainsaid. The fourth, albeit disputed word is '*urr*'. I believe it to mean the number one, as in the old word *orra*. So we end up with '*the* blank *the* blank, blank, blank *city of Arl* blank, blank, blank *must* blank *one*.'" He paused and beamed triumphantly. "As I say, exciting isn't it."

Eldore nodded soberly. "It must be for someone of your calibre. I can see you are the perfect man to replace Verryl, and I'm sure that if anyone can translate the text, it's you – with Hevalor's assistance, of course."

"Of course," the Lore-Master beamed. "Come on then Hevalor, let's set about solving this riddle at once and leave the sick in peace." He took hold of the Overseer's arm and started to pull him away. After a last, lingering look at the boy and then a polite parting nod to Eldore and Morjeena, Hevalor acceded and the two men took their leave.

"Lord Eldore," Sharna called softly. Eldore turned and smiled at her questioningly. "Thank you," she whispered, her arms wrapped protectively around her son.

"There's no need for thanks; Yewan and I are old friends now, aren't we boy?" He gave Yewan another wink which the lad returned with just as little success as before.

Then D'harid arrived. He came striding over to them, an enigmatic grin on his battered face and Eldore's large, heavy hammer in his hands. He greeted the muscular lord with a friendly, "Eldore," then turned to the two women and bowed graciously.

"My ladies," he said formally. Gretya's face burned crimson-red. She felt awkward and embarrassed at being addressed with the same high honour as the Lady-Regent; but at the same time, there was perhaps just a hint of delight in her eyes. "It's good to see you all looking well," D'harid continued. "It seems there's been no lasting effects from your strange ordeal – for any of you," he added, glancing at the boy.

"None at all," Eldore replied. "In fact, I've never felt better; I feel as though I've the strength to take on a whole army singlehanded!"

"Then it's a good thing I brought along an old friend of yours," D'harid grinned as he struggled to hold out the mighty hammer.

Eldore took it from him and effortlessly tucked it into his belt. In his powerful grip the heavy weapon seemed to have no weight at all. "I take it you've brought it to me for a reason?"

"Indeed. I was hoping you'd be well enough to join us at the rampart; your presence would work wonders in bolstering the men's courage and resolve."

"Why, has something happened?"

"Yes and no," the Vice-Master replied cryptically. "Obviously there's been a great deal of muttering after your...erm...incident," he shot a sideways glance at Yewan. "But that'll calm down as soon as you reappear. As far as the bridge is concerned, on the face of it little has changed. Although the fires have now died down, there have been no further attempts to take it, and we've managed to block it mid-span with a barricade of old carts. Unfortunately, that effort has cost the lives of many a brave man, but I'm afraid it was a necessary action. The barricade is well pitched and oiled and should keep the enemy at bay – for a while at least when they next attack."

"But?"

D'harid gave a wry smile. "You already know my concerns; I've had a bad feeling for some time; a nagging sensation that we face something more than just soldiers."

Eldore studied him for a while. His battered features were tired and strained but his eyes and voice were as calm as ever. He was still the same competent and confident man he always was – but there was something...

"Something's happened, hasn't it?"

"You read me too well, my friend. A light has been seen in the enemy camp; several times it flashed like green lightning. Those men who fought the lich army say it resembles the red light of the evil general." He shrugged. "It may of course be nothing, but it worries me nonetheless."

"What's going on?" Yewan asked in a small, scared voice. "Have we been attacked again?"

Of course, Eldore thought. *The boy has no knowledge of anything that has occurred since the storm.* He smiled and ruffled his hair. "Don't worry," he said reassuringly. "Everything's going to be just fine. Morjeena will tell you all about it while I'm gone." He turned to his wife. "But gently?" he pleaded.

"Of course," she replied. "Gretya and I will sit here and tell him all he *needs* to know."

"Thank you." He kissed the top of her head and squeezed her hand. "I'll be off now, take care of Gretya."

Gretya looked horrified. "What do you mean? You can't go off to battle, you've only just woken up."

Morjeena put a consoling arm around her shoulders. "It's alright," she soothed, then smiled at Eldore. "Don't worry, I'll try and explain it to her."

Her husband nodded his gratitude and then slapped D'harid on the back.

"Right then, let's go and see what's afoot. Perhaps the green light will flash again and we'll see that it's nothing to fear."

D'harid snorted sceptically and the two men started for the door. Before they reached it, however, Eldore heard Yewan call his name. Something in the boy's voice stopped the muscular lord dead in his tracks and forced him to turn around and face the young child.

As their eyes met, Eldore gasped; for just as when he'd approached Yewan in Pump Square, the boy's gaze drilled into his mind, invading his psyche and violating his private thoughts. But when he spoke, unlike then, Yewan's voice was his own – albeit filled with a power that made Eldore's hair stand on end.

"There's a lesson in everything for all to see," the boy intoned forcefully. "Be wise, Eldore, and learn; remember the storm."

As he finished speaking, the boy blinked and seemed suddenly to come to himself again. Then seeing Eldore's appalled expression he became scared and pressed himself back into his mother's arms.

"What's the matter?" he asked timorously. "What's wrong?"

Eldore swallowed hard. "Nothing," he replied tightly. "Nothing at all." He then turned and hurried after D'harid, following him down into the city.

CHAPTER FORTY-EIGHT

The northern half of the city of Sirris was for the most part swathed in darkness. But here and there a pool of light spilled out onto the street from the few houses where a lamp still burned. These were the homes that had been commandeered as billets for the many off-duty militiamen, and every time Eldore and D'harid passed through one of these glowing oases, the Vice-Master stole a glance at his silent companion. Eldore's face had glowed with a healthy vitality before they'd left the viltula, but now his features had a worrying, deathly pallor. Added to that, his expression was a complex combination of shock and fear, tinged with faint hope and wonder. Something had obviously happened to the young noble but it was something D'harid had somehow missed.

To Eldore himself, the world seemed to have suddenly lurched into the unknown. He'd been certain that Yewan was completely back to his old self, but after that strange, inexplicable outburst, could he really be sure? No, something of whatever had possessed the boy was definitely still inside him. And what had it said? It had repeated some of the old proverb that had been Eldore's mantra for most of his life; the mantra he'd secretly been delighted to see had irritated his brother so much.

"There's a lesson in everything for all to see, but only the wise will learn." And the 'Yewan-thing' had told him to be one of the wise and to learn; but to learn what? "Remember the storm," it had said. Again and again, he ran the events of that terrible tempest over in his mind, and although there had been many lessons to see, which of them was he to learn from?

The sudden strident call of horns from the direction of the river jerked him back to reality. The two men looked at each other and in unison said one word: "Attack!"

* * *

The wooden rampart that sealed the city from the bridge approach was only lightly manned when the assault began. It had seemed inconceivable that the enemy would attack before dawn, so it had seemed prudent to allow some of the soldiers to rest while they could. This assumption had proved a false one however, for a dozen Keshtari footmen had charged up to the makeshift barricade and had begun rapidly to dismantle it. Almost immediately, the few Arlien archers still at their posts had sent a volley of flaming arrows onto the bridge, igniting the barricade and turning it into a sudden and fierce inferno. Most of the attackers were forced to stumble back to the safety of the southern bank, but the foremost soldiers were not so lucky. Five of them, smeared in pitch from their efforts to shift the upturned carts, were engulfed in the fire and instantly became horrifying, human torches. They staggered around the bridge, screaming in pain and terror until at last they fell to the ground and mercifully lay still. Once again, the calm, serene, unambitious D'harid had turned fire into a ghastly and terrible weapon of war.

The brightly blazing barricade illuminated the far bank and revealed the true number of the forces gathered ready to flood across the bridge once the makeshift obstacle had been cleared. The southern riverbank and city approaches were seething with the shadowy figures of countless ferocious warriors. The brilliant yellow flames glinted menacingly on their spear tips and their long, sharp-edged swords. Instinctively, the Arlien bowmen targeted the massed ranks of the exposed soldiers and began raining death down on their heads – a rain that rapidly became torrential as more and more archers returned to their posts. The vulnerable soldiers desperately tried to escape the storm by forcing their way back into the city, but such was the press of men squeezed into the surrounding streets, there was no way to evade the lethal hail that was mercilessly cutting them down.

It was at this point that D'harid and Eldore arrived on the scene. They ran through the confusion of men rushing to take their positions and then heaved themselves up onto the fighting-shelf that ran all the way along the rampart. The Vice-Master took less than a heartbeat to evaluate the situation before calling out to the duty officer. In an uncharacteristically curt voice, he commanded him to stop the fierce barrage at once. The officer, an aged section leader of the regular armshost, instantly hurried off, barking out his orders as he went. Within moments, the archers stilled their bows and the raging storm of death ceased. In the sudden respite, the invaders quickly regained their discipline and began once more to prepare for their assault. The gentle breeze carried the sound of their movements across the rushing, twinkling water to the ears of the shuffling Arlien militia. Above the clank of armour and the rattling of swords, they could clearly hear the shouted commands of the enemy commanders as they brought their men to order. The defenders marvelled at the many different languages used by the forces arrayed against them. As well as the common tongue spoken with the distinctive Keshtari accent, there was, among the many other discernible dialects, the hypnotic lilting flow of the desert nomads. Most disturbing of all, however, the Arliens could clearly hear the hard, guttural voices of the few surviving fierce and ferocious barbarians.

For a while, D'harid watched the enemy, studying their formations and gauging how long it would be before they were ready. But then he became aware of the Lord-Regent standing at his side and gazing at him with an expression of shocked disbelief. The Vice-Master met his eyes and with a wry smile motioned that they should retire back into the city where they could talk more privately. They jumped down and pushed their way back through the gathering militiamen and made for the nearest empty house that had a lamp burning inside. They entered it, shut the door behind them and quickly searched the few rooms to ensure they were alone. Sure enough, the militiamen who'd been using the place as a temporary billet had rushed back to their positions leaving a tempting uneaten plate of bread and goat's cheese on the table. As well as the food there was also a welcome flask of mead. The two men took a seat and while D'harid helped himself to the victuals, Eldore sat and silently watched him with a brooding, thoughtful expression on his face.

"Well?" D'harid said after a good swallow of the honey-ale. "Speak your mind."

"Why did you spare the lives of our enemies?" Eldore asked bluntly. "After all, we had them trapped and helpless; we may never have such an opportunity again."

"You believe I was wrong to hold back?"

"Yes, I do."

"Yet you didn't attempt to countermand my order."

Eldore sat back in his chair. "I could have, but what would be the point? There's little sense in commissioning a military commander then overruling him at the first opportunity; especially when his tactical skills have proved to be beyond reproach."

D'harid gave one of his calm, enigmatic smiles. "You speak wisely my friend. I hope your brother rules as king with the same insight as you rule as his regent. My decision to withhold our arrows wasn't taken lightly. I can assure you, my bones ached to avenge the deaths of the men I sent across the river yesterday. But nevertheless, I had no choice. Consider this: if we'd shot every arrow we have and every arrow had taken down one man, we would have killed at most a third of those that stand against us. How many thousands would then remain to storm the bridge unopposed? And once across the bridge, how long would our stockade hold them back? True, we could then retreat to the Refuge, but you already know my concerns about that."

"But surely it makes sense to kill as many of them as we can?"

D'harid sadly shook his head. "Ah, my friend, you misunderstand our position. We have no hope of victory here now. It matters not whether we kill as many as a thousand or as few as only one. Our purpose is not to defeat them but to hold them at bay for as long as we can. Our *only* task now is to stay alive until Eh'lorne has finished his work in Hornvale and returns here to save us with the Talisman. And that may be many days from now."

Eldore frowned. "You make our position sound hopeless; you sing a far more pessimistic song than that which you sang earlier."

D'harid shrugged. "I sing the lyrics as they're written on the song sheet; and although the words may sound pessimistic, the music at least has an optimistic melody. We know that the bridge *can* be held – if we are determined and have enough arrows. The stockade is stout and with Mordan's blessing, may withstand more than one attempt to breach it. And who knows, maybe I'm wrong; maybe the uneasy feeling in the pit of my stomach – the felling that we face a supernatural power – is nothing more than indigestion."

"In that case," Eldore replied grimly, "I hope for once you *are* wrong!"

But D'harid wasn't wrong; in fact, he couldn't have been more right. For earlier that evening, just as dusk had deepened into a cold, star-studded night, two small groups of tiny, child-like figures had entered Cor-Peshtar from the western pass. Under the early cloak of darkness, they'd made their way across the fertile valley-plain and had headed towards the beleaguered city. Each of the two groups consisted of six sellufs walking inline, one outlandish figure closely following another. The creature at the head of each line carried a staff; but rather than the plain sect-staffs such as Eh'lorne and Bandil had encountered, these were more akin to those wielded by the huge warrior-magi in order to lead Limnash's bestial lich armies. The only visible difference – other than being tailored to suit the sellufin's short stature – was that the gemstones at their tips were emerald-green not ruby-red.

Although both the red and the green crystals had been created by the sellufin, it was not just in colour that these precious-looking stones differed from those of the red-armoured generals. The rubies had been crafted to contain Limnash's power, to act as vessels to project his influence far

THE TALISMAN OF WRATH

beyond his natural reach. They even gave him the ability to see through his general's eyes. The emeralds on the other hand, were pure sellufin and contained nothing whatsoever of their powerful god-king. Indeed, Limnash had been deliberately kept ignorant of the green crystals' real nature and intent.

Before Mylock had presented the king with the Spite-Stone, all three sellufin sects had secretly united the strength of their sect-staffs to infuse three carefully grown emeralds, not just with their own power, but also with some of the evil, pebble-shaped artefact's malicious puissance. Although Limnash knew and approved of the three green-tipped staffs, he had no idea of their true provenance or purpose.

But the purpose of the two crystals on this particular night was perfectly clear. Limnash himself had charged the twelve sellufin with the task of bringing order to the inevitable chaos brought about by so many potent and disparate armies squabbling over the spoils of victory. But when the twelve creatures had entered the scorched remains of west Sirris, it had quickly become clear to them that the battle had not gone as expected. The manner with which their arrival had been greeted however, was exactly what had been forecast and planned for.

They'd entered the devastated city through one of the streets that had been at the centre of the conflagration, and although the area was now in deep shadow, their large, nocturnal eyes had registered every detail of the disaster that had taken place there. Without a word they'd walked slowly through the smoking ruins, silently observing the piles of blackened, incinerated corpses stacked unceremoniously in the side streets and in the smoking remnants of doorways. From the design of the charred cadavers' armour and helmets, it was clear exactly which side had suffered such catastrophic losses.

After following the street directly north for a while, they'd turned right and headed into the unburned intact quarter of the city. It wasn't long before they'd come into contact with the first soldiers of the occupying army. The men – five somewhat drunk desert nomads – had spilled out onto the street from the lamp-lit house they'd seized as a billet, only to be confronted by twelve demonic imps straight out of their most frightening folklore. The dark-skinned mercenaries had screamed in terror and had scurried away, crying out to their comrades that the *derath-somarr* – the soul-snatcher devils – had risen up amongst them.

It hadn't been long before a great number of the fiercely superstitious nomads had come charging at the twelve sellufs. The courageous mercenaries had screamed out magical defensive charms while viciously swinging their long, curved swords. Unmoved, the two leading sellufs had merely raised their staffs and had loudly barked out one harsh word of command. Simultaneously, the two emeralds had flashed, immediately bringing the frenzied warriors to a stunned halt. They'd stood looking at each other with dazed and bemused expressions on their faces, appearing to all intents as though they'd just woken from a particularly unpleasant dream.

Twice more the sellufs had been attacked, each time by groups of various and mixed races. Each time the same flash and command had restored order, bringing the charging warriors under control. What none of the soldiers realised was that when Limnash had addressed them before the campaign had begun, a subjugating trigger-word had been implanted in their minds; a word the sellufs now spoke to pacify and to dominate them all.

All that is, apart from the Keshtari footmen. These soldiers had no need of a subliminal trigger. They'd already been aware of the sellufin's existence, and their appearance at Sirris was not entirely unexpected. The reaction amongst these Keshtari warriors however, varied wildly depending on whether they were regular soldiers or reluctant conscripts. The fiery-eyed zealots had drawn as close to the uncanny creatures as they'd dared, but those that had been forced to bear arms had simply crept away and cowered in the darkest corners of the empty houses.

Once the sellufs had pacified their aggressors, they'd interrogated their respective leaders to ascertain exactly how what should have been an easy conquest had gone so badly wrong. They'd taken overall command and had organised the initial night-time assault on the bridge. Standing in their two distinct groups safely downstream, they'd watched as the small advance-party had attempted to clear the barricade. When it had burst into flames the six creatures in each separate group had huddled together, quietly conversing in their harsh, complicated tongue. After a short while, the two staff bearers had left the huddles, meeting a few strides away and putting their heads together in a low, earnest discussion. Eventually, one of the sellufs had nodded curtly, returned to his five compatriots, and had then reluctantly led them towards the bridge. It was not in their nature to take such direct and overt action, but Limnash's objectives apart, their own agenda demanded that this battle be over as quickly as possible.

As soon as the rain of arrows had ceased, they'd approached the rapidly reorganising ranks of Limnash's army. The massed, disparate forces had parted to allow the six tiny figures to pass through and walk right up to the foot of the stone-built crossing. There they now stopped and formed themselves into a triangle with the staff bearer forming the lead point. Each selluf then laid a hand on the shoulder of the one at his side or in front so that every one of the creatures had a physical link to another. The lead selluf then drew himself up to its full diminutive height, and using both hands, it thrust the jewel-tipped staff towards the sky. All six then began quietly and coarsely to hum, each in a separate monotone of a different pitch that melded to form one single harmonious chord. In spite of the sharp, rasping gruffness of their voices, the uncanny sound was haunting in its beauty. It was as though a talented artist had taken filth and dirt and used their different hues to create a great and wondrous masterpiece. As the volume of their eerie song began to rise, so the emerald began at first to glow, then to shine brighter and brighter. Within just a few heartbeats, the light took on a tangible form of power that began to whirl around the six tiny creatures in a terrifying green tornado. As the tempest grew fiercer and stronger, the formation of sellufs began to walk slowly and steadily across the bridge.

Across the river, horns began to cry out the alarm and a storm of arrows began to fly. But not one of the deadly missiles found their target, for the puissant vortex merely flung them aside as easily as swatting a fly from the air. D'harid and Eh'lorne arrived back at the rampart just as the sellufs reached mid-span, and a heartbeat later, the bright emerald whirlwind struck the burning barricade. It extinguished the flames and scattered the upturned carts like leaves in a gale. The largest and heaviest of the impromptu obstacles was flung high into the air, finally crashing back to earth deep in the city behind the horrified defenders.

Eldore's mind raced as he watched the unstoppable progress of the approaching disaster. All around him, panic was beginning to set in and despite the several duty officers' firm commanding cries of "Hold your positions!" the militiamen were on the point of abandoning the stockade and running for their lives. And why not? What possible use was it to stand and on a rampart that was certain to be torn apart at any moment? But run to where? The Refuge? Not even that fortified haven could stand against the fury of the sellufs' emerald-tipped staff. Nothing, it seemed, could stop Limnash's most trusted and powerful disciples from at last giving him a quick and decisive victory.

CHAPTER FORTY-NINE

Eldore glanced at the faces of the men standing with him on the ledge of the rampart. The scintillating green light illuminated the fear in their eyes and turned their faces into grotesque, ghoulish masks. Even D'harid seemed transfixed and horrified as he stared out at the approaching supernatural tornado. Eldore took him by the shoulders and spun him around so as to look at his face. To his relief there was no sign of panic in the Vice-Master's eyes, but the man's usual aura of confident serenity had given way to a look of helplessness and deep regret.

"I'm sorry, my lord," he said with an impotent shake of his head. "I have no idea how to counter this devilry. This was my worst fear and I have no answer to it."

Eldore nodded. It occurred to him that this was the first time the unorthodox, self-assured old soldier had addressed him with any real formality. He looked back at the bridge and bit his lip; the selufs would be stepping onto the north bank at any moment now. He closed his eyes and muttered a desperate prayer for help – any kind of help!

Yewan's face suddenly sprang into his mind. The memory of the boy's strange, penetrating stare sent a cold shudder running down his spine. He could almost hear the uncanny tone of the lad's parting words: *"There's a lesson in everything for all to see. Be wise Eldore and learn; remember the storm."*

The storm! Of course; remember the storm. His hand flashed up to the pouch hidden beneath his tunic. He'd almost forgotten the small leather bag of red earth; yet without doubt it had held the great storm at bay, leaving his forge an island of calm in the howling, malicious gale. And was it possible that it had also helped Bandil's Stone to heal his wounds? Another quick glance along the rampart revealed that the men's fear was about to turn into full-scale panic.

Instantly, he made his decision and turned back to D'harid. "I must stop this," he declared. "You must hold the line here as long as you can." He hesitated for a moment then added firmly, "And let no man follow me; I mean no one, understand?"

The Vice-Master nodded. "As you wish," he replied grimly.

Eldore took a deep breath than launched himself over the parapet. In his haste, he completely missed his footing and as he landed, he fell awkwardly and heavily onto his face. In spite of the pain and terrible sense of impending doom, somewhere in the back of his mind he grinned as a memory from another time, another life flashed before his eyes. He remembered when just a few short years ago he'd had a similar fall. He could clearly see his brother standing over him, clutching his sides and roaring with laughter. "By Mordan, Eldore," he'd teased. "For all your strength you have the grace and agility of a drunken ox!" If

Eldore had been aware that Bandil had recently stood laughing and teasing Eh'lorne in the exact same manner, the comic irony would have been almost too much for him to contain.

He climbed hurriedly to his feet and regained his composure. His face turned deadly serious as he realised that the sellufs had now taken their first steps onto the northern bank. He pulled his hammer from his belt, squared his shoulders, and then charged recklessly towards the shining green vortex. In spite of his conviction, he couldn't help flinching as he crossed the whirling threshold of the sellufs' power. But just as he'd hoped, the destructive malice of the uncanny tornado caused him no more hurt than had he just stepped from deep shadow into brilliant sunlight.

Unimpeded, he threw himself at the startled sellufs and in one movement, he snatched the staff out of the hands of its bearer while simultaneously crushing its skull with his hammer. Instantly, the raging tempest eased, rapidly slowing until within a single heartbeat, it was nothing more than a calm, though still bright, glow. Eldore raised his weapon high ready to bring it crashing down on the five remaining creatures, but something about their manner stayed his hand.

They'd dropped their arms to their sides and were standing motionlessly waiting for the inevitable, fatal blow. Their sharp, ugly faces – made even more hideous by the gemstone's spectral green light – held no animosity and betrayed not the slightest trace of fear. Instead, their large sad eyes gazed up at him with an inexplicable expression of surprised admiration. The sudden silence from the armies on both sides of the river only added to the heavy tension hanging in the air. He wavered for a moment then lowered his hammer, sparing the lives of the five evil-looking beings. They were unarmed and child-like, and no matter how grotesque their appearance, in contrast to his brother's feelings of disgust, they filled his heart with a strange sense of pity.

For a few moments the committed foes stood facing each other until as one, the sellufs bowed. As they did, they kept their eyes fixed firmly on Eldore's, demonstrating that they bowed not in deference, but out of deep respect. When they straightened, the nearest selluf held out its hand.

"Give me back our staff," it said in a tone that although neutral, carried a great weight of authority.

Eldore examined the potent weapon closely then looked back at the creature waiting patiently with its hand extended.

"And why would I be mad enough to return to *you* the means of *our* destruction?" he asked incredulously.

"Because I give you my word that if you do, the five of us will stand aside and take no further part in this conflict."

Eldore looked across the river to where the shadowy hordes stood poised ready to attack. He then glanced behind him at the hastily prepared stockade. In the gem's emerald radiance, he could clearly make out the many strained, terrified faces peering over the parapet. Even the helmets, swords, and spears glinting in its light couldn't hide the shortcomings of the inexperienced militia.

He shook his head. "No, I can't gamble your word against the annihilation of my entire race. I think it best that I hold onto your staff and keep it safely out of harm's way." He gave the selluf's dead comrade a pointed look. "Unless you wish to try and take it back by force."

"You have no choice but to hand it to me," the selluf persisted calmly. "You cannot keep it, for its power would instantly corrupt your people and bring ruin down upon their heads. Even if all the armies that stand against you left these hills and never returned, your destruction would be even more assured."

"It doesn't seem to be corrupting me," Eldore sneered contemptuously.

It was the creature's turn to give his dead companion a pointed look. "You are...*unusual*," it said deliberately choosing the word with great care.

"Then I'll destroy it!"

The selluf smiled condescendingly. "That will not be possible," it said as if explaining some obvious fact to a small disbelieving child. "The crystal is sellufin-made and only the sellufin can unmake it. As I say, you have no option but to return it."

Eldore felt a fierce and boundless indignation rise up within him; the absurdity of the confrontation was almost beyond comprehension.

"I will NOT return it!" he cried angrily.

The selluf was unmoved. "You *must*," it replied calmly.

"NEVER!" Eldore roared throwing the staff down onto the cobbled ground. With lightning speed, he raised his arm high over his head and then struck the shining crystal a mighty blow with his hammer. In a blinding flash, the huge emerald was completely crushed leaving nothing more than some tiny green shards lying in a bed of coarse white powder.

In the sudden ensuing darkness and before the sellufs could react, he turned and sprinted back to the stockade. After the bright light of the crystal, the deep gloom left his eyes totally blind but with his Arlien mind-sight, he could clearly make out the wooden palisade and could 'feel' the dozens of willing hands reaching down to lift him over the parapet.

Behind him, unseen in the dark shadows, the five sellufs could clearly see his departure. To their large, nocturnal eyes, the night was as bright as day. But in return, had any man been able to see the creatures, he would have witnessed the inconceivable spectacle of five of the most ancient and knowledgeable beings in history standing shocked and immobile, frozen in slack-jawed amazement. They simply could not comprehend how an impotent, mortal man with no discernible source of power could accomplish something so impossible. After some time of deep, contemplative thought, and without a further sound, the five sellufs turned and invisibly retraced their footsteps across the river.

Back at the stockade, once he was over the parapet Eldore was welcomed with loud cheers of relief and triumph. Men were shouting his name and jostling precariously on the narrow fighting-shelf in their efforts to pat him on the back. Such familiarity with someone of his high rank and standing would normally be unthinkable, but under the circumstances, Eldore was happy to indulge this over-exuberant display of gratitude.

By the dim light of the widely spaced torches and braziers below the ledge, Eldore spotted D'harid trying to push his way toward him through the tight press of men.

"Come on, back to your posts," the Vice-Master shouted impatiently. "The war's not over yet; we've still got work to do." Other officers along the stockade took up the cry and soon the men reluctantly retook their positions still grinning with relief after their deliverance from the tiny demons' sorcery.

D'harid drew close to the Lord-Regent and peered deep into his eyes.

"Well done, Lord Eldore," he said quietly. "Now perhaps we can withdraw a way so you can explain to me what in in Mordan's name just happened."

"There's nothing to explain," Eldore started to say but he was cut short by the fiercely incredulous look on the Vice-Master's face. He drew a deep breath and then nodded. "Very well then, come on."

He jumped down and led D'harid away from the stockade and into the shadows of a narrow alleyway between the lines of the nearest houses. After a quick look around to ensure they couldn't be overheard, D'harid turned on Eldore and insisted that he give a satisfactory explanation.

"So what exactly was that all about?" he demanded. "And what in all creation were those…those things?"

Eldore sighed. "Honestly, I have no idea what they are; but I'm sure they're not one of Limnash's abominations. They had an ancient feel to them; something…" He tried to find the right word but, in the end, could only give a helpless smile and a lame shrug.

"That's not good enough," D'harid pressed grimly. "Were they imps or demons, or perhaps some kind of evil grotesques conjured by the enemy's dark arts?"

"I've already told you, I don't know."

"I see," the Vice-Master replied sceptically. "You have no idea what they are, yet you knew enough to engage them in a lengthy conversation. Tell me, my lord, how exactly did they persuade you to spare their lives?"

Sudden realisation dawned on Eldore as to the nature of D'harid's concern. "Don't worry, my friend," he smiled. "I haven't been bewitched. I spared them because there's something…" He frowned, seemingly unable to express exactly what it was about them that had moved him to pity. "There's something sad about them. It felt as though to slay them would violate one of Mordan's most sacred laws."

"And yet they come here to annihilate Mordan's children. It would seem a strange sort of law that prevents his own people from defending themselves against extinction."

"I would tend to agree with you, but then you didn't see their faces. They were shocked and amazed that I was able to penetrate their light storm, *and* they said it would be impossible for me to destroy their weapon, yet I did."

"Then they lied!" D'harid stated coldly. His normally calm composure had been completely overwhelmed by his deep anxiety concerning sorcery.

Eldore thought for a moment then shook his head. "No, I'm positive they were speaking the truth."

"In which case they were wrong," D'harid replied in a voice more akin to his old assured manner. "But whether dishonest or just mistaken, the fact is that you *did* destroy it and we're still alive – at least until morning."

"You think they'll wait until dawn this time?"

"I do; but then I thought that before, so my opinion is no guarantee. Therefore, this time I intend to err on the side of caution. I'll keep all the men at their stations for the rest of the night."

"I think that would be very wise my friend. In which case, if I've managed to allay your suspicions satisfactorily, I suggest we go back to the wall and take our own positions in the line."

With a grunt of agreement from D'harid, they started back towards the stockade. They'd only gone a few steps, however, when the night was once again rent by the strident cry of horns.

"Wrong again!" D'harid spat with a disgusted shake of his head. They sprinted back to the palisade and breathlessly heaved themselves up onto the platform.

At first glance the situation that greeted them was dire, for with no barricade to slow them down, the enemy had stormed across the bridge and were now attacking the stockade itself. To make matters worse, the Arlien stock of arrows was now so depleted that the archers were almost no hindrance to the enemy at all. The invaders flooded onto the northern riverbank where dozens of crude assault-ladders were quickly moved to the fore and thrown against the wooden wall of the palisade.

But contrary to all appearances, the circumstances were not quite as hopeless as they seemed. The stockade was well built and strong, and the defenders were many and determined – buoyed up as they were by Eldore's recent heroics. As soon as a ladder was put in place, it was pushed away and the men on it fell back into the throng where both ladders and men were broken and crushed underfoot. The valiant defenders mercilessly hacked down any of the enemy that did manage to scale the wall

THE TALISMAN OF WRATH

before they could strike a telling blow. For all the overwhelming odds against them, there was every chance that the line would hold and the assault would eventually be repulsed.

But then a blinding green light from within the seething mass changed everything. The second group of sellufs had approached the stockade shielded from sight by the darkness and the great press of men behind them. Once they were close enough, the sinister imp-like beings had ignited the bright puissance of the remaining crystal. The soldiers standing between them and the palisade then parted as the potent creatures prepared to unleash their power.

The six sellufs drew a deep breath and then in one voice, they barked out a loud, harsh word of command. An impossibly bright beam of light burst from the shining emerald and struck the palisade with a deafening crack. A devastating explosion pulverised a substantial section of the stout wooden wall sending dozens of militiamen hurtling through the air like broken dolls. Countless others were killed or horribly wounded by the wickedly sharp, flying splinters. Before the stunned defenders could react, the invaders came pouring through the breach, cheering and roaring triumphantly. The sellufs stood stock still like a brightly lit island while the attackers flowed around them like a rushing, mighty river.

But then the shocked Arliens came back to life. They leapt down from the ledge, recklessly throwing themselves at their raging foes. But as Eldore and D'harid turned to do the same, the muscular lord suddenly stopped short and gave a loud, tortured cry. He staggered across the platform then tumbled over the edge and crashed heavily to the ground. It was only by good fortune that he avoided crushing some of his own men or impaling himself on one of their weapons.

D'harid dropped to his side and with some difficulty, managed to drag the prostrate lord to the relative safety afforded them by the shelter of the ledge. With a mighty effort, he managed to lift him into a sitting position and prop him against the wall.

"Are you wounded?" he asked, his voice full of desperate concern.

Eldore, struggling to regain his breath, shook his head and indicated that he was just badly winded by his fall. D'harid stayed kneeling at his side but his frequent, frantic glances toward the raging battle betrayed the conflict of his desire to stay with his injured friend and the need to go and join his men.

"It's...it's Eh'lorne," the stricken lord gasped at last.

"Eh'lorne? Is he hurt?"

Again, Eldore shook his head. "Just the opposite; he wields the Talisman and the shock of it caught me off-guard."

"If that's the case then it's excellent news; but it hardly helps us here." He motioned towards the frenzied encounter raging just a few strides away. "I must re-join the fight. Have you recovered? Are you with me?"

Eldore managed a deep breath then got to his feet. Unable to stand up straight beneath the low ceiling of the fighting-shelf, he cast around to where he'd dropped his hammer. It took just a few heartbeats to locate it, and once he'd retrieved it, the two men charged into the fray.

The situation though, was now hopeless. The enemy were flooding through the breach like an unstoppable tide and any thought of an ordered, tactical withdrawal to the Refuge was a fantasy beyond reason. The Arlien militia, was no longer a cohesive army, and had degenerated into small scattered islands of men surrounded by a sea of vicious malevolence. They were now nothing more than ineffective groups of armed civilians, hopelessly enveloped in a chaotic and frenzied free-for-all.

Eldore and D'harid soon found themselves alone standing back to back and surrounded by the last of the bare-chested barbarians. They were screaming for blood to avenge the vast numbers of their slaughtered countrymen. As valiantly and skilfully as the two men fought, their end was both inevitable an imminent.

But then the air was torn apart by the deafening yet silent sound of the distant Great Horn. It echoed through the mountains, carried by the raging cold fire of the Talisman of Wrath. The sky exploded with the argent brilliance of the king's standard, lighting up the whole valley-plain more clearly than the full moon on a cloudless night. Tiny scintillating flakes of ice floated with the breeze and the very ground seemed to tremble in awe. The Arlien defenders lifted their heads and looked up in wonder amid cries of, "The king, the king. Eh'lorne is with us!"

The various effects on the invading armies, although immediate and profound, were nothing as dramatic as the effect on the bestial lich at Hornvale. Although almost everyone clamped their hands to their ears in a vain attempt to keep the sound out of their minds – and many of those screamed and howled with pain – only a very few actually turned and fled. The most surprising consequence, however, was the influence the sound had on a small proportion of the Keshtari conscripts. Several hundred of them threw down their weapons and stood staring up at the sky with smiles on their faces and tears streaming down their cheeks.

Meanwhile, amidst the agitated men outside the breach in the stockade, stood the six sellufs. The staff's gleaming emerald still shone as brightly as ever, and the uncanny creatures remained exactly as they were, still in formation and seemingly unaffected by the sound of the Horn. Fascinated, they looked up at the sky, at the men they commanded, and then finally, they looked at each other. Whatever their thoughts, their expressions betrayed little more than surprised curiosity.

When the sound of the Horn eventually faded and the various combatants came to their senses, it quickly became clear that the battle was far from over. If anything, the enemy now threw themselves into the fight with an even greater ferocity and determination. Despite the fiery king's standard fluttering across the night sky, it was an undeniable fact that Eh'lorne's victory in the north could do nothing to prevent the extermination of the Arlien race.

But then the wolves arrived. They came in their hundreds and in their thousands; more wolves than could possibly exist in the whole of the mountains – for in fact they came from everywhere. Every single wolf had come; from the northern wilds, to the eastern wilderness, and right down to southern kingdom of Mah-Kashia. Even the brooding presence in the Dark Shadow Forest had surrendered its wolves – all save one pack that by luck or design had served a different purpose. From the moment Eh'lorne had snatched the Talisman from its resting place under Mordan's Finger, they'd answered its call and had loyally obeyed the command laid down at the dawn of time.

Now they came flooding into the southern part of the city from across the plain of Cor-Peshtar, and even more of them raced down the path beside the eastern gorge and along the northern riverbank. Snapping and snarling they launched themselves into the fray, ripping out throats and scattering their human prey in bloody, terrified confusion.

The sheer savagery of the beasts' ferocious onslaught was staggering, yet their furious aggression was not indiscriminate. Not a solitary Arlien soldier was singled out for attack and even those Keshtarim who had abandoned their weapons were spared. But the rest of Limnash's invading armies received no such forbearance or mercy; and although many a wolf fell to the edge of a sword or axe, there was no escape for their quarry.

Untouched by the rampaging predators, however, the six sellufs warily surveyed the bloody drama being played out around them. The five subordinates turned questioningly to their leader, but he shook his head and lowered his staff. With a dismissive gesture, he led his small troop back over the bridge to where their five comrades stood waiting patiently for them.

Beyond the breach, Eldore stood amidst the miraculous, bloody deliverance and tried to catch his breath. Everywhere he looked the magnificent, lithe beasts were running amok and routing the enemy. He shook his head in wonder; never had he imagined that salvation could come from such an unexpected source.

Wolves, he thought. *Wolves*! If only Bandil could have been here to witness it. Surely the old hermit would forever regret having missed such an opportunity to be close to the animals he'd most wanted to meet.

Someone tapped him on the shoulder and he turned to see D'harid's bemused, blood smeared face smiling at him. The bewildered Vice-Master pointed to the nearby stockade and with a nod of understanding, Eldore followed him over to it. The two men climbed up onto the fighting-shelf and from that vantage point, they surveyed the battlefield.

"Can I really believe my eyes?" D'harid asked, his voice choked with emotion. "I'm not dreaming am I? It is victory, isn't it?"

"Yes, my friend; by your guile and with Mordan's intervention, we have a victory."

"Then I am satisfied; my men have been avenged and perhaps my years of guilt have been absolved."

"Guilt?"

D'harid sighed. "It's a long story and one that I'm not yet ready to share. Suffice it to say, there's a reason for my reluctance to accept high rank."

Eldore let the subject drop. He put his arm around the Vice-Master's shoulders and looked out across the river. Suddenly, he stiffened as he spied the two groups of sellufs. Now reunited, they were heading back into the city unimpeded by any wolf's tooth or claw. Indeed, it appeared the animals were afraid to even come close to the evil-looking sellufs. His jaw clenched as he watched the Arlien people's most dangerous and powerful enemies escape into the shadowy remains of the scorched, narrow streets.

EPILOGUE

Although the hour was very late, the dazzlingly lit throne room was packed with people. All were carefully chosen zealous worshippers of Arl's powerful god-king. The crowding was made to seem worse by another fact. No one dared draw too close to the rough flagstone path that ran through the centre of the hall from the open double doors to the great throne itself.

The reason for their reluctance was obvious and understandable. The remaining sects of sellufin were standing on the path lined up behind their staff bearers in two columns. The sellufs at the head of the columns were the two sect leaders and they carried the two sect-staffs. The staffs were identical in form to the one Eh'lorne and Bandil had encountered. Identical apart from the fact that unlike the one Mylock had tried to remake, these were not made of black ebony. One of the staffs was carved from deep-red mahogany, while the other was fashioned from bleached white birch. The sellufs in each column numbered forty-nine out of the normal sect total of fifty-five; the missing six from each sect were away on their mission to bring order to Sirris.

But whatever their race, whether human or sellufin, all eyes were fixed expectantly on the beautifully handsome, white-robed figure sitting on the ornate oak and leather seat of power. Limnash sat poised on the edge of the throne with one of his two potent artefacts held in each hand. In his right hand, the Star of Destiny blazed brighter than ever, while in his left he held the evil Spite-Stone. It nestled in his palm – the same innocuous looking pebble that Mylock had presented to him almost five years ago now. His head turned slightly from one side to the other as if he was looking around the room, carefully surveying the adoring crowd. But in actual fact, his cold, dead eyes were firmly closed. His lips moved constantly as though in deep conversation with several invisible beings standing closely arrayed before him.

Captivatingly framed by the cascading waves of his dark, flowing tresses, his delicately masculine features became increasingly marred by a mercilessly cruel and triumphant smile. As time wore on and the volume of his voice began to rise, more and more snippets of his strange monologue became audible. Eventually, the whole of the decidedly one-sided conversation could be heard. The louder his speech became, the brighter the Star shone and the more ruthlessly sadistic his smile became. The usual velvety-soft tone of his powerful voice became coarsened by a harsh, impatient avarice.

"That's it," he sneered exultantly. "Gather them for the strike. Now, attack!"

A moment or two later the callous smile slipped and he frowned thoughtfully. "Clever," he muttered. "Very clever. Now who could have prepared such an ingenious trap?" Then he laughed derisively. "No matter. Whoever he is, all he has done is to delay the end and their inevitable destruction."

But then his expression changed again, only this time to one of angry surprise.

"What's this? They taunt us with laughter? They presume to..." Suddenly he stiffened and his voice grew fierce and commanding. "Control them! How dare you let my mighty army run from such an insignificant display of defiance."

Gradually he relaxed and then settled back into the throne. "That's better," he said soothingly as his face lost some of its hard malevolence and his smile took on a beatific quality. "Now all we have to do is wait; the flames will soon die down and then our success is assured." With his eyes still closed he rested his head against the high back of the throne and began softly to hum a pleasant, merry tune.

Without warning, he shot forward and looked over his right shoulder. At first his eyebrows arched with incredulous surprise, but then he roared with laughter.

"Oh wonderful!" he cried joyously. "Such futile valour, such admirable courage." His expression suddenly hardened. "Crush them!"

He remained with his head turned to the right for some time while his breathing became taut with excitement. He sat greedily licking his lips while his face was a study of rapacious bloodlust. Suddenly, he startled all those present as he swung around to his left and gave a loud horrified shout.

"No!" he cried. "It can't be! Quickly, stop him – all of you." He jumped to his feet. "I said stop him!" The blood drained from his face turning his even, golden tan a deathly white. Appalled and helpless, he watched his carefully laid plans fall apart before his supernaturally enhanced eyes.

Then, from far across the wide plains of Keshtar, the air was rent asunder by the silent and majestic sound of the Great Horn.

S. P. MUIR

Every man and woman fell to the floor, screaming and writhing in pain as the Talisman's power scorched them with cold fire. Down in the city beyond the open doorway, the blazing royal banner illuminated the streets and avenues, shining down on the remainder of the city's adult population. They'd been standing outside their homes, patiently waiting for the news of their god-king's victory. But now they were also suffering the agony of the Horn's effect. However, amongst the many thousands afflicted by the Talisman's power, hundreds of others were standing erect and transfixed, gazing up at the sky with rapturous tears in their eyes.

Back inside the hall, the Star of Destiny became so cold that it began to sear Limnash's hand. With a sharp cry of pain, he flung it to the ground. By sheer luck, he managed to drop the Spite-Stone at the same time, thus preventing his instant demise. Wide-eyed and bewildered, he stood staring at his blistered right hand with a stupefied look on his disbelieving face.

When the wondrous and dreadful sound ended, he came to his senses and looked around the throne room. His lips twisted into a furious snarl as he saw his subjects sprawled on the floor and weeping and wailing in their anguish and pain. Burning with fury, he strode through the hall towards the source of the light shining down on the city. He barged through the two lines of sellufin, knocking the tiny creatures aside as he went. He then stormed through the wide-open portal and out into the palace's elevated courtyard. There he stopped and stared up at the blazing banner with its single, seven-pointed star and howled with rage.

The intrigued sellufs looked at each other curiously then calmly walked outside to join their furious deity. For a few moments, they too carefully studied the sky before once again looking at each other with questioning expressions. Finally, they looked enquiringly at their two staff bearers who, after exchanging a brief glance, then nodded their assent. Immediately, the entire company turned and began to walk indifferently away. As soon as Limnash realised they were leaving, he stiffened and angrily shouted at their retreating backs.

"Where do you think you're going?" he demanded. The sellufs seemed not to have heard him and continued walking in the direction of the courtyard's filigree gates. "Are you deaf?" he cried, his fury reaching even greater heights. "I asked, where are you going?"

Again, there was no answer until apoplectic with rage, he roared at them, "I COMMAND YOU TO STOP!"

The leader of the red sect and bearer of the mahogany staff paused and then slowly turned to face the irate god-king.

"I demand to know where you are going," Limnash said for the third time.

The selluf cocked its head. "Demand?" it asked expressionlessly. "That is too strong a word and wholly inappropriate. Where we are going is none of your concern."

Limnash could not believe his ears. "HOW DARE YOU!" he bellowed taking a threatening step forward. "You cannot speak to me with such insolence; I AM YOUR GOD!"

The selluf smiled gently as though to placate the tantrums of a small child. "There are many gods, oh divine one, but most are nothing more than mindless idols of wood or stone. Some gods may *appear* real and powerful, but although raised up to glory by their disciples, they are in the end just mortal men, doomed to grow old and eventually to die. But you are none of these; you are without doubt, truly a god. You were immortal and powerful long before my race came to worship you; and then we elevated you further still. So yes, oh exalted one, you are *a* god, but whether you are to remain *our* god is no longer certain."

Limnash's face turned puce and he seemed to be in danger of exploding. "Blasphemy!" he thundered. "What other god could you have? Who else in all the earth can rival my power and majesty? Do I not stand before you in glory and splendour?"

"Indeed, you are most splendid and possess great majesty. You are the one we call, '*The Flesh God*'; but there is another god worthy of our worship. We name that one, '*The Silent God*' for he has not spoken to us aloud for millennia now." Casually, the creature pointed up at the shining sky. "But it could be possible that he speaks to us once again."

"I would rather destroy you than have you worship another god!"

"I'm sure you would – and you have the power to do so if you wish – but it is unnecessary. I assure you that for the present, we will worship no one. We will instead stand aside and watch and wait. All you would achieve if you destroy our two sects is to drive my people into the arms of your enemies. Never forget, *'a common foe makes for strange bedfellows.'* Have your enemies not wounded you enough without adding *us* to your woes?"

Limnash lifted his head indignantly. "They may have wounded me at the Horn, but I have annihilated them at their pathetic city."

"Perhaps, perhaps not. You have already failed there once; who is to say that they haven't humiliated your armies again? Not until my brethren send word will we know for sure."

"I am not beaten!"

The selluf smiled indulgently. "No, you are not; far from it in fact. And although your losses are grievous – even catastrophic if they have defeated your assault on their city – you are still *very* powerful. And despite their triumph or triumphs, their victory will have cost them dear and their hand is now seriously weakened."

"Then you must help me raise another army and then march against them once more."

THE TALISMAN OF WRATH

With a sad shake of its head, the selluf sighed. "Have you learned nothing from this disaster? The Silent God has claimed those hills as his own and even we will not risk entering them again. No, oh divine one, you have no choice but to stay here. So gather your forces and prepare your defences; rest assured, your enemies will come to you soon enough." Again, the creature studied the shining banner in the sky. "Whatever has happened at their city, there is a new king in the Sacred Hills and his claim to your throne is strong."

It suddenly fixed Limnash with a penetrating warning look. "So build your walls high, oh great one, for when he comes – and he *will* come – he will wield the Talisman of Wrath against you and there will be a War of Destiny."

The selluf then smiled. "But if you prevail – and there is every probability that you will – we will return to worship you once again. Then we will serve you with all our might, and together, oh great one, nothing can stop you from conquering the whole world."

With that the selluf turned and walked away leaving the god-king of Keshtar staring impotently after him.

S. P. MUIR

Printed in Great Britain
by Amazon